The Wild Ride

Ride! the voice commanded.

Karigan dared not disobey. She squeezed The Horse's sides just as the first arrow was loosed. The Horse leaped into a gallop. Blue of sky, green and brown of wood, rushed by in streaks. The buildings of a village were a smear they left behind. Two arrows, she knew, sang behind her and would not stop till they found their mark.

Wind buffeted her, loosened the braid in her hair. The rhythm of The Horse's hooves pounded through her body, but for all she knew, they flew.

There were other pounding hooves, other riders abreast of her, filmy white and transparent. Trees and buildings did not hinder them, they traveled right through. They called to her with far off voices in what was like a battle cry: *Ride, Greenie, Ride! It's the Wild Ride!*

Cold arms slipped around her waist from behind. *Ride,* the ghost of F'ryan Coblebay whispered. *It's the Wild Ride.*

DON'T MISS:

FIRST RIDER'S CALL

The sequel to GREEN RIDER

KRISTEN BRITAIN

GREEN RIDER

DAW BOOKS, INC.
DONALD A. WOLLHEIM, FOUNDER
375 Hudson Street, New York, NY 10014

ELIZABETH R. WOLLHEIM
SHEILA E. GILBERT
PUBLISHERS

First paperback printing, April 2000

20 19 18 17 16 15 14 13 12 11

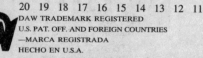

DAW TRADEMARK REGISTERED
U.S. PAT. OFF. AND FOREIGN COUNTRIES
—MARCA REGISTRADA
HECHO EN U.S.A.

PRINTED IN THE U.S.A.

ACKNOWLEDGMENTS

Book dreams do not become reality without the support and inspiration of several special people whom I wish to thank:

Cheryl Dyer, who insisted I read *The Lord of the Rings* at a young age, leading to my discovery of other authors and their tales, and eventually inspiring me to craft tales of my own. Cheryl is my steadfast friend, sounding board, and first reader. Her support so early on was essential, and still is today.

Terry and Jeri Goodkind, for their friendship, hospitality, chairs, and . . . well, they know. Terry's quest for excellence in his own work, and his high standards of quality in all aspects of his life, continually inspire me.

My agent, Anna Ghosh, for championing a "green writer," and for her hard work in finding the right home for this book.

My editor, Betsy Wollheim, and assistant editor, Debra Euler, for their enthusiasm and patience, even after the die had been cast.

Keith Parkinson, for the beautifully rendered cover art.

Author John Marco, for comparing notes and sharing advice, and for listening with empathy to my harangues about noisy upstairs neighbors and squirrels (sometimes one and the same).

Author Lynn Flewelling, for sharing with me advice and her experience in this mind-boggling world of publication.

Batwing and Percival, who imitate office equipment all too well (paper shredder and paper weight respectively) and offered me companionship during the long and lonely efforts of writing a novel-length manuscript. They keep me humble.

And finally, Karigan G'ladheon, for shouldering her way into my life and sweeping me along on one heck of a Wild Ride.

For my parents

❧ GRAY ONE ❧

The granite was cold and rough against the gray-cloaked man's palms. It was good, solid granite, from the bones of the earth itself. He traced barely perceptible seams between the huge blocks of the wall. It was the seams, he believed, that held the key. The key to the wall's destruction.

The wall towered above him to some unknown height. It was many feet thick, and it followed Sacoridia's southern border for hundreds of miles, from the East Sea to Ullem Bay in the west. It protected Sacoridia and the rest of the lands from *Kanmorhan Vane,* known in the common tongue as Blackveil Forest.

The wall had endured for a thousand years. It had been built after the Long War at the turn of the First Age. For a thousand years, the denizens of the dark forest had grown restless, had festered, trapped behind the wall.

Now the Gray One must call on them and end their exile. He would bring these nightmares back into the daylit world. He would bring them slowly. Slowly at first.

The wall was bound with such deep magic that it prickled his hands. The magic was ancient and powerful, even for the works of those long-ago humans. Today humans understood none of it. They knew little of what their ancestors had been capable of. Nor did they know what they, the citizens of present-day Sacoridia, were still capable of.

A good thing.

He brushed the layers of magic with his mind. Magic

had been melded into each block of granite from the moment it was quarried, through its cutting, finishing, and placement. The mortar had been inlaid with strengthening spells not only to ensure that the wall stood for all time, but to prevent magic from breaking it.

Oh, the spell songs the stonecutters must have sung as they hammered drills into the rock and refined the mortar mixture. The wall was magnificent, really. A great accomplishment that had taken generations of humans to complete. A pity it must be destroyed.

The Gray One smiled beneath the shadows of his hood. He would return the world to a state it hadn't known since before the Long War, far beyond the First Age, a time lost to memory; a time when humans lived in primitive bands that stalked herd beasts and game. There had been no kings back then, no countries, no organized religions. Just superstition and darkness. During the Black Ages, as that long-ago time was now called, they had had a better understanding of magic than they did today.

The Gray One looked up. The pink clouds of dawn were fading, and birds squabbled in the trees. His collaborators would be growing impatient for his return. He supposed they had every right to be impatient: they were mortal.

He closed his eyes and shielded himself. He began to follow songs of quarrymen and stonecutters wrought in a tongue modern Sacoridians would not recognize. The music sprang from the earth's bones; it wove strands of resistance, barriers, and containment.

The echoes of hammers wielded by stonecutters centuries ago clamored in the Gray One's head. The blows jarred him, rang deep in his mind. He gritted his teeth against the pain and probed deeper.

Men and women sang in unison. Their song intensified as his thoughts rippled along the seams. He caught the harmony of their ancient voices, allowed the cadence of the hammers to invade his mind, and he sang with them.

His body swayed to the rhythm, and dripped with perspiration. But his body was a distant thing now, an after-thought, for his mind was deep within the granite. He flowed within the pink feldspar and crystalline quartz, within the pepper flecks of hornblende. He felt powerful enough to withstand the Ages, untouched by the weathering forces of nature. He could endure anything. But he must surpass this power. He must become stronger than even the granite to break the wall.

His voice found its own harmony running counter to the rhythm within the wall. *All great things must fall,* he sang. *Sing with me, follow me.*

Far away, his forefinger tapped the new rhythm on the wall. It wasn't enough yet to disturb the hundreds of hammers, but it helped create discord. But did he detect uncertainty in the song? Did some of the hammers lose the rhythm?

A splintering akin to the spring cracking of lake ice scattered his thoughts. He lost his bearing. The song and rhythm faded, his solidarity with the wall wavered.

His body absorbed his mind like a sponge. The force sent him flailing backward, stunned and unwieldy in his corporeal form. When he remembered how to use his legs and arms, he inspected his handiwork.

Yes, yes, yes! A hairline fracture in the mortar. The wound would grow, and he could come back and break the D'Yer Wall!

Now he must return to the camp where the humans awaited him. Cracking the wall had sapped a great deal of his energy—there was barely enough left to transport him. He would be in bad shape for the rest of the day, but the soldiers would be impatient to hunt down the Green Rider. Soon he would be done with this intrigue the humans so valued, but for now, it served his purpose.

As he slung the longbow and quiver of black arrows over his shoulder, he felt someone's gaze upon him. He looked wildly about but saw only an owl roosting on a branch above. It blinked, extinguishing its moon eyes, and twisted its head away, as owls do.

The Gray One had nothing to fear from an owl preoccupied with its early morning hunt. He spread his arms wide to begin the summoning. They trembled from the effort of having cracked the wall. "Come to me, O mortal spirits. You are mine to hold, bound to me in this world. Walk with me now and take me where I must go."

He willed them to him, and they couldn't resist his call. A host of spirits, like a watery blur, gathered around him. Some sat mounted on horses, others stood afoot. Among them were soldiers, old men, women, and children. Ordinary citizens stood beside knights. Beggars huddled next to nobility. All were impaled with two black arrows each.

"By the arrows of *Kanmorhan Vane,* I command you to walk with me now. We will walk on the quick time roads of the dead."

⇜ DEAD RIDER ⇝

Karigan G'ladheon awakened to the chitter of waxwings and chickadees. Mourning doves cooed and jays defended their territories with raucous song and fluttering wings. Above her, the sky opened up like an expansive dusky canopy that winked with stars. The moon hung low in the west.

Karigan groaned. She lay at the edge of a fallow farmer's field, behind a hedgerow, and her back wasn't taking it well.

She pushed damp hair away from her brow. Everything was wet with dew and her clothes stuck to her like a cold and clammy second skin. She remembered aloud why she was here.

"To get away from Selium."

Her own voice startled her. Aside from the birds, the countryside was wide open and empty and silent. There would be no tolling of Morningtide Bell here, nor the familiar creaking of floorboards as her fellow students moved around in her old dormitory building preparing for a day of classes.

She stood up and shivered in the chill spring air. Indeed, she was "away" from Selium, and would get farther away still before the day was done. She gathered her blanket and things, stuffed them into her pack, stepped over the hedgerow, and started walking. She carried little more than a hunk of bread, some cheese, a change of clothes, and some jewelry that had belonged to her mother—the only objects precious enough to her to carry away. All the rest had been left in the dormitory in her haste to leave Selium.

She walked briskly to stave off the chill, the gravel of the road crunching beneath her boots. The rising sun, with its bands of orange and gold, drew her east.

As she walked, the glistening grasses of farm fields transformed into thick stands of fir and spruce blotting out the newly risen sun and darkening the road.

This was the edge of the Green Cloak she entered, an immense wood that grew thick and wild in the heart of Sacoridia. Its more tame borders marched in snatches and thickets right down to the shores of Ullem Bay and the foothills of the Wingsong Mountains. The bulk of the wood was dense and unbroken, save for villages and towns that made islands of themselves in its interior, and the occasional woods road that, from an eagle's view, she thought, must cut through it like a scar.

Such roads were often in conflict with their surroundings. It didn't take much for saplings to start growing in the middle of woods roads and winter blowdowns to topple across them, eventually obscuring the least used. A carpet of rusty pine needles softened Karigan's footfalls and gave this road an abandoned look, though it was the main thoroughfare leading into Selium from points east.

Karigan walked till her stomach growled. She sought out a warm patch of sun surrounded by solid, cold shade, and washed down chunks of bread and cheese with handfuls of water from a gurgling stream next to the road. It wasn't the choicest water, but it would have to do.

Afterward, she splashed cold water on her face. She felt altogether bedraggled after just one night on the road, and she longed for the hot baths and full meals the school served up.

"Don't tell me I miss it. . . ." She glanced over her shoulder as if the entire campus, with its templelike academic buildings looming over the city from atop its hill, might pop into view.

It was curious how a night on the road made yesterday's events seem somehow less significant, less hurtful.

Karigan half-turned, gazing back down the road which, within a day's walk, ended at the school. Her hands tightened into balls and she clenched her jaw. She would show the dean.

Kick me out of school, will you? Let's see how you like confronting my father. She grinned, imagining her father, his expression livid, towering over a shrinking Dean Geyer.

Then her shoulders sagged and her grin faltered. It was no good. She had no control over her father. What if he agreed with the dean that her punishment was just?

She kicked the ground and pebbles skittered across the road. *Gods, what a mess.* She hoped to reach Corsa before the dean's letter did, so she could tell her father her side of the story first. Either way, she would be in deep trouble. Maybe she ought to hire herself out on a merchant barge and stay away for good. After all, that's what her father had done when he was a boy.

She jammed her hands into her pockets, and with head bowed, ambled along the rutted road at a reluctant pace.

She startled a baby squirrel sitting on an old lightning-racked stump. It pipped and squealed, its tail abristle. It stamped in place, then darted from one edge of the stump to the other, as if too frightened to decide which way to go.

"Sorry I scared you, little one," Karigan said.

Chittering, the squirrel dashed into some underbrush and scurried noisily through the leaf litter of the forest floor, sounding like some much larger beast.

Karigan walked on humming an off-key tune. However, when the sounds of the squirrel did not abate but, in fact, grew much louder, she froze.

The racket shattered the woods. Trees and shrubs shook as if some wild creature—many times larger than a squirrel—thrashed in the twined branches and undergrowth. Crazed catamounts and rabid wolves played through her mind. She hadn't a weapon with which to fend off the beast, and she couldn't run either; her feet seemed to have taken root in the ground.

She drew a ragged breath. Whatever the nameless beast was, it charged her way, and fast.

It burst from the woods in an explosion of branches. Karigan's breath hissed in her throat like a broken whistle.

The creature loomed huge and dark in the tree shadows. It huffed with great wheezings through flared nostrils like some infernal demon. Karigan closed her eyes and stepped back. When she looked again, a horse and rider, not some evil dragon of legend, staggered onto the road. Twigs and leaves fell from them to the ground.

The horse, a long-legged chestnut, was lathered with sweat and huffed as if from a hard run. The rider slumped over the chestnut's neck. He was clad in a green uniform. Branches had lashed trails of blood across his white face. His broad-shouldered frame twitched with fatigue.

He half dismounted, half fell from the horse. Karigan cried out when she saw two black-shafted arrows impaled in his back.

"Please. . . ." He beckoned her with a crimson glove.

She took one hesitant step forward.

The rider was only a few years older than she. Black hair was plastered across his pain-creased brow. Blue eyes blazed bright with fever. With the two arrows buried in his back, he looked as if he had fought off death longer than any mortal should have.

He was of Sacoridia, Karigan was certain, though the green uniforms were far rarer than the black and silver of the regular militia.

"Help . . ."

Each step she took was shaky as if her legs could no longer support her. She knelt beside him, not sure how she could aid a dying man.

"Are you Sacoridian?" he asked.

"Yes."

"Do you love your country and your king?"

Karigan paused. What a curious question. King Zachary was relatively new to the throne and she knew little of his policies or methods, but it wouldn't do to sound disloyal to a dying servant of Sacoridia.

"Yes."

"I'm a messenger . . . Green Rider." The young man's body spasmed with pain, and blood dribbled over his lip and down his chin. "The satchel on the saddle . . . important message for . . . king. Life or death. If you love Sacor . . . Sacoridia and its king, take it. Take it to him."

"I—I . . ." One part of her wanted to run screaming from him, and another part felt drawn to his need. Running away to Corsa, instead of waiting for her father to collect her at Selium, had held an irresistible air of adventure that she had anticipated. But real adventure now looked at her with a terrifying visage.

"Please," he whispered. "You are—"

The last words died inaudibly as blood gurgled in his throat and sprayed his lips, but she thought she caught a breathy *the one*. The one what? The only one on the road? The only one to take the message?

"I—"

"Dangerous." He shuddered.

Everything around fell silent in an expectant hush, as if the world held its breath for her decision.

Before Karigan could stop herself, she said, "I'll do it." She heard the words as if someone else had drawn them from her.

"You s-swear?"

She nodded.

"Sword. Bring it to me."

The horse shied from Karigan, but she caught his reins and drew the saber from the saddle sheath. Its curved blade flickered in a patch of sun as she held it out before her. She knelt beside the messenger again.

"Wrap your hands around the hilt," he said. When she did, he placed his hands over hers. It was then she saw his gloves were not dyed crimson, not originally. He coughed, and more blood flecked the corners of his mouth. "Swear . . . swear you'll deliver . . . the message to King Zachary . . . for love of country."

Karigan could only stare at him wide-eyed.

"Swear!"

It was as if she already looked upon a ghost rather than a living man. He would not allow himself to die until she swore the oath. "I swear . . . I'll deliver the message for the love of my country."

Although she had sworn, the Green Rider was not ready to die yet. "Take the brooch . . . from my chest. It will ident . . ." He squeezed his eyes shut in pain till the spell passed. "Identify you as messenger . . . to other Riders." The words were gasped as if he were forcing air in and out of his lungs by sheer will to extend his life. "Fly . . . Rider, with great speed. Don't read m-message. Then they can't tor-torture . . . it from you. If captured, shred it and toss it to the winds." Then, because his voice had grown so faint, she had to lean very close to hear his final words. "Beware the shadow man."

A cold tremor ran through Karigan's body. "I'll do my best," she told him.

There was no response from the messenger this time though his eyes still stared at her, bright and other-worldly. She gently pried his fingers from her hand and closed his eyes. She hadn't seen the winged horse brooch before, but now, pinned over his heart, it glowed golden in the sun. Absently she wiped bloody finger marks off her hands onto her trousers and then unclasped the brooch.

A curious sensation, not at all unpleasant, as if all her nerves sang in unison, tingled throughout her body. The gold warmth of the sun embraced her, and drove the shadowy chill away. There was a fluttering like great white wings beating the air, and the sound of silver-shod hooves galloping. . . .

Moments later, the sensation receded, and she realized the sound was her own excited heartbeat, and the sun had risen sufficiently to widen the patch of light she stood in. Nothing more. She pinned the brooch to her shirt.

She then sensed, like a breeze whispering through a

hundred aspen trees, invisible lips that seemed to murmur, *Welcome, Rider.*

Karigan shook her head to clear it of such fancies, and turned to practical matters. What to do with the messenger's body? She couldn't just leave it lying there in the middle of the road exposed to carrion birds and passersby, could she? She wouldn't want to stumble across a body in the middle of the road during her travels. It just wasn't right to leave it there.

She grimaced. The body was too heavy for her to drag into the woods by herself, and how would she bury it? She most certainly hadn't packed a shovel. It seemed wrong to leave the body out in the open, but . . . she had to try. Then, as if a voice said to her, *Don't waste the time,* she backed away from the body and took up the reins of the horse.

And still she hesitated. The least she could do was leave the saber with the messenger to show how bravely he had died. But what if she met up with the people who had struck him with the arrows? She would need some kind of defense, even if a saber wasn't any good against arrows. Practicality won out, and she slid the blade back into its sheath.

The messenger had told her to fly, but running the horse to his death would serve no purpose. She would walk him and mount up only when he seemed at least partially recovered.

The horse was a sorry-looking beast. His legs were long but thick; obviously he had been bred to run fast for distances with no thought to aesthetics. His neck reminded Karigan of her father's descriptions of some long-necked wild beasts he had seen on one of his voyages. The horse's coarse chestnut hide was crisscrossed with old scars.

"I wish I knew your name," Karigan told him as they plodded along.

The horse curved his neck to look, not at her, but behind her. She glanced back, too. The messenger's body had already fallen behind a bend in the road, and there was nothing to see besides the pointy shadows of spruce trees shrinking as the morning progressed.

She shuddered. The messenger's twisted, tortured form would stay in her memory for some time to come. She had helped lay out the corpses of old aunts and uncles for funerals, but they had died peacefully in their sleep, not with arrows driven into their backs.

This message business was a huge change of plans. Home was out of the question. Karigan bit her lip. Her father would be aggrieved enough by her suspension from school, and now she was running off on some reckless errand without having considered the consequences.

She could almost hear her aunts enumerating her deficiencies: *Feckless,* Aunt Gretta would say; *Willful,* Aunt Brini would add; *Impulsive,* Aunt Tory would declare. Aunt Stace would sum it all up with, *G'ladheon,* and all the aunts would nod knowingly in mutual agreement.

Karigan thrust a strand of hair behind her ear. She could not help but concur with her aunts' assessment. It seemed she always made the wrong choices—the kind that got her into trouble.

It was too late to turn back now, though. She had made a promise. She had sworn to the Green Rider she would take the message to King Zachary himself.

She had visited Sacor City once as a young child, and at the time, elderly Queen Isen, Zachary's grandmother, reigned over Sacoridia. Zachary's father had ascended the throne only to fall ill and die a short time later. Zachary's ascension to the throne had been challenged by his brother, Prince Amilton, but why, she did not know. She assumed all royals engaged in squabbles whenever power and prestige were at stake.

Now her ignorance annoyed her. What could be happening in the land that meant a life-or-death message for the king? What did the message contain that was so vital someone was willing to kill for it? She longed to look at the contents of the message, but the Green Rider had ordered her not to.

Belatedly, she wondered how much danger she had

put herself in. She was all alone amidst the wild forest lands of Sacoridia. She carried a message for which a man had been pursued and killed. She let out a trembling sigh, suddenly yearning for home; to be held in the safety of her father's arms and to hear her aunts gossiping in the kitchen. She missed the big old house in Corsa and the predictable and unimportant concerns of everyday life that pulsed and flowed through it.

The recklessness of her decision to carry the message truly set in. With a sinking feeling, she knew it would be a long time before she saw home again.

Three wooden arms branched from a cedar signpost planted in a grassy island in the middle of the intersection. From the south arm hung a shingle indicating the River Road. More shingles, carved with the names of towns along the way, hung beneath it. If Karigan were going home, she would take this road.

The middle arm pointed to the well-maintained Kingway which bore east, the most direct route to Sacor City and King Zachary. Her father had said the Kingway would one day be paved all the way from Sacor City to Selium, increasing commerce and prosperity for all the villages situated along it.

The third arm pointed toward an ill-kept, overgrown track. The one shingle hanging from it bore one ominous word: North.

Estral, Karigan's good friend at school—her only friend at school—had hinted there was more activity up north in recent months and that King Zachary had reinforced the borders with armed patrols. But Estral, who pursued the craft of the minstrels and seemed to come by incalculable amounts of information from unguessable sources, never said exactly where the trouble was emanating from. Mysterious Elt Wood lay due north, but somehow she couldn't fathom anything from that strange place deigning to bother Sacoridia.

The horse had finally cooled down enough for Karigan to mount up. The saddle was a tiny thing compared to what she was used to. A light saddle made sense if you wanted to travel speedily, which she supposed most messengers did, but it would take some getting used to. It felt like there was nothing between her rump and the horse's bony spine.

The message satchel was strapped to the front of the saddle, and a bedroll, two small packs, and the saddle sheath to the cantle. She would investigate the contents of the saddlebags later when she was well down the Kingway. Maybe there would even be food inside one of them.

She adjusted the stirrup irons to a comfortable length, settled into her seat, and squeezed the horse's sides. He didn't budge. She kicked more insistently, but he stood his ground.

"You're a stubborn, ill-trained horse," she said.

The horse snorted and walked toward the North Road of his own volition.

"Hey!" Karigan pulled back on the reins. "Whoa. Who do you think is in charge here?"

The horse stomped his hoof and shook the reins. Karigan tried guiding him toward the Kingway again, but he refused. When she let up, he gained a few more steps toward the North Road. She dismounted in disgust. She would lead him onto the Kingway by foot if she had to. The horse tossed his head back and jerked the reins out of her hands. He took off down the North Road at a trot.

"Hey, you rotten horse!"

More horrified than angry that the horse was running away with the important message, she chased after him. He looked back at her as if to laugh and kept jogging for nearly a mile. Then he waited patiently, cropping the grass that grew in the road, for an infuriated Karigan to catch up. When she was just within an arm's reach of the reins, he swished his tail and trotted off again, leaving her to shout a number of curses in his wake.

The third time, Karigan made no attempt to grab the

reins. She stood huffing and puffing before him with her hands on her hips.

"All right, horse. Maybe you know something I don't. Maybe the Kingway is more dangerous because it's the most direct route to King Zachary. We'll try this road for a while."

At this compromise, the horse allowed her to gather up the reins and mount. He responded to her commands as a well-trained horse should, and Karigan frowned at his duplicity.

"That's right, you rotten horse," she said. "Pretend nothing happened."

He then adopted an uncomfortable gait that jarred every bone in her body.

"I do believe you're doing this on purpose."

The horse made no indication he had heard her, and continued on in his ambling, bouncing, potato-sack gait. Karigan clucked him into a canter which was equally jarring, but would make better headway. If foes were on their trail, she wanted to keep as far ahead as possible.

Red squirrels raced across the road before them. "Road" was laughable. It served more as a streambed when the ditches were too overgrown or filled with debris to drain properly. When Karigan reached King Zachary, she resolved to inform him what a sorry state the road was in, and demand that taxes be put to good use in repairing it. Well, maybe not demand. One did not demand anything of a king, but she would make a strong recommendation nevertheless.

Later that afternoon, she slowed the horse to a halt and dismounted. She threw her pack to the ground and searched through the saddlebags to see what would prove useful during her journey. To her delight, she found not only dried beef, bread, apples, and a water skin, but a thick green greatcoat, caped at the shoulders. Though it was a little long in the sleeves, it fit fairly well.

"Now I won't go cold." She took the food and water and plopped on the ground for a feast, and groaned.

"Am I sore." She glared at the horse who nibbled innocently at some grass.

After her light supper, Karigan wrapped herself in the greatcoat. She dozed off, and in a dream, imagined that a filmy white figure approached the horse and spoke to him. The horse listened gravely to every word. She heard nothing but a low whisper. *Who are you?* she wanted to ask. *Why do you disturb my rest?* But her mouth would not work, and she couldn't shrug off her slumber.

A nudge on the toe of her boot woke her up. The horse gazed down at her and whickered. It was dusk.

"Are you telling me it's time to go?"

The horse waited for her on the road.

"All right. I'm coming, I'm coming."

They trotted along the road again, the flutelike song of thrushes echoing in the twilight. The horse compelled Karigan to ride through the night. It was an uncomfortable ride although his gait lacked its former tooth-rattling agony.

As she rode, the woods and the abandoned road began to take on a new, ominous character. Tree limbs clinked together like old bones, and clouds blanketed the moon and stars. Her breath fogged the air, and she was glad of the warmth the greatcoat provided.

A number of times she glanced over her shoulder thinking someone was following behind. When she saw no one, she pulled her coat tighter about her and tried singing some simple songs, but they died in her throat.

"Can't keep a tune anyway," she muttered. She urged the horse into a canter, but still the unseen eyes seemed to bore into her back.

❧ DISAPPEARING ACT ❧

By the time morning arrived, bleak and gray, Karigan rode hunched in the saddle. She was exhausted, but the sensation of being watched had disappeared with first light and she finally felt safe to stop and rest.

She slid from the horse's back onto wobbly legs and groaned. Riding class had been one of her best, but nothing had prepared her for endurance riding. Too tired to even eat, she loosened the horse's girth so that he might have some comfort, wrapped herself in her stained blanket, and fell into a deep sleep.

She guessed it was late morning when she awakened. Gray clouds foretold showers to come. She leaned against a gnarled ash tree and slipped her chilled hands into the pockets of the greatcoat, and found, to her surprise, a piece of paper. Curiously she unfolded the crisp, white sheet. It was a letter written in bold script, addressed to one Lady Estora.

"A letter from our dead messenger?" she asked the horse. He blinked at her with long lashes.

She hesitated to read it. It wasn't addressed to her, or intended for her, and she feared invading someone's privacy. But the messenger was dead, and reading it wouldn't do him any harm. If she could find out who Lady Estora was, she might be able to deliver it to her

one day. With this rationale, she felt better about reading
it—until she realized it was a love letter. Her cheeks
burned as she read:

> *My Dearest Lady Estora,*
> *How I miss you these last few months; your ready*
> *smile and merry eyes. My heart aches with the*
> *knowledge that it will yet be a long month to the*
> *day before we see one another again. My brother*
> *insists it's not love, but what does he know of it? He*
> *has never loved a soul.*

Karigan scanned the private, loving sentiments until
she reached the final paragraph.

> *It is dreadfully lonely without you and to keep my*
> *spirits light, I think fair thoughts of you planning*
> *our spring wedding. Do not worry—dark arrows*
> *couldn't possibly keep me from you.*
> *With Loving Devotion,*
> *F'ryan Coblebay*

Karigan clutched the letter to her chest and sighed
wistfully, imagining that Lady Estora was the most beautiful woman who lived and how distraught she would be
over her beloved F'ryan Coblebay's death.

F'ryan Coblebay. The messenger for whom she swore
she would deliver a message to the king. The dead Green
Rider. He was no longer nameless. How ironic his last
line about dark arrows.

The horse jerked up his head, his ears pricked forward.

Karigan shook herself out of the reverie. "What's
wrong? What do you hear?"

He pawed at the road. His uneasiness was enough of
an answer for Karigan. She thrust the love letter back
into her pocket and cleared up her things. Hooves clip-
clopped distantly down the road.

She stepped into the stirrup to mount the horse, but
the saddle slid beneath his belly. The contents of the

saddlebags spilled onto the road. She cursed and pushed
the saddle to its rightful place behind the horse's withers,
and stuffed the bags with their displaced goods.

A sudden gust took her blanket and it tumbled down
the road with a life of its own. Karigan sprang after it,
feeling like a clown as the wind took it just out of her
grasp. Finally she pounced on it and ran back to the
horse with the crumpled mass.

This time, before mounting, she tightened the girth,
skinning her knuckles on the metal buckles. She sucked
on them, tasting salty blood. Sweat trickled down her
sides. The hoofbeats were drawing nearer.

There was no telling exactly how close the riders were,
or even if they were the ones who had pursued F'ryan
Coblebay. She was determined not to find out.

A fine mist fell and tendrils of fog reached out of the
forest as Karigan and the horse galloped along the road.
She didn't know what else to do except follow the road.
If they cut through the forest, its dense growth would
hamper their speed. If the people following behind were
hoping to waylay the message she carried, they might
have a tracker among them who could find her just as
easily off the road as on. If she remained on the road
and an archer with black arrows was among the group,
surely she was an open target. No easy answer came
to her.

They ran hard. She began to wonder how long the
horse could endure this pace without rest. The fog, at
least, would provide some cover. And where were they?
Where did the road lead besides north? The stream of
doubts flowed through Karigan's mind. She bent low
over the saddle, queasy with uncertainty.

When they came upon an enormous fallen spruce
blocking the road, Karigan was prepared to pull the tireless horse aside, but his stride did not flag. As he gathered himself beneath her, she grabbed handfuls of his
mane and closed her eyes. He launched over the spruce.
Branches slapped his legs and belly. Upon landing, his

front hooves dug furrows into the soft road surface. A lesser horse would have refused.

Rain pelted down, the sky darkening as if it were evening rather than late morning. The road turned into a quagmire of mud, and the horse slipped and labored through it. When they reached a stream flowing across the road, instead of under it through a collapsed culvert, she pulled the gasping horse to a halt.

"Running through this mess will only break one of your legs," she said.

She guided him upstream. A tracker wouldn't be able to find hoofprints in rushing water. If they were lucky, the rain would wash away their prints on the road. The Horse, as she decided to call him for lack of any other name, seemed to approve, or at least he did not resist.

Karigan pushed away branches hanging over the stream, receiving an extra drenching from water accumulated on each limb. They picked their way over slick moss-covered rocks and through deep mud.

A granite ledge, mottled with green lichen, large enough to hide behind, loomed out of the mist. The road couldn't be seen through the fog, but it was close enough that anyone passing by could be heard. Karigan concealed herself and the horse behind the ledge, and stood miserably in the downpour awaiting some sign.

Though only moments passed, the waiting was interminable. Karigan dismounted and, tired of the rain pounding on her head, drew up her hood. She leaned against the coarse, wet granite, berating herself for having left Selium at all.

When she left Selium, the possibility of encountering genuine danger had never occurred to her. Sure, she had wanted an adventurous life like her father's. And here it was, nothing at all like she dreamed it would be.

If something happened to her, she would be unable to clear her name in Selium. More distressing still, the people who cared about her would have no clues to her disappearance. She closed her eyes and could see her father scouring the countryside for her, calling her name, grieving. . . . Her throat constricted, and she swallowed hard.

The Horse tensed beside her, his ears pricked forward. Voices could be heard from the road, faint at first, then clearer as they drew closer.

"No sign of any horse here."

"I don't like it. The Greenie's dead and you can't tell me the horse has the smarts to deliver the message by himself."

There was a long silence before the first voice replied. "Sarge, in my estimation, a ghost rides that horse. How do we stop a spirit rider?"

Sarge snorted. "You know I forbid that kind of talk. Don't let the captain hear it either. That's the problem with you rustic fools, you're all superstitious."

"Things was getting uncanny," the "rustic fool" answered. "These woods, the dead Greenie, and the Gray One. Ice cold, he is. It's not reg'lar."

"I don't care if it's regular or not. We follow the captain's orders and right now our orders are to find that horse and destroy the message. Understand?"

"Yes, Sergeant."

Sarge grunted. "Spirit riders. You rustics have lively imaginations. I've never heard such nonsense. Now look for tracks. Captain doesn't carry that whip as an ornament, you know. You don't want his leather licking your hide, I assure you."

So at least four searched for the message. Where were the other two if they weren't with the sergeant and his companion? Whose soldiers were they? Their accents were Sacoridian to the core, but surely the king's own militia would not be involved in trying to block a vital message from reaching him. Some of the wealthier provinces armed their own small contingents, as did major landowners. Would any of them have something to lose if the message reached King Zachary?

"Sarge! I got something. Looks like a hoofprint in the mud."

"Sharp eyes, Thursgad."

Karigan unconsciously grasped the winged horse brooch pinned to the greatcoat. It warmed at her touch. Trees shifted around her in the gently wafting mist like the shapes of armed soldiers. Branches jabbed at her like swords. Should she make a run for it? Could speed and surprise allow her and The Horse to escape? She remembered all too vividly the black-shafted arrows protruding from F'ryan Coblebay's back.

Trying to outrun the soldiers would be fatal. She would hide behind the granite ledge and flee only if she had to. If the soldiers believed the messenger horse was acting on his own, all the better. She unsheathed the saber and stood by the horse's side, ready to mount, just in case.

"I can't figure out which way the horse went," Thursgad said.

"Think like a horse. Shouldn't be too hard—they've got small brains like yours. They'd take the easiest route."

"You mean . . . straight down the road?"

"Whadya think I mean? Is your brain even smaller than a horse's? Yes, the road. Straight ahead. This hoofprint confirms it came this way."

"But if a spirit rider guides him—"

"Thursgad, you fool. Didn't I say none of that rustic nonsense?"

Their voices faded down the road. Karigan heaved an enormous sigh of relief and sheathed her saber. She swung herself up into the wet saddle, grimacing as cold rainwater soaked through her trousers.

Then she sat in indecision. Using the road might mean running into those who searched for her. She could cut through the woods and head east, but the woods would slow her down. She frowned. If she hadn't skipped so many geography classes, she might be able to think of some other route than the road.

The Horse whinnied sharply and danced beneath her, his hooves sucking in the mud.

"What now?"

The driving rain had changed to a penetrating drizzle.

It fell away in layers like veils to reveal the approach of a mounted figure. The rider was much like one of Thursgad's spirit riders, gauzy and indistinct in the shifting fog, molded of mist, insubstantial as air. His tall white stallion faded in and out of the opaque fog.

The Horse pawed the mud and snorted, every muscle in his body taut, willing Karigan to give him his head to flee as instinct told him he must. Her arms ached with the effort of holding him in. She sat rooted, fascinated by the stranger. Then she remembered F'ryan Coblebay's final words: *Beware the shadow man. . . .*

As the rider neared, his form solidified and sharpened. No ghost was he, and his demeanor did not suggest he was a man of the shadows. He sat erect in the saddle. He stared at her with one intense green eye, the other covered by a black patch. Rain beaded on his bald head, but he seemed unconcerned. Beneath a plain charcoal cloak he wore a gold embroidered scarlet tunic. It was the uniform of one of the provincial militia.

The man halted the stallion's fluid movements with an imperceptible twitch of the reins. Karigan watched him through her tunnellike hood. Water plunked rhythmically from the rim onto her arm.

The leather of the man's saddle creaked as he leaned forward. His eye searched her. "My men seem to believe you're some sort of spirit rider," he said in a gravelly voice roughened by a lifetime of shouting commands. "Who is beneath the hood?"

Karigan was too paralyzed by fear to speak. Why hadn't she let The Horse run when she had had the chance? She grasped the brooch again.

The man's green eye flickered. "I see from your hands that you are of the flesh. Though one Greenie is dead, another carries on the mission. If you don't wish to shed your earthly flesh like Coblebay, I suggest you hand over the message satchel you carry. And you will tell me who gave Coblebay the information."

Karigan sat frozen, holding the reins tightly, feeling as if someone clenched her in a steely grip. The Horse's neck was lathered with sweat, his eyes rolling wildly. Only her tight hold prevented him from bolting.

The cold rain soaked through to Karigan's skin and the clamminess of it made her shiver. The sodden greatcoat weighed her down and made movement an effort.

The man raised a brow and Karigan imagined the great gaping socket beneath the eyepatch widening. "My governor is most displeased by this. Someone has abused his trust, and all his plans will go to ruin if he doesn't learn the name of the traitor."

Karigan remained still.

"I see." He pulled what looked like a live snake from beneath his cloak. It was a coiled whip. "Since you do not volunteer the information, I shall have to persuade you."

Karigan panted, and loosened her hold on the reins. Whatever had held her back now eased its grip on her. The whip unraveled in the man's hands, and he cracked it expertly.

"I will have you know that the hands that wield this tool of persuasion are well-practiced. Perhaps you've heard of me. I am Immerez. Captain Immerez."

Karigan had never heard of him, though a true Green Rider might know him by reputation. Her knuckles turned white around the brooch. She swallowed hard. If only she could snap her fingers and turn invisible! The brooch pulsated with sudden heat beneath her hand.

Captain Immerez stiffened, the whip going limp in his hand and his one eye wide open. "Where . . .?" He bent close again, his eye darting about. "Where are you?"

Karigan's mouth dropped open. Had he gone suddenly and inexplicably blind? Yet he seemed to see clearly. He just couldn't see her. She looked at . . . no, looked through her arm. It was there like a faint shadow, but definitely transparent. She jabbed her arm with a finger. It was solid enough. . . .

Whatever rendered her invisible had affected her vision as well. The deep greens of soaked moss and pines became shades of gray. Immerez's scarlet tunic darkened to a shadowy maroon. Shapes grew indistinct as if a thick cloud obscured her sight.

Immerez's eye still searched for her. He unsheathed his sword, undoubtedly attempting to test by touch.

The shackles of indecision and fear fell away. The Horse needed no prompting as she gave him his head. They bounded down the stream, and she let instinct guide him, the grayness in her eyes lacking enough contrast or depth to distinguish rocks from water.

Once they nearly fell headlong, and Karigan was thrown onto The Horse's neck. He almost fell to his knees, then scrambled for his footing, slid through mud, and picked up the pace again. They careened around boulders and between trees in a breakneck dash that would have mortified her riding instructor. All the while, Captain Immerez's high-strung stallion splashed behind them.

An eternity passed before they reached the road. Karigan could only guess how the struggle downstream had taxed The Horse, yet he flew into a flat-out gallop when they reached level ground.

Thursgad and Sarge, at least the two men whom she guessed were Thursgad and Sarge, appeared ahead, riding their own horses at a slow jog. Should she turn back? The whip whizzed past her ear. Immerez was just strides behind. But she was invisible. How could he . . . ? She blew past the two men ahead and got an impression of their amazed expressions.

"The horse!" they shouted.

Though she was invisible, The Horse was not. As she rode around a bend, she wished for him to be invisible, too. The Horse vanished from the pursuers' sight, leaving behind only the echo of pounding hooves.

Karigan rode on, feeling as if she were submerged beneath some gray sea, with water pressing in all around.

She felt as if she fought the tide; her lungs ached for air. In the grayness, a gloom clung to her which she felt she would never be free of, as if she would drown in it. She was so exhausted. Exhausted and wrung out with despair in the never ending gray, gray world.

Then color shimmered like a newly created thing. A path opened up on the side of the road painted with rusty red pine needles and vibrant green hemlock, pine, and spruce trees. Tiny white bunchberry flowers grew in patches along the path. The sun broke through the clouds, and though it appeared just a lighter shade of gray elsewhere in the woods, along the path it showered through the trees in brilliant beams of gold.

Karigan reined The Horse along the path and slumped on his neck. She could see right through his chestnut hide to the forest floor. He halted, and she slid off his back onto a moist patch of sphagnum moss. She was too exhausted to even remove the sodden greatcoat.

As she drifted into sleep, she wished to be whole again—not transparent like some living ghost.

⋘ GRAY ONE ⋙

The rising sun was hidden behind the height of the great wall. One could look up and up, and even higher, but never really see the top. It was magic, of course. Where the real granite stopped, a magical shield continued in a seamless illusion of a towering wall. The D'Yers had designed the wall to seemingly surpass the sky and reach for the very heavens. There were flying things the Sacoridians and the League had wanted to keep on the other side.

The Gray One's original crack had spread its spidery fracture lines into the surrounding seams of mortar, weakening a section of wall about the size of a doorway. This went far beyond his expectations—that the cracks would grow more than a few inches. He was closer to breaking through than he could have hoped for.

Time. Time had made the spells brittle and the mortar vulnerable. Without the touch of a mage to maintain the wall, it had weakened. Even now silvery runes shimmered on the granite blocks around the fractures. The runes were ancient Sacoridian and Kmaernian characters. They were runes of alarm; they warned of the fissures, of the weakening of the wall. They revealed unraveling spell songs, and rhythms that had been corrupted.

No one would know about the wall until it was too late. It was already too late. The D'Yers hadn't bothered with patrols for centuries, and even if they became aware of the cracks, they wouldn't know what to do. They would have to seek a scholar to decipher the runes, and a very learned master he would have to be. The language of Kmaern was lost with its people, extinct from the tongues of the living for centuries.

Even if the D'Yers could translate the runes, they would have no understanding of how to rebuild the wall. Like many other things, they had lost the craft. There was no threat to the Gray One's plans.

He splayed his fingers against the cold wall. It prickled, but without the intensity of before. He willed his thoughts down through his shoulders, down his arms, and through his fingertips. His consciousness spread across the wall like cracks, and he felt the resonance of his song still working in the rock and mortar.

The old voices had grown uncertain, and the beat weaker. With any luck, his song would spread along the entire length of the wall of its own volition and decay the spells that bound it together. In time, the wall would crumble to the earth and the power of *Kanmorhan Vane* would spread unhindered across the lands. Not only would the Gray One win access to those great powers, but the lands would surrender to him under the threat of darkness that lurked in the forest.

He sang the unweaving, steadily corrupting the old spells, chipping away at mortar with his thoughts, convincing the granite it had been subject to thousands of years of freezing and thawing, to wind, rain, and snow.

Finally, he weakened it enough.

The Gray One moved each limb experimentally where he lay on the dewy grass. His body proved a hindrance at times, but it managed to absorb the shock with no damage. His mind had experienced the worst strain while singing the counterspells, and when body and mind reunited after hours of unweaving, he had collapsed. His head throbbed worse than at any time during his earliest training.

It was midmorning; the soldiers would be anxious to

find the messenger horse. Let them wait. They would find their quarry soon enough. First he must examine his work.

The fissures had spread along every seam across a width of about six feet. They had spread upward, too, to wherever the wall peaked. The Gray One placed his palms against the wall, and this time he pushed. The cracked section teetered and swayed, balanced on edge. The wall fell over with a shower of mortar and chipped rock; the ground rumbled like thunder as giant blocks pummeled the earth. Tremors shook beneath his feet.

When the dust had settled, rubble sat in a heap where a once impermeable section of wall had stood. Not only was the physical barrier down, so was the corresponding magical barrier that had shielded above it. The real wall was only ten feet high, whereas the magical shield extended far into the sky. His broken section would now serve as a portal.

Black tree limbs twisted and writhed in a shifting vapor beyond the breach. Much of the forest remained cloaked by fog. Unknown wild creatures screeched within. Soon. Soon some of them would find their way through the wall and into Sacoridia.

He wanted to explore the forest, but there was no time. He turned away from *Kanmorhan Vane* with some regret.

I will enter one day. But now is too soon. I must lay the groundwork.

A fluttering of wings on an old ash tree caught his eye. An owl launched from its perch and flew swiftly away to the east, soon disappearing in the distant sky.

It is sensible to leave, he thought. *This will soon be no place for owls or other creatures to live.*

He called his ghostly slaves to attend him. They swam in an indistinct mass before him. These had once been individuals with their own paths in life, their loves and hates, their skills and talents and dreams. Some had been good citizens, and some had been criminals. Indiscriminately, the Gray One had cut short all of their lives. All so they could serve him.

One stood off by itself, more rigid and defined than the others.

"Coblebay," the Gray One said. "You couldn't resist my call this time."

The spirit wavered as if drawn by the Gray One's words, then redefined himself. *I still resist.*

"Won't you help me take the quick road?"

I've come to see what you've done.

"Magnificent, isn't it?"

The spirit's face remained impassive.

The Gray One knew what energy it cost the spirit to appear to him, and yet resist. He stretched out a hand. "You will serve, not defy me." The magic of his command vibrated in his throat. The binding song flowed through his mind.

The spirit faded, began to drift toward him.

"Yes," the Gray One said. "You serve me." But even as he said it, he lost strength in his legs and staggered, barely maintaining his feet. The strain was too much. He asked too much of his body after having breached the D'Yer Wall. He would have just enough power and strength to travel. Reluctantly, he let F'ryan Coblebay go, and watched him vanish.

He wondered at the spirit's stubborn nature. It was strong, and it had its own agenda that impelled it to resist him.

❧ SEVEN CHIMNEYS ❧

Someone prodded Karigan's ribs.

"Stop it, Estral. I'll go to class tomorrow." She moaned and rolled over onto her back. The rich scent of loam filled her nostrils and the sun beat on her face. She blinked her eyes open. Clouds smeared the sky like fingerprints. This wasn't her dorm room.

Thump, thump. This time on her shoulder.

Karigan blinked again. Soldiers pursued her. Soldiers who would stop at nothing to possess the message she carried.

She sat bolt upright, and the world spun. She gasped in terror, feeling around herself for a rock, for anything with which to defend herself, expecting at any moment to feel the sting of Captain Immerez's cruel whip. But when the dizziness passed, two elderly ladies, not Captain Immerez at all, stood before her. She rubbed her eyes to make sure.

"The child is alive," said one.

"I can see that very well for myself," said the other.

Karigan shook her aching head to make sure she wasn't dreaming, but the two still stood there staring at her in fascination, lively eyes animating crinkled elfin faces.

The plump one wore a dress of burnt orange and had a white apron tied around her ample hips. A kindly smile rounded her cheeks into robust humps. Her companion, in contrast, wore a sterner expression on her narrow face. She was dressed in deep velvet green with puffy sleeves, a black shawl draped over her shoulders. She leaned on a cane of twisted hickory, which she had used to prod Karigan awake. They both looked as if they were out for a stroll in one of Selium's manicured parks, not standing in the middle of the wilderness.

"Do you think we ought to take the child in?" the plump one asked.

"She does look harmless and frightfully out of sorts. It would be rude of us not to invite her to tea."

"That would surpass mere rudeness, I fear. It would be uncivilized. But what of the others?"

"They must be invited, too."

Karigan glanced over her shoulder to see who they meant, but only The Horse stood there.

"Letitia will have a thing or two to say about the mud."

The thin one rolled her eyes. "She always has a thing or two to say."

"The child does look like she's in need of a good scrubbing. She is very muddy."

"I agree. It would only be proper for her to be presentable, and Letitia wouldn't have so much to complain about." The woman then turned her sharp eyes on Karigan. "Come, child, and bring your friends. It's nearly time for tea and you mustn't keep us waiting."

The two ladies turned their backs to her and walked down a surprisingly well-groomed trail. A well-groomed trail? The last she remembered was a tangle of underbrush. She watched The Horse follow the strange old ladies, his ears twitching back and forth as if he listened to their nonsensical chatter rising and burbling like birdsong. The woman in green halted and looked over her shoulder.

"Child, are you coming or not? It would be terribly impolite of you to be late. Look, your companions are joining us."

Karigan looked, but still couldn't see anyone but The Horse. She could only wonder who these eccentric ladies were and what they were doing in the middle of the woods.

They appeared harmless enough, and The Horse seemed to trust them. She snorted at herself: was she to rely on horse instinct this whole strange journey? It was her stomach, though, that decided her. It rumbled in an empty, cavernous way, and the thought of tea and cake was heartening. Legs wobbly and head pounding, she climbed to her feet and trotted to catch up with them.

The woods gradually grew more cultivated. The path broadened into a full-scale road wide enough for two amply outfitted coaches to pass one another. It was well maintained, too, compared to the North Road. Someone had cleared dead wood and the snaggle of underbrush from the bordering woods, lending the area an aura of order and balance unlike the chaos of the untouched wilderness. Neatly trimmed hedges lined the road.

They crossed a stone bridge which spanned a chatty stream. Warblers trilled in the woods about them. The pounding in Karigan's head subsided; weariness lifted from her shoulders.

The road ended in a loop at a stately old manor house built of stone and timbers. Several chimneys puffed balsam smoke into the air, and windows rippled in the sunshine. Vines crept up the sides of the manor house, blending it harmoniously into the woods. Several outbuildings of like character, including a small stable, were spread out behind it. It was an oasis in the middle of the Green Cloak.

The two ladies mounted the steps to the front porch which wrapped around the house. "Welcome to Seven Chimneys," said the woman in green, as if addressing an assembly rather than just Karigan.

Karigan counted the chimneys and came up with nine, not seven.

"It was built by our father long ago," the woman continued. "Come." She extended her hand. A fine tracery of veins like rivers on a map looped around her thin wrist and across the back of her hand. "Our servants will see to your friend, the horse."

No servants appeared, but The Horse walked toward

the stable as obediently as if led. The two old ladies certainly were peculiar, but they didn't seem threatening, and so she followed them into the house.

The floors were a light stained oak, and the walls were papered with intricate, flowery designs. Rich hangings, anonymous portraits of men and women garbed in armor or fancy dress, and hand-braided carpets adorned each room they passed through, all miraculously unfaded by time or sunlight.

Heavy furnishings were intricately carved, not a surface left untouched. One such chair in the corridor had a back carved in the likeness of a tree, its armrests and legs all leaves and sinuous, winding branches and roots. A red velvet cushion covered the seat.

Cheerful fires glowed in each fieldstone hearth they passed, and Karigan's damp chill began to be replaced by warmth.

"Letitia has set a bath for you, child," the plump lady said. "She will be none too happy about the mud you've let in, but don't let her annoy you. If she couldn't complain, she wouldn't enjoy life at all. Isn't that right, Miss Bayberry?"

"Indeed. Mud season is the bane of her life, poor dear, and sends her into a snit every year. We endure, however. It is impossible to find good help out here." Miss Bayberry paused in front of a door and took a deep breath. "Well, then, child, we shall lend you a nightgown and robe after your bath. Letitia will see to the cleaning of your clothes."

They led her into a stone-flagged room where yet another hearth merrily crackled with fire. A solitary window looked out into the garden. Sunlight filtered through its upper pane, which was stained in the deep hues of wild blueberries and cast liquid splashes of blues and greens on the slate floor.

Plumes of steam rose from a brass hip bath in the center of the room. It wasn't what Karigan was used to, with Selium's porcelain tubs and piped water, but in her present state, the hip bath looked heavenly.

Miss Bayberry pointed her cane at the tub. "Take your time, child. Relax—you look thoroughly done in."

The two left, pulling the door shut behind them. The voice of the plump one drifted back to Karigan from somewhere down the corridor: "I think our etiquette has improved over the years, dear sister."

The other made a muffled agreement.

Karigan disrobed, untidily dropping her clothes on the floor. A bucket of cold water and a dipper stood next to the tub. She ladled enough cold water into the bath to make it bearable, but it was still shockingly hot as she submerged.

Sprigs of mint floated on the water, the scent soothing and relaxing her. Her body quickly adapted to the heat, and her taut muscles loosened. Before she became too languid, she set about cleaning several days' accumulation of grit from herself. Her long hair wasn't easily managed, but she struggled with it till it was clean and fully rinsed.

She sighed blissfully and eventually dozed off. When she awakened, the bath water was still comfortably warm, and sunshine still glimmered through the window as before. Yet, she couldn't help but think hours had passed.

Her clothes had disappeared, but the promised nightgown and robe hung from pegs on the wall, a comb placed on a side table, and a pair of soft suede slippers were on the floor below.

They do think of everything.

When she was dry, robed, and her long hair was combed out, the pleasant smell of mint lingered on her skin and hair. As if on cue, Miss Bayberry tapped on the door.

"Child, are you prepared for tea?"

Karigan cracked the door open and smiled. "Yes, I'm ready."

"Very good. Bunch awaits us in the parlor."

Bunch?

Miss Bayberry, leaning on her cane, led Karigan to the

most elaborate room of all. They sat on a plush sofa which faced yet another hearth. The sofa's armrests were carved with floral patterns and hummingbirds. Sunlight beamed through a broad window casting the room in a warm amber tint.

The plump one, "Bunch," Karigan supposed, carried in a silver tea service on a tray and set it on a table before them.

"We use the silver for special guests only," she said. "Not that we receive guests very often, special or otherwise. Usually a wayward stranger lost in the woods. I trust you found the bath satisfactory."

"Oh, yes—splendid!" It wasn't a word Karigan typically used, but it seemed appropriate in this house of rich furnishings, and in the company of these two ladies.

Bunch poured tea. "Honey and cream? No, not you, my dear Bay. You know what cream does to your digestion."

Miss Bayberry *hrrrumfed* her opinion.

Butter cookies, scones, and pound cake were served with tea, and while the ladies discussed the oddities of weather and gardening, Karigan's mind brimmed and swirled like the cream in her tea, especially when Bunch poured a fourth cup which she placed before an unoccupied chair.

Miss Bayberry noticed Karigan eyeing the teacup. "I am sorry your other companion could not join us, but Letitia would not have him in the house. She was adamant."

Karigan couldn't take it any longer. "Companion? What companion? I've been traveling alone."

"Oh, my dear. You must be terribly unobservant."

"Or dense," Bunch said, not unsympathetically.

"I was referring, of course, to your companion whom you call The Horse. I assure you that though he did not join us for tea, he is being well tended by the stableboy."

"The Horse." Karigan shifted in her seat wondering if the women were mad. "And the other?"

Bunch and Bayberry exchanged surprised glances.

"If you don't know, dear," Miss Bayberry said, "then it may not be our place to tell you."

"Oh, come now, Bay. She will think us daft old fools. My dear child, a spirit accompanies you."

A swallow of tea caught in Karigan's throat and she choked violently.

"Oh!" fretted Bunch. "I told Letitia to leave the nuts out of the scones."

Miss Bayberry struck Karigan soundly on the back.

"A *what* accompanies me?" she sputtered.

"My," Bunch said. "She's deaf, too."

"A SPIRIT!" Miss Bayberry hollered through cupped hands.

"Please," Karigan said, her back stinging and her ears ringing, "I can hear fine."

"Ah." Miss Bayberry crooked a skeptical brow. "You are accompanied by a shadow. A specter, a ghost, a shade. You know, dear, a spirit." Her apparent ease with the topic was unnerving. "He follows you. You, or something about you, binds him to the earth."

Karigan paled. She had heard stories, of course, of dead relatives visiting those still alive and loved. There were many tales of spirits haunting buildings in Selium, but she had never given them much credence.

"Now you've gone and done it, Bay. You've upset the child."

"H-how do you see this spirit?" Karigan asked.

"Quite simply, the same way we see you." Bunch twisted her teacup in her hand. "He wears green and has black hair hanging to his shoulders. Two black-shafted arrows protrude from a blood-dampened back that will not dry."

"He calls himself F'ryan Coblebay," Miss Bayberry said.

Karigan's hands trembled. How could they know what he looked like or how he had died unless . . . unless they really could see him? They could have gotten his name off the love letter which had still been in the pocket of the greatcoat. . . . The greatcoat had disappeared from the bathing room with the rest of her clothes.

Miss Bayberry placed a comforting hand on Karigan's wrist. "Not to worry, dear. Master Coblebay is only trying to watch over you, to see that his mission is carried out. After that, he will pass on. As it is, he tends to fade in and out. His link with that which is earthly is rather limited. One day, you too, may see."

Karigan shook her head in disbelief. Here she was, in this incredible manor house, with two old, eccentric ladies who could communicate with ghosts. Either they were cracked, or they were seers, or some other sort of magic was at work. "Who are you?" she asked. "And what are you doing out here in the middle of nowhere?"

Miss Bayberry rapped the handle of her cane on the little table. Scones and cookies bounced, and teacups clattered. "Bunch! Did we forget introductions? Did we?"

An expression of horror swept across Bunch's plump features, and she covered her mouth with her hand. "Oh, Bay. In our haste to please, we forgot. It has been so long since anyone has visited. Can you forgive us, child, for forgetting this one basic propriety?"

Karigan stared dumbly.

The ladies must have perceived her reaction as forgiveness, for they both released sighs of genuine relief.

"Well, then," Miss Bayberry said, "let us introduce ourselves properly. We are the Berry sisters. I am Bay and this is my sister Bunch."

"Our dear father, the late Professor Berry, gave us names that made us sound like some of the local vegetation," Bunch said with a chuckle. "Terms of endearment, really. They are but nicknames."

"We were born," Miss Bayberry said, "with the names Isabelle—"

"And Penelope," Bunch finished. "Though we rarely use our true names."

"We loved our father a great deal. It was he who built this house in the midst of the Green Cloak's wilds. He

said it was the only way to absorb the power of nature
and bring to the wilderness an element of civilization.
What with no towns nearby, and the unpredictability of
living near the northern border, it was not an easy life,
especially for our mother. Child, there wasn't even a road
back then."

Miss Bunchberry smoothed a crease out of her linen
napkin. "When our father built Seven Chimneys, he
sought to provide Mother a respectable estate. He spared
no expense for her, and even brought along the entire
household staff from our original home in Selium."

"Selium," Karigan said. "That's where I began my
journey."

"Are you a scholar?" Miss Bayberry asked.

Karigan frowned. "No." She hadn't been much of anything at Selium.

"Ah, well. Our father was. He was a master of many
disciplines—so many that he just wore a white uniform
with a master's knot. None of the single disciplines have
white uniforms, you know, and Father was the only one
to wear it. Soon he studied disciplines that were no
longer taught . . . or approved of."

Miss Bunch leaned forward. "The arcane arts," she
whispered.

A tremor ran up Karigan's spine. Magic was a topic
to be shunned by most Sacoridians.

"Who is telling the story?" Miss Bayberry demanded.

Miss Bunchberry pouted.

"Don't interrupt again." Miss Bayberry cast her sister
a severe expression, then cleared her throat and continued. "Father started to study the arcane arts. He spent
years poring over old books and scrolls in the archives,
first to learn the history of magic, then to learn its appli-
cation. The latter made the Guardian of Selium nervous.
You see, after those incursions made by Mornhavon the
Black, who used such terrible powers during the Long
War, people have been phobic of magic, as if using it
would restore Mornhavon, or someone like him, to
power.

"The Guardian finally demanded that Father either stop trying to awaken magic, or leave the city. As you may have concluded, Father chose to leave the school."

Karigan was incredulous. First ghosts, now magic. These two old ladies must be daft. Her hands shook a little as she set her empty teacup on the table before her.

"Was . . . was your father successful?" she asked. "At awakening magic, I mean. . . ."

"Yes and no," Miss Bayberry said. "He had no natural talent. Either you are born with innate talent, or you can possess a device which provides or augments powers. Mornhavon the Black had natural powers, but he augmented them with a device called the Black Star. Father did try to create magical devices, but he wasn't very successful because the magic wasn't within him. The arcane arts are elusive. Still, he was able to accomplish some things. I expect you know all about magic."

"Uh, no."

Miss Bayberry raised both brows. "But surely you must know since you carry a magical device."

"I—"

Karigan looked at Miss Bayberry, then Miss Bunchberry. Their faces were flat, their eyes questioning. The house creaked in the stillness.

"You are a Green Rider, are you not?" Miss Bayberry asked.

"No, not exactly."

The ladies exchanged glances and rounded their mouths into O's.

"Our question to you, then," Miss Bunchberry said, "is who are you?"

Karigan shifted uncomfortably in her seat under their intense gazes. It was as if the room had suddenly iced over. She realized she would have to do some fast talking or . . . Or what? What could these two possibly do to her? With all the talk of magic and ghosts, better not to find out.

In acknowledgment of their penchant for propriety,

she stood up and bowed the formal bow of the clans: one hand over her heart, and bending deeply at the waist.

"I'm Karigan G'ladheon of Clan G'ladheon," she said. "At your service."

"A merchant greeting," Miss Bunchberry said in hushed tones to her sister.

Miss Bayberry remained unmoved, absently caressing the smooth handle of her cane. "You'd best tell us your story, Karigan G'ladheon."

Karigan cleared her throat uncertainly. She glanced at the fire, finding some comfort in its warmth and cheerful crack and pop. "I, uh, left Selium rather abruptly." She took a deep breath. "I was a student there, and the dean suspended me. Indefinitely."

The sisters maintained their stoic expressions. Somehow it seemed terribly important to be honest with them. If she admitted her doubtful background, they would be more willing to trust her. Still, it didn't make the telling any easier.

"The dean suspended me because I skipped classes and such. He said my, uh, attitude wasn't good." Blood crept up her neck and colored her cheeks, and still the ladies stayed mute, neither condemning her nor offering comfort. "The main reason he suspended me was because there was this fight. And I won."

She could still see it clearly, the throng of students pushing and shoving around the practice ring to see what was happening, Timas Mirwell prone on the ground, spitting dirt, the tip of her wooden practice sword against the back of his neck. *You are dead,* she had told him.

Miss Bunch lifted a brow. "You were suspended for winning a fight?"

"I beat the heir of the lord-governor of Mirwell Province." At the time, she hadn't felt remorseful about challenging him to the fight, then thrashing him. He had humiliated her in a number of other ways since the first day she arrived at school, and she had finally had enough. But now, under the steady scrutiny of the Berry sisters, she had a new perspective. She felt childish.

"All right," Miss Bayberry said with a dismissive gesture. "You've established you were not the most desirable student which, in the end, caused you to leave Selium. Did you not think to face your problem?"

Karigan's cheeks grew warm again. "I was too angry. I ran away. That's when I met F'ryan Coblebay."

"Ah," said Miss Bunchberry. "This is what we were wondering about."

Karigan wiggled in her seat and felt the weight of their gazes on her again. But she had nothing to be ashamed of with this part of the story. She told them of how she encountered F'ryan Coblebay, dying with two arrows in his back, and anxious for her to carry his message to the king. She was careful about what she told them—it wouldn't do to reveal more than necessary. She wished she hadn't let the message satchel out of sight. She finished with her narrow escape from Captain Immerez and his men.

The sisters glanced at one another as if mentally conferring. The room warmed considerably.

"The spirit . . . that is, F'ryan Coblebay, wasn't able to tell us so much," Miss Bayberry said. "You've explained yourself quite adequately, dear child. Yours is a brave undertaking. Many would have quailed at carrying such a message under such serious circumstances." She must have noticed Karigan's stricken expression for she added, "Rolph the stableboy immediately placed the message satchel in the guestroom where you will be spending the night. No one has broken the seal of the message. Your other things await you there as well . . . except the device which is in our immediate care."

"The . . . device?"

"Yes, the arcane device. The one that caused you to fade out when you faced those brigands on the road. The brooch, child."

"Oh!"

"It isn't a particularly powerful thing," Miss Bunchberry said. "It may even be more trouble than it's worth. Letitia brought it to Bay and me when she set about cleaning that muddy coat of yours. Poor soul just can't abide mud. She'd clean it from the ground if she could."

"Ahem, sister," Miss Bayberry said. "Keep with the topic."

Bunch sent Bay an annoyed glance, then continued. "Father had no one but us to confide his discoveries in, and to teach. Seven Chimneys wasn't a proper school like Selium, but it didn't keep him from his calling. Teaching, I mean. That's why Bay and I are able to recognize arcane magic like the brooch. It is probable you accidentally invoked its one single power: fading out."

Miss Bayberry produced the brooch in her upturned palm, seemingly out of the air. "We would like you to try to invoke the power of the brooch so we can see how potent it is."

Karigan sat up startled. For all the sisters' fetish for propriety, and seeming ingenuous natures, she sensed an underlying intelligence of which she was allowed to touch but a small part. There was an intensity about them, like a bright burning fire within, but hidden behind a facade of proper social deportment, lightly sugared scones, and fine silver. Was their simplicity a deception, so as not to betray their hidden wisdom? Or was it that their father had taught them well? There was little about them, she decided, that was simple.

"I'm not sure I can make the brooch work," Karigan said. "I don't know how I did it the first time."

"Just try for us, dear," Miss Bunch said. "Try to remember what you did just before you went invisible."

Karigan took the brooch with some hesitation. It was cold and heavy in her hand, the winged horse ready for flight as ever. She tried to remember the moments leading to her serendipitous ability to become invisible . . . Captain Immerez sitting upon his white horse in the rain, his one eye trying to see through her hood; a whip unraveling in his hand. She shivered. She had no idea what had triggered her invisibility except a strong desire to disappear.

"Oh!" Miss Bayberry straightened next to her, her eyes glittering. "The child has positively faded."

"She is one with the upholstery," agreed Miss Bunchberry.

To Karigan, the room had become leaden, all the furnishings, and even the fire, just shades of gray. Except the Berry sisters. Their eyes were as blue as ever—as blue as blueberries—and color and light danced about them, just like the colors of the trail that had led her to Seven Chimneys. Why the variation? The grayness weighed on her, just as before, and she wished herself visible again.

"We have learned much," Miss Bunchberry said.

"Child, your brooch isn't terribly powerful, just as we suspected. It gives you an ability to fade out, or more accurately, to blend in with your surroundings. It wasn't particularly potent here in the parlor because of the amount of sunshine coming through the window. It must have been extremely effective in the dark forest with all the rain and fog."

Karigan nodded, her temple throbbing. Maybe the terrible weather had been an advantage in her confrontation with Immerez after all.

"I can see also that the device saps energy from the user. That is often the fault with magical devices, and even innate power. There is always some cost to use it, and for the trouble, it's often not worthwhile."

Karigan hooked a tendril of hair behind her ear. The brooch had proved its worth already. She dreaded to think what would have happened if she hadn't used it when she met Immerez. "I still don't understand how this brooch . . . how magic works."

Miss Bunchberry poured another cup of tea to help "restore" her. The steaming liquid extinguished the throbbing in her head.

"Of course we've just tried to explain magic," Miss Bunch said. "The little we gleaned from our father's teachings, anyway. But one can't explain magic, really."

"It exists," Miss Bayberry said, "as flowers bloom in the spring."

"As the sun rises and sets," Miss Bunchberry said.

"As the ocean rolls . . ."

"And as stars twinkle in the night."

"You see, child," Miss Bayberry said, "magic is. The world fairly glows with it. Rather, it did before the Long War, and for a while afterward. All we have left now are shards and pieces."

Miss Bunchberry folded her hands decorously in her lap. "Child, we thought from all appearances you were an indoctrinated Green Rider. The magic accepted you, and the messenger service does take young ones, you know. Only Green Riders and magic users could recognize that brooch. To the ordinary person, the brooch would look like something other than its present form. Maybe a cheap piece of costume jewelry, or nothing at all. It is a way of setting apart the false Green Riders from the real Green Riders."

"I don't understand." Karigan had never seen the brooch as anything but a winged horse. She had known it was pure gold—what kind of merchant's daughter would she be if she couldn't recognize true gold?—but she had thought nothing of it.

Miss Bayberry stirred some honey into her tea. "The brooch has accepted you. It wouldn't permit or tolerate you to wear it if it didn't perceive you as a Green Rider."

Karigan was aghast. "But it's just metal." And she was not a Green Rider.

"With some very strange spells designed within it. I'm not sure how the brooch accepted you as a Green Rider, but it may have been the duress of the situation when young Coblebay passed his mission on to you." Miss Bay tapped her spoon on the edge of her teacup. "Fortunately, the brooch found you worthy."

Or unfortunately. Karigan hardly felt worthy of anything at the moment, and such talk made her dizzy. "I have a lot of questions. . . ."

Miss Bayberry reached over and patted her knee. "We

understand, child. You left Selium under undesirable conditions only to find your life complicated by a dying messenger with an unfinished mission. I know my sister and I have said some unlikely things, but we are trying to be helpful for we have known some Green Riders in our lifetime—friends of our father's—who shared with him what they knew of magic. They were the best kind of people."

The sisters had said unlikely things, indeed! Ghosts? None that she could see. And magic? Karigan's fingers tightened around the gold brooch. She felt the urge to hurl it into the fire along with F'ryan Coblebay's message. Why had she taken on his mission? *I must have been out of my head . . . or daft.*

Maybe she could leave the message with the sisters and absolve herself of all responsibility. Suddenly the brooch flared with heat in her hand, and she dropped it onto the floor. She blew on her stinging palm.

"What happened, dear?" Miss Bunchberry asked.

"It burned me! I was thinking about getting rid of it and it burned me!"

"Arcane relics often have a mind of their own, and when they've made up their minds about something, well, there is no changing them."

Karigan groaned. How could an inanimate object have a mind of its own? She tentatively picked up the brooch. It was as cold and immutable as ever, and only her still stinging palm proved the brooch had burned her. Was she losing control of her life to a horse, a ghost, and a brooch?

"Poor child," Miss Bayberry said. "You ought to be settled into a life of ease and courting as with all girls your age. But I can see in you too much fire for such a life. Yours is an open road filled with excitement and, yes, perils.

"Never forget you are a creature of free will. Free will is everything. You may choose to abandon your mission. Choice, my child, is the word. If you carry that message against your will, then the mission has already failed. Do you understand?"

Karigan nodded. She had chosen to carry the message. Even F'ryan Coblebay had given her the choice. To believe she had been forced against her will to carry it was to admit defeat before the mission had even begun.

❧ PROFESSOR BERRY'S LIBRARY ❧

Miss Bunchberry showed Karigan to her father's library so that she might amuse herself in a restful way before supper. The shelves along each wall were filled from floor to ceiling with books, their spines dyed in bright yellows and reds, deep blues and greens. Older tomes covered in plain, worn leather stood out amidst the color. Embossed titles in gold and silver gleamed on the bindings in the remnant shreds of daylight.

If Karigan were more of a scholar, she'd feel as if she had stumbled upon a veritable wonderland. The collection was greater than even Dean Geyer's.

Thought of the dean made her frown.

A bay window looked out into the formal gardens below where a bronze statue of the fabled Marin the Gardener, in her weathered, elderly visage, watched over the grounds. Sparrows and chickadees darted to and fro, feeding on seed left on the statue's outstretched hand. The popularity of Marin was greatest along the seacoast where it was said she had once inhabited an island in the Northern Sea Archipelago. Some island cultures deified her as the Mother of all Nature, while those inland tended to think of her as more of a sea-witch who brought good luck to the gardener, and kept a limited area in balance with itself. A winter for every summer, the stories went.

Her presence in gardens was supposed to bring a

bountiful harvest of foodstuffs, and to promote the growth of colorful and glorious flowers. Lovage, delphinium, comfrey, and others grew beneath her beneficent gaze. Violets and bluets bloomed about her feet. In an adjacent plot, a vegetable garden was laid out in neat rows, tender shoots seeking the sun, and leaves unfurling over tantalizing secrets just beginning to take shape beneath the soil.

A brass telescope mounted on a tripod looked out through the bay window toward the sky. An expensive object to possess, even for someone as wealthy as Karigan's father. The ground glass alone was probably equivalent to two barges of his finest silks.

A fire crackled in a snug hearth, casting a warm glow over the room. The library was a very homey place in all.

A collection of objects displayed on a mahogany table drew her to the center of the room. A navigator's astrolabe stood next to the pitted skull of some unknown creature. A beautiful harp set with emeralds, sapphires, garnets, rubies, tourmaline, and diamonds glistened in the firelight. There were many things that weren't set in any particular order: a whale's tooth with fine scrimshaw etchings of a sailor and a fair lady, a hunk of melted, glassy rock of unknown origins, a rusted dagger with a polished pearl handle, a gold coin indented with tooth marks . . . endless things to entertain a curious mind.

A miniature ship encapsulated in a bottle fascinated Karigan. It rocked in a frothy sea, square-rigged sails billowing, seemingly in a breeze. Tiny figures moved about on deck or climbed the rigging. A light fog moved in on the ship, and moved out. The waters calmed some, and the sails slackened.

She was tempted to uncork the bottle to see if the sea would pour out. She suppressed the impulse, but not before another caused her to grab the bottle and shake it. The "sky" darkened; foamy waves lashed the deck, and the ship pitched and careened. Rain fell in sheets. Ant-sized sailors scrambled for handholds, and she imagined she could hear their cries above the crashing of the sea. *Drop the aft riggin', boys, an' watch the top'sle, she blows down!* the bosun cried. Then, *Man overboard!*

The sailors staggered and crawled astern, groping from handhold to handhold, doing all they could to keep from being washed overboard themselves, but by the time they reached the poop deck, their companion had vanished beneath the roiling waters.

Karigan hastily replaced the bottle and stepped back repelled, trying to reassure herself that the ship's lifelike qualities had all been the effect of some illusion or magic, and that the tiny figures on board had never been in peril.

In time, the tempest subsided and the seas calmed. The crew dropped anchor and set about making repairs to sails and rigging. Karigan heaved an unintended sigh of relief.

Next she picked up a clear, round crystal. Dazzling silver rays flickered to life from within, and spread warmth through her aching muscles more effectively than the bath had. She fancied it was a captured moonbeam such as children chased, as she had once chased, on silver moon nights. She never heard of anyone ever capturing one. It was said that only Eletians were quick enough, but no one knew if the fair race that once inhabited the Elt Wood still existed.

Karigan did not believe moonbeams could be captured, but she could not explain how light flowed from the crystal. She held onto it for a time, allowing the heat to soothe her.

The lap harp drew her attention next. It was as old as anything she had seen in the museums in Selium, and ornate enough to satisfy any royal. She strummed the gold strings, and was stunned by its true tones and human voice. Single strings produced perfectly pitched individual voices; combined strings sang in unearthly harmonies. It was like having the Selium Chorale right in the room with her.

I bet Estral would like this.

Karigan wasn't proficient at playing any instrument,

but no matter which string she struck, the harp made her sound like a master. The beauty of it kept her playing at great length. Every object in the room resonated around her. The light in the crystal brightened, and the little sailors sat or stood in an attitude of listening, their ship becalmed in a mirrorlike sea. Karigan shivered and detached herself from the instrument. The whole room seemed to dim and sag in disappointment.

The shadows grew long outside, and as dusk fell and darkened into night, pinpoints of starlight dotted the sky. The glow of the fire, which never needed stoking, and the crystal kept the library light and cheery. There were other objects on the table, but Karigan refrained from touching another. Everything was strange.

Instead, she turned her attention to the shelves. Despite the absence of Professor Berry, there wasn't a speck of dust on the books. Obviously they were still treasured and well cared for. She ran her forefinger along the spines of the books; they smelled faintly of leather and ink, but without a hint of mustiness. There were books covering all angles of Sacoridian history from *The Foundation of the Sacor Clans* to *The House of Hillander: A Guide to Practical Monarchy in Our Times.*

A large section was devoted to Rhovanny. One intriguing book was titled *The Architecture of the Royal House of Rhove Illustrated.* Karigan's father had once been to the castle in Randann and had described to her the wonders of the king's house. In the book, she found handpainted illustrations of some of the details he had described, such as the roof of the castle which reflected light like the corona of the sun. In the old days, the effects revealed the sun goddess' favor of the royal family to the common folk. The book disclosed the roof to be tiled by thousands of mirrors.

Some tomes were so old that the words were handinked in a script Karigan found agonizing, or impossible, to decipher. Many were in strange languages, or ancient versions of modern languages.

One such book was titled *Translations from Ancient*

Eltish. Eltish was, or had once been, the language of the Eletians. She thumbed through the volume. The lettering, printed in fair Eletian characters, shimmered in the light of the crystal. She pronounced words which had been translated phonetically into the Common, and the harp hummed with each syllable she spoke. She hastily closed the book and shelved it.

Undaunted, Karigan climbed a ladder which rolled along the stacks on runners. She found books on the arts and sciences. One row was devoted to the arcane arts. When she opened one of the books, she found only blank pages. No wonder magic was arcane!

The rest of the books on the shelves seemed rather dull. Several dealt with etiquette, and she doubted they had belonged to Professor Berry's original collection.

She left the stacks and paced around. She stretched taut muscles as she walked. Too many days in the saddle, and too many nights on the ground. The floor creaked beneath her feet, and she wondered when Miss Bunchberry would return for her.

She paused when the telescope caught her eye again. It gleamed more gold than brass in the flickering firelight, and aroused her curiosity. It was a rare opportunity for her to look at the stars. At school, the star masters hoarded the looking pieces, allowing only a special few to gaze through. She bent over and peered through the eyepiece.

Stars streaked across the lens as she adjusted the scope's position and focus. She located the Sword of Sevelon, a constellation of seven stars in the shape of a cross like a sword, and nearly as easy to find as the Ladle. The scope's range was amazing. Only the scopes in Selium's observatory compared in distance and clarity.

Legend had it that a great hero by the name of Sevelon had once served the god and goddess by attending to their affairs on earth, and dispensed justice as the immortals saw fit. In popular legend, Sevelon often manipulated events so they benefited her fellow mortals, and kept the immortals humble. After many lifetimes of good work,

Aeryc and Aeryon rewarded Sevelon by allowing her to ascend the crystal staircase to the heavens to dwell with the immortals among the stars.

When she reached the final landing, she cast her sword aside for all time, and it could now be seen still tumbling across the night sky. It was dominant in spring, the sword tipped up in the "salute" position, and as the seasons progressed into early winter, the sword spiraled until the tip was planted downward in the "warrior at rest" position. The sword then left the skies, only to emerge large and brilliant again the following spring.

Interestingly, Sacoridian legend depicted Sevelon as female, while Rhovan legend characterized her as male, despite the fact that a female statue of Sevelon stood in the great hall of the king in Randann. Whether male or female, Sevelon's exploits served as stories with morals told to the children of both countries. Sevelon was depicted as knightly, courageous, and good, while the god and goddess were depicted as capricious, using humanity to suit their own whims. Karigan had often wondered if Sevelon was as pure as the stories made her out to be.

Just as she thought to turn the telescope elsewhere, the stars swam in her eyes. Try as she might, she couldn't focus or blink her eyes clear. A scene began to unfold, and though she tried, she could not pull away from the eyepiece.

Evergreens wheeled, merged, and spun like a kaleidoscope in the eyepiece. Fragments of an image fell into place and created a picture of the all too familiar woods of the Green Cloak and the desolate stretches of the North Road. A red squirrel paused in the road, then scurried across and into the undergrowth and shadows of the woods. A raven alighted at the top of a spruce, the bough bending under its weight. It squawked once and flapped its wings, watchful. All else was still.

Although Karigan couldn't place the section of road, it looked familiar. But then, there wasn't much to distinguish one part of the endless stretch of the Green Cloak and the monotonous miles of curving road from another.

Movement caught the corner of her eye, and the telescope obligingly zoomed in at a dizzying rate only to reveal herself. She watched herself lead The Horse away from F'ryan Coblebay's body. The Horse plodded dispiritedly behind her, his head bowed, while she walked on seemingly deep in thought.

I remember this.

As they rounded a curve in the road, something behind them caught The Horse's attention. The Karigan within the vision looked behind, too, just as she had done that day, but saw nothing. The Karigan who observed through the telescope, however, saw a shadowy figure following behind, bent and in green, with two arrows protruding from his back.

Before she had time to consider it, the vision dissolved as if flushed with water, only to reveal another. Bright sunlight washed the new scene, but she couldn't determine anything else about the setting. The soldiers Sarge and Thursgad had their backs to her and obscured her view. The telescope moved in slowly, allowing her to peer over their shoulders.

Captain Immerez sat on the ground soaked in blood which gushed from his wrist. His severed hand lay on the bloodied ground, stark white, and with the fingers still curled around the handle of his whip.

Revolted, Karigan tried to jerk away from the eyepiece, but she was held fast.

I will kill that Greenie. Immerez's whisper came breathy and close into her ear.

Like the turning of a page, the scene changed. Darkness flooded Karigan's eyes like puddles of black ink. Then Immerez's face appeared, a glowing orb, his features chiseled by shadows and flickering light, as from a candle or fire. He moved his face close to hers, rotating his head sideways to gaze at her with his one eye. The shadows shifted across his features and darkened half his face. He smiled.

A sticky wetness dripped into her eyes and Immerez turned into a luminescent blur. She blinked rapidly and

the contours of his face sharpened. He pulled back and
was surrounded again by the blackness. He thrust his
handless stump in front of her face, the wrist now
equipped with a metal hook. He turned it carefully and
slowly so she might see it from all angles. It gleamed in
the unknown light source.

Immerez then pressed the hook into the flesh just
below her eye. She gasped at the sharp, cold pain.

Well met, Greenie, he said.

Pain ripped just below her eye. She made a strangled
noise of terror, wanting to scream, but her voice was
muffled and it was difficult to breathe. She wanted to
paw at her cheek, but as if her hands were bound, she
was unable to move them. Her breath rasped raggedly
and quickly in her ears. The pain . . .

Then Immerez's face folded in on itself, and the pain
ceased.

The next scene blossomed sky blue, with slow moving
clouds trailing along in a chill spring breeze. Karigan
stood amidst the green of the practice field at Selium. It
was pocked with worn, dirt practice rings. A crowd
thronged around her. She held the point of her wooden
practice sword at the back of Timas Mirwell's neck as
he lay prone on the ground before her.

You are dead, she said.

Timas spat dirt. The roar of the onlookers subsided to
painful silence. *G'ladheon,* he said, *that was dirty swordplay—against the rules!* He climbed to his feet wiping dirt
and spittle from his mouth. He was a small young man
and had to look up at her.

I dunno, Timas, an onlooker said. *Whether it was
against the rules or not, she got kill point.* There was a
murmur of agreement from the crowd.

Karigan, the watcher, struggled to release herself from
the eyepiece, but still she could not move. *Must I relive
this?* As if in answer, the scene continued uninterrupted.

It wasn't fair! Timas cried.

You just haven't learned that kind of swordplay yet,

said someone else, and many in the crowd laughed. *At the top of your class indeed.*

Timas sputtered in anger. Karigan flashed a grin at her audience and dipped into a low, self-mocking bow. Timas sprang upon her unguarded back and swatted the wooden sword across her shoulders. Stunned, she fell to her hands and knees. Sharp pain flared across her back. The crowd watched in silence, unable to react.

What's happening here?

The crowd gave way to a stocky man with steel gray hair. Arms Master Rendle grabbed Timas around the chest and pressed on his wrist to force him to drop the practice sword. He let go only after Timas stopped struggling and kicking.

Then he clasped Karigan's hand and hauled her to her feet. *You all right?* he asked gruffly.

Karigan watched the rest, how Master Rendle humiliated Timas for his unwarranted attack by assigning him a month of drudge chores; how the arms master remarked on her abilities with a sword and offered to take her on as a private student. Yes, it was all familiar to her, but what she hadn't seen before, what she hadn't noticed, was Timas Mirwell watching from a distance as she and the arms master conversed, his expression one of unadulterated hatred.

Karigan shivered. Timas had gotten his revenge by taking his case to his relatives of status who lived in the city who, in turn, took his case to the dean and the trustees. Karigan had initiated the fight. She was the one to blame.

The scene faded out, Rendle talking to her softly, and Timas' glare radiating across the practice field to her like a flare of pure hate.

Karigan fought to pull away from the terrible visions, but the telescope wasn't done with her yet.

The brightness of day darkened to night. Little could be seen except a rider, cloaked and hooded in gray, mounted on a shadowy horse. She felt unexplained attraction, coupled with fear, toward the rider. She was drawn inexorably closer to him. He twisted toward her.

Though she couldn't see his features beneath his hood, she felt his cold gaze as if he could see her where she stood in the library. Icy daggers of fear pierced her heart.

Who are you? he demanded. *Who watches?*

She felt unseen eyes search for her, and felt his smile. *The mirror goes both ways,* he said.

Karigan's mind screamed in fear.

The telescope, or maybe it was her own will this time, wrenched her out of that scene. But no sooner was she out than she was plunged into another. A tall man with almond-shaped brown eyes gazed at her sadly. She couldn't make out his surroundings, but she had an impression of a room of stone walls like a keep or a prison.

Kari, the man said, *I need you. I need you here. Please don't accept that mission. It's dangerous and I can't bear the thought of losing you.*

This man needed her? Who was he that he should speak to her so? She tried to call out to him, to reach for him, but she could not move or speak. *What mission?* she wanted to ask. *What danger?*

His image shimmered, then vanished, and she felt inexplicably bereft and alone. Stars filled the eyepiece once again. Released from the spell of the telescope, Karigan fell to her knees weak and breathless, her whole body shaking and drenched with sweat, her head throbbing.

She cupped the crystal in her hand and staggered over to an overstuffed chair by the unending fire. She curled up and heaved a sigh as the warmth of the crystal wrapped around her.

⋙ INTRIGUE ⋘

Karigan had not realized she'd fallen asleep in the big chair until she awakened to find Miss Bunchberry gently shaking her wrist. "Supper, dear child. Letitia has outdone herself."

Karigan stretched and yawned, and nearly walked out of the room with the crystal cupped in her hand, before she remembered it and replaced it on Professor Berry's table of oddities. Of all the objects in the library, the crystal seemed to be a source of light and warmth, and possessed no twisted qualities like the telescope. The silver light extinguished as her fingers released it. The room grew dark and uninviting without its radiance.

"I daresay," Miss Bunch said as she led Karigan out of the room, "it's been a long time since I've seen the moonstone aglow. It will not work for Bay or me."

"Moonstone?"

"Oh, yes. It holds a silver moonbeam."

Hairs prickled on the back of Karigan's neck. "You aren't telling me it's really—"

"Of course I am. It was given to Father by an Eletian years ago." Miss Bunchberry smiled, and her eyes became dreamy. "I rather fancy the story of Laurelyn the Moondreamer and how she built a castle of silver moonbeams, don't you? Silvermind it was called. My father wanted to go find it, but other projects diverted his attention, and before he knew it, he was too old for adventuring."

Laurelyn the Moondreamer. Karigan had heard the story as a tiny child, and had forgotten it long since. In her memory, she could hear the words as she sat wrapped in her mother's protective arms. "Tell me 'bout Laur'lyn, Momma. Tell me again." Her request was met with a warm chuckle. "Maybe you will build your own castle of moonbeams one day, Kari." And the story would be repeated till she fell asleep.

"Have I made you sad?" A startled expression crossed Miss Bunchberry's face. "Are you in pain?"

Karigan wiped away a tear. *Yes, and yes.* Aloud she said, "I'm fine."

Aromas of roast goose and baked bread drifted through the house, reminding her of Midwinter Festival: loud music, wild dancing, and plenty of imbibing. Her father always invited the cargo master and crew, and all the closest kin of Clan G'ladheon. Her mother used to preside over the affair, an element of calm and dignity amidst the frenzy of merrymaking. Her mother, with her high forehead and rich brown hair, the one parent everyone saw when they looked at Karigan.

The tears brimmed in her eyes again, but her solemn thoughts were dashed when she saw Miss Bayberry sitting primly at the head of a ridiculously long table that rivaled, in length, any in the dining hall at Selium. The silver was in use again, and the table was positively heaped with food. Karigan wondered exactly what clan had been invited to feast with them.

"Please be seated," Miss Bayberry said.

Fortunately, the three settings had been placed at one end of the table, rather than at opposite ends. Otherwise they would have had to shout to one another to carry on a conversation.

Miss Bayberry dropped a cloth napkin on her lap. "F'ryan Coblebay couldn't join us though we did the proper thing and invited him. It seems he expends far too much energy when in contact with that which is earthly, and he wishes to reserve it for times when he's truly needed." She sniffed, indicating how she felt about that. "The Horse couldn't join us either. Letitia was resolute that she would not have him in the house. To help compensate, Rolph has been feeding him premium grain and the sweetest hay."

"As you can see," Miss Bunchberry said, "we've observed proper etiquette. Letitia wouldn't have us dine in the kitchen, though Bay and I normally sup there. What fun it is to see Mother's old table in use once again. From time to time, relatives or my father's old colleagues would descend upon Seven Chimneys. Letitia would cook and bake all day in anticipation. Those were grand times."

Goose and sauce were passed around, along with the last of the winter squash, legumes, mushrooms, and dressing. A slice of warm bread spread with creamy honey butter melted in Karigan's mouth. It was like a traditional Midwinter Feast, except it was spring. Miss Bayberry poured Rhovan red wine in each goblet and Karigan could only guess at the vintage.

It was like spending an evening with a pair of spinster aunts, eccentric as they were, but oozing comfort and a sense of home. The canny intensity Karigan had witnessed before seemed to dissipate as the evening wore on and the wine bottle made its rounds.

When they had eaten all they could, they removed to the parlor where glasses of brandy awaited them, and the fire roared in the hearth as cheerfully as ever. Karigan sank into the sofa with the hummingbirds carved on the armrests, her goblet in one hand, and she told tales of her mostly silly classmates and Selium. Bunch and Bay raised eyebrows upon learning that the hot springs could be pumped directly into a bathtub.

"It was so long ago that we lived in Selium," Miss Bayberry said. "I don't think half the school or museum buildings you described were there when we were. Otherwise, the city hasn't changed much." She swirled her brandy in her goblet and smiled in a self-satisfied way. "Child, you have enlivened this house more in one day than we have been able to in years. My sister and I will remember your visit for some time to come. I can only hope that you have found your stay with us equally interesting."

Karigan nodded emphatically. Interesting was an understatement.

"Miss Bunch tells me you spent the afternoon in the library. What did you think?"

"It was . . . unusual."

Miss Bayberry cast a severe glance at her sister. "Bunch, did you just leave her there? Did you explain nothing? Give no forewarning?"

"But Father's old things are so harmless—"

"That is not the point. We caused our guest undue surprise. That was not proper."

Miss Bunchberry gazed sulkily at her lap. "The moonstone lit at her touch." Her voice was nearly a whisper.

Miss Bayberry scrutinized Karigan anew, and something of that hidden intensity reignited—and it wasn't just the glow of the wine or brandy. "My dear child, that stone has shone no light for many a year. How you called upon the moonbeam to glow I can only wonder. Do you have any idea?"

Karigan shook her head, wary. "No. I—I was just curious about the objects on the table, and when I picked up the crystal, it lit up." She wondered if she had somehow offended Miss Bay, but the old woman's expression was glad.

"What else did you observe?"

Karigan described her experiences with the bottled ship and the harp. "They were very odd." She shuddered, remembering the tempest she had caused. "I mean, they possessed qualities that were so real. I know it's illusion . . ." Her statement was met with lingering silence. "It was illusion . . . wasn't it?"

Miss Bayberry leaned forward and, evading the question, asked, "What else did you observe?"

Karigan licked her lips, a little nervous now. "Well, the harp sounded so human, unlike the lap harps my friend Estral plays, and she has access to the finest instruments in all of Selium."

"My dear child, arcane objects are . . . unusual. Of course, when you first observed the things on my father's table, they seemed relatively normal. After handling them a bit, you discovered otherwise. The bottle, the moonstone, and the harp are a few among several devices Father collected over the years in order to comprehend magic. He discovered, like you, that arcane objects can take on some very lifelike qualities.

"That harp has a very dark history. It was originally made by the finest craftsmen at the turn of the First Age, for a wealthy aristocrat. It was carved as no other instruments of those times, and inlaid with precious jewels, themselves cut by masters of lost Kmaern for whom rocks and gems were living things.

"The aristocrat was pleased by what he saw, but not with what he heard. When strung, the instrument sounded like any other well-crafted harp. The aristocrat, it seems, could not live with a harp that was not extraordinary. Remember now, this was a dark time. Magic was more accessible and understood back then. Mornhavon the Black was at the height of his power, and dark magic had a profound influence on many people. It was difficult to wield any magic without the taint of the dark, so strong was Mornhavon."

Miss Bayberry paused to take a sip of brandy. She carefully replaced her goblet on the table before her, clasped her hands, and bent toward Karigan to resume her story. "It's not known if the aristocrat had innate powers himself, or if another did the work for him, but he had the finest singers known in the lands, including Eletians who have the fairest voices of all, brought to his keep. Using methods unknown today, he extracted the voices from the singers and melded them into magical strings. Child, what you heard were voices from centuries ago."

Karigan remembered, with clarity, the crystalline voices of the strings . . . strains of some ancient past forcibly carried into the future . . . like ghosts. "What happened to the singers?"

Miss Bayberry tilted her head, looking beyond Karigan, a sadness in her eyes. "There is no record, but you can believe that if they survived the process, they lived without that which they loved most—their ability to sing."

The more Karigan learned about magic, the less she liked it. It seemed to bring nothing but evil and grief. "The telescope—"

"Oh . . ." Miss Bunchberry groaned. "Not the telescope. I do think, my dear Bay, that we should remove the lenses and crush them beneath our heels."

"Nonsense, sister. That telescope was one of Father's most treasured pieces. Tell me, child, did you see far when you looked through the eyepiece?"

Karigan noted there was no question of whether or not she had gazed into it. "I saw very far. Too far." She described the series of images as they had appeared.

"A sprinkling of the past, present, and future," declared Miss Bayberry. "Such a device could erode one's sanity if one had constant access to it. Father possessed a tremendous will to resist using it when he had major decisions to make. Believe me, he felt the lure, but he also felt it was human temptation more than the device itself that called to him. Indeed, no one should see too much of their own history or future."

Miss Bayberry fixed her piercing blue eyes on Karigan. "Remember, child, your future isn't made of stone. What the telescope showed you was what may happen if the present line of events continue."

Put that way, it sounded to Karigan as if the current of her life was out of her control. It wasn't a welcome idea. "Do you look into the telescope?" The sisters seemed to know so much about everything.

"Heavens, no," Miss Bayberry said.

"We've no need," Miss Bunchberry added.

The ladies would say no more about the telescope or anything else in the library. Miss Bunch left the parlor briefly, and returned bearing a wooden game board and multicolored pieces. She set them on the table before them.

"Are you familiar with Intrigue, child?"

Karigan had recognized the game immediately—it was all the rage in Selium. Two kingdoms battled for dominance, each piece possessing a different ability. Arranging the pieces in various patterns created offenses or defenses.

The pieces, in this case, were made of ivory or bone, dyed in the traditional colors of red, green, and blue, and carved in the likenesses of kings, messengers, spies, soldiers, and so on. The game was most difficult when played as a Triad, with a third player who was random—the wild card with no set loyalties one way or the other. The other two players could petition the Triad for allegiance, but the Triad could choose not to take sides and play for its own benefit. It was the never knowing of what the Triad player would do that made Intrigue exciting.

Exciting, if you liked the game. Karigan didn't. She lost every time she played. "I've played Intrigue a few times, but not often with a Triad." Estral had been her only friend at Selium. There was never a third person to play with.

Miss Bunchberry clapped her hands. "Splendid! Bay and I haven't played with a Triad in a long time either. Child, you will be the Triad, and if this first game doesn't last long, we can switch."

Splendid. Karigan remembered to smile, and because propriety was so important to the ladies, she said, "I'm honored."

"That's good. I offered to a guest first as was proper."

Miss Bayberry nodded in solemn agreement.

They played long into the night, each taking a turn as Triad. The gentle sisters transformed into ruthless opponents and Karigan found herself, as usual, on the defensive. Miss Bay took a general and three of her knights. Miss Bunch killed her queen and abducted a spy. She watched their pieces march across the star-shaped board and annihilate her kingdom, and she wondered, with a bemused expression, if she and Estral had been too kind to one another. The sisters did not spare an inch where Estral would have allowed a concession.

Karigan didn't consider herself a ruthless person. Rather, she considered herself wise to the ways of survival. The swordplay "tricks" the cargo master had taught her, the stories her father had told her of his perils and adventures as a merchant traveling in far-off lands, her experiences far away from home among aristocrats . . . these were basic learning experiences for life. She had never thought of employing ruthless tactics in a harmless game of Intrigue.

When the third and final round was won by Miss Bunchberry, the older woman sank back into the sofa with an ecstatic giggle. "That was just so fine. I could play endless games, but I know it's late." As if to accent her words, the last embers of the fire crashed in the fireplace, sending a flurry of sparks up the chimney.

Miss Bayberry's lips were set in a taut straight line. She had won two of the three victories, yet she seemed none too happy about it. "I think the child wasn't putting her all into the game. Perhaps she believed she was doing the polite thing by letting us win."

Karigan blushed, as she often did, somehow feeling guilty. "I did try . . ."

"Tsk. Not hard enough. You've much intelligence for such a youngster. Use it. Many of the situations you come across in Intrigue aren't too far removed from real life. Many of the aristocrats use it as a teaching tool for their children, and it may have been developed for that exact purpose."

Miss Bunchberry looked scandalized by her sister's outburst. "Bay, you really oughtn't criticize our guest."

Miss Bayberry rolled her eyes in annoyance. "Bunch, sometimes one must go beyond the bounds of propriety and speak her mind." She jabbed her cane at Karigan. "Child, use your brain. Think on your feet. Being polite and reserved is how we were raised, but we learned the hard way that the rest of the world isn't that way. I've perceived from conversation that you comprehend such things, like that swordplay with whatsit . . . that Titmouse, or whatever his name was. In other words, child, propriety has its place, but don't let your guard down. In real life, you never know who the players of Intrigue really are, or what they stand for."

The words echoed in Karigan's mind as she followed Miss Bunchberry and the glow of the oil lamp up the stairs to the second story. Weren't Miss Bayberry's words much like what Arms Master Rendle had told her one evening after sword practice, as she repaired fighting gear at the field house? "Do not make the mistake you made with Timas, lass," he had said, pipe smoke curling above his head and up to the rafters of the field house. "Never assume the enemy is down and then turn your back on him. You will pay for it with your life."

In other words, expect others to play dirty. Miss Bayberry's words, and Arms Master Rendle's, hung heavy with her, but every time she thought of Timas as "Titmouse," she was reduced to giggles.

"This is the east gable guestroom," Miss Bunchberry said. "You will see the sunrise from here and the morning sun will fill your room with warmth." She lit another lamp for Karigan's use. "Letitia has aired the place out and put fresh water in the pitcher next to the wash basin. She will draw a hot bath for you in the morning, as well."

"If I could see your Letitia, I'd thank her for her delicious cooking and all the details she has seen to." Karigan thought it rather odd she had seen no signs of servants, especially the often talked about Letitia.

"We will pass your praise on to her—if she hasn't heard already. Now—"

Karigan put a hand on Miss Bunch's wrist before she could go on. "Why can't I meet Letitia?"

Miss Bunch brushed a gray curl from her face and

looked at Karigan in surprise. "You want to know why . . . why you can't meet Letitia? Isn't knowing that she is here to serve enough?"

"No. In my clan, the servants are practically part of the family. It only seems fair to thank Letitia in person."

Miss Bunch clucked her tongue. "Dear, dear," she muttered. But when she saw Karigan's look of resolve, she said, "We are not fond of relating painful stories, child, especially when one's father is at fault. It was an accident."

"An accident?" Karigan's brows drew together in a perplexed line. "What was an accident?"

Miss Bunch's eyes shifted and she plucked nervously at the hem of her apron. "Letitia's invisibility was an accident. Oh, dear." Miss Bunch drooped into a chair as if overcome.

Karigan's mouth hung open aghast. "Invisible?"

"Very invisible. Far beyond what you are able to attain with your brooch, child. Completely, irreversibly, transparently invisible. She is more akin to an energy, or a ghostly presence, for we cannot hear her either. But we know she's there, for the house is tidied when neither my sister nor I have lifted a hand, our meals are prepared for us, and so on. We know when she is less than happy, for she starts sweeping up a tumult like a great dusty tempest. And it's not just Letitia."

"Not just . . . Letitia?" Karigan looked all around her, wondering how many invisible servants might be in her room this very minute. It made her skin crawl.

"Well, there's Rolph the stableboy, and Farnham the groundskeeper, too."

"And you said they are invisible by accident?"

Miss Bunch nodded mournfully. "Indeed, child. You see, Letitia was forever nagging Father. He tired of her pointing out the mud he tracked in from the garden, or the coating of magic dust he left in the library which she had to wipe up. He was consumed by his scholarship, and scraping off candle wax from tabletops, or leaving papers in orderly piles were not foremost in his mind.

"One day, as Father was in the library hard at work studying some form of magic or another, Letitia stood in the doorway with her hands on her hips. *At it again, eh Professor?* she said. *A spill of that vile liquid in yon beaker will ruin the finish of your fine table and then where would we be? And after Herschel refinished it for you last month.*"

"Uh, who's Herschel?" Karigan asked.

"Herschel was our handyman. Was with the family for a hundred years, it seems. We believe he has passed on. . . . Things break now and then, and no one fixes them." Miss Bunch emitted a sad sigh. "If he were lying dead somewhere, there was no way for us to see him." She paused for a few moments, then continued her story. "Letitia nagged at Father until he commanded her to silence. *I need quiet, woman,* he said, *not your endless nattering.*"

"Letitia is not one to just sit quietly while the chaos of clutter, dust, and bubbling fluids threaten to overwhelm her sense of domestic orderliness, but she had pressed him too far this time. *Sir,* she said, waving her dust rag in emphasis like a law reader about to present some crucial evidence to an arbiter, *may I remind you that you threaten the sanitary concerns of this household, and you with two little daughters under your roof?* She followed up that reproof with a *tsk, tsk, tsk.* And that's when it happened."

"It?" Karigan asked.

Miss Bunch fanned her face with her hand. "Yes, it. She *tsked* one too many times, and Father lost his patience. Remember now, their run-ins had been going on for a very long time, and the tension between them both had built up over the years. Father shouted, *Servants should not be seen or heard!* Well, that did it! We haven't seen or heard any of the servants ever since. Not one of them. But we know they're there."

"Wait." Karigan held up her hand. "Your father said that servants should not be seen or heard, and Letitia and the others just disappeared?"

"Well, no, child. Dear me, but I don't tell stories as well as Bay. I left out one crucial fact. The 'vile' liquid Letitia feared that would ruin the finish of Father's table was volatile with spells. The spells responded to his command unequivocally. He could not countermand it."

Karigan was aghast. "And the servants stayed with you even after your father . . . turned them invisible? Weren't they angry?"

"Of course they were upset, child. And terribly so. But they stayed in hopes that Father would find another spell to reverse the curse. He searched to exhaustion and illness to find one, and never stopped until he died. He was terribly remorseful, and I think the servants knew it. And yes, they stay on with us. Where else can they find positions, invisible as they are?"

"And so, that's it?" Karigan said. "Letitia and the rest will be invisible to the end of their days?"

Miss Bunch nodded with a solemn expression on her face. "We try to treat them as well as possible, and continue Father's search for a cure. We have picked up a thing or two about magic along the way, but so far nothing that will help the servants. Alas, there may not be an answer."

Karigan had no response this time, and Miss Bunch pulled herself out of the chair and patted her on the shoulder. "As I said, it is a painful story, one that we will never be free of. In the meantime, we go on as we must, and," she added in a whisper, "we take care about what we say about whom. You never know who is listening in!"

Miss Bunch moved to the doorway. "If you need anything, just call. I sleep down the hall. Bay can't negotiate the stairs very well lately, poor dear, so she has taken a back room downstairs. Sleep well. Breakfast will be served when you wake."

Karigan was left alone in the room which, like all the others in the house, was well-appointed. A porcelain pitcher and bowl stood on a wash stand. The heavy bureau, carved intricately with pine boughs and cones, was draped with hand-embroidered linens. A huge cedar chest, full of coarse wool blankets, sat at the foot of the bed. A pieced quilt with a diamond-shaped motif flared like a starburst. She looked in satisfaction at her clean clothes neatly folded on the edge of the bed. She took the winged horse brooch from her robe pocket and pinned it to the lapel of the now spotless greatcoat.

She checked the greatcoat for the love letter and found it intact and undamaged. Miraculously, or perhaps meticulously, the vigilant Letitia had removed it during the cleaning process, and replaced it after. The message satchel, too, had been placed on the bed. She hadn't dared to open the leather case before, and though she felt the sisters could be trusted, she did so now. Inside was an envelope sealed with the wax imprint of a winged horse. All items accounted for, she could now sleep in peace.

But then she caught sight of herself in the dresser mirror. Her image was like a ghost flowing by, her long white nightgown billowing behind her gauzy and luminous. She backed a few steps to gaze in the mirror. She found herself mostly unchanged from her travels, if a little thinner in the cheeks.

There was a blemish beneath her left eye. She leaned toward the silver glass for a closer look. It wasn't a blemish exactly, but a reddened crescent-shaped scratch just above the cheekbone, and just below her eye.

She remembered the image of Immerez through the telescope, and the feel of his cold, metal hook against her cheek. She touched trembling fingers to the mark, and turned away from the mirror. It was coincidence and nothing more. She could have gotten the scratch from thrashing through the underbrush, or from her own fingernail. She could have gotten it from anywhere.

Exhaustion was leading her to strange fancies, and she delayed going to bed no more. The bed was like the one her grandmother had used. It was so high that a stool was stashed beneath to help one climb into it. Karigan sank into the down mattress and clutched the blankets about her. It was hard to believe she had been with the sisters for only a day.

This afternoon, she had been asleep on a patch of moss, not even sure how she had gotten there. Tonight, she lay in true luxury between crisp, cool sheets smelling as fresh as if they'd just been pulled off the line. She blew out the lamp on the nightstand and sighed in satisfaction. It had been a strange day, but there was nothing extraordinary about this gabled room or the comfortable featherbed.

Karigan nestled under the covers. The house was draped in silence, but outside peepers cheeped in their springtime chant. The last sound she heard as she drifted into a heavy slumber, was the *hoo-hoo-hooing* of an owl in a tree below her window.

In the morning, The Horse waited outside for Karigan. She had awakened to the warm glow of the rising sun, as Miss Bunchberry had promised she would, certain that she had slept hours upon hours. Yet, the sun was still low when she finally roused herself. Even when she took her time bathing, and breakfasting on the elusive Letitia's cooking, the morning advanced very little. Time seemed . . . well, flexible at Seven Chimneys. She had slept in and taken her time in every endeavor, and yet, she was still getting on with her travels bright and early.

The Horse was tacked, the saddlebags bulging to capacity. His chestnut coat glowed in the sun—someone, probably the invisible Rolph, had given him a bath and thorough brushing, and he looked handsome despite his gangly shape. Karigan gave him a companionable slap on the neck.

"Before you go, child," Miss Bayberry said from the front step, "we've a few things for you."

Karigan glanced at the bulging saddlebags and felt the extra weight in her pack. "You've already given me so much—all the food and a change of clothes. . . ."

"Nonsense, child. Those are just provisions. You have a little growing to do, and Bunch and I are concerned about your proper nourishment. We would like to give you some gifts. Very simple gifts." She held forth a tiny sprig with dark green leaves. "My namesake, bayberry. When you find resolve failing you, when hope is lost, or you miss the deep scents of wild places, take a leaf and rub it between your fingers. The scent will refresh you, and perhaps you will think of me."

Karigan smiled as she took the bayberry. The freshly cut branch was fragrant.

Miss Bunchberry had a shy smile on her face. She held in her palm a flower with four white petals. "Bunchberry is my namesake. There is a small patch in the woods behind the house just pushing up out of the ground with the spring. If you are in need of a friend, pluck a petal from the flower and let it drift in the wind. Perhaps you will also think of me. It won't wither soon, child, as a good friendship should not."

"One more thing, child," Miss Bayberry said. She pressed something cool and smooth into Karigan's hand. Thin slivers of light beamed through her fingers, even in the bright sunshine.

"The moonstone!" Karigan cried in awe. "I can't take this. It was your father's."

"Don't be silly," Miss Bayberry said. "It has taken to you. I daresay it never lights up for Bunch or me. And as for it being Father's . . . well, I'm sure he would have wanted you to keep it."

Miss Bunchberry nodded in agreement. "Take it. It will light your way and keep you warm. It was the moonstones, they say, that held back the dark forces during the Long War. It should serve you well. May the moon shine brightly on your path."

"Thank you . . . thank you." Karigan's eyes grew moist. "Is there anything I can do for you? Take word of you to kin in Sacor City?"

"My, but she's taken to the part of being a messenger, hasn't she, Bay?"

"Definitely, but I'm afraid that we have no kin in Sacor City. Just a cousin down south and you wouldn't want to meet her."

"Miss Poppy is very cranky," Miss Bunchberry said.

"And that doesn't even begin to describe her. Child, you need do nothing for us, for you've done so much by giving us a little company, and as I mentioned before, Green Riders assisted our father in his search for knowledge. We are simply returning the favor. If you are back this way, do visit. Just watch out for brigands and thieves on the road."

Karigan didn't think the sisters had gotten the better end of the deal, but this wasn't one of her father's bargaining sessions. She looked the manor house over, at the windows reflecting the woods, and at the chimneys puffing smoke. "Why," she asked, "do you call this place Seven Chimneys?"

"You mean when there are more than seven chimneys?" Miss Bunch asked. Karigan nodded. "Why, seven is a magical number. Nine is not, and Father wouldn't use a name for his home that wasn't magical."

Karigan chuckled and mounted The Horse. "I don't even know how to get to Sacor City from here."

"East by north, child," Miss Bayberry said. "East by north will get you there."

When it was apparent no further information was forthcoming, Karigan reluctantly turned The Horse down the road. Glancing once over her shoulder, she saw the two sisters standing side by side as they watched her leave. She waved, and they waved back. She wished, with a sigh, she could linger.

All too soon, Seven Chimneys and the sisters disappeared behind a bend in the road, and shortly after, the road turned into a deer trail. She reined The Horse around, but found that the road was really gone, as if it had never existed. She circled around in the underbrush, but could find no evidence of it.

"A road can't just vanish," she muttered. But then again, neither could a girl and a horse.

❧ MIRWELL ❧

Tomastine II, Governor of Mirwell Province, sank wearily into his worn, hide-up-holstered armchair, facing a stone hearth large enough to walk into. The fire would do his bones good. It would relieve his joints of aches accumulated over an active lifetime of hunting and warring.

Blast the cold damp, he thought.

The Great Arms of Mirwell, two war hammers crossed over a mountain crazed with cracks and fissures, on a field of scarlet, drew one's eye above the massive mantel. The creation of the Arms, according to the family chronicles, coincided with the formation of the Sacor Clans before the Long War. Clan Mirwell's ancient roots were imbued with crushing opponents, of possessing the strength to strike down the very mountains. The Mirwells had never governed their province with a bejeweled scepter of gold, but with an iron hammer of war.

Even so, over the generations, the province had grown quiet, almost sleepy. Two hundred years ago, however, it had not been that way. The clans had torn at each other's throats for land and the glory of the family. Clan Mirwell had absorbed more land into its borders than it had lost, and acquired a reputation for savage brutality. Ah, the glory, when you knew what a man thought and he expressed it with his blade, instead of today's spineless politicking of court eunuchs who stabbed you from behind with words.

The high king of old was no more than a clan lord himself, sitting on a pretty throne watching all his liege lords—the clan chiefs—gut each other. The clan chiefs had eminent control over their lands and all those who lived within their borders. Once a year, in the rare display of peace, the chiefs swore their fealty to crown and country, paid their taxes to the realm, and that was that. Although the chiefs of Mirwell were often the close confidants of the kings, and served as advisors.

Then King Agates Sealender, the last of his line with no heirs born to him, died of old age, and clan chief Smidhe Hillander, of Clan Hillander, ascended the throne. That's when history went awry. Mirwell combed his fingers through his lank gray hair. Yes, everything changed with Clan Hillander.

King Smidhe tamed the lands with his own forces, created permanent boundaries, and decried bloodshed between clans. He proclaimed the clan chiefs brothers and sisters, and said that the country of Sacoridia could never survive if it did not stand as one. There were other ways, he said, than bloodshed, to find glory.

Indeed, the clans had never seen such unity since the Long War. King Smidhe said the founding clans of Sacoridia, when they created a high king, had never intended the chaos beset by the Sealender line. Mirwell snorted. King Smidhe pacified the clans. The chief of Clan Mirwell had fought the new way, but the king's soldiers had come to him and Clan Mirwell was pacified, too. Mirwell's soldiery had been decimated or run into the Teligmar Hills until they surrendered. The honor of the clan had never been clean since.

King Smidhe bestowed the clan chiefs with new titles—they became lord-governors, and new industry was encouraged. Commerce blossomed as timber was harvested and granite quarried. Eventually the paper-making process was discovered and the printing press invented. King Smidhe even encouraged good relations with neighboring Rhovanny and trade developed among lesser clans whose merchant fleets plied coastal waters, elevating Sacoridia's reputation as one of the wealthiest countries on the continent.

The old high king was called the Great Peacemaker, and Province Day was established as a national holiday celebrated throughout the country in the summer to commemorate Sacoridia's unity, and the man whose words were carved into his tomb in Sacor City. They read: *There is greatness with unity. Only if we lift ourselves above our base and bestial natures shall we stand as one.*

The fire hissed and steamed with rain that seeped down the chimney, and Mirwell shook his head. The raging blood of his clan had never been truly gentled. Tournaments and hunting diverted some of the blood lust, but there wasn't the same glory to be had. Oh, there were occasional forays into the Under Kingdoms. Mirwell had been on a few himself. But even now ties had been forged with those savages, and there was nothing. Nothing until now.

The governor was determined to raise his clan to its former glory, to once again attain a place in concert with Sacoridia's kings, to expand forth its boundaries that now felt too crowded. He would control commerce and the distribution of wealth. And he would do it the old way: by force.

Mirwell sighed, glancing at the crumpled letter on his lap sealed with the dean's mark. Before shaking the very foundations of Sacoridia, he would first have to deal with his son, his only progeny despite a succession of wives and mistresses. Actually, he would deal with his son second. Someone was here to see him.

"Report."

Captain Immerez stepped into the flickering light. It gleamed off his bald head. He had spent no small amount of time waiting for his lord's notice. Mirwell was perfectly aware of this. Immerez's face remained neutral, however, and his bow was deferential, despite the misery his wet, muddy uniform must have caused him.

Immerez was young yet. He could stand it. The youngsters could traipse through the wilderness in all weather conditions, none the worse for wear. Mirwell had paid his dues in that way. The bear head mounted on the wall attested to his strength in the old days, and he was now content to manage his province by his fireside and let the young ones do the work, just as his father had before him.

"My lord-governor," the captain said. "We've killed the messenger."

"Good." The captain could always be depended on to carry out his directives. He had been hand picked from hundreds of young soldiers years ago to help in raising Mirwell Province back to glory. "And what did you find out about a spy?"

Immerez shifted uncomfortably. His one eye darted to and fro, and he licked his lips. Rain pattered against the window. "We were unable to extract that information before he died."

"What? I don't find that satisfactory."

Immerez held his chin up. "The only way to stop him was to kill him."

Mirwell drummed his fingers on the armrest of his chair, which was carved in the likeness of a catamount's head, and rubbed smooth by the years. "Meanwhile, someone may be loose within my household, imparting information of my plans to the king. Where's the message?"

Immerez swallowed.

"Well, man, what is it?"

"The message . . . it—it got away."

"The message got away? What did it do? Sprout legs and run?"

"Yes, my lord. I mean, no, my lord."

Mirwell rubbed his grizzled eyebrows with his thumb and forefinger. "Explain."

"We chased Coblebay for days, and even more after we injured him. The day we thought we finally had him, he eluded us yet again. He rode like a demon, as if his horse had wings. Unnatural, if you take my meaning. He should've died days earlier. He rode off the trail and into the woods. We lost all trace of him, as if he'd disappeared completely."

"How do you know he's dead?"

"We found him eventually, on the Selium Road."

"So where's the message?" The governor's voice was tinged with impatience.

"With the horse." Before the governor could bark another question, Immerez explained, "Someone took the horse. That fool Thursgad thought Coblebay's ghost still directed it, but we caught up with the rider, cloaked in a Greenie greatcoat, and very much of the flesh. This Rider *did* vanish."

"Greenie tricks, eh? I've heard they have uncanny abilities, but they are close-mouthed about it. Zachary keeps that woman by his throne. You know the one."

"Mapstone?"

"That's the one. Mapstone." He snarled her name. "He keeps her by his side and she looks at me like she can see right into my soul. I heard of Greenie magic when I was a boy and always knew to keep my mind clear around her, and my words honest. No sense in taking a chance, and I'm glad I haven't. Only a Greenie could disappear like that. What do you plan now?"

Immerez released a long breath, as if relieved by the governor's apparent understanding. "My men and the Gray One continue to track this new Greenie. I request additional help. I thought it would prove advantageous if we include a couple of Prince Amilton's people in the chase. After all, it is for him we are treading such a dangerous path."

"A couple of Amilton's folk, eh? Which ones did you have in mind?"

"His Weapons."

Mirwell chortled. "How very shrewd of you, Captain. We'll make our would-be king feel a little vulnerable without them, eh? And how very appropriate. They are already traitors to the realm, so by necessity they will be careful. By all means, broaden the search."

"What if the prince should protest?"

"Does he have any choice? Without our help, he won't be able to claim the crown as his." The fire popped, and the captain blinked. Mirwell ran his fingers through his beard where four white streaks cut through the gray like clawmarks. "You must stop that Greenie, Captain. We must prevent that message from getting through. If it does, our plans could fall to ruin, and the reprisal would be harsh indeed. We mustn't alert Zachary to his impending assassination. Find out also who the spy is, if one exists, by whatever means necessary."

"Yes, my lord." Immerez started to bow, but Mirwell stopped him with a gesture.

"And Immerez, if you fail, I shall carve out your other eye from its socket myself, and display it in a jar on my mantel until it withers away."

Immerez's cheeks blanched. He knew it was no casual threat. He completed the bow and turned smartly on his heel, leaving the library in brisk even steps.

Mirwell chuckled. Immerez was generally a competent man, but a threat wouldn't hurt. It was no secret the governor could have housed a museum of body parts taken from those who had displeased him.

The letter from Dean Geyer crinkled as he unfolded it for another read through. His idiot of a son had lost a swordfight with some merchant girl and had retaliated by involving the Selium Mirwells. It seemed his cousins had things under control. The girl in question was suspended from school for the fight, causing her to run away. Mirwell, never fond of merchants, grinned. Maybe his boy held some promise after all. But governing a great province, a province that was destined to become even greater once they rid Sacoridia of King Zachary, took more than simple retaliation and meanness of spirit.

The girl's name was G'ladheon, a name of the old days, but not an original Sacor Clan, and certainly the name of a lesser clan. A merchant clan . . . He had heard of it before, he thought, but it was one that did not frequent Mirwell Province.

He rang the bell at his side and presently his aide, Major Beryl Spencer, joined him. Her bow was crisp, but elegant. Ah, if he were only twenty years younger, maybe the two of them could have bred a robust, intelligent son. But he had grown too crusty, and another heir now would not only ruin all his hard work with Timas, but would complicate things inordinately.

"My lord?" Beryl perched on the edge of a chair and held a quill and paper ready to record his command, or to script a letter.

"I've an assignment for you, Spence," he said, using his pet nickname for her. "My son has gotten into trouble with a girl of a lesser clan."

"Shall I offer the clan reparation on your behalf, or shall we acknowledge the child?"

"Child? What? Oh, no, not that kind of trouble." It was an amusing thought that made him chuckle, and almost erupt into a belly laugh. Beryl's perplexed expression prolonged it. "No, I doubt the runt is capable of siring a child. I'd like you to find out about a merchant clan called G'ladheon. Find out who they are and what their home province is. I want to know how powerful they are should they seek retaliation."

"Yes, my lord. Anything else?"

"Send word to Dean Geyer that I need *dates,* not just names. I thought the man to be intelligent, as scholars are supposed to be."

Beryl's eyes were questioning. "In regard to . . . ?"

"He'll know what it's about, and tell our messenger he must reply immediately. Dismissed, Major."

"Yes, my lord."

Beryl bowed and left him. An efficient woman, that Beryl. Mirwell liked to surround himself with efficiency. Efficiency meant competence, and competence meant that his goals would be achieved. He had but to command. He glanced at Dean Geyer's letter again. There was a natural history class full of high-blooded children at Selium, some of them the sons and daughters of clan chiefs. Interesting that the G'ladheon girl's name should be on the class list. In an odd way, Timas had saved her life by causing her to run away.

The field trip sanctioned by the dean would insure that

none of the aristocratic children would pose a threat to Prince Amilton's ascension to the throne. Oh, there were others out there, thick-blooded aristocrats ready to take the throne, but they would be dealt with individually if necessary. Children were but a small sacrifice for a greater cause.

Mirwell wadded up the letter and tossed it into the fire. He watched the paper ignite and blacken around the edges, seeming to fold into itself until it was no longer there. This plan of his had to be thought through, and he had been thinking about it for decades. Only with the help of the Gray One had it seemed possible for it to become reality.

Beside his chair, a little table held an Intrigue board set with blue, green, and red pieces. Few were moved from their starting positions on the edges of the board, for only one man played this game.

Mirwell removed a green messenger from the perimeter of the red court. The pieces were ancient, at least very old, and made of enameled lead. The features on the pieces had been blurred by the fingers of generations of his family.

He laid the green messenger on its side. "You are dead," he said.

Then he moved another green messenger into the fray. He positioned three red soldiers, two red knights, and a blue assassin behind it.

SPAWN OF *KANMORHAN VANE*

Several days passed, punctuated only by the occasional spring shower. Karigan and The Horse drifted between the North Road and the cover of the endless forest, backtracking several times in hopes of confusing Immerez and his men should they pick up on her trail again. Every so often, she felt as if she were being watched, and was seized by an unnerving urge to glance repeatedly over her shoulder. But she never saw any evidence of pursuit, and The Horse didn't seem concerned at all. Could it be that the spirit of F'ryan Coblebay still followed?

At midday, she sat on a rock while chewing on a piece of dried meat. The Horse wandered nearby, cropping at grass that grew in the road and swishing his tail at flies. Karigan slapped at her own neck. The biters had emerged in abundance after all the wet weather.

After only a few days on the road since her stay at Seven Chimneys, she missed all the little comforts provided by the Berry sisters—the soft bed, hot tea, fragrant baths, and especially the conversation. It had been all very civilized. She kept the gifts bestowed upon her by the sisters close to her. The moonstone remained in her trouser pocket, and the bayberry sprig and bunchberry flower were tucked in an inner pocket of the greatcoat. Whenever she removed them, they were uncrushed and unwilted, and yet, she wasn't surprised.

The Horse nickered and looked toward the sky, blades

of grass sticking out of the corners of his mouth. Karigan followed his gaze, shielding her eyes against the glare of the sun. Far above an enormous eagle circled. His size and dull coloring indicated he was one of the rare gray eagles who lived in the Wingsong Mountains. They were seldom seen so far from their mountain realm, and never at close range. Her natural history instructor, Master Ione, would give up his master's knot to see what she now watched.

The eagle rode the currents, rising higher and seeming to float on the air, then swooped lower as though watching something. Karigan could imagine the feathers on his wings rippling, and the wind roaring in his ears. What breathtaking sights he must see from so high up! Could he see beyond the expanse of the Green Cloak to the sea? Could he see the spires of his own mountain peak home?

The eagle's circle widened—he was definitely searching for something—prey most likely. He hovered for a moment, as if frozen in time, before veering southward and out of sight. The Horse snorted and resumed his grazing.

At dusk they followed a deer trail to find a campsite for the night. Karigan winced at the thought of sleeping on the ground again, certain that her back would never be the same after so many nights of rocks and roots. Her precious, albeit bedraggled, blanket from Selium helped, but it was certainly no feather bed.

Biters buzzed in her ears. It was feeding time, and they chewed on any bit of flesh she left uncovered. The Horse shook his whole body to relieve himself, and almost dislodged Karigan from the saddle in the process.

She scratched at a new row of welts on the back of her neck, wishing for a jar of priddle cream, obtained from the horrible smelling priddle plant, more often called stinky weed. Despite the pungent odor, or because of it, it was by far the best repellent against biters. Wishes were as solid as air, however, and she was no more likely to come across a pot of priddle cream as she was to sleep in a feather bed.

Without warning, The Horse stopped dead in his tracks and laid back his ears. Karigan paused her scratching.

"What's wrong?" she whispered. "I don't see anything."

There were any number of things in the deepening shadows of the woods that could spook a horse, though this horse was not easily spooked. Karigan waited for a moment, and when she didn't hear or see anything, she urged him forward. He resisted and stepped backward instead.

"I still don't see—" Off to their right, the underbrush rustled. "—anything." The last word crept out in a whisper.

Karigan's eyes darted from shadow to shadow, searching for the source of the noise, but silence hung thick in the woods as if all the creatures within waited with bated breath for something to happen. The reins became slimy in her sweaty hands. The Horse shifted uneasily beneath her.

Just when she decided she must have imagined the noise, a creature larger than her horse exploded from the underbrush, scattering leaves and branches into the air, and hurled itself at them in a silvery streak.

The Horse reared, dumping Karigan out of the saddle.

Karigan groaned. The whole world moved and bumped in her head . . . her aching, groggy head. The greatcoat and her shirt were bunched up beneath her shoulders, and the ground scraped and dug into her bare back. There was a terrible pain in her ankle. Her arms trailed behind her in the forest litter. Trailing, moving, bumping. No, the movement wasn't in her head at all. Her foot must be caught in a stirrup and The Horse was dragging her.

Her eyes fluttered open, and she had to crane her neck

to see. A huge pincerlike claw, not a stirrup, clamped her ankle. The claw was attached to a saucer-shaped body armored by a metallic carapace supported by six jointed legs. A flat tail arched over the creature's body with a stinger the size of a dagger protruding from its end oozing with venom. Two black orbs glinted in the moonlight, moving on the end of eyestalks. A mandible worked where its mouth was, and two slender antennae felt the path ahead as the creature ambled crablike deeper into the woods. A second claw snapped at The Horse, forcing him to keep his distance.

Karigan almost lost consciousness again, but she fought it off. Oblivion, no matter how inviting, was not going to help her. Instead, she screamed.

Then like a frightened animal snared in a trap, she squirmed and thrashed and snarled, but the claw held her fast, and in fact tightened and cut into her ankle. She moaned with the pain. She sat up even as she was being dragged, and tried to loosen the giant claw with her hands. The shell was as hard as a knight's plate armor, and the claw wouldn't budge. Her toes began to feel numb. She fell back, puffing from the exertion, letting her hands trail in the leaf litter. Her head throbbed so and she felt as though she might vomit. Where was the creature taking her?

Gods . . . She stifled a helpless sob, her breathing ragged. Her heart thumped against her rib cage. *Calm down, calm down. Think.* She forced herself to take deeper, longer breaths, to relax her muscles as much as possible, just as Arms Master Rendle had trained her. "Caving in to fear will be your death," he once said. "There is no room for it on the battlefield. Being afraid is healthy, but fear is an enemy." She continued with the breaths and thought about how she could help herself.

Her head bounced on a rock and sparks of light burst before her eyes. She groaned and felt the back of her skull. She winced as she touched one egg-sized bump—from when she fell off The Horse, she guessed—and a small one from the rock. Rocks and roots continued to scrape her back as she was dragged along. Would this nightmare never end? How could she help herself?

Her hand trailed along another rock and she fumbled with it, but she couldn't get it firmly into her grasp. She searched for other rocks, but they were too small to have any effect, or too lodged in the ground, or too big for her to handle. She grappled with another that seemed right, and almost lost it when she ripped a fingernail on it. But she didn't give up till it was firmly in her hands.

It was not easy to aim, being hauled along the ground on her back as she was. Using the strength of both arms, she heaved the rock at the creature, issuing a grunt as she released it. It glanced harmlessly off the creature's carapace and dropped to the ground with a thud. She succeeded only in drawing the creature's attention to her. It swiveled its disk body about to look at her directly. The eyestalks bobbed above her, then the feelers swung over and probed her midsection.

"Stop it!" Karigan cried.

The jabbing was painful, and at times, ticklish. She grabbed one of the feelers and the other whisked away. It was rough and cold in her hand, and as thick as a broom handle. The creature considered her for a moment, then shook her till she was certain her foot would be severed from her ankle. She dropped the antenna, tears of pain slipping down her cheeks.

The Horse took advantage of the diversion and met the creature head on, rearing up and pounding his hooves onto the hard shell. He moved deftly out of the way of the stinger to evade the snap of the claw. When he came too close to the creature's eyes, it was alarmed enough to drop Karigan's foot and pay full attention to the annoying mammal that threatened it. How astonishing, Karigan thought, that The Horse hadn't run off, much less had stuck around to defend her.

A moment passed before she realized she was free, and that her foot was still attached to her body. She tried to stand on it, but fell back to the ground with a cry. Too much feeling flooded into her foot all at once. She stood up again, this time hopping on her left foot, and not daring to put weight on the right.

"Horse!"

The Horse was too preoccupied with fighting for his own life to help. The creature, unburdened of Karigan, moved quickly from side to side, and swiveled to stop him. The Horse's hooves thudded the ground as he turned and swerved, bucking at the creature, then rounding on it and snapping his teeth. His efforts could have killed a man or woman, but proved futile against the armor plating of the creature. He was showing signs of exhaustion, breathing labored, and foamy sweat dripping on the ground, and he stumbled with increasing frequency.

Karigan hopped away in an attempt to keep ahead of the two combatants. If The Horse failed, there was nothing to stop the creature from getting her.

She hopped and loped heedlessly, pushing through underbrush, and checking over her shoulder to see how The Horse fared. As the moon fell behind some clouds, an almost palpable darkness took hold of the forest and she could discern little about her. Maybe the blow to her head contributed in some way, by darkening the edges of her vision.

With her uncertain footing and dim sight, she stumbled into something sticky, like a giant cobweb. She tried to walk out of it, but it clung to her, and snapped her back, entangling both legs and most of her body. She struggled, but the stuff only stuck to her more.

What is this?

The moon began to edge out from behind the cloud and she saw a white, weblike filament stuck to her arm and legs. In fact, it was tautly woven between several trees.

Oh, gods, a giant spiderweb.

Her only hope now was The Horse.

Something quivered down the length of the web. The moon had moved far enough out from behind the cloud to penetrate some of the deep shadows with light, revealing other creatures trapped like Karigan. A doe kicked, trying to free herself. It looked like she had been at it for some time. Her head sagged in exhaustion, and her body heaved in staggered breaths. Birds, squirrels, bats, a raccoon, and even a *wolf* were ensnared.

The wolf snapped at the air and howled, a rending howl that churned Karigan's insides. His call wasn't answered, and he whimpered. Karigan had heard howls like that on freezing winter nights. They had terrified her. Yet, all she could do now was pity the wolf.

On the ground behind her, almost hidden beneath a bush, was a heap of ivory bones, luminous in the dusky forest, and freshly stripped of flesh. Next to the bush was a pile of round, fist-sized objects, each the same tarnished silver of the creature. Was it her imagination, or did a couple vibrate? She passed her free hand over her eyes, uncertain of the reliability of her vision. It felt like someone was drubbing her head with a hammer, and she was dizzy.

More bones were scattered near the spherical objects, and she began to suspect that, like a fly caught in a spider's web, the creature was not done with her.

Sounds of the battle between The Horse and the creature drew closer—the racket of hooves on carapace, the cracking of tree limbs, The Horse's hard breaths, the snap of claws . . . The Horse backed through the underbrush, and Karigan could see the rise and fall of the creature's claws as it herded him toward the web.

"Horse!" Karigan shouted. "It's a trap!"

The Horse hesitated and glanced in her direction, as if suddenly understanding his predicament. The creature struck him with its tail, embedding the stinger into his neck. The Horse crashed to his side, and he didn't move.

"Nooo!" Karigan wailed.

The creature prodded The Horse's belly with an antenna. When he didn't respond, it emitted a clicking sound, perhaps of approval. From The Horse, it sidled to the webbing, and moved up the line from the doe to the raccoon, then to Karigan. Eye stalks wavered as it inspected its prey. It poked her ribs with an antenna, and softly whistled to itself.

Karigan jerked away and slapped her free hand at the antenna. "Get away!" But already the creature's attention was on the spherical objects. It nudged one or two with its claw to a more satisfactory position, then trundled away.

Karigan moaned. All was lost without The Horse. She was trapped and there was no escape. She hadn't expected it to end this way. She thought she would reach Sacor City, and hand over the message directly to the king. She'd be a hero! If she was to be stopped, she thought it would have been by Immerez and his men, and they were horrible enough to contemplate. This monster was totally unexpected.

Moments passed and the wolf cried out with his dreadful howls. How long before the creature returned? How long before it would return to feed?

The scent of bayberry drifted to Karigan from her coat pocket. The little sprig of bayberry must have been crushed during her struggle with the creature, and now it did what Miss Bayberry said it would: "When you find resolve failing you, when all hope is lost, take a leaf and rub it between your fingers. The scent will refresh you, and perhaps you will think of me." Hope swelled within her, and with it, courage. While she still lived, there might be a chance.

Miss Bunchberry had given her a bunchberry flower: "If you are in need of a friend, pluck a petal from the flower and let it drift in the wind." She wished fervently that she could now be in the care of the Berry sisters. She needed a friend.

A crack split the air somewhere behind her. At first she couldn't identify its source, then she glanced at the spherical objects. They vibrated and hairline fractures grew and spread across their smooth surfaces. Karigan sagged, but the webbing held her up. The spheres were eggs.

Antennae poked through. Tiny claws tapped on the

insides of shells, and slimy silver bodies, miniatures of the parent creature, emerged wet and glistening. They slid over their brethren, one on top of the other, and scurried toward the web, attracted to the heat they sensed from those trapped in it. There was no doubt of what would be doing the feeding.

A creature crawled onto the toe of Karigan's boot and she kicked it. It spun a yard away, but in a flurry of legs, feelers, and claws, it scurried toward her again. The animals struggled, too, but in their panic, only entangled themselves farther into the webbing.

An almost human scream drowned the moans of the animals. Karigan's nerves stretched taut. The raccoon. She closed her eyes as if to silence its anguished cries. When the cries diminished, she opened her eyes again.

Three hatchlings crawled up her leg. She growled and shook them off, more angry now than fearful. The creatures had no right. *No right.* The hatchlings closest to her feet made a sickening crunching sound beneath the heel of her boot.

The bunchberry flower was in her hand. She couldn't remember having pulled it out. The fragrance of the bayberry was intoxicating. *If you are in need of a friend, pluck a petal* . . . She would need an army of friends. She shook her leg, but this time the hatchlings hung on with their claws, antennae feeling the way up her leg.

She lowered the flower to her other hand which was stuck in the web, and pried off a single petal. . . . *and let it drift in the wind.* As soon as the petal left her fingertips, a breeze swept it up, avoiding the webbing and entwined tree limbs, and carrying it out of sight above the treetops. Karigan sighed. At least she would die remembering her friends.

She shook her leg again. The creatures had climbed up as far as her hips and now employed their stingers. Her legs began to go numb. Yet she vowed she wouldn't die without a fight. She shook and writhed her body, ignoring the stings, and brushed some of the creatures off with her free hand. Each hatchling that fell off was a victory. She ground them into the earth with the heel of her boot.

A screech echoed over the whimpers of her fellow victims, and some great winged thing crashed through the canopy of the trees. Karigan cringed under its shadow. What horror had come to join the feasting of the little creatures? Then she saw the outline of an eagle—a huge gray eagle.

"The web!" she screamed at him. "Watch the web!"

She felt the beat of each powerful backstroke of his wings. The span of his wings had to be as long as she was tall—wonderful for the great heights of the Wingsong Mountains, but not practical in the woods.

I will help you. He settled on a stout branch above her head.

"What?"

In the oldest folklore, the kind children adored and skeptical adolescents scoffed at, there were stories of creatures with an intelligence equal to a human's, who could speak into the minds of others. Karigan herself had pleaded with her mother to tell such tales, but now, a skeptical adolescent, she wasn't sure that she had actually heard the eagle. Master Ione had never said anything about animals or birds using mind speech, so surely, she had heard nothing at all. The eagle was nothing more than an illusion gazing at her. Her pounding, addled mind, and the poisonous stings were making her see and hear things.

I will help you. The voice was deep and guttural, and very real.

Awed, Karigan could only stare at him, her mouth gaping. If the old stories were true and the eagle really spoke to her, did she direct thoughts of what she wanted to say to him, or did she speak aloud? Could he hear her thoughts?

Direct me. The eagle perched as implacable as a statue, though his "voice" was tinged with irritation.

Karigan opened and closed her mouth, fishlike, unable

to utter a word. Even if he could read her thoughts, they'd be an unintelligible jumble.

She did not know what to tell him. If he tried to fight the creatures, he could easily get tangled in the web, or the creatures could sting him, or . . . She looked hopelessly about for an answer, shaking a couple of hatchlings from her leg almost as an afterthought. She looked at The Horse's still body. He had fallen on the saddle sheath. If the eagle could reach her saber . . .

"My sword," she said. "It's beneath the horse. If you could pry it out and—"

The eagle, guessing her intent, launched from his branch to The Horse. He stood on the ground, his head cocked as if deciding how best to proceed. Karigan couldn't watch. Tiny silver disk shapes swarmed all over The Horse.

Her right leg was completely numb. At least she couldn't feel the pain in her ankle.

"Ow!" A hatchling bit her beneath her left knee. She shook her leg so violently that the hatchling smashed against the nearest tree trunk. She breathed hard with the exertion, and hung limp in the web like a marionette.

Here is the sword. The eagle hovered just above her, the hilt of the saber grasped in a huge talon.

She extended her free hand as far as possible. The eagle lowered the saber carefully, trying to avoid becoming enmeshed in the web. She couldn't quite reach the hilt, and had to grab the blade instead.

"Ow!" It bit into her fingers and palm, and she almost dropped it. But her fear of the creatures was greater than the pain, and she kept her grip on it. She shifted it with her other hand, so she could grip it by the hilt.

Your horse still lives, the eagle said. *I will do what I can for him.*

The Horse was alive! Joy surged through Karigan and she slashed through the sticky web and released herself. However, her numb right leg failed to support her and she fell face to feelers with a dozen hatchlings. She scrambled to her left foot and hopped back a step. She brushed or cut off any hatchling that still clung to her.

You must kill them all, the eagle said. Using his sharp beak, he plucked a hatchling from The Horse and smashed it against a rock, much the way she had seen gulls crack crabs open along the seashore. *You must do it now while their shells are still soft. They harden as we speak. Kill them all.*

There must have been hundreds of the creatures scattered all over the forest floor. First she attacked those hatchlings affixed to the hapless animals caught in the web. The doe and the raccoon were dead, their flesh efficiently stripped down to the bone. Then she released the birds and bats that were too high up for the creatures to reach.

The wolf still fought, but the weight of the hatchlings attached to his blood-soaked fur weighed him down. He yelped with every movement, his tongue lolling out the side of his mouth, and yet Karigan paused. Too many people had told her, when she was little, that wolves killed the sheep people depended on, that wolves would eat a man if driven to hunger. Wolves, they said, were evil—products of Mornhavon the Black.

The wolf gazed at her with defiant amber eyes, as if challenging her. As if challenging her to release him. Just as suddenly, his eyes rolled back in a spasm of pain, and his hind legs sagged beneath him.

Without another thought, Karigan brushed the creatures from his fur with her saber. His sides heaved as he panted. Where the creatures clung to him with their mouths or claws, she speared them through the shells. When she had them off the wolf, she hacked them into pieces, their phlegmy yellow blood soaking into the ground. The wolf collapsed, his eyes half closed in exhaustion. Karigan slashed down the web to prevent any other animals from becoming ensnared.

Balanced on one foot, she single-mindedly hacked at the creatures. Without a ready source of meat, many just scurried in circles, their claws clicking at empty air. Some helped her cause by feeding on their brethren.

Agile as Karigan was, it was difficult to chase the creatures down on one foot. Her blade bounced off shells that grew harder with every passing second. Soon, the eagle deemed The Horse safe enough to be left alone, and took up the hunt, tearing the creatures apart with his powerful talons. His keen eyesight assured that not one hatchling escaped.

The Horse's chestnut hide was nicked and streaked with blood where the hatchlings had bitten him, but as the effects of the sting waned, he could lift his head and move his legs. Karigan wiped her yellowed blade on a clump of moss. The ground was littered with destroyed hatchlings. The wolf had disappeared in the mayhem.

Sensation crept into her right leg like the sting of a hundred hornets. She didn't even want to think about what the parent creature had done to her ankle with its claw.

"What are these creatures?" she asked the eagle.

They've come from Kanmorhan Vane. *All things there are corrupt.*

"Kanmorhan Vane?"

The Blackveil Forest which your country borders, he said. Kanmorhan Vane *is its Eltish name. A friend of mine, an owl, told me there is a breach in the D'Yer Wall through which the creature came. I've been tracking it for two days.*

Blackveil Forest figured in more stories about evil than Karigan had heard about wolves. She was inclined to believe those stories in light of her encounter with the creatures; stories of how Mornhavon the Black sickened the once verdant forest with his magic. Everything that dwelled there, it was said, became evil. After the Long War, Aleric D'Yer had begun a wall along the Sacoridian border where Blackveil threatened to spread its roots, even though the evil of Mornhavon the Black had been vanquished.

A block of granite from the wall was on permanent

display at the Langory Museum in Selium, though she doubted many paused to consider its significance. The wall had stood for so long that it was taken for granted, and most information about Blackveil was held as superstition. After all, how could a mere wall prevent such a dark force from encroaching across the border? The stories about Blackveil, Karigan thought, could not have been exaggerated if the parent creature had come from there.

When you see your king, the eagle said, *you must warn him of the breach. If the one creature made it through, others are bound to follow.*

When you see your king . . . Karigan wasn't at all confident she would succeed after this experience, but she felt more hopeful than just a few minutes ago.

The eagle cocked his head, as if listening. In the moonlight, his gray feathers were not dull, but rippled with subtle blues, greens, and golds.

I hear the parent, he said.

Karigan froze. The hand that held her saber shook.

It must not live, the eagle said. *I will help you as well as I can.*

"What?"

You must slay the parent, he said, annoyance in his voice. *It mustn't be allowed to lay any more eggs.*

"How am I supposed to—"

The underbelly is soft. So is the tissue between the joints.

Vegetation rustled as the creature drew nearer. How was Karigan to reach the creature's underside? She would have to be beneath it before she could reach with her saber.

Avoid its blood, the eagle said. *It's not diluted like that of the hatchlings. It will burn you, and maybe poison you if you touch it.*

They didn't have to wait long. The creature scuttled into the clearing, driving a terrified red fox before it. When the creature saw the carnage of its young, and the destroyed web, it screamed in rage, a high-pitched whistle racking the forest. Karigan dropped her sword and clapped her hands over her ears. The fox kept running, and without a web to stop it, was safely free of the creature.

The whistle faded and Karigan uncovered her ears. The creature charged her. She stumbled backward and landed hard on her buttocks, gaping at the creature looming over her, its antennae whipping the air above.

The eagle dove between the creature's flailing claws, narrowly escaping being snapped shut in one pair. The creature shook tail feathers from its claw and hissed in fury. It swatted at the eagle with its tail.

The eagle dove at the creature's eyes. *Don't just sit,* he chided Karigan from mid-flight. *It must be killed.*

She curled her fingers about the hilt of her sword. An invisible pair of hands slipped under her arms and helped her up from the ground. There was no time to think about the unseen help as the creature made steady progress toward her, despite the eagle. The weight on her right foot sent the hornets prickling up and down her leg.

A claw whistled within inches of her nose. She ducked and felt the whoosh of air as it clamped shut where her head had just been. A frontal assault, evidently, was not the most advantageous. She limped away from the creature's line of sight and lethal claws, but it was quick. A claw struck her across the shoulders from behind, knocking her face first into the ground. She gasped for breath, trying to gain her bearings.

Messenger!

Karigan turned at the eagle's warning. An open claw descended on her, but a flurry of fur darted from the vegetation and straight at the creature. The wolf!

The creature paused its attack at this new distraction. The wolf snarled, wove between the creature's legs, and caused it to stumble.

Again, the invisible hands helped Karigan to her feet and handed her the sword. She ran-limped to the creature's rear, but it was too quick and swiveled around to attack her directly. The tail whistled overhead. Sweat slicked her back and every step on her bad foot was agony. She couldn't get close enough to the creature's belly without facing the claws or tail.

The wolf positioned himself before the creature. He glanced at Karigan with his defiant eyes, then leaped up and caught a feeler in his mouth. It broke with a crack. Oily black blood spilled from the severed appendage, and the wolf dropped the broken piece, his mouth foaming. Pain enraged the creature, and it snapped up the distracted wolf in a claw.

"No!"

Karigan moved between the claws, and holding the saber two-handed, chopped into the joint of the pincer that clutched the wolf. The claw and wolf crashed to the earth.

The creature whistled and hissed. Now Karigan dared to approach closer, hacking when legs or the other claw came too close. The eagle continued to harry it from above, constantly at its eyes, even more so now that there was one less claw to worry about.

Karigan dismembered the second claw and ducked beneath the body. Without ceremony, she thrust the saber into the leathery undershell and disemboweled the creature. Foul smelling blood and black ropy innards poured from the wound. The ground sizzled beneath the guts. She jerked the saber free and backed into the open night air. The creature shuddered, tripped over its own legs, and collapsed onto the ground. Karigan waved away the stench that rose up about it.

Her wrists began to burn. "My skin!" Black blood seared her wrists.

The eagle flew over to her. *Water. You need water to bathe in. I saw a stream this way.*

Karigan dropped her sword uncaring. Tears of pain filled her eyes. She limped through the woods behind the airborne eagle, stumbling from exhaustion. Branches snagged at her greatcoat and slapped her face. The dense canopy of the woods blotted out moonlight, and she fell twice. Groaning with the pain, she climbed back to her feet.

Quickly, the eagle said. *It's not far.*

"My water skin would have been closer."

It would not have been enough. And he flew ahead over the trees.

After another fall, Karigan remembered her moonstone. When she removed it from her pocket, it lit the woods around her like brilliant daylight. Her pains diminished as she held it, and travel through the woods became easier.

The promised stream appeared, a glimmering ribbon in the light of the moonstone. She set the stone on a fallen tree trunk and dropped to her knees in the soft mud of the stream. She plunged her wrists, sleeves and all, into the cold, soothing water. Her whole body felt hot, as if she had bathed in the creature's burning blood. She splashed her face with stream water.

I hope for your sake we were not too late.

Karigan looked at the eagle. His feathers showed a veritable rainbow of colors in the light of the moonstone. "What do you mean?"

The blood—its poisonous effects.

It was like listening to someone else's conversation from far away. She cupped water in her hands to slake her sudden thirst.

Creatures such as we fought tonight haven't been seen since the Long War. The eagle preened a little, then watched her impassively as she dunked her whole head into the water.

Her thirst quenched, at least for the moment, she stood up, wobbling with dizziness.

What are you doing? the eagle asked.

"The Horse . . . he needs me. And the wolf."

Karigan limped back through the woods, stumbling and falling despite the assistance of the moonstone. It seemed to take years to reach the clearing where the carnage of the battle lay. The creature's carapace had darkened in its pall of death. She felt numb all over. Only the eagle's loud protests prevented her from stepping in a puddle of black blood.

The Horse watched her approach. He lay on his side with his legs tucked up against his belly, and though his neck was grotesquely swollen where he had been stung, his eyes were bright. The wolf, on the other hand, did not move. Karigan cried in rage and pulled at the claw that still clenched him, rocking it back and forth. His eyes were empty of defiance and life.

"I won't have this!"

She dropped the claw and found her saber on the ground. The blade was still black with the creature's blood. She carried it over to the creature. The Horse whinnied in alarm, but she ignored him. She swung her sword again and again at the creature, but it bounced off its shell.

The eagle flew at her face, pushing her away. *Foolish human. It's dead.*

"Leave me alone!" She swung the sword erratically, nearly catching the eagle in midair, but gentle hands took it from her. She wasn't sure if she could see the hands or not, but they were cool to the touch. They led her from the clearing and helped her lay down.

She closed her eyes and fell into dreams of thousands of silvery creatures stinging her, making her drink black blood, of fire and burning. When she opened her eyes again, F'ryan Coblebay stood next to the eagle, flickering like a candle in a breeze. She could not hear their words as they conversed, only whispers that may have been the branches of trees rattling together like dry bones. They glanced down at her, talking about her, she was sure, as if she wasn't there.

"Talk to *me* . . ." She had meant to yell, but her lips and mouth were so dry the words were no more than a raspy breath.

She saw the wolf. Like F'ryan Coblebay, there was a luminous quality about him, an otherworldliness. He looked right into her face, his amber eyes challenging her once again. Challenging her to what? She could not maintain that gaze, and she closed her eyes. She fell into a dark slumber with tiny silver-shelled creatures feeding on her mind.

⊰≫ SOMIAL OF THE
ELT WOOD ⊰≫

The nature of her dreams changed abruptly. She heard fair voices in song and talk around her. The voices weren't intrusive, but soothing, though she could not understand the words. She awakened once, and a myriad of stars brightened the sky like beacons, and silhouetted the tops of evergreens. She lay in a great round clearing softened by deer moss that looked like clumps of snow in the starlight. Stars flickered among the trees . . . no, not stars, but *moonstones* . . . dozens of them. She was not alone.

Light followed in the wake of folk tall and slender, who glided across the clearing and disappeared among the trees. She sat up with a start that set her head ringing.

"Easy, youngling," a quiet voice said. A gentle but firm hand on her shoulder eased her back down. "There is nothing to harm you here. You've the good fortune of being found by friends in your time of need. You need not fear the Tree Kindred of the Elt Wood."

As Karigan drifted back into sleep, she heard the eagle say, *My Lord Drannonair of the Mountains calls me. I confess I've no wish to get mixed up in the affairs of earthbound creatures, and it was time I left.*

The quiet-voiced one laughed, and it was a sound of joy. "But, Softfeather, you are always betraying yourself!"

Someone put a cool hand on Karigan's burning forehead, and she fell into deep slumber. She dreamed of feasting, of fair folk amidst the moonstones singing and laughing, and dancing to music that could not be heard. The women, clad in long and simple dresses, spun and danced with fluid grace as if their movements were some flowing language. If so, what were they saying? The swaying, dipping, leaping figures were strong in her vision, but after a time, they faded into the moonstone light.

The singing continued for a time, and though Karigan didn't know the language, it seemed she understood the words nonetheless:

> *By bright of light in Laurelyn's step,*
> *By the brilliant light of Moonman's beam,*
> *We leave the shadows of the night,*
> *In the realm of poison dreams.*
> *Our hearts will lift at the hour,*
> *When the light conquers the dark,*
> *And when poison from the heart is driven,*
> *We dance in a glade in Laurelyn's step.*

The song faded, and the men entered the clearing and picked up on the rhythm of the unheard music where the women had left off. They danced for a short time, but could have as easily surpassed the Ages.

Karigan dimly perceived a change of light from dusk to dawn. Stars still dangled above as the sky transformed into the blue blush of day. The dance went on and the strains of a song she could not hear carried through her dreams. When the dance stopped and the women reentered the clearing, Karigan moved to join them, but the cool hand on her forehead cast her into a deeper sleep where dreams would not disturb her.

When she awakened again, stars still dotted the sky and moonstones shimmered in the woods as before, and the clearing was not so far removed from her dreams, except now it was empty of dancers. It was all she could do to open her eyes, so overcome with weakness was she.

"So you are with us again, youngling."

Karigan recognized the voice, but the speaker wasn't within her vision. When she struggled to her elbows, the clearing and stars spun.

"None of that," the voice said. "You are too weak yet."

Hands pressed her shoulders down. When the spinning ceased, a young man such as she had never seen before knelt beside her. At least, he was young in appearance, though the weight of years could be felt through his mild manner. Long hair shimmered silver in the starlight, though she could not be sure that silver was its true color. Wide bright eyes of pale gray set into a fine-boned face gazed down at her merrily. He was slender like a reed, but not bereft of heft and muscle.

"Who—" she croaked. Her mouth and throat were parched.

He lifted a skin of water to her lips and helped her drink. It was cold and clear as if it had been drawn from the root of all waters, from a mountain spring that flowed into a sunny glade where the trees around it grew taller than any she had ever seen.

"I am Somial," the man said. "I am Somial of Eletia, or the Elt Wood as your folk would call it."

Karigan choked on the water. Eletia! "Eletians are legend," she whispered.

"If that is so," he said with a smile, "I must then be a legend."

"Estral always claimed there were still Eletians around, but I never believed her."

"Your Estral, then, is most wise."

"The Horse—" She tried to sit up again, but Somial pressed her firmly to the ground.

"He fares well," he assured her. "We have been caring for him most diligently."

Karigan struggled no more. She hadn't the strength to. "A long night," she murmured.

Somial arched his right brow. "Yes. This night and the last two."

"I've been—?"

"Yes, messenger. Your fight only just began when you slew the creature of *Kanmorhan Vane*. Softfeather told us of your courage. Such courage is not often found among your folk, nor such resilience. The poison of the beast raged hot and thick through your veins."

Karigan couldn't get over the feeling he was secretly laughing at her, but his gaze and tone were sincere enough. "Softfeather? Who—?"

"The gray eagle. He, too, is a messenger of sorts among his folk."

Karigan closed her eyes. The lights around her had begun to dim and flare, and dim again. How was it the Eletians had come to be here at this time? Were they just another fever dream?

"How did you find me?"

Somial said, "We are *tiendan*, hunters, or watchers for the king. We walk the lands, even outside our beloved Eletia. Long it has been since last we traveled Sacoridia's fine northern forest. Our king and his son have sensed a great unease in the world, and the creature of *Kanmorhan Vane* only confirms some unrest of the dark powers. We would that we could have come to your aid sooner, but we only knew of you when we saw the light of the *muna'riel*. Curious that a mortal should possess one. We don't know what to make of it."

"You mean my moonstone?"

"Yes, your moonstone. You have been touched by the light of Laurelyn. It makes you a friend of the Elt Wood, though our king cares little for your kind."

"It was a gift," Karigan said, a little defensively.

"And a worthy one. As is this." He held in his palm, a tiny white petal. With a clear ringing laugh, he tossed it into the air and it might have vanished, but to Karigan, it seemed to become a star. She couldn't hold on any longer, and as she slipped again into slumber, Somial said, "Your wounds were grave, the poison is still within you, but you shall be well soon. Do not fear the night or the creatures within. We shall watch over you, Karigan of Sacoridia, till you have regained the strength to continue your endeavor."

"Can you take my message to Sacor City?" she asked in a groggy whisper.

"Your path lies long and dark," came the quiet reply. He brushed damp hair from her forehead. "But you've the will and strength, and the *muna'riel.* Laurelyn's light can shatter the strength of the dark powers. Yours is not our mission, youngling. We seldom venture where humankind dwells."

"Youngling . . ." she protested.

"Though I am young among my folk at nigh on two hundred years, you are younger still." He kissed her forehead, a gesture that reminded her of her mother, and as she slipped into oblivion, she thought she heard him say, "May Laurelyn light your way."

Karigan drifted off and did not know how long she slept, and though the sleep was deep and healing, she was always aware of the rhythm of the music. The Eletians watched over her, and thus reassured, her sleep was peaceful.

When she did awaken, the clearing was awash in the glow of late morning sunshine. Experimentally she moved each limb. Her right leg was still sore, and when she inspected her ankle, it was bruised black. There were numerous purple marks on her legs where the hatchlings had stung her, but the swelling was gone and the marks were not very painful.

Her wrists were wrapped in a gauzy material where the creature's blood had burned her. In all, she felt as anyone else coming out of illness: weak but renewed, and grateful to be well.

There was no sign of Somial or any other Eletians in the area. They had tended her wounds well. She lay on her bedroll wrapped in her blanket, her head pillowed on the greatcoat, just as she had slept so many nights during her journey. Maybe Somial and the Eletians had been dreams, but her tended wounds proved otherwise.

Nearby, The Horse's tack and her packs lay on the ground, and beside them, the unsheathed saber which glared in the sun. Someone had cleaned it of black blood. She shivered as she remembered that night, and wondered how many nights had since passed.

A loud rattling of branches on the outskirts of the clearing made her heart leap. She took up the saber expecting another creature to attack her, but relaxed when The Horse emerged from the trees. She staggered to her feet and limped over to meet him halfway across the clearing. When she saw no evidence of his sting wound, she wrapped her arms around his neck. He nickered softly.

"Never thought I'd be so happy to see you, you stubborn old horse."

Karigan lingered another day and night in the clearing trying to regain the old strength that still eluded her. There was no trace of the Eletians, though when she slept, she could still feel the rhythm of their silent song.

❧ AMBUSHED ❧

The world beyond the clearing was oppressive. Biters swarmed in clouds about Karigan and The Horse, stealing away any pleasure they might have found in the budding of wildflowers, and the trills of warblers recently arrived from the south. Deciduous trees, few and far between the spiky sun-stealing spruces, strained to open their leaves.

The weather alternated from cold damp to summerlike heat and heavy humidity. Karigan opted to wear the greatcoat often despite the heat as her only defense against the biters. The cuffs were all burned through and tattered from her confrontation with the creature of *Kanmorhan Vane*. Still, it offered a sense of security.

They cantered long on the road as much to outpace the biters as to make up ground. The Horse's gait was tireless, his tail whisking behind as they loped along. Whether it was relief from biters or a sense of spring that drove him, it was hard to say. For all their speed, they were no less cautious in covering their tracks, for she knew Immerez and his men still sought her and the message she carried.

If they were cautious on the road, they were equally cautious off. No longer did they blindly follow deer trails to find a campsite. Karigan chided herself over and over for ever having done so in the first place. Following deer trails at dusk was like walking into a predator's trap. Encountering the creature of *Kanmorhan Vane* at what was suppertime for most predators had been no mistake. Who was to say some bear or catamount, equally as dangerous, wasn't waiting at the end of some other deer trail for an easy meal?

Between Immerez and the creature, Karigan felt like prey in more ways than one.

After a week of swift travel, she began to find signs of human habitation. Though the road had in no way improved, it was grooved with wagon wheels and hoofprints, all recent. Every so often, travelers rode or walked down the road, and she and The Horse concealed themselves in the woods and watched those who passed by.

There were grim men with thick beards and broad shoulders dressed in buckskin, their horses or mules burdened with pelts. Merchants in bright garb sat on wagons laden with goods. Though they were not nearly as prosperous looking as the leading merchant clans of Sacoridia, they were heavily armed and guarded, their cargo masters casting stern expressions over the road.

At the sight of merchants, whether they were of a clan or not, Karigan felt pangs of homesickness. All merchants longed for spring after a winter of little or no travel and no haggling or dealing. Spring brought increased commerce and an opportunity to see old friends. Karigan had accompanied her father on many spring journeys which often included fairs. She would sit proudly with her father atop the foremost wagon of a long wagon train on its way from one town to the next. But she was not with her father. She was alone on a dangerous road and fairs were a distant dream.

Other armed travelers passed down the road, but she couldn't decide if they were brigands, mercenaries, or both. They were male and female, some jolly and lighthearted in conversation, others grim and stern like the merchants' guards, and yet others possessed a downright disreputable air. Their clothing was soiled and their bodies reeked, even off the road where she stood.

What conversation she picked up was more often foul than not. She didn't know whether to feel glad to see others on the road, or alarmed. Carrying the life-or-death message, given to her by a murdered Green Rider, made her suspicious of all who passed by.

The message. The all important message. What did it say? She was dying to take a look at its contents. She had already risked her life to carry it—didn't she have a right to read it even though F'ryan Coblebay had told her not to?

Karigan pulled The Horse to a halt, disregarding the cloud of biters that massed around her head. She unfastened the message satchel and drew out the envelope. "King Zachary" had been written on the front in quick, uneven strokes. She frowned. *This isn't for me.*

She turned it over and took a look at the wax seal. It remained uncracked and unblemished despite its hard journey. A bead of sweat glided down her forehead and pattered onto the envelope. She wiped it away carefully with her sleeve.

I could say it broke along the way. . . .

Maybe she could slip the tip of the saber beneath it, then after she read the message, soften the wax and reseal the envelope. But that would distort the perfect imprint of the flying horse and it would be obvious she had tampered with it.

There's only one way, she decided.

She held the wax seal between her thumbs ready to crack it, one eye closed and a grimace on her face as if she didn't want to see it happen. Then The Horse shifted beneath her and flicked his ears back and forth. Voices, barely audible, floated to her from behind. She sighed, actually relieved by the diversion, and dropped the intact message back into the satchel.

She guided The Horse into the woods and tied him up well out of range of the road. She crept back to the road and crouched behind a rock. Two people, a man and a woman, walked into view. They moved as smoothly as cats, their ease of movement belying powerful shoulders and sword arms, and legs rippling with muscles.

They were both dressed in the same plain leather jerkins. Gray cloaks, patched and travel-stained, hung from their shoulders. They wore no devices to identify militia or mercenary company.

Bandits or plainshields, Karigan thought. *Poor bandits if that is what they are.*

Despite the drab and worn look of their gear, the patches had been carefully sewn and the leather was oiled. Long swords bumped against their hips as they walked.

Their poor state probably had little to do with their prowess as fighters. They did not waste movement with superfluous gestures even though they appeared to be in deep discussion. . . . Deep, heated discussion.

"I tell you, Jendara," the man said, "I caught a whiff of a horse."

His partner looked at him askance. Ringlets of russet hair flowed down her back. "You're just hungry," she said. "You are imagining things."

"What about those droppings we saw back there?"

"Look, there've been several travelers up and down this road. Who's to say that last pile of horse manure belonged to the one we're looking for?"

The man's face was grim. It was coated by the beginnings of a spiky yellow beard, and the lines of tension could be seen clearly beneath it. "I'm tired of this walking. We should be with our lord."

The couple drew abreast of Karigan's hiding spot and walked by.

"I don't like it either," the one called Jendara said. "But we must do as we are told."

"Chasing ghosts and horses. It is not what we swore to do."

"The sooner we're done, the sooner we return to our true duty."

Then the two were gone. Karigan stood up and brushed pine needles from her trousers. Their conversation was enough to convince her she had no desire to encounter them on the road, especially with the reference to chasing ghosts and horses. She would stay here this night, and maybe the next, but she liked having them ahead of her less than behind.

A few days later on a sweltering afternoon, Karigan gave in to the heat. She folded up the greatcoat and fastened it behind the saddle with the bedroll. It was like midsummer in the southlands in the shade, and even the biters seemed to wane in the heat. She rolled up her shirt sleeves and squeezed The Horse on.

All at once, the bushes beside the road shook and The Horse swerved out of the way, nearly unseating Karigan. She held onto his mane, but a man burst out of the bushes and seized The Horse's bridle. The Horse jerked back, but the man's hold was secure.

"Dismount," he said.

Karigan cursed silently. This was the man she had observed on the road the other day, but where was the woman, Jendara? She reached for her saber, but felt the pressure of a sword tip against her spine.

"Were I you," the woman said from behind, "I would obey."

Karigan licked her lips, tasting the salt of perspiration. If she could urge The Horse into a run, maybe the man would release the bridle and the woman wouldn't have time to—

"Dismount!"

The sword tip pressed harder into her back. She dismounted. The Horse made to bolt away, but the man yanked on the bridle.

"I've heard of you, smart steed. If you don't obey, I shall sever the tendons in your legs."

The woman regarded Karigan with eyes as steely as her sword. Today her lush hair was bound by a strip of cloth. "You don't look like a spirit rider to me."

The man snorted in contempt. "Ghosts do not exist, and they certainly do not ride horses. Those Mirwellian fools are over superstitious."

Karigan's eyes widened. Surely they meant Immerez, Sarge, and Thursgad . . . and they were *Mirwellians!* Nothing good ever came out of Mirwell.

The man, still holding the bridle, reached over to the message satchel. He undid the leather thong, peered in, and nodded. He let the lid drop and secured it back down. "This is it."

"Remove your shoulder pack," the woman said.

Karigan reluctantly slipped it from her shoulder to the road. It was an inglorious end to her mission. She was caught, and the delivery of the message thwarted by mercenaries working for Immerez.

The other mercenary was already looking through the saddlebags, laughing in delight at the food remaining from the Berry sisters. The woman looked in disdain at the soiled blanket and clothes she found in the shoulder pack.

"I told you there would be little spoils," she said. "Greenies aren't known for being rich."

"We've the food, Jendara, and a new horse, and all the gold the Mirwellian will pay us. What's this?" He untied the greatcoat from its fastenings and unfurled it. "Looks warm enough . . . but, ach! I wouldn't want to be seen in a filthy Greenie coat. This bauble on front, however . . ." He gazed speculatively at the brooch.

Jendara spotted something shining from the tangle of blanket she had pulled from Karigan's shoulder pack. "What might these be?"

Karigan cried out in alarm. "Don't touch those! They're mine!"

In her hand, Jendara the mercenary held finely wrought rings and bracelets set with gems. She was entranced by the way they glittered in the sun. "They're yours no longer, Greenie."

"Those were my mother's—" Her voice broke off in a sob. They were the only objects of intrinsic worth that she had taken with her when she fled Selium.

The man unclasped the brooch and let the greatcoat fall to the dusty road. His grin revealed a gap between his two front teeth. "A bit gaudy, but it might be worth something. We didn't fare so badly after all, did we Jen? Perhaps our luck has changed."

The Berry sisters had told Karigan the brooch wouldn't tolerate the touch of another, yet it glimmered coldly in the sun, the same as usual, as the mercenary weighed it in his palm. Then again, according to the sisters, Professor Berry had never mastered magic, so who was to say there were no gaps in their knowledge?

Jendara was too busy admiring the jewels on her fingers and wrists to answer.

"And a saber. A Greenie saber, but one should never leave behind a weapon. The king's smiths do a fine enough job on their blades."

Karigan's throat constricted with grief and anger as Jendara drew on her finger the troth ring Stevic G'ladheon had given his bride Kariny twenty-five years ago. It was gold and set with a diamond that flared like a star in the light of day. The clan emblem of a ship at full sail upon the sea was etched into the gold band. The etching had been made three years after the wedding when Clan G'ladheon had been formally recognized by the merchant's guild and a representative of the queen.

The emblem represented Stevic G'ladheon's most profitable ventures, most achieved by sailing far seas, and backed by a hardworking bloodline that once made its life in the islands of Ullem Bay. The jewels Jendara now admired were Karigan's only material link with her former life, and her mother.

"You won't take those," she said.

"I don't think you can stop us." Jendara laughed. "We will take good care of your things, and the Mirwellians will take good care of you."

Karigan clenched her hands into fists, her cheeks blushing hotly. She had not killed that unnatural creature only to be put into the hands of Immerez. The creature had been more dangerous than these two. She leaped at Jendara with an animallike snarl, but even as she did so, the other mercenary's hilt cracked against the back of her skull and she fell into darkness.

Karigan awakened with a throbbing head. Her tender wrists, not yet fully healed from the burning blood of the creature, were bound cruelly tight behind her back, leaving her fingers numb. She lay prone on the dead leaves and moss of the forest floor. She assessed her body for further damage, but found none besides her smarting head and strangled wrists.

She carefully surveyed the scene around her through cracked eyelids. In the lengthening shadows of late afternoon, The Horse stood hobbled and untacked a short distance away. His head hung low in a dispirited way.

Jendara and her partner sat before a cookfire eating from Karigan's rations. They had heaped her things into two piles: the things they could obviously live without, namely her travel-worn clothing, and another pile of things they intended to possess, mainly the sword and jewelry. The man twisted the moonstone in his fingers, but it didn't light up. Evidently, they had been through her pockets, too.

"Curious, this crystal," the man said. "Probably a cheap bauble of glass, but fair enough."

"You're no judge, Torne," Jendara said. "See how it catches the light? A fine crystal, I judge. What I find curious is that a simple Greenie possesses all this excellent stuff. Maybe she's really a thief."

"Now what would a thief be doing delivering messages to the king? You heard what she said about the jewelry being her mother's."

"I guess you're right, but she's a stupid Greenie to be carrying these jewels on a road such as this."

Karigan closed her eyes. The thought of the mercenary Jendara wearing her mother's troth ring made the bile rise in her throat. How could she get it back? Even if she did manage to loosen her bonds, how could she ever hope to escape two thoroughly trained mercenaries? Arms Master Rendle had taught her much in the few sessions they had had together, but she possessed neither the practice nor the strength to match Jendara and Torne.

"What are you thinking, Greenie?" Karigan opened her eyes only to find them level with the toes of Torne's boots. "I can tell you aren't asleep."

She spat on his boots.

"I'll say one thing for you," Torne said, "you may not be a spirit rider, but you are spirited!" He laughed at his own joke while Jendara cast him a disgusted look as if she had to endure his humor more than she wanted. "Tomorrow we continue our travels so we can meet up with Captain Immerez. I expect you to be on good behavior, thief. Yes, you will be a thief, girl. Folks on the road will be less likely to take pity on you. One word about Green Riders and I'll put you in the spirit world." He guffawed again, and before Karigan could move to lessen the blow, he kicked her in the ribs.

Pain exploded through her body as Torne's laughter assaulted her ears. Each breath she took ripped her side. In a haze of pain, she thought she saw F'ryan Coblebay, white and gauzy, standing among the trees. She closed her eyes, and when she opened them again, he was gone.

Karigan trudged through ankle-deep mud with her head bowed. A storm stirred up the treetops and rain pelted from the dark sky. A crack of lightning shattered the darkness. At first Torne wasn't going to give Karigan any protection from the weather. They had no extra cloaks, and he did not want to give away her "identity" by letting her wear the greatcoat. Surprisingly, Jendara insisted he let Karigan wear it.

"The horse and gear will give her away anyhow," the

mercenary woman said. "We can say she stole it all. She's a thief, remember? Besides, there can't be too many idiots on the road on a day like this." She glared at Torne significantly since it had been his idea to travel despite the storm, instead of holing up somewhere dry.

Torne relented, but by the time Karigan was permitted to wear the greatcoat, she was already soaked through. She drew the hood up over her head with her tied hands, and searched the pockets for the bunchberry flower and sprig of bayberry in vain. The mercenaries must have discarded them as worthless. She sighed in despair. There was no hope of help this time—she'd have to find her own way out.

The damp caused her ribs to ache dully, but the sharp pains had subsided and she could breathe easier. Her wrists were swollen red beneath the bandages. Torne had not allowed her to wrap a fresh dressing around the burns.

"How'd you get burned anyway?" he asked. "Clumsy with a campfire?"

The question wasn't even worth the dignity of an answer. A campfire, indeed! She wished another creature would attack—then see if Torne could do as well as she had. She fantasized about huge claws squeezing his midsection, squeezing him so hard that his eyes popped out.

Lightning struck somewhere nearby with a deafening crack. The Horse snorted and sidestepped nervously. Karigan grimaced as a tingling sensation crept its way up through her feet all the way to the roots of her hair. The thunder rumbled away and Karigan thought, *Idiots. They don't have the sense to find cover in a lightning storm.*

She was mollified by the fact that if any one of them were to be scorched by lightning, it would be Torne or Jendara for the swords they carried at their sides. It was not an unpleasant thought.

Even now, oblivious to the dangers of the storm, they took turns riding The Horse. At first he pulled away, but Torne threatened to sever his tendons again. Karigan commanded him to be still. He looked at her with wide eyes and snorted defiantly, but tolerated being mounted. Neither mercenary sat upon him for long, however.

"One must have a bottom of steel to ride this beast," Jendara declared. "I suppose he will serve as a pack animal."

The Horse tossed his mane at the insult. Karigan smiled smugly to herself—his gaits were smooth as butter when desired.

They continued down the road as thunder drummed low and far away, over some distant part of Sacoridia.

The mercenaries were not very generous with *her* food supplies, Karigan thought. They crouched beneath some trees by the road at midday. The rain had dwindled to a steady drizzle and the last bit of storm had rumbled away an hour ago. Already the biters were stirring to a frenzy in the damp.

Karigan's stomach growled as she picked pieces of mold off the crust of hard bread Torne had tossed her. Torne smacked his lips over dried meat as if it was a feast. Jendara was a bit more dainty, but not much. The two must not have eaten in a while. What kind of mercenaries were they if they couldn't hunt up the occasional hare or squirrel? Even she had learned a thing or two about trapping and hunting from the cargo master, though it wasn't a skill she used often.

"What are you glowering at, girl?" Torne demanded.

"You look hungry. Didn't they teach you wilderness survival in mercenary training?"

Torne's eyes blazed. "Jendara and I were soldiers of the highest order. We had no need."

Karigan raised a brow. "What order might that be?"

"We weren't always mercenaries, girl. It's none of your business."

Karigan guessed they had not been mercenaries for very long, and the fact they were no longer a part of this "high order" was a sore point, at least for Torne. She thought hard about what the two could have been before they became swords for hire. Guards, she supposed, but even guards were subject to survival training . . . unless they never left a specific post, or were of so high an order they were waited upon by servants.

"The Mirwellian fools told us you can disappear," Jendara said. "When are you going to disappear?"

Despite the mercenary's mocking tone, Karigan perceived a hint of uncertainty. It wouldn't hurt to play on it, but it also renewed her concern for the brooch. Torne had taken to wearing it on his cloak. "I'll disappear when I'm good and ready to."

Torne guffawed. "Those idiots lost her in a heavy fog. Disappeared, indeed."

"Immerez is no idiot," Jendara said quietly, "though he thinks it was some Greenie trick, not a spirit rider."

"Is that so, Greenie girl? You know some Greenie tricks?"

"Maybe. You might not take me as a spirit rider, but a spirit rides with me."

"What's that supposed to mean?"

Karigan shrugged innocently, a twinge of pain tugging at her ribs.

"I won't have any of this spirit stuff!" Torne was over to Karigan in a bound, and he cuffed her across the face.

She fell to her side and shook her head, tasting blood from a cut lip. What was left of her midday meal was a mess of crumbs on the ground. She forced herself back into a sitting position.

"You're nothing but a ruffian," she told Torne, "and a coward."

Torne only laughed. Karigan had the satisfaction, however, of knowing she had planted a seed of uncertainty in his mind. If only she could get her hands on that brooch. At present, however, it did not seem likely.

They passed through numerous settlements cut out of the woods. They were too small, really, to be called villages. Woods folk in plain dress worked about their cabins. They hung laundry in the sweet spring air, tended gardens where enough sunlight crept through the forest canopy to nourish vegetables, and they split wood.

Torne used some of the coppers he had taken from Karigan's pockets to purchase meat and bread, boasting all the while to the settlers about the thief he and his partner had snared. More often than not, food was offered the mercenaries for free when they heard this fabrication.

Karigan received nothing except scowls and curses about thieves who preyed on law-abiding Sacoridians who were trying to scrape out a living in the wilderness. Some looked her up and down, disbelieving one so young and innocent looking could be a notorious thief.

"That's part of her method," Torne explained at one settlement. "She seems innocent, but when you are not looking . . ." He spread his hands wide, allowing the settlers to come to their own conclusions. "Do you see this horse, and the coat she wears? Murdered a Green Rider, she did."

Disturbed exclamations passed among the settlers. Just about everyone in the tiny community stood around the mercenaries and their captive. Visitors came seldom and they were hungry for news.

Karigan guessed these were all very decent folk, and she couldn't blame them for their accusing, if not fearful, expressions. They had probably been victims of brigands more than once. Seldom did the king's law pass through these isolated spots, except at tax time.

Torne was an adept storyteller, too. Despite the blatant lies, Karigan didn't dare breathe a word. Jendara held her close with a dagger tip digging into her back. It was frustrating having people so close who could help her, but they had been turned against her by Torne's words.

"Bad 'nough with groundmites crossing the borders," one man muttered. He removed his leather cap and smoothed his hair back. "Don't need our own kind killing and thieving."

"Groundmites?" Jendara asked in surprise, echoing Karigan's own thoughts. "Crossing the borders?"

"Aye," the man growled. "Killed a family not five miles from here on the Putnal Trail. And not a sign of king's soldiers anywhere. We sent one of our lads to the city to find help. The rest of us sleep uneasy with what weapons we have close at hand, and keep watch during the night."

"Wise precautions," Jendara said. "Groundmites crossing the borders . . ."

"Aye, worse still, some of our hunters found the carcass of an unnatural creature and its spawn." Karigan snapped to attention as she listened. "We wouldna believed it were they not our finest woods folk who found it, and honest to the core. Whatever slew the creature must be even more dangerous. Sank its great fangs into the creature's belly, it did. Makes you wanna believe the old minstrel tales of Mornhavon and the Blackveil Forest."

Karigan wanted to laugh out loud. Maybe she ought to name her plain saber "Fang" the way the great warriors named their blades, or carried blades bearing long lineages and ancient names. If they only knew who had really slain the creature!

The crowd babbled about the old evil, ancient prophecies, and the Long War. Karigan became absorbed in her own thoughts. Estral, ever the fountain of information, had mentioned trouble on the borders. But groundmites? She had scarcely believed groundmites would dare leave their dens in the far north after they had been slain and scattered after the Long War with the fear of the League driven into their hearts.

Now she felt no disbelief that the groundmites, legendary minions of Mornhavon the Black, which were not quite human, but beastlike creatures that were terrible in battle, were roaming across Sacoridia's borders. There was no room for disbelief—not after Immerez. Not after the creature of *Kanmorhan Vane*. Things were happening in the world, and her beloved Sacoridia no longer seemed very secure.

A tug on her coat snapped her out of her reverie. A little boy with tousled sandy hair gaped up at her with solemn brown eyes. He couldn't have been more than six years old.

"You really kill someone?" he asked in awe.

Karigan glanced about. The settlers and the mercenaries were too deep in discussion to notice. She then looked down at the little boy. "No."

"You lying?"

"No."

"Din' think so." He grinned at her brightly, then ran off to join his mother who stood off a ways with a cluster of other women. She put a protective arm about his shoulders and scowled at Karigan.

Jendara and Torne were invited to share dinner with the settlers. Visitors bearing news from abroad were enough cause for celebration. The feast was held outdoors, for no dwelling in the area was large enough to hold more than a small family. Pots of priddle cream were passed around and smoke candles lit to stave off ravenous biters.

However, no one passed Karigan any cream, and she was tied to an ash tree out of range of the smoke candles, her mouth securely gagged with an old rag. As if to augment her misery, the smell of roasting meats drifted all around her. Her stomach roiled. The hard heel of bread Torne had tossed her earlier had done little to ease her hunger pangs.

One of the settlers stood guard a little way off. He seemed more intent on watching the festivities, his notched and rusted blade loose in his hand. She could hear music, mostly a simple pipe and drum, and laughter and clapping from dancing folk.

She allowed a few tears to trickle down her cheeks. If only she still possessed the winged horse brooch or the bunchberry flower.

How she missed the Berry sisters. And Estral, and her

father. Where was he now? What was he doing? Was he searching for her, or did he assume her dead? Would she ever see him again? The tears poured down her cheeks now and she sobbed hard, gasping for air through the gag. She was so alone! How did she ever get into this mess? She would never wish for adventure again—she just wanted to go home.

Under different circumstances she might have found the night quite pleasant. A milky moon rose far above the trees, and stars speckled the sky. The laughter of the settlers had a homey feel, but only made her more lonely. She took a deep, rattling breath and blew it out her nose slowly. A soft breeze dried her tears and whispered of summer yet to come. It would have been easy to feel happy here, comfortable, if she hadn't been tied to a tree and gagged.

I wish I could help you.

The words drifted to her as if upon the breeze. She looked wildly about her and strained to see behind the tree, but no one was there.

I—ish—help you.

Karigan sat up alertly.

I—you—danger—the road. We spoke—ger.

Karigan grunted through the gag, unable to respond.

—no strength—help now. Wish—could—elp.

Karigan squirmed, fighting against her bonds. Was it F'ryan Coblebay trying to communicate with her? Was she crazy to think she heard the voice of a ghost?

—not—er—wish—help.

"Mmff fog elp wone ga me anna wheah!" was all she could say through the gag.

There was giggling all around her. Karigan looked up and all the young children of the settlement gazed at her the way they might at some intriguing beast at the Corsa Zoo. In the forefront was the little boy who had spoken to her earlier that day.

"Are you a muhdrer?" asked a tiny girl with her forefinger hooked in her mouth. "What's a muhdrer?"

"Hush, Tosh," the boy said knowingly. "She's not a murderer. She told me so."

"Maybe she's crazy," another boy said. "My old aunt was crazy and they locked her in the attic."

The rest of the children were duly impressed.

"What's a muhdrer?" the tiny girl asked.

"Means she killed someone," the first boy said.

Karigan cleared her throat, and they all jumped.

The boy looked surreptitiously around, then gazed at Karigan with a very serious expression on his face. "You have to promise not to talk. Not loud, anyway."

Karigan nodded emphatically.

The boy looked around again, then pulled the gag out of her mouth. She took some deep breaths, then said, "I didn't kill anyone."

The children jumped again at her voice, but they seemed willing to believe her.

"What are you all doing here? Won't you get in trouble for talking to me?"

"Dad's too sleepy. Drank too much cider." Then the boy pointed to the guard whose back was still turned to them. "You gotta keep real quiet, 'member? Then we won't get in trouble. We came to look at you."

Now Karigan did feel like a strange beast in the zoo. "Well, then go away. I don't like being stared at. It's not polite." The Berry sisters would approve.

The children giggled, especially when she made an ugly face. They skipped away, chattering excitedly among themselves in hushed voices. They had done the forbidden by speaking to her, and were full of it. Only the sandy-haired boy remained behind, and Karigan now saw he held a dish heaped with scraps of food.

"I couldn't eat it. You can have it."

Karigan was about to compare herself to a beggar dog, but was too hungry to care. She lowered her face to the dish while he held it, and ate greedily. She licked the plate clean. She wasn't even sure what it was she had eaten, but her stomach felt full for the first time in days.

"What's your name?" she asked him.

"Dusty."

"Thank you, Dusty. Thank you."

He smiled shyly, then without warning, stuffed the gag back in her mouth. He ran off to join his friends. Karigan watched after him with regret. She had been about to ask him to untie her. Except for one trip to the latrine to relieve herself, she had been left tied to the tree in the cramped position.

When morning came and Torne made her stand up, she nearly fell to her knees. He stood by impatiently while she rubbed some feeling back into her legs.

The greatcoat weighed more than before, and the pockets bulged against her thighs. When Torne wasn't looking, she slipped her hands into a pocket and found it stuffed with what felt like dried meat, cheese, hard bread, and an apple. Dusty and his friends must have filled her pockets while she slept. They didn't want to see her go hungry!

When she could finally walk without too much discomfort, Torne secured her wrists in front of her. He leaned over and whispered in her ear, "One word from you, and Jendara's knife will slide right into your back. Should I gag you?"

Karigan shook her head. One night of that foul gag in her mouth had been quite enough.

The three of them walked from the settlement with Torne in the lead, Karigan in the middle, and Jendara leading The Horse very close behind. The folk patted Torne and Jendara on the back, or shook hands, wishing them goodspeed. Karigan was wished a good hanging.

The children were there, too, and waved their good-byes emphatically. Karigan winked and smiled at her miniature benefactors in return. An angry father who noted the exchange threw a stone at her, which missed her shoulder by a handsbreadth, but she didn't care. Even with the animosity of the settlers surrounding her and the grim outlook of days of travel with Torne and Jendara, something good had happened here: she had made new friends among the children when all others scorned her, and when she had been at her loneliest.

When they were out of earshot of the settlers, Torne chuckled. "Suckers. Feed 'em a story and you can get anything you want." The Horse's saddlebags were crammed with food. "Maybe we ought to do this sort of thing full time."

Jendara shrugged her shoulders indifferently. "It's annoying dragging a prisoner around." She glanced at Karigan.

Karigan wondered, once again, who the two had been prior to becoming mercenaries.

❧ WEAPONS ❧

Karigan received her answer later that afternoon. The day dragged along until The Horse froze in his tracks, his ears laid flat. He sidestepped nervously and patches of sweat darkened his neck and flanks. Torne hauled on the reins as if he could forcibly drag The Horse down the road. When The Horse stayed anchored to his spot, Torne cursed and threatened him.

"He senses something ahead," Karigan said, weariness weighing her words down. She could not have cared less if the mercenaries walked into some sort of trouble, but Torne's hand was on the hilt of his sword and it looked as if he was going to use more than threats to move The Horse this time.

"Go on, Horse," she said.

The Horse flickered an ear at her, but balked no longer. They walked on and soon discovered what had stopped him. Strewn across the road, and alongside it, was a jumble of bodies.

"King's soldiers," Jendara said without emotion.

In a flash, the mercenaries unsheathed their swords. That was when Karigan saw the black bands on their blades which marked the two as swordmasters. As such, they probably were, or had been, either tomb guards, or the king's personal guards, truly an elite order of soldier. They took oaths which bound them for life to the royal family, and even beyond life. Some were bound to protect the dead in the Avenues of Kings and Queens from desecration, and to guard against potential grave robbers lured by the priceless relics of ages long past entombed with royalty. No too few guards were interred near their wards.

They were the finest swordfighters found in all Sacoridia. Arms Master Rendle had told her that such guards, even without their blades, were human weapons. In fact, they were often referred to as *Weapons*.

Karigan had been too shocked during the ambush to notice the bands on their blades before. Their status as Weapons explained their ineptitude in the wilderness, but not why they were now scraping around as mercenaries.

Weapons were revered for their skills, and though they did not live in absolute luxury, they lived at least as well as the lower nobility, in large houses with servants to attend to their needs.

Even after retirement, they held honored places in the king's court. Many often became counselors to the king, or trained the next generation of guards bound to the royal family. Karigan found it hard to believe Torne and Jendara had left Sacor City and their privileges voluntarily.

Crows flew squawking into the trees as Jendara and Torne picked their way among the bodies. Larger carrion birds hopped, wings extended, only a few paces away. The Weapons checked pockets and packs of the dead for valuable trinkets or coins, but the two were out of luck. Whoever had slain the soldiers had done a thorough search already. The breeze shifted and Karigan gagged on the stench of rotting corpses.

"Looks like they were ambushed by groundmites." Jendara sheathed her sword as if groundmites were no cause for concern.

"The Gray One has been busy," Torne said. He beckoned for Karigan and The Horse to follow.

Karigan covered her nose and mouth with her hands, and tried not to look down, but she had to look where she stepped. Bodies lay twisted and entwined, and it was impossible to tell where one stopped and another started.

Crawling beetles created a sense of movement among the dead.

The silver of uniforms glared in the sun as if to mock the pride and honor with which the soldiers had once donned the colors of Sacoridia. Grim faces bloated in the sun unseeing. Carrion birds had picked out their eyes.

Among the human dead were a few not-so-human remains. Karigan couldn't tell if it was death that made the skin of these large creatures yellowish brown, or if it was their natural coloring. The skin was covered with patches of mud-colored fur. Open mouths, as if in the midst of howling at the moment of death, were armed with sharp canines. Their ears were pointed and furred like a cat's. Groundmites.

Three human heads were impaled on lances by the roadside. What remained of a captain hung from a tree, his stomach split and gutted. Two black-shafted arrows with red fletching pierced his heart. Karigan vomited.

It took considerable time to coax The Horse across the corpse-strewn road, much longer than she could bear. She wanted to run, to leave the grisly scene far behind her. But she knew it would return to her in her dreams, no matter how far away she went.

"That horse would never survive a battle," Torne said, watching the miserable Karigan tug on the reins.

"Greenies are worthless in battle." Jendara's voice was full of contempt. "They gallop across the countryside on horses, is all. I'm surprised they even carry swords."

Karigan felt as green as her greatcoat, and kept walking even after she had come to the end of the carnage. The mercenaries trotted to catch up with her. Behind them, the carrion birds flopped back among the corpses to resume their feeding.

Karigan was sick several more times. Blood and gore clung to her boots and no amount of scraping them on the road seemed to rub it off. When a stream appeared alongside the road, she ran to it so fast that even quick Jendara could not route her. Karigan stood there in the stream, her eyes closed, willing the rush of water to cleanse her feet, and her mind.

"Back on the road," Jendara ordered.

When Karigan opened her eyes, she was staring down the black-banded blade. Torne stood in the middle of the road, his head thrown back in laughter. "A murderer who can't stand the sight of blood!"

Karigan ignored him and locked her gaze with Jendara's. "Were you a tomb guard, or a king's guard, Swordmaster?"

Jendara squinted, as if the glare off her own blade blinded her. A frown tugged at the corners of her mouth. "I do not guard the dead."

"Then why do you betray the king?"

"I do not betray the king, not the rightful king."

Karigan raised her brows. The only sound was the stream flowing around her ankles. Just what had Jendara meant by *that*? "There is only one king. Zachary."

The blow was so fast Karigan didn't see it coming. Jendara slammed the flat of her sword on Karigan's collar bone and sent her nerves ringing with its force. She splashed to her knees, cold water soaking through her trousers.

"I serve the rightful king," Jendara hissed. "Do not forget it." She grabbed Karigan's collar, hauled her out of the stream, and shoved her down the road.

Torne was laughing again, or perhaps he had never stopped. Karigan staggered after her captors, dizzy and empty from vomiting repeatedly, but relieved her boots, at least, were clean.

Days came and went—Karigan lost count of how many. Hands tied before her, she trudged along with the mercenaries. She was only able to keep on because of the food Dusty had slipped in her pockets. She nibbled at it when the mercenaries weren't looking, or were asleep. Even with the food in her pockets, she dreamed of feasting on goose and fresh baked bread, of sugared apple fritters and sharp cheese.

One night while Torne snored on the opposite side of the campfire and Jendara sat at watch with her back to Karigan, Karigan slipped her hand into her pocket. Her mouth watered in anticipation and her stomach rumbled—Torne had given her nothing to eat all day.

She pulled out a strip of dried meat. She chewed and swallowed hastily, yet savored every bit. So intent on the food was she, that she did not notice Jendara gazing at her until it was too late. The swordmaster's eyes glinted in the firelight.

Karigan tensed, readying herself for another blow, for more pain, for Jendara to rouse Torne. She stuffed the rest of the meat strip into her mouth, not willing to be denied one last morsel. She glared defiantly at Jendara.

The swordmaster, however, did not twitch a muscle. She did not wake Torne, nor did she leap over to Karigan and strike her, or demand that she empty her pockets of the hidden food. She spoke not a word. She simply blinked her eyes and turned her gaze back to the depths of the night woods, her back rigid. Karigan was not about to question her motives.

When Karigan didn't dream of food, she dreamed of retrieving the brooch, and fantasized about what she would do with the saber if she were invisible. She dreamed also of her mother's ring, which Jendara wore. Sometimes she dreamed that her mother chastised her for her carelessness. Other times, her mother held her in a warm embrace, the seal of Clan G'ladheon seeming to come to life behind them—the roar of the ocean, the creak of ship timbers, the cry of gulls. . . . Then she would awaken to a reality much stranger than all her dreams together. How did a simple schoolgirl ever get into such a mess?

Travelers on the road watched the trio curiously. Torne told his story many times, Jendara sticking her knife tip into Karigan's back lest she speak out. Torne's embellishments, Karigan thought, were getting a little wild, and if he wasn't careful, he would one day betray himself. One afternoon he pulled aside an old trapper riding a mule.

"Down the road you'll come to a terrible sight," Torne warned the man. "King's soldiers slain, every last one."

The trapper rubbed his bristly gray beard, eyes wide. "All dead, you say? How?"

"Groundmites," Torne said. "Surely you've heard of them raiding the borders."

"Aye, but . . ."

"You will see. But see also, this girl." Torne pointed at Karigan and the trapper followed with his gaze.

"I see her."

"*She* is responsible."

The trapper plucked at the laces of his coarse wool shirt. "Responsible? She is? For what?"

"The massacre."

"I thought you said groundmites—"

"She led them there," Torne said fervently. "She led the massacre, she slew many of the guards herself. And what she did to the captain . . . Unspeakable." He shook his head.

The trapper raised a skeptical brow and cleared his throat as if to say something, then he eyed Torne's sword and thought better of it.

"We take this girl, this *traitor*," Torne spat the word, "for judgment in Sacor City. She eluded us at first, but we caught her, planning another raid with her groundmite cohorts on an innocent settlement."

"Aye, well, must be goin'. Good day t'ya." The trapper slapped his mule into a hasty trot trailing a plume of road dust behind him.

Torne beamed his gap-toothed grin at Jendara, pleased with his own performance. She groaned and rolled her eyes.

Some folk Torne told the story to were all too ready to believe it, and suggested a roadside hanging for Karigan. Torne protested and declared himself a good citizen

willing to let the king's law decide her fate. She wondered *what* king he was talking about.

Jendara was tiring of his stories as well. "Do you have
to blather on to everyone we meet? I never took you
for the minstrel type."

"I am not a spineless minstrel. I am being neighborly.
Besides, it unsettles folks to see a girl tied up by two
warriors like us. Especially when she wears that green
coat." Karigan had refused to remove it, no matter how
warm the weather, for fear Torne would discover her
hidden caches of food and take it away from her.

"Well, I'm getting tired of the story. If you don't watch
yourself, you'll overembellish and give us away. Your
tongue is not nearly as glib as a true minstrel's."

"My sword work is what's glib."

Jendara looked away from him with a frown of disgust
on her face.

Dusk shadowed the road. A mounted figure appeared
ahead of them riding at a walk, his movements smooth
and fluid. Torne squinted his eyes, then unexpectedly,
whooped in recognition. He ran forward to greet the
horseman. Karigan's heart sank. Immerez? The Gray
One Jendara and Torne murmured about?

In the hands of Immerez, her chances of escape
slimmed considerably. But as the rider approached, she
saw he wasn't Mirwellian at all. He wore no scarlet, but
a leather jerkin emblazoned with an eagle grasping a
human skull in its talons. A mercenary.

"Garroty!" Torne cried. "What chance meeting is
this?"

The other man grinned and the effect was grotesque.
His face was misshapen by dozens of scars and a wad of
tobacco stuffed in his left cheek. Gray-brown hair hung
in a ponytail down his back. His arms were ropy with
muscles and veins. The eagle and skull were tattooed
onto his left forearm like an oversized bruise.

"The Talons have given me a fortnight's leave and I'm traveling. Good to see you, Torne." His voice was gravelly and low. "I see you travel still in beautiful company." His eyes drifted first to a smoldering Jendara, then rested on Karigan. "And who is this?"

"A Greenie we're delivering to the Mirwellians. For profit."

"Ah, yes. Profit." He leaned over his horse's withers and spat tobacco. "You are a merc's pride, Torne, seeking profit. But you were not very good at it when I took you under my wing when you fled the city, were you?"

"We've improved, I assure you."

Garroty snorted. "Profit is of little meaning to you except if it helps sustain you in service to your master. This smells more like politics to me."

"What do you know of politics?" Jendara asked. Her countenance suggested he knew nothing.

"I know who you work for, beautiful."

Jendara bridled. "You will address me by my name."

Garroty shrugged.

"Why don't you camp with us tonight?" Torne asked eagerly. "We could catch up on things."

"Why don't you keep going?" Jendara suggested, an unfriendly smile on her face.

"I accept your invitation," he said to Torne. He turned to Jendara. "Nothing could keep me away from your lovely companion."

Karigan wished he would follow Jendara's advice. The Weapon's animosity toward him made her nervous. Garroty's easy seat on his battle horse, his ugly grin, and all too interested glances, did not reassure her at all.

Torne and Garroty stayed up front, conversing about weapons and war, other mercs they had both known. Garroty remained arrogantly mounted while the others walked. Torne had to crane his neck to look up at his friend. Jendara strode behind with Karigan, leading The Horse in brooding silence. Karigan wondered what caused Jendara to loathe the mercenary so.

They walked until nightfall, and settled beside the road

around a little campfire. Karigan leaned against the rough bark of a pine, huddled in her greatcoat. She wanted to stay as far away from Garroty as she could, but his coarse laughter assaulted her ears and echoed down the road. He spoke of profitable campaigns his company had engaged in.

"I tell you, Torne, some of those villages in Rhovanny are ripe to pluck, especially in the wine country. And the wenches there don't carry swords." He grinned at Jendara. She glared back.

"Sacoridia is a bit too peaceful for profit," Garroty said. "That's what I think. There is always something happening down in the Under Kingdoms, though. Petty lords trying to reshape the map. The year has been good for many merc companies."

"Stick around, my friend," Torne said. "There are those in Sacoridia who would change things as well."

"Maybe so, but Zachary is a strong leader. It would take a united front, maybe more, to bring him down. The governors might not like him a lot, but the common folk do, and what the governors don't need is an uprising among the common folk. Nothing would get done. The harvest would rot in the fields. Paper makers would stop their mills. The governors' wealth would dwindle. Simple as that."

"Then what are you and your company doing here in Sacoridia," Jendara said, "if it's so unlikely there will be an uprising?"

"Aah. Now we come to it. Rumors, beautiful. Rumors, no doubt begun by your employer, and designed to create unrest. I've even heard of a woman who has convinced a good many common folk that Sacoridia has no need for any king at all—not enough to start a rebellion, but enough to spread dissent. And her ideas are catching on.

"The Talons are here in case an uprising does occur in Sacoridia. It would prove more profitable than anything that has ever happened in the Under Kingdoms. Imagine, the governors uniting to bring down the king.

Talk about profit! If your employer is as good as he claims, the peace Sacoridia has enjoyed for centuries will be shattered. There is nothing better than civil war if you're a merc. Captain Heylar of the Talons has eyes and ears in the courts of most provinces. Wouldn't hurt to encourage a profitable situation now, would it?"

Karigan listened to this with wide eyes. Much more was going on in Sacoridia than she had ever dreamed. Did this sort of speculation always go on, or was there really a threat to Sacoridia's peace? There was always intrigue—the Berry sisters had said as much. Intrigue was as much a game in real life as it was on a board. But surely, threats to the king were not commonplace. Nor the threat of civil war.

"You expect mercenaries can encourage the governors in civil war?" she asked Garroty. His smile was feral in the dancing light of the fire. It made her feel like dinner, and she was sorry she had drawn his attention.

"So, the Greenie speaks." He leaned to the side and spat. "Of course we seek to influence what would be in our best interests. Civil war means work. Work means profit. Men of the Talon Company are wise in the ways of such things. They merely encourage the governors to do what is *right.* And should they do what's right, Talons will be strategically placed to negotiate contracts with the highest bidders. It's more convenient to hire a company of well-trained soldiers than to raise a rabble army of commoners."

Karigan shook her head. Outsiders were trying to create a civil war in Sacoridia for *profit.* As the daughter of a merchant, she understood the nature of profit, but at what cost? The very idea was gruesome.

Quite suddenly, she felt an urgent need to reach the king with the message F'ryan Coblebay had entrusted her to carry, but she was caught up in a hopeless situation, held captive by two swordmasters, and now accompanied by a seasoned mercenary.

❧ MIRWELL ❧

Warm air flowing through an unshuttered window cleared out stale air which had accumulated in the library chamber throughout the lengthy northern winter. What a change mild air was, and for once without that damp, chill wind.

A bee droned along the flowered vine growing just outside the window, and the air smelled of fresh green things and lilacs. The square of sky framed by the window was brilliant and clear. On such days, it was said, you could see Mount Mantahop of the Wingsong Range from the fortress gate towers. Mirwell scoffed at that—in all his years he had never seen it. The range was just an indistinguishable line of nubs and bumps far, far away on the horizon.

He sipped from his goblet of rhubarb wine and stared into the embers of the day fire, allowing the wine to warm him from inside. Despite the influx of summerlike warmth, the old stone fortress was dim, and if you weren't careful, in a perpetual state of damp and mildew. Mold grew in the dark corners which his servants battled constantly with soap and scrub brushes.

The damp made his bones ache. He could never seem to keep warm, not satisfactorily anyway, and he suspected it was unhealthy to reside in the dank fortress. His personal mender advocated he leave his library chamber and soak up the sun outside, but there was too much to do. This was no time for catnapping in the sun.

The efficient Beryl Spencer sat across from him in a straight back chair, her nose buried in half a dozen sheaves of paper. She must be nearsighted. He would have to look into getting her fitted for a pair of specs, but he hated the idea of wrecking her lovely oval face with glass and wire. Besides, the lenses would no doubt cost a pretty fortune.

"The clan is presently headed by Stevic G'ladheon," she said. "It was his only daughter, Karigan, who provoked Lord Timas. She hasn't been seen or heard of since running away."

"Tell me about the clan," Mirwell said, intrigued by how Beryl's scarlet uniform deepened her rosy, healthy cheeks.

"It's based in Corsa. No surprise there. Corsa is home to many merchant clans due to its outstanding deep water harbors. G'ladheon invests heavily in shipping, but is not a dominant holder in any single ship."

"Wise of him. The more diverse his holdings, the less risk to his fortune. He does have a fortune, doesn't he?"

Beryl looked up at him with those pale green eyes of hers, glistening like the gems that were her namesake. "Stevic G'ladheon is perhaps the single wealthiest person in all the provinces. Last year's Merchant Guild's Year End Reckoning had him the highest grossing member."

"Therefore, not a man to anger if his wealth is any indication of his influence. What does he deal in?"

Beryl scanned her papers. "Textiles and spices mainly. Some lumber and paper. Much of his trading is done inland via river cog and wagon train. He has strong ties with Rhovanny, and has even traded ice in the Cloud Islands. Very clever of him to find such a market in the tropics. According to some of your relations, my lord, he doesn't venture often into Mirwell Province."

"No wonder I've heard little of him. Do any of my relations consider him a threat?"

"No, my lord. Though, just in case, they traced some of his personal history. He is the clan founder—Clan G'ladheon has existed for some twenty years."

Mirwell snorted. "A bought clanship, I've no doubt."

"G'ladheon worked hard for it, starting with small

merchant families to learn the trade. He's intelligent to
have accumulated such wealth over so short a time." Was
that admiration in Beryl's voice? "Here's an interesting
bit of information. About thirty-five years ago, he served
on the merchant vessel *Gold Hunter,* which used tactics
of questionable legality during peacetime to acquire
goods for trade."

"Explain."

"The crew practiced piracy, my lord. Mostly around
the Under Kingdoms. They wreaked havoc with the
sugar and tobacco trades."

Mirwell raised his brows. "More interesting by the moment. Any idea of what capacity he served as on this
vessel?"

"No, my lord."

"What became of the ship?"

"It was sold and reregistered as *SMV Avren's Pride,*
and became something of a coastal scow transporting
granite and lumber. It was lost somewhere in outer
Ullem Bay fifteen years ago."

"I see no immediate threat from this G'ladheon fellow." Mirwell sipped his wine. It was just the right
amount of dry balanced with sweet. It did not rival the
fine vintages produced in the lake country of Rhovanny,
but in a pinch it would do. Vintners couldn't seem to
grow grapes in Sacoridia's sandy soil, so cider and fruit
wines served as staples. Unless Rhovan was to be had,
of course.

"Good work, Spence. Keep the information on hand
just in case he turns into an overwrought father. Should
he cause us trouble, I'm sure our good friend aus-Corien
of the Under Kingdoms would be interested in hearing
about him. And we may have our own uses for the
information."

"Yes, my lord. Anything else?"

Mirwell rubbed a sweaty hand on his thigh. He could
think of countless "things" she could do for him. He felt
a certain thrill at the idea of what she could do for him
tingle all the way down to his loins. Would voicing his

desire wreck her fealty and efficiency? Or, would it bind her closer to him?

Phaw, randy old man, he thought, not displeased by the response of his libido. But she was too effective as his aide and he feared ruining her devotion. Should she make the first advance herself, however. . . .

She never would. He was a grizzled old man and she was more intent on making a place for herself in his court hierarchy with pure hard work. She had moved swiftly up the ranks during her term in Sacoridia's regular militia, and had given it all up to serve her governor and home province. The chance she had taken paid off, and here she was working her way up in his own provincial militia. Ambition was a trait Mirwell admired, and honest ambition rare enough.

Ah, well. At least I can enjoy my dirty thoughts.

"My lord?"

"Eh?"

"Anything else?"

Now she must think him a dotty old fool leering at her like that. "Send in Amilton," he said, then amended, "*Prince* Amilton."

"Very well, my lord."

Mirwell watched after her with longing and regret, and observed how her every movement was graceful, yet held a stillness like a deer in the woods: alert but calm, and not prone to excessive motion. She reminded him of the Weapons, but their movements were always precise and lacking beauty.

Ah, if he were a younger man, then maybe, but now he must set aside his thoughtful maunderings and get on with his great work. The glory of his clan was more important than anything else, and Amilton had been insistent about seeing him today. Mirwell had put him off all morning, and most of the afternoon. By now, the prince would be angry enough to spit venom.

"There are ways," the governor told the bear head mounted on the opposite wall, "of showing who is in control. Subtle ways, mind you."

The bear had once exerted her control on him in a none-too-subtle way. It was she who had maimed his right side. He had been careless during the hunt, had gotten between the mother and the cubs. The bear mauled him, and it was perhaps his injuries which had prevented him from siring another son, though he was always certain to blame his wives. He could not be perceived as weak in any of his ventures. Too bad the wife who bore Timas had been so short and mean. The boy had acquired her temperament and size.

Half-dead and ravaged from bear claws and teeth, Mirwell had hunted down and killed the mother bear with nothing more than his own stubborn will and a dagger, just to prove he was not weak. He skinned her and ate of her raw heart, still warm and pulsating with blood. As he chewed, bear blood gushed in runnels down his beard and neck, and into his gaping wounds, blending with his own streaming blood. This, he thought, made their strength one.

Then, out of pity, he killed the mewling little cubs, too little to survive without their mother. Of the bear pelts, he made a mantle to wear on state occasions as a reminder to others of his strength.

Prince Amilton entered the chamber, glowering. His bodyguards, simple Mirwellian guards, posted themselves outside the doorway. Not that he needed guards in the governor's house, but he had become dependent on his two Weapons who usually never left his side, and now they were somewhere out in the great wide wilderness tracking the Greenie and leaving him, in his mind, vulnerable.

Regular militia made a poor substitute for one used to the fanatical, servile devotion exhibited by Weapons. Mirwell liked the idea of a more vulnerable Amilton. It made the prince more malleable.

Amilton was dressed in elegant silks with a purple scarf tied prettily around his collar—useless clothes more suited to impressing court butterflies than anything else.

He did attract his share of female attention, but to what practical end?

The governor preferred a military look himself, and no one in his court, not even the ladies, wore such lavish fabrics or colors. Amilton looked a butterfly in House Mirwell.

Mirwell touched his brow and inclined his head, not deeply, but not insolently either. He was excused from a full formal bow because of his old hunting wounds.

"Wine, my prince?" he inquired.

Amilton waved a contemptuous hand at Mirwell and faced the fire. Mirwell poured him a gobletful anyway, and with great effort, limped over to the hearth to give it to him. Amilton took it wordlessly—and poured the contents on the floor.

Mirwell watched unblinking. "How may I serve you, my prince?"

Amilton turned on him, his expression haughty. His face was narrower, more sharp and severe than his brother's, but he had the brown, almond-shaped eyes that characterized Clan Hillander.

"You shall not serve me the bottled urine you call wine."

"I beg forgiveness, Liege. Rhovan is difficult to come by, and we save it for more . . . extravagant occasions." It was no wonder the late king had chosen Zachary to rule—Amilton was a spoiled fop.

"You seem reluctant," Amilton said, "to update me in the affairs concerning my brother."

"Missives from Captain Immerez are few. He is hard on the road to ensure our plans go forward without mishap. You know as much about his progress as I do."

"It seems I could have sent my own assassins months ago and have had done with it."

"Of course we've tried that avenue to no avail—it lacked finesse. The assassins were promptly thwarted."

"Yes, because you've permitted spies into your house who learned your plans. And my brother knows where I am."

"If your brother knew the source of those assassins, don't you think his Weapons would be upon us now? And why should he care where you are, so long as it is far away from Sacor City? My liege, we only suspect there is a spy in House Mirwell."

"I believe my brother was suspicious enough of those last attempts to put a spy here. How do you know our next attempt won't fail?"

"Every precaution is being taken, Liege. You must trust me in this."

"I sincerely hope you don't fail this time, Tomas." Amilton left his goblet on the mantel and moved restlessly about the chamber. He paused by the open window which looked over the training fields of the provincial militia, and allowed the implied threat to hang in the air before he spoke again. "And you trust this Gray One?"

"Explicitly. He is of the old powers, and his alliance will bring such influence and glory to us that we can't even begin to imagine it."

Amilton leaned against the windowsill, arms crossed, his trim, angular figure silhouetted against blue sky. "I don't particularly care for his ways. The groundmites, you know. But the Gray One's forces ought to convince the other governors and nobles to ally with me."

"His forces are great enough to take a province at a time, if necessary," Mirwell said. "And he has offered you powers?"

"Not precisely. I fear he may betray us and offer them to my brother first."

"It would be easiest for the Gray One, in his own self-interest to do so."

"I agree."

"Let us not fret," Mirwell said. "He'll have trouble convincing your brother that the D'Yer Wall should be crushed. Zachary is far too scrupulous."

"And I'm not?" Not even a trace of a smile could be found on Amilton's lips.

Wisely, Mirwell didn't respond. He was growing used to Amilton's little tirades.

"My father took what was mine by right of succession, and gave it to my brother. Do you know the humiliation I experienced when *he* was pronounced heir? I wanted to gut him right there in the throne room; right there in front of my father and his counselors, and those smirking lord-governors and clan chiefs. He was always favored in Father's eyes. He always exceeded me in his studies, he excelled in hunting and riding. He revived the old Hillander terrier breed, and his kennel is the envy of the country."

"He sounds very impressive," Mirwell said. "But a man cannot be judged by his kennels."

Now Amilton did smile, but it was fleeting. "If I'd the sense, I'd have seen to my father's death before he had a chance to announce an heir. I'd be king now, and I would have the control over my brother's life, instead of he over mine. Then we would see who the exiled one was!"

Mirwell gazed down at his Intrigue board. Little had changed on it since Immerez last reported. He picked up the red king, its enamel paint chipped and scratched, and rotated it in his fingers.

"Hindsight, my prince, will not change the future. There is no use dwelling in it. Your brother does lack certain qualities which are in your favor."

"Such as?"

"Such as ambition. You and I share that particular quality, and it is always the downfall of one who is as scrupulous as your brother. We will make Sacoridia great, you and I." He set the red king on the fringes of the green king's realm.

Ambition was a healthy attribute for a man in his waning years. It kept him thinking young, and prepared his clan for the ages to come. Once Amilton ascended the throne, Adolind and L'Petrie Provinces—the poorest and richest provinces in Sacoridia—would be incorporated into his own. Adolind because it bordered him to the north, and it contained millions of acres of virgin timber—enough to feed paper mills and shipyards for the next few centuries; and L'Petrie for its harbors, fishing fleet, and prosperous trade city—Corsa. It was also on the southeast corner of his border.

There would be little resistance, if any. Both provinces had militia that were laughable at best. And if there was a problem? The Gray One and *King* Amilton would back him up with their forces.

"You will prevail, my prince," Mirwell said. "You will prevail."

That is, he thought, *if Immerez stops that Greenie in time.*

⇜ STEVIC G'LADHEON ⇝

Stevic G'ladheon caught wind of a bad omen as he rode his sorrel stallion through the gates of Selium. An undertaker's cart stood pulled to the side of the street. The ancient nag harnessed to it dozed in the sun oblivious to the flies that swarmed around her tearing eyes, and that which lay beneath the blanket in the cart.

The undertaker, an old man with a stubble beard, leaned against the cart on his forearms. His worn clothing, hole-ridden trousers, and a frayed waistcoat held together by patches, were smeared with mud and dirt as if he had just returned from grave digging. Stevic G'ladheon, whose own clothing was of the richest fabrics and finest make, wrinkled his nose.

A woman in green joined the old man. Her hair, like new copper, was bound in a single braid down her back. A winged horse was embroidered in gold on the left sleeve of her shortcoat, and a saber girded at her side.

"I can smell what's in that cart from here."

Stevic smiled grimly at his cargo master, Sevano, who rode next to him on a gray mare. "It's not what I think of when I think of Selium," Stevic said. "I'm surprised they let that undertaker through the gates."

As they rode past the cart, the woman lifted the blanket. She clapped her hand over her mouth and nose. Whether she was shocked to see the corpse of someone she knew, or was reacting to the stench of decay, he couldn't tell.

"Found 'im on the side of the road," the undertaker

said in a gruff voice. "Had to have been there a while, I reckon. Woulda left 'im there, but I'm not that way. Some fellas would let a corpse rot in the open if someone weren't there to pay for a proper burial. I can give you a real decent deal on a pine box if you're inclined."

"Was there any sign of a horse nearby?" was the surprising response.

"Nothin' but my old cob here within miles, Cap'n. Now how 'bout that box?"

The woman dropped the blanket and grabbed him by his lapels. His eyes bulged and his arms dangled helplessly at his sides as she shook him. "Did you see anything lying near the body?" she demanded. "A satchel of any kind? Tack?"

"N-no! Nothing . . ."

Stevic and the cargo master hurried past the unpleasant scene at a trot. After a while, Stevic pulled on the reins and looked back. The undertaker had disappeared, and the woman held two arrows at eye level. A frown tugged at the corners of her mouth.

Sevano followed Stevic's gaze. "Green Rider," he muttered. "Always like a raven before the storm, bearing ill news wherever one turns up."

It sometimes seemed true that the king's messengers bore only bad news: from strife, illness, and death to new taxes. Some likened crossing the path of a Green Rider to meeting disaster. Stevic knew otherwise. Years ago, a Green Rider had brought news of Queen Isen's approval for the chartering of Clan G'ladheon. The Rider had stayed on to witness the confirmation ceremony, and turned out to be a jolly entertainer during the reception that followed.

Stevic and Sevano rode through the late afternoon bustle of Selium. Crafters hawked their wares in stalls, and tourists milled around street musicians who played ballads for coppers. Steam rose from vents in the roofs of bathhouses. Despite the outrageous rates chalked outside on slates, long lines formed outside, and business was thriving. If not for the hot springs, commerce in the city would be considerably slower.

Students, in their indigo, green, maroon, gold, and brown uniforms, created a motley scene as they wove in and out of the crowds, or sat on the front steps of the art museum. Some shared notes and gossip while others sketched. Some played involved games of Intrigue as pigeons cooed and stalked the steps in search of handouts.

The old longing swelled within Stevic's chest as he took in the scene—a wistful longing to be a student here, himself. He hadn't the wealth when a youth to study at Selium. Indeed, his family had dragged what meager living they could out of the sea. At a young age he could master a sloop and haul weighted nets alongside his brother and sisters. As he spent a portion of each day gutting or scaling fish to be dried, he dreamed—oh, how he dreamed—of the Golden Guardian searching in his poor village for hidden talent, and finding it within him.

Alas, it remained a dream, for the Golden Guardian had never come to his obscure village. Stevic saw the life of a fisherman as the bleakest possible future, and no longer able to endure the stink of dead fish and their scales clinging to his skin, he ran away.

Instead of a refined education immersed in the arts and history, he was educated through life experience in the employ of various merchants. He learned to read and tally figures—his first employer had seen to that—and traveled to places he could never have imagined, but he missed a classical education.

In the midst of the conviviality of Selium's main thoroughfare, and absorbed by his own regrets, he almost forgot the unpleasant summons that had brought him here. The charges against Karigan were preposterous, of course, and he planned to straighten it all out with Dean Geyer. If nothing else, currency would convince the dean of his mistake.

Pink apple blossoms drifted into the street, filling the air with a far sweeter fragrance than the corpse down by the gates. Stevic had traveled lightly, though tempted to bring along a caravan of goods now that the spring trading season had opened and people were in the mood to buy. However, his daughter's plight was more important, and he made what speed he could, bringing along Sevano, who was talented with a sword despite his age, and welcome company. Up the Grandgent River they had sailed from Corsa, on one of Stevic's own cargo barges. They had left it unburdened of goods for speed. From the river, it was a two-day ride to Selium.

Stevic sent Sevano to arrange for rooms at the Harp and Drum, where he stayed whenever he was in town. The inn was clean and tapped into the city's famous hot springs. Each evening, students performed in the common room. The inn provided an opportunity for aspiring minstrels to practice their craft in a real situation, and to earn coppers and silvers for tuition at the same time.

Stevic had hoped Karigan would take a liking to music making, but it appeared she hadn't the aptitude for it. Exactly what she had an aptitude for remained a mystery, though Dean Geyer hinted in his letter that it was for nothing but trouble. Stevic had crushed the letter in his fist and thrown it into the fire. His daughter was headstrong, but she was also intelligent. One just had to know how to direct her energies.

The closer Stevic got to campus, the quieter the street became, as the mercantiles, inns, bathhouses, craft booths, and tourists fell behind. Grand houses now huddled close together on both sides of the street. They were old and similar in style to the academic buildings with pretentious columns supporting overhanging roofs of red clay tile. Sharp angles and corners cast stark shadows against pale walls. Scenes carved in relief ornamented entryways. Over one door, the god and goddess glowed in the sunlight. Narrow, tall windows remained darkened by shadows like empty eye sockets.

Though the houses were similar in style to the academic buildings, the academic buildings were even older. The city had grown up around the school, and the name Selium was interchangeable between the two.

Stevic rode beneath the P'ehdrosian Arch which marked the entrance to campus. He admired the scroll work and detail carved into its marble facade. On the keystone was a half-man, half-moose creature blowing on a horn. His features were scrubbed away by hundreds of years of harsh winters, and his body, like the rest of the arch, was splotched with lichens.

Was the p'ehdrose a mythological species, or a lost race? It was like asking if the god Aeryc rode the crescent moon in the evening. He couldn't see it happen, therefore he could not know in truth. Once he had thought Selium contained the answers to all such questions, but time and maturity had taught him the answers were all open to interpretation. If he believed the p'ehdrose existed, did it make it so?

His fingers dragged along the inscription inside the arch as he rode beneath. He couldn't read the ancient Sacoridian script, but he remembered that the words roughly meant that knowledge brought peace. In fact, the school had risen from the ashes and death of the Long War with the optimistic goal of ending all war with knowledge. A lofty ideal? Not really, considering Sacoridia had been a relatively peaceful nation for hundreds of years. Other countries, once members of the League that had crushed down the dark forces of Mornhavon the Black, were less peaceful than Sacoridia, but still sent children to be educated here. A sign of hope for future generations not to be discounted.

At the school's stables, Stevic handed the reins over to a boy and tossed him a copper.

"Thank you, my lord," the boy said in astonishment. Evidently tips were uncommon.

"I am no lord, boy. Remember that."

"Y-yes, my . . . Yes, sir!"

Stevic strode toward the administration building, with its golden dome and marble colonnade, his royal blue cloak flowing behind him. Well over six feet tall, he was an imposing man with a set chin and wide shoulders. Brown hair, flecked with silver, hung long and loose.

Despite his rich silks and the presumed leisure which accompanied wealth, he wasn't in any way soft. His body, for all its height, was hard and compact from years of hoisting cargo. Most merchants of his status sat in their offices counting their currency, but Stevic was different. He would not make his men and women do what he himself could not do. It wasn't uncommon to see him on the docks, sleeves rolled up, throwing heavy kegs up to a cog's crew.

It also wasn't uncommon for him to be called a lord, for his bearing and composure, his self-confidence and commanding presence, were those of a nobleman. He would have none of it. He was proud of his simple roots, proud of the hard work that had attained the success he now enjoyed. He scorned royalty on the most part, and he was heard to mutter, more than once, that royals didn't have the sense of a horse's ass.

A gold ring flashed on Stevic's finger as he entered the dim administration building. It bore the clan emblem, the twin of the one his beloved Kariny had once worn. Upon her death it had been passed on to Karigan. Whenever he looked at his daughter, he saw Kariny. Her high forehead and bright eyes . . . Karigan had not inherited her quiet ways, however, but her father's own temper.

Stevic's footfalls echoed loudly in the lobby. It was a domed rotunda with a veined marble floor. Bronze statues and busts of past administrators, stern and staid scholars, and severe looking craft masters, frowned at him from their alcoves. Offices branched off in either direction in rows of oak doors.

A bald-pated clerk sat at a desk, crouched over a sheaf of papers. Stevic stood before him some moments before the clerk acknowledged his presence with a sniff and nasal, "Yes?"

"I'm here to see Dean Geyer."

"Dean Geyer is in a meeting." The man stuck his nose back into his papers and proceeded to ignore Stevic.

Bureaucrats, Stevic knew, could be worse than aristocrats. As a merchant, he had dealt with his share of tax collectors and trade officials. "I will see the dean now."

"Have you an appointment?"

"Of sorts."

"There are no appointments scheduled on the roster at this time." The clerk didn't even glance at the appointment book on his desk.

"I received a letter from Dean Geyer instructing me to visit when I arrived."

"Do you have it with you?"

Stevic frowned. "I—it was destroyed."

"I see." Though Stevic towered above, the clerk still managed to look down his nose at him. "Dean Geyer is busy. Either you have an appointment or you do not."

Stevic wondered if the clerk gave the royals the same runaround, or if they received special treatment. He placed his hands on the clerk's neat desk and leaned down so he could look the man in the eye. "You will create an appointment for me *now,* or by Breyan's gold, I'll inform the dean that his clerk is reading poetry rather than attending to his duty."

The clerk licked his lips and gulped nervously. "Very well, but the dean will be annoyed."

"I pay this school handsomely so my daughter can attend. I expect some of that tuition goes toward your salary, and that of the dean. I do not think it unreasonable that the dean see me. *Now.*"

"Of course, my lord."

So, the clerk *did* treat royals the same way. Perhaps he wasn't so bad after all. "I am no lord. I am Stevic G'ladheon, chieftain of Clan G'ladheon. At your service." He put his hand to his heart and bowed slightly, as was customary.

The clerk sniffed as he took in the fine clothing. "Oh. A merchant, I suppose. Very well. Follow me." He hoisted his robes of office and strode across the lobby, his sandals whispering on the marble floor.

They mounted two sets of spiraling stairs carpeted with rich red pile, and zigzagged through numerous branching corridors before halting before enormous double doors of oak. The clerk hesitated and glanced over his shoulder at Stevic. Noting the merchant's expression of resolve, he licked his lips and knocked.

"Who is it?" barked a voice from within.

"Dean Geyer, I—"

"Oh, Matterly. Come in."

The clerk shrugged and pushed the doors open. Dean Geyer, a distinguished looking man with snowy hair and bright blue eyes, sat at his vast desk, just about to insert a mast into the upper deck of a large model ship.

"I see how busy he is," Stevic whispered to the clerk. Matterly reddened.

The dean cleared his throat when he noticed Stevic, and pushed the model aside. He stared at the clerk, awaiting an explanation.

"Chief Stevic G'ladheon to see you, Dean," Matterly said. He backed out of the office without another word, pulling the doors shut as he went.

Stevic ignored the impressive collection of books on the dean's shelves, and the rare hand-drawn maps framed on the wall that would have ordinarily intrigued him. He stepped right up to the desk and focused his attention on the ship model, examining it carefully. "I've sailed a few of these square riggers myself," he said.

"I, uh . . ." Geyer ran his fingers through his white hair and chuckled nervously, like a child caught with his finger dipped in the honey pot. "I tried sailing once or twice, but uh . . . the sea sickness, you know."

Stevic scrunched his brows together. "You've glued the bowsprit to the stern." He clucked in dismay. "And see here—" he pointed to the rear of the model, "—you've put the jib where the spanker belongs."

He stood straight, feet spread and hands on hips, and turned his attention on the dean. He surveyed the dean as critically as he had the model, as if something was out of place. Geyer swallowed and twisted a length of twine around his little finger. He tried to speak, but under Stevic's stern appraisal, no words came out.

"I beg your pardon for this intrusion, Dean," Stevic said finally, "but your letter demanded immediate attention. I haven't even been to see my daughter yet."

The dean paled and seemed to quiver. Then he mastered himself and pointed at a chair on the other side of his desk. "Of . . . of course. Please sit. You must be weary after such a long journey. From Corsa if I'm not mistaken."

"You are not mistaken." Stevic pulled up a leather upholstered chair. "And I will sit, though I'm not tired. What I really want, Dean, is answers. Why is my daughter being expelled from school?"

Dean Geyer changed the arrangement of his glue pot and carving knives on his desktop, and picked up an unattached model mast which he rolled between his fingers. He seemed unwilling to look Stevic in the eye.

"Not expelled, not exactly. Suspended. You see her grades were dwindling, and she'd been picking fights with other students."

"Those are no reasons for a . . . suspension."

"I'm afraid they are. We do not abide schoolyard brawls. Fighting is not in keeping with the principles of the school."

"Brawls?" Stevic said. "My daughter does not participate in *brawls*."

The dean pushed his fingers together in a triangle. A smile fluttered on his lips. "A fight, then. A fight which she initiated. Fortunately, the other student involved was not hurt."

"I don't believe it."

"Perhaps you do not, but the student's family complained to the trustees. You must also know she was not doing well academically." The dean relaxed as he explained Karigan's shortcomings. "She hardly attended her classes, and even when she did, her grades were still mediocre, not in keeping with our standards. That alone would be enough for dismissal. With this as her background, and a fight she provoked as cause, the trustees determined Karigan should spend some time at home and reconsider her reasons for being here."

Stevic's face flushed an angry red. "My daughter is not mediocre. Nor is she a bully who goes about provoking fights."

Geyer spread his hands wide to indicate the matter was beyond his control. "As a parent, you are entitled to feel that way about your child. Needless to say, the trustees have formed another opinion about her. It is hoped that upon reconsidering her behavior of the past, she will change her ways and return to Selium . . . in time."

Stevic gripped the arms of his chair, feeling as if he would explode. "I would talk with your trustees. If I don't receive satisfaction, my donations to this institution will cease. I will talk to the Golden Guardian himself if I must, but first I wish to see my daughter. I have yet to hear her side of the tale."

Geyer blanched again. "She isn't home? You . . . you haven't . . . seen her?"

"Of course not. I told you. . . . What's going on here? Where is my daughter?"

The dean mumbled to himself and looked around his office as if seeing it for the first time. Stevic felt he would strangle the dean with a strand of the model ship's rigging for all he could not seem to say anything. Geyer gathered his courage, but couldn't bring himself to look in Stevic G'ladheon's eyes. "She ran away. I was the last to see her."

Stevic struck the flat of his hand on Geyer's desk. Papers flew off and the ship model shuddered. A freshly glued mast toppled over and clattered onto the desktop.

"My daughter is *missing?*" Stevic lowered his voice to a hoarse growl. "I thought more of Selium than this." He pointed a shaking finger at the dean. "I hold you responsible for her being missing. I demand to see Guardian Fiori at once."

Geyer cringed in his chair. "The Guardian isn't—"

Stevic didn't wait to hear the rest. He threw the double

doors open, stormed out of Dean Geyer's office, and searched up and down corridors for the Golden Guardian's office. He flung doors open, startling administrators and disrupting classes. He pushed clerks out of his way when they blocked passageways. Exclamations and curses followed in his wake.

When he thought he had searched every office, he found another corridor branching off from one of the main ones. He struck off down the poorly lit corridor not slackening his stride. Candles ensconced on the wall sputtered at his passing. The rich red pile disappeared, revealing scuffed and scarred floorboards. Finally, he came upon a door adorned simply with the symbol of the golden harp. He opened it and entered.

The office was a disarray of musical instruments. They hung on the walls, lay on shelves, and leaned in corners. Some were in pieces, or had broken strings curling crazily from tuning pegs. Countless books were stacked on the floor—there was no space on the shelves for them. A thick layer of dust coated everything, and the scent of resin hung thick in the air.

"This is the Golden Guardian's office?" Stevic said with incredulity.

"As a matter of fact, it is."

Beyond the plain pinewood desk in the center of the room, a girl in a uniform of indigo with a white apprentice knot at the shoulder, looked up with sea-green eyes from the book she had been reading.

"I beg your pardon," Stevic said, "but I need to see Guardian Fiori."

The girl's book thumped closed, and she sighed. "I'd like to see him myself, but he's the only one who knows where he is."

Stevic waited for an explanation, but the girl seemed to have sunk into her own thoughts and didn't go on.

"Ahem," he prompted. "What do you mean?"

"He's doing what a minstrel does best. He's journeying. He could be in the northlands, Ullem Bay, or Rhovanny for all I know. He never knows where he'll be until he's there. He has been gone up to a year, and longer than that before I came to live with him.''

Stevic reckoned himself open-minded, but this girl was no older than his Karigan. It was rumored the Golden Guardian was well into his sixties, and though it was not unusual for older men to wed younger women prime to bear children, this age discrepancy was criminal.

He stalked over to a dusty window that overlooked the campus. A bell chimed four times, resonating through the floorboards, as if it must be very close. Students poured out of buildings and onto the square below, changing classes. Karigan should be among them, but she wasn't. Where was she? On the road home, he hoped. A pigeon perched on the windowsill.

"Some governor Fiori is if he isn't here to watch over his interests."

"Pardon?" the girl asked. "I don't hear well. It's best if you face me."

Stevic turned in surprise. This wasn't Fiori's wife at all, but his daughter! He reddened in embarrassment. "You're Karigan's friend, aren't you? Young Estral?" Karigan had spoken of Estral, saying that she was deaf in one ear from an accident, but still a fabulous musician.

The girl nodded with a smile. "And you're her father." Then her face grew serious. "You haven't seen Karigan, have you?"

"No. I expected to find her here. Either a message she had run away didn't reach me before I left Corsa, or the dean didn't bother to send me one." The anger began to build within him again, like a fire scorching his belly. "I hold Dean Geyer responsible for this. If anything has happened to Karigan—"

"It's terrible." Estral's shoulders sagged and she rested her chin on her hands. "I wish . . . I wish she'd come back. I miss her. It hasn't been the same here without her. I've no one to talk to, and the other students pester me worse than usual. She used to sort of protect me. I don't know why she ran away. Did you know her grades

were improving, and that Arms Master Rendle had taken
her on as a student just before she was suspended?"

"Your story differs from the dean's," Stevic said. "You
say Karigan left no clue as to where she went?"

"No. And I wouldn't blame the dean too much. He's
a little out of touch, and perhaps too much at the sway
of the trustees. After all, it was an aristocrat Karigan
fought."

"An aristocrat?"

"Lord-Governor Mirwell's heir. He was humiliated
after she beat him at swordplay."

"Never heard of anything good coming out of Mirwell." Stevic's caravans rarely traveled there. The common folk were, on the most part, too poor to purchase
his goods, and the wealthy were more interested in arms,
which he didn't sell.

Estral continued, "It created a sensation all over
town."

Stevic grinned mirthlessly. "Sounds like something she
would do."

Estral shook her head. "She never knew it, but she had
more friends than she ever realized because she stood up
to bullies like Timas. A lot of the students here are not
of noble blood or wealth, but are full of talent. Father
makes a point of searching for such children and bringing
them to Selium. They are often at the mercy of those
such as Timas."

"And instead of playing along, she stood against the
ruffians." Stevic rubbed his chin. "Yes, that is like her."

The office door creaked open. Stevic started in surprise
as the Green Rider he had seen earlier with the undertaker walked in. She still clutched the arrows, black-
shafted, he saw, her brow furrowed with anger.

"I wish to see Guardian Fiori," she said. The corners
of her eyes were creased from too many years in the
sun, and her cheeks were sprinkled with faded freckles.
Her hair, which had looked so intense outside, now appeared a burnished auburn with a streak of gray sweeping from her temple. Hazel eyes sparkled alertly, no

doubt taking in every detail of the Golden Guardian's disheveled office. Her nose was disjointed as if it had been broken once, and a badly healed scar ran raggedly down her chin and neck in a brown line until it disappeared beneath her collar.

"I'm sorry, but he's away," Estral said.

The lines across the Rider's brow deepened. "You are being honest with me? I can sense falsehoods if I so choose." She fingered a brooch on her shortcoat. Stevic hadn't noticed it before, and even now couldn't seem to make out its shape or design.

"I've no reason to lie to you," Estral said. "My father is traveling."

"Your father! You're not one of those idiot clerks—please forgive me." Her voice was chagrined, and it was difficult to imagine her as the same woman who had shaken the undertaker by his lapels. Stevic wondered if she had given the clerk Matterly similar treatment. "I was hoping he could help me identify this talisman." She held the arrows aloft. The steel-barbed tips were encrusted with dry blood. "There are words carved on them in a language I can't quite make out, but I have my own thoughts. They've the feel of magic. Very old magic."

Estral gazed at them with some interest but didn't ask to hold them. "I'm sorry Father isn't here. Maybe Master Galwin could help. He's a historian and the school curator. He studies the lore of old magic. Where did you find them?"

"In the back of one of my finest Riders." She sighed. "We believe he was bringing us a message of some significance." Then, as an afterthought, she introduced herself. "I am Laren Mapstone, captain of His Majesty's Messenger Service. Your father has been very helpful to me in the past. That is, dealing with objects of antiquity and magic."

"Ach," Stevic said. "Magic is evil." He made the sign of the half moon with his fingers to ward off any magic that might be conjured up just by mentioning it.

Captain Mapstone gave him a long, measuring look.

Her head did not even reach his shoulders, but her bearing made her seem equally tall. "And who are you?"

"Chief Stevic G'ladheon, at your service." He bowed deeper for her than he had for the clerk.

"Oh. A merchant. Obviously with backward views. Magic is magic. It's the user who makes it evil or good."

"I still wouldn't touch it."

The Green Rider's lips drew back into what could have been a smile. "There are those who still touch magic and use it, despite the denial this country has been immersed in for the last several centuries."

Before Stevic could retort, the door creaked open again. This time, a man of wiry and well-muscled build walked in. His hair was steel gray, but his mustache and eyes were as black as night. A pipe protruded from his shirt pocket.

"Pardon my intrusion, Estral," he said, "but I hear that Karigan's father is here."

Estral nodded toward Stevic. "That's him, Master Rendle."

"Arms Master Rendle?" Stevic stepped past Captain Mapstone to greet the man. He forgot to bow.

"Pleased to meet. We've a few things to discuss."

Estral's chair scraped the floor as she stood up. "Guess I'm not going to get anything done here. Nobody ever bothers to come back here except when I have to study."

"If you could direct me to Master Galwin . . ." the Green Rider requested, and followed Estral out.

The arms master watched after them. "A dangerous job that Rider has."

"How's that?"

Rendle shook himself as if he hadn't realized he'd spoken aloud. "Can you imagine riding all hours of the day at the mercy of weather during all seasons? Can you imagine bearing a message through dangerous territories, or taking bad news to a short-tempered lord who wouldn't think twice about killing you? Can you imagine carrying a message someone doesn't want delivered? The lifespan of a Green Rider is very short. That captain is about as old as I see them get."

"That's all very well, but it's their job. Why, sometimes it's no better for a merchant traveling with a load of goods. Unless you've a full complement of guards. I know plenty of merchants who have been killed for—"

"Aye, it's their job, and Green Riders are the closest to insane as I've ever seen."

Unsettled by the arms master's words, Stevic watched out the dusty window as Captain Mapstone and Estral crossed the courtyard down below. "Tell me about my daughter."

Arms Master Rendle leaned against the Golden Guardian's desk, his arms folded across his broad chest.

"By the end of the fight," he was saying, "I saw enough to recognize she had some natural talent with the sword. It was the way she moved. It was raw and instinctual, but I saw promise. You must understand that most of the students who come to me are there mostly because it is part of their coursework, or a clan tradition to receive weapons training. They hone traditional skills it is unlikely they will ever use. Minstrel students are more musician than warrior, but weapons training is required for them. The Guardian believes they should be prepared for the world they wander in, and I quite agree. But it is rare to find a student with actual interest and talent."

Stevic stared out the window. The courtyard had fallen into shadow and silence, empty of students. Even the pigeons seemed to have fled the grounds, giving it a gloomy and abandoned feel. "I had hoped Karigan would find a talent for something, but I never expected the sword."

"Ah, but the sword is just a beginning. I had heard about her from her other instructors. Complaints, mind you, except from her riding instructor, Master Deleon. Del said she excelled at riding. When I saw Karigan put Timas Mirwell on the ground, I thought maybe I could get her to work for something else and the sword would be just a beginning, that it would inspire her to seek out whatever it was she wanted to do with her life."

Stevic turned his gaze to the arms master. "I am fortunate my daughter had such an instructor."

Rendle grinned. "She was fortunate to have such a father."

Stevic raised a brow.

"I once asked her what she wanted to do with her life," Rendle said. "She told me, something adventurous. She wanted to be a merchant like her father. It is not many children who choose to follow their parents' footsteps."

Stevic stilled, letting it sink in. Then he slowly shook his head and turned back to the window and the shadows. He felt buffeted by a variety of emotions: elation, fear, sadness, desperation. *Where was she?* "She never told me." His voice was taut.

Rendle said nothing until he was certain Stevic had mastered himself. "We continued training every day. It seems someone had worked with her before, the cargo master—?"

Stevic nodded. "Sevano."

"Her skills were less than basic, but she was an eager student, always at the practice field early. She worked harder than any student I've had the privilege to teach in a very long time. Her skills improved quickly though she seemed discouraged by what she saw as a lack of progress. Unfortunately, her training was cut short."

"The suspension you mean."

"Aye." Rendle removed his pipe from his pocket and patted his side as if in search of something, and frowned. "My tobacco pouch. Hmmm . . ." When he couldn't find it, he stuck the pipe back in his pocket. "Despite the fact Timas Mirwell attacked her after their swordplay, and despite Del . . . er, Master Deleon and myself speaking on her behalf before the trustees, Karigan was suspended."

Stevic left the window to stand before Rendle. "I've heard the dean's explanation, but why do *you* think she was suspended?"

"I am Rhovan born," Rendle said. "My mother was of Rhovanny, my father of Adolind Province. I spent a goodly part of my life on the Wanda Plains growing more weeds than crops, and fighting off groundmites and other raiders. We were too concerned with day to day life to worry about what the clans were doing in Sacoridia. Politics . . ." Rendle leaned forward and in a low voice he said, "At least one trustee is of Clan Mirwell. Mirwellians don't take kindly to dishonor. Karigan dishonored the governor's son, thus the entire clan, and they will remember such an insult for a century if need be."

If need be. Stevic took a deep swallow of his ale and set the tankard down on the knotty pine table with a *clunk*. It was late afternoon at the Harp and Drum, and no one had begun to entertain yet. The music would start during the supper hour. He didn't think he would have the heart to listen to it anyway.

Only a few other patrons sat quietly at tables, sipping wine or ale, as drowsy sunlight filtered through the windows. Stevic twisted the gold ring on his finger, ignoring the steaming fresh bread and cheese plate the innkeeper set on their table.

"You think about Kari," Sevano said.

Stevic nodded. "She's my daughter . . . just a baby."

"Oh, no—no baby is she! Young, yes, but no baby. You know she's got herself into plenty of scrapes before. It's just like her to go home on her own. No waiting around for you to arrive, not with the humiliation this suspension must have caused her. I know G'ladheon pride, I do." He chuckled. "If you were her, you'd do the same."

Stevic smiled. "I did do something similar when I was her age. I joined a merchant barge, but—"

"But she is still your baby." Sevano shook his head. "She has jumped from her nest, her wings spread. You would prevent this?"

"No, of course not. I . . . Well, you heard all the whisperings of strange things happening as we traveled here. By Breyan's gold, Sevano, strange things were happening all winter. The tree folk have been seen outside of the Elt Wood for the first time in at least a hundred years, and you heard about groundmites crossing the borders just as I did. Are you saying I shouldn't be worried about my daughter?"

"No." The older man stared into his tankard and listlessly picked up a piece of yellow cheese which he tossed back onto the plate. "I worry, too. But remember, I taught her many things about survival, and that Rendle sounds like a good man. I'm sure she learned much from him."

"You both taught her swordplay. I don't expect she has a sword of her own."

"I taught her much more than the sword, I did. She could use her bare hands to defend herself. Like a niece she is to me, too, though no blood do we share."

The two sat in silence for many minutes. The very air pressed on their shoulders. They were awakened from their individual reveries as the door creaked open and blinding sunlight poured into the common room. A young man stepped across the threshold, hesitating a moment until his eyes adjusted to the dim interior. He was dressed in a waistcoat of green over a white linen shirt. His breeches and the coat he carried draped over his forearm were green as well. A saber sheathed in a plain black scabbard was strapped to his waist.

Stevic watched as the Green Rider searched the depths of the common room. The messenger's eyes registered in sudden recognition and he strode toward them, the soles of his boots making no sound on the wooden floor. Stevic wondered what the Rider would want with them, but he didn't stop at their table. Rather, he continued on to the booth behind them. Stevic couldn't see who the young man sat with because of the high backing of the booth, but he instantly recognized the voice.

"Connly," said Captain Mapstone. "Good to see you. How was the road?"

The Rider murmured something imperceptible, and Stevic strained to hear.

"I need you to contact Joy about F'ryan and his missing message. We need every available Rider scouring all roads and towns. Those who are on a run must keep their eyes open. There's no telling where that message is, or if it even still exists. Maybe someone took it from him, or maybe his horse is running loose with the message still snug in its satchel. We must find out. Also, be sure to warn Joy of the manner of his death."

Connly murmured some more, but Stevic couldn't make out a word of it.

"I don't know," Captain Mapstone replied. "Though I think it very odd that his brooch was missing. It could—"

Whatever she was about to say was cut short by a clamor outside. Stevic looked out his window, but could only see people rushing into the street. "What do you suppose that's all about?" he asked Sevano.

"Dunno." Sevano took a final swig of ale and wiped his sleeve across his mouth. "Let's have a look."

Stevic was reluctant to leave the conversation he had been eavesdropping on, but the booth had become silent anyway. Undoubtedly, the two Green Riders were distracted by the shouting from outside as well. Stevic pushed his tankard aside and followed Sevano out into the glare of sunshine. He pushed through onlookers to see what was causing such excitement, and stopped in shock.

A fallen horse and rider lay in the middle of the street. Blood foamed from the heaving horse's mouth. A youth of dark complexion lay dazed beside it, one leg pinned beneath the horse. Some of the onlookers attempted to free him. The boy seemed oblivious to what was happening around him.

"They killed them," the boy cried. "They killed the master . . . Master Ione . . . everyone. They killed everyone but me! Monsters . . . like men, but not . . ." The boy's sobs rang out over the stunned crowd.

"I believe that's Urath of the Under Kingdoms," a woman said behind Stevic's right shoulder. "Son of aus-Corien, pack leader of T-katnya. He was on a field trip with his class."

"Someone ought to inform the dean," a man said.

Stevic turned away. The boy's whimpering carried over the chatter of the crowd. The boy's face was clear of tattoos, making him an adolescent who hadn't yet made the great hunt, the traditional rite to become a man of the pack. "He's Karigan's age," he said to Sevano.

"Aye. Well do I know it."

Captain Mapstone watched the commotion from the steps of the inn. Her expression was thoughtful. Stevic walked over to her purposefully, and she shook out of some uncomfortable reverie as he approached.

"Groundmites," she said. "Those monsters he saw were groundmites."

Stevic felt his stomach lurch. Where was his daughter? "Captain, I would ask a favor."

She raised a copper brow. "A merchant always seeks favors at no cost to himself, which he rarely repays."

Stevic's cheeks burned in anger. "Perhaps it's true with some merchants, just as it's true with some minstrels, soldiers, craftmasters, farmers, and ferrymen, but I am not of that nature."

Captain Mapstone's expression remained unaltered and she did not apologize. "What favor do you ask?"

"It would . . . It would mean much to me if your Riders could watch for a young girl, the same age as this youth here who now lies in the street. She has disappeared and—and she's my daughter. I believe she is traveling toward Corsa, but who can say if something ill has befallen her?"

The captain blinked, but it was her only change of expression. "Green Riders aren't in the habit of searching for runaways, Chief, and at the moment we're involved in—"

"I implore you, Captain." Stevic's voice cracked as he spoke. "My daughter has been missing for weeks. She is all I have left since . . . since my wife died. . . ."

"Surely taking the girl's description and passing it on to your Riders won't distract them from their duty." Stevic had forgotten Sevano behind him, and was suddenly grateful for his presence. "It is but a small thing to ask. She is young and alone. What if she meets up with groundmites like that lad yonder?"

"I will more than repay you if your people can find Karigan." Stevic looked hopefully at her. They were now eye level, the steps she stood on helping her to meet his gaze. He saw her expression soften just the least bit. "I will make donations to your unit. I'll—I'll re-outfit your Riders."

Now there was a perceptible hint of a smile on her face.

She turned toward the interior of the inn. "Connly! I need you to take a description. Come listen, and listen well." As the young man trotted to the doorway, she turned back to Stevic and said, "I intend to keep you to your end of the bargain."

⤜ SWORDMASTERS ⤛

Karigan and her captors walked in the same formation as they had the previous day. Garroty sat upon his horse, talking down at Torne who strode beside him. Jendara, leading The Horse, walked next to Karigan. Karigan had spent an unpleasant night listening to Torne and Garroty swap tales and make suggestive, if not entirely vulgar, comments about her. She hadn't slept all night, and now her eyelids sagged as she stumbled down the road.

Her wrists itched. Either they were healing from the burns, or they were getting worse. The rope that bound her wrists made it impossible to check beneath the old, dirty dressings that covered the wounds.

Jendara had kept silent all day. Torne and Garroty directed some comments her way, too. She merely scowled at their backs, as if to burn holes through them with her eyes.

"I'd castrate those two."

Karigan tripped over a rock. Jendara's speaking aloud was unexpected enough. Her words, even more so. "Why don't you?"

Jendara chuckled. "Two of them against me, and one a swordmaster at that? The odds are a bit precarious, don't you think?"

"I'd help."

"Very helpful you would be. I doubt you can even lift that sword fastened to your saddle. All they need Green-ies to do is ride."

Karigan, of course, had little idea of what Green Riders were capable of, but was certain she could surprise even Jendara with a few of the skills she had learned, whether Jendara was a swordmaster or not.

"This road goes on forever," Karigan said.

"It was built long ago to breach the northern wilderness." Jendara's reply was again unexpected. "Where do you think all the pulp that makes paper comes from? There isn't nearly the expanse of woods to the south."

Ribbons of sun dropped through the trees, leaving puddles of light on the road and in the woods. Karigan caught movement in the woods out of the corner of her eye. She looked closely, but at first she couldn't focus on the shape. She blinked, and the shape slowly defined itself into a man, another traveler walking abreast of them in the woods, fading in and out of the shadows, weaving between the trees, striding swiftly and unhindered through the underbrush, as if he were on a smooth road.

His passage was silent, not a snap of a twig to be heard, not a single bird flushed from cover. Tall ferns and tree limbs swayed in a breeze—not from the touch of the man who seemed to pass right through without brushing a thing. The Horse whickered and watched the traveler, his ears pricked forward.

"What does he see?" Jendara asked. She looked right at the traveler and . . . through him. Torne and Garroty chattered, oblivious to the newcomer.

Karigan narrowed her eyes and saw the traveler's pale face, and two arrows sticking from his back. F'ryan Coblebay. He turned to her, still keeping pace with them. His mouth worked as if he were trying to tell her something, but she couldn't hear words. He kept speaking until he passed through the shadow of a tall hemlock and disappeared.

The Horse champed the bit and sidestepped in a skittish way. Maybe he could hear the voice of the ghost.

Watch as she might throughout the day, Karigan saw no further signs of F'ryan Coblebay. What message had he been trying to convey? Jendara had asked, at one point, what it was she saw, or expected to see, in the woods.

"Just ghosts," she said matter-of-factly. "A spirit follows me."

Jendara frowned. The two men overheard, and while Garroty guffawed loudly, Torne growled. "I ought to cut your tongue out. Your superstitious talk won't work with me."

"You actually sound worried, Torne." Tobacco juice slapped the road. Garroty wiped his mouth with the back of his hand. "Are you superstitious? You, a swordmaster and grown man?"

Torne glowered. "Of course not. Those Mirwellian fools brought it up first, and this Greenie is trying to make us nervous. Won't work, Greenie, won't work."

Karigan shrugged. She had spoken plain truth which she believed Torne and Jendara must have sensed despite their protests, for they began searching the woods with their eyes, and their pace had picked up.

Garroty chuckled. "All of this plain living has gotten to you. Why, if you had stayed with the Talons a little longer, we could've taught you a few things."

"We are comfortable where we are." Now Garroty had managed to prickle even Torne. "As comfortable as we ever were in Sacor City. Why *we* were sent on this mission, we don't know and will not question. What my lord wills, my lord receives, and time spent with the Talons has nothing to do with it."

"You are infants lost in the woods," Garroty said. "I bet your horses were stolen right from under you." At Torne's glower, he let out a great "Hah!" and, "I guessed right. And if you took that leather jerkin off, I bet I could count your ribs. Weapons and swordmasters indeed. You may survive in the court, but out here is where it counts."

Karigan could nearly see the smoke pouring out of Torne's ears. With a yawn, she listened closely as Garroty and Torne continued their debate.

"The problem with you Weapons," Garroty said,

scraping bristly hairs on his cheek, "is that you're all honor and ceremony. Honor and ceremony may work in court and in battle, but it won't do much good out here. Even the Blood Guard of Rhovanny leave the court once in a while to see what the world looks like."

"Ceremony is deeply traditional among Weapons of the Order of Black Shields," Torne said. "Ceremony instills discipline. Besides, who needs to know of the real world when the court is the real world? Jendara and I . . . well, our circumstances are special."

"Ah, and if any of Zachary's soldiers see you and recognize you, you'll be hanged as traitors—at the least."

"We aren't traitors, Garroty."

"I suppose that depends on who you work for, then. Zachary or his brother. But hear this, Swordmaster, Zachary is the one in power. He was the one named heir by his father, not Amilton, no matter the usual order of succession. What you've done is high treason, and if you get caught and strung up, you will be let off easy, I assure you. If I recall history, there was a traitorous Weapon named Saverill who was slowly tortured for weeks, and then chained to the prison tower for the vultures to feed on. He was still alive."

"We know the consequences of our loyalties," Torne said. "Tales of Saverill the Traitor were drilled into our memories when we were mere pledges at the academy. You don't have to remind us."

Garroty shrugged. "Don't misunderstand me. I'm all for fighting on behalf of the highest bidder, even if the stakes are a little high. What I am simply trying to say is that you, a Weapon whose honor and ideals go beyond payment, should make very sure the stakes are worth the price you may have to pay, and that you will succeed."

"The stakes are worth it," Torne said barely above a whisper, "and we will succeed."

Another blob of tobacco juice hit the road in reply. The debate ended there.

The shadows of evening deepened, and the air became heavy with dew. Fireflies blinked, falling like flurries of light between the trees. Thrushes sang their evening songs, and as night descended, milky moonlight spilled into the woods. Torne led them off the road and into the clearing where they set up camp.

Karigan was thrown her usual hard chunk of bread, and was thankful as ever for the cache of food in her pockets given to her by little Dusty. The cache wouldn't last much longer, and soon she'd go hungry again, unless she escaped. Her stomach grumbled as the scent of meat drifted from the mercenaries' cookfire. Torne tossed pieces of dried meat into the stew pot.

Garroty stared at Karigan during the whole meal, stew dribbling out the corner of his mouth, which he roughly wiped away with the back of his hand. Repulsed, Karigan looked elsewhere, trying to focus on more pleasant thoughts. Maybe her father was looking for her by now. Surely Dean Geyer had sent him a message about her running away. Well, that wasn't exactly a pleasant thought either. Her father was going to be irate when he found her. After all, it was the beginning of the spring trading season; any delay in sending out the caravans or barges could prove costly.

Torne stood up and stretched. "I'm going to scout for Immerez," he announced. "That fool should have caught up with us days ago." He buckled on his sword belt, wrapped his worn cloak about his shoulders, and strode out of camp.

"Watch out for ghosties!" Garroty taunted, chuckling heartily. Torne's step faltered as he disappeared into the night.

Silence filled the clearing. Garroty pinched a wad of tobacco from his belt pouch and stuffed it into his cheek. His gaze drifted from Karigan to Jendara, and back again. He leaned back onto his elbows, chewing at his ease. Jendara's expression was stony as she drew her sword from its sheath. From a pouch she removed a soft cloth, oil, and two whetting stones. The hiss of blade against stone filled the clearing.

"I love women who carry weapons," Garroty said. "The danger of it excites me."

The hissing ceased. "You're a foul man, Garroty. Be silent before you lose something very precious to you."

Garroty laughed. "It sounds like a challenge to me."

"I've been wanting to unman you since I first laid eyes on you."

"Then go at it, woman. I'll have fun stopping you."

Karigan tensed as Jendara gripped the hilt of her sword and leaped lightly to her feet. Garroty did nothing, and Jendara hesitated.

"Well, woman, come on. I'm waiting."

Jendara snarled. "Stand up. If you're a warrior, you will fight like one."

Garroty chuckled and slowly pushed himself up from the ground. He stood with his arms spread out wide. "I'm standing, woman. Come for me, and I'll show you *my* blade."

A howling pierced the forest, almost human in its cry, followed by the trampling of foliage. The horses whickered nervously.

"What was that?" Jendara asked.

Garroty shrugged, unconcerned. "Probably some wolf looking for dinner." Then with a wicked grin he added, "Maybe it's found Torne."

Jendara muttered under her breath, looking from the mercenary to Karigan. "I'm going to check it out," she said. Glaring at Garroty, she added, "Leave the prisoner alone." She held her sword before her, and stepped uncertainly into the darkness in the direction of the disturbance. Karigan looked pleadingly after her retreating back.

When Jendara was out of sight, Garroty shook his head. "Foolish woman. Just a coyote chasing a hare, I'll reckon. The horses are quiet now, like nothing happened. No matter." He turned his eyes back on Karigan. "It will give us a little time alone."

"Don't come near me." Karigan's voice quavered as she spoke.

Garroty was across the clearing in three strides. He seized her arm, and lest she cry out loud enough for Jendara to hear, he clamped a sweaty hand over her mouth. He yanked her to her feet, and before she could squirm away, he wrapped his arm around her chest and held her securely. If only her hands weren't tied!

"I've been waiting for this." His hot breath filled her ear damply as he spoke, and smelled of stale tobacco. Garroty dragged her beyond the clearing into the dark of the forest. She kicked and writhed, but the man must have a hide like boiled leather. She raked his shin with the sole of her boot—a trick taught her by the cargo master—but it didn't faze him one iota. Most people would have screamed with pain.

Minutes passed like hours as Garroty dragged her, and then threw her to the ground. The barest shred of moonlight fell across his face, revealing a sickening grin. "I've been waiting for this," he whispered. With a childlike giggle, he unbuckled his sword belt and dropped it to the ground. Karigan rolled over and started to crawl away, but Garroty caught her in the small of her back with his foot, and ground her into the dirt. She gasped for air.

"If you fight," he warned her, "I can easily break your spine." He let his foot rest there for a moment, pressing down when she moved the slightest bit. Then he pulled it away, caught her under the ribs with his toe, and rolled her onto her back again. Karigan gasped for breath, her side throbbing with pain.

Garroty fell to his knees and straddled her. The stench of his unclean body was overpowering, his very sweat reeked of tobacco. Tobacco drooled from his mouth and stained her shirt. Karigan shook uncontrollably.

Fight, fool!

It was a voice Karigan remembered. The voice she had heard that night in the settlement. Garroty's hands now pinned her shoulders to the ground. His expression was rabid.

Fight! the voice commanded.

Yes, fight. The cargo master had taught her several tricks should she ever be in a situation such as this. She lunged and sank her teeth into Garroty's wrist. He screamed and yanked his hand away, almost snapping her head off her neck with the force.

He growled and struck her across the face.

The blow sent reverberations ringing through her body, and she blinked dazedly. Garroty examined his wrist. This distraction might be her only chance—he was vulnerable with his legs spread above her as they were. She locked both hands into a single fist and punched upward. Garroty's jaw fell slack as if uttering a silent cry. His eyes bulged like a fish's, and he clutched his crotch.

Karigan poised to punch his ugly face in, when she heard Jendara's laughter. The swordmaster sheathed her blade and crouched beside them. "Seems I underestimated you, girl. You don't need a sword to unman this idiot." She chuckled mirthfully at Garroty. "You like dangerous women, do you? It seems to me it would be of service to all women if we permanently crippled you." She reached for her dagger.

Garroty's face swelled with such blood that Karigan thought it might explode. Instead, his fist slammed into Jendara's face. The impact sent her flailing backward, her head striking the ground hard. She didn't move.

Garroty grunted in satisfaction and leered down at Karigan. "This is going to be more interesting than I thought. When I'm through with you, I'll finish off with her whether she wakes up or not."

Not willing to leave himself unprotected a second time, he grabbed both of Karigan's wrists, and knelt across her legs.

Karigan thought desperately. She thought back to summer evenings in an empty warehouse on her father's estate where the cargo master practiced swordplay with her. For one lesson, he left the wooden practice swords leaning against the wall and devoted the session to what she could do with her bare hands.

"Now, Kari," Sevano had said, as she sat cross-legged

on the dirt floor. "There may be a time when no weapon you've got. I'm gonna show you how to use your hands and feet to maim, and if need be, kill some thug who tries to harm you. But first, let me tell you where it's gonna hurt him most. . . ."

She had tried Garroty's shins and groin already. What was left? She couldn't pinch the nerves in his hands, and she couldn't kick—she was too immobilized by him to do anything. Sevano would disagree, though. She thought frantically.

Once she decided, she breathed a short prayer and gathered herself up. Propelled by her elbows and shoulders, she slammed her head into Garroty's face. Not a precision move, but it would have to do. There was a muffled cry and he fell back clutching his nose. Blood was splattered across his face. He curled into a fetal position on the ground, writhing in pain.

Karigan dared not breathe, fearing she had not damaged him sufficiently, and that he would be back on her to finish what he had begun. But he didn't get up, and after several minutes, he stopped moving altogether.

She crawled to him on knees and elbows, and saw that his chest did not rise or fall. The cargo master had said that if the nose was bashed into an assailant's head, the bone would shatter and pierce the brain, killing him. Karigan had killed a man.

She had killed Garroty and was appalled because it did not bother her.

Jendara still lay unmoving, rivulets of blood trickling down her cheeks from her nose. She wasn't dead, for she breathed, but she didn't look likely to wake up in the next few moments. This was Karigan's chance for escape.

She espied Garroty's discarded sword and drew it. She rubbed the rope that bound her hands against the blade, carefully so she wouldn't slice herself. With relief bordering on joy, she watched the rope fall away—her hands were free!

She hastened to her feet to run to The Horse, but paused. The ring of Kariny G'ladheon gleamed in the moonlight on Jendara's hand. Karigan slid it off the swordmaster's callused finger and onto her own. It had always been a little loose on her, but now it fit perfectly.

A twig crunched behind her. Karigan whirled around.

"This is quite a scene." Torne's face was more grim than she had ever seen. "Somehow—I'm not sure how—you've killed my friend and hurt my partner." His sword *shooshed* out of its sheath.

Defend yourself, the voice thundered in Karigan's head. Jendara's sword, still sheathed at her side, was closest. She grabbed the hilt and drew it. The black band seemed to disconnect the blade from the hilt. The sword was of the best balance she had ever held—of course, it belonged to a swordmaster.

"Foolish girl," Torne said. "You are no swordmaster. You dirty her blade by touching it, but you will die on mine."

Torne thrust without preamble and Karigan barely deflected it. She tried to remember the exercises Arms Master Rendle had drilled into her head, and the hints and tricks Sevano had taught her, but Torne was relentless and all she could manage was to duck and block the onslaught of blows. Each strike from Torne jarred her body and numbed her arms from her fingers to her elbows. If there was any time she was going to die, it was now.

Torne's speed and rhythm was a dance. Karigan had never seen anything like it, and was enthralled by his deadly skill. His feet barely shifted, he never swung the blade more than required. His economy of movement was grace itself.

After just moments of swordplay, Torne raised his sword for the death blow, but time stilled. Cold filled Karigan's body—not a chill really. It was like being a glass filled with cold water. Then there was something else . . . an awareness of another.

Her arms were buoyed by another's strength, and her reflexes guided by another thought process. Her own awareness grew dim, and she became a bystander in her own body. Or was it her own body? Two points of severe pain in her back twisted her insides.

The action resumed, and the would-be death blow was miraculously blocked. *Raven's sweep to the side.* The voice echoed from far away in her head. The same voice that had told her to fight and defend herself. The same voice that had tried to speak to her at the settlement.

One and two and three and upthrust, five. The voice and her body matched and countered the rhythm of Torne's attack. She recognized some of the techniques named, but many more were new to her. All of the various moves, the balance and steps, the angle of the cutting edge, fell into place within her in a way they hadn't when taught by Sevano or Master Rendle.

Was that shock registering on Torne's face as she blocked a particularly difficult thrust? Was that sweat that dampened his brow?

Oversweep, Crayman's Circle, three and four and swipe!

She watched in amazement as the tip of her sword slashed across Torne's leather jerkin. Although it only made a long cut in the leather, his face blanched as if it had been his own flesh.

"Who are you?" Torne panted, his eyes wide in . . . fear.

. . . two and three and Raven's Sweep redoubled!

The move threw Torne against a tree, his arms and sword tangling in the evergreen boughs.

Butcher's Block, one-two-three.

Torne barely avoided being chopped in three. Each swing of the sword caused the pain of arrows in her back to twinge, and the bleeding to start anew . . .

"Who are you?" Torne demanded again.

Burn, brooch, burn! By the flying horse, burn!

Torne screamed. He groped with his free hand for the brooch on his cloak. He grasped it, but jerked his fingers away with a cry. The distraction was enough.

Ice Slide now!

The blade ran through Torne's jerkin and out through

his back, impaling him to the trunk of the tree. His limbs jerked and flailed. Karigan's nostrils flared with the metallic scent of fresh blood.

"Who are you?" This time it came as a whisper, barely heard over his raspy breaths.

A voice that was Karigan's spoke words that were not her own. "I am a Green Rider and swordmaster initiate. You are spared Saverill's fate, traitor." The hand that held the hilt twisted the sword, and Torne's eyes rolled into the back of his head. The presence within her turned to Jendara and reached for her dagger.

Stop! Karigan struggled to expel the presence from her, but it was like trying to disgorge her own guts. *Leave me.*

The presence drained from her, and she sighed as warmth flooded through her body again. F'ryan Coblebay stood before her.

I saved your life, he said. *She is a traitor and must die.*

"It is for me to decide," Karigan said, "if she should die." She gazed at Jendara lying on her back, neck naked to any blade she might draw across it. The blood was drying on the Weapon's face, but she breathed normally and looked to be asleep. Karigan remembered when Jendara made Torne let her wear her greatcoat against the cold rain. Jendara had let her keep her hidden cache of food and had never told Torne about it. She knew Jendara would have killed Garroty to keep him from hurting her.

F'ryan Coblebay's form flickered once. *You must kill her.*

"You kill her."

I cannot unless I enter—

"I won't allow that." Karigan clenched and unclenched her hands at her sides. "I will not be used."

I saved your life.

The night's events started to catch up with her. Her body trembled, and she felt cold all over again. The idea of someone else controlling her affairs infuriated . . . and terrified her. "It seems to me you set me on this course in the first place. You and that brooch."

F'ryan Coblebay dimmed and flickered. *No, not I. You were called.* He looked up at the sky, then walked away, vanishing completely in the dark, but his voice lingered like an echo, . . . *you were called* . . .

Karigan sighed, feeling light headed from the whole experience. She wanted to get away from the carnage as soon as she could—Garroty's crushed face and Torne's impaled body—but she needed the brooch back, too. Jendara murmured incomprehensibly and twitched on the ground. She would have to be quick.

Torne was pinned to the tree like a cadaverous scarecrow, his arms snagged at odd angles among the evergreen branches. The brooch clung by a thread to his cloak. With a shudder, she plucked it away. It had burned a hole right through his cloak and jerkin, and had branded a red shadow of the winged horse on his flesh.

The Berry sisters had been right in a sense—the brooch would tolerate no others to handle it, except Green Riders. It had merely waited for the most advantageous moment to inflict its wrath, when commanded. She shuddered again and pinned it to her shirt.

She fled the carnage, pausing only to collect the belongings that had been taken from her. She and The Horse galloped away, disappearing as they went. If Immerez was to have met them days ago, he may be nearby. It wouldn't do to be snared again, just as she was escaping.

Jendara crawled to the edge of the clearing. Something like thunder and lightning crackled through her hurting head, but she was determined to stop the Greenie. It wasn't revenge. She applauded the end of the miserable Garroty's life. And though there had once been friendship with Torne, he had gone sour long ago, and tolerance was all that remained. It was the directive of her lord to waylay the message, which meant waylaying the messenger.

Who was this girl who could overpower men so much stronger than she? Torne, pegged to the tree with her own sword, was nothing worse than she had seen in battle, but the expression frozen on his face, an expression of utter amazement, would haunt her for some time to come.

Jen was amazed herself. Who would have thought the girl capable? And the brand on Torne's skin . . . Exactly who were they dealing with?

Jendara's dagger shone dully in the moonlight as she reached the edge of the road. With the throbbing in her head, standing was impossible. Her stomach knotted in nausea.

She caught a flurry of movement on the road, and the pounding of hooves. She watched the girl and horse leave at a gallop, then fade out into nothingness. Jendara curled up on the ground, resting her head on her arm.

What were they dealing with?

❧ WAYSTATION ❧

They galloped through the night, The Horse's hooves echoing dully on the road. The gray world passed as a blur, and Karigan relied on The Horse to find the way. Holding onto his mane and keeping her seat was all she could manage under the weight of invisibility. When the night changed to a lighter shade of gray, The Horse slowed to a walk and halted.

"What?" Karigan was unable to lift her head from his warm neck.

The Horse glanced both ways up and down the road, then with a swish of his tail, he stepped into the woods. No path existed here, not even a deer trail, yet as they passed through the woods, no underbrush or low hanging branches snagged them, and the ground was clear and level.

The Horse skirted a granite outcropping, and something snapped within Karigan. The world repainted itself in the colors of early dawn, and the weight of invisibility lifted from her and raised her spirits.

Snug against a granite ledge, a tiny log cabin, with a fenced paddock and attached lean-to shelter, came into view. She was nearly on top of it before she saw it. There was no sign of life anywhere near the cabin except the morning song of birds.

"What is this place?" Karigan asked The Horse. She dismounted, falling to her knees in fatigue. He nuzzled her shoulder reassuringly. The brooch had sapped Karigan's energy painfully, and it was some time before she could stand again, and even then, she had to lean against

The Horse for support as they walked to the cabin. A winged horse was carved on the door.

"Is this a Green Rider . . . shelter?" she asked.

The Horse whickered and nudged her back. She unlatched the door and stumbled inside. The one room cabin was musty from lack of use, and dust swirled about her boots with each step she took. Green Riders probably didn't travel this way often.

The interior was cloaked in darkness with the shutters fastened closed, but she had reclaimed her moonstone along with her other belongings, and now used it to light the building. Silver light stretched to all corners of the cabin, and lifted some of her fatigue and heartened her as if to remind her that she was truly alive.

A straw mattress lay on a simple bed frame against the far wall, a shelf above held some candles, a lamp, and even a few books. Wood was stacked next to a stone fireplace with snowshoes propped on the mantel. More shelves held jars sealed with wax and cork.

A cedar-lined closet contained blankets, pillows, and some clothing. Karigan tore off her own shirt, stained with Garroty's tobacco juice and, now she saw in the light, flecks of blood. Throwing it to the floor, she grabbed a white linen shirt from the closet and pulled it over her head. Then she pinned the brooch on. She felt less dirty now, having broken one more thread that had bound her to the mercenaries.

She took some bedclothes from the closet and heaped them on the table. Using what little strength she possessed, she beat on the mattress, raising all manner of dust. She staggered out of the cabin sneezing.

The Horse watched her expectantly, his ears at point. When the fit passed, Karigan untacked him. "Sorry I made you wait, Horse," she said. Her father and her riding master had both insisted that the horse that bore you must be seen to before yourself. She should have taken care of him before investigating the cabin. After all, he had carried her through the night for who knew how many miles, while she had clung to him witless under the spell of the brooch. He deserved her consideration at the very least.

Once untacked, The Horse walked into the paddock and under the roof of the shelter. Again, he watched her expectantly. Karigan followed and gazed about. A large bin containing a stash of grain and two buckets was attached to one of the walls. The grain appeared, if not fresh, unspoiled; no beetles or worms crawled in it.

She scooped some of the sweet-smelling grain into one bucket, then took the other in search of water. She did not have to go very far. A spring bubbled behind the shelter, trickling into a stream that ran down an embankment. She drank of the clear cold water, unclogging her throat of road and cabin dust, then filled the bucket and took it to The Horse. With those tasks accomplished, she returned to the cabin, wrapped a blanket around herself, and fell to the bed. She was asleep in an instant.

Karigan awoke with a shiver. Her breath fogged in the cool, damp air—not at all unusual in a northern spring, but not altogether pleasant. At first she thought it was the same morning as that of her arrival, but this morning was drizzly, whereas yesterday had promised warmth and sun. With the blanket still wrapped around her, she found a tinder box on the fireplace mantel, opened the flue of the chimney, and stacked wood on the hearth for a cheerful blaze. It wasn't long before the cabin filled with warmth.

She traded the blanket for her greatcoat and stepped outside to see to The Horse. She refilled his grain and water buckets, the pure ordinariness of the activity creating a sense of security that she hadn't felt for ages. Maybe she could stay hidden in this place and let the world continue without her.

The scent of wood smoke lured her back into the cabin. She had filled a kettle with spring water and now set it over the fire. It had been days since Jendara had let her bathe in a muddy stream, and her fastidious nature insisted upon bathing as a priority that morning. As she waited for the water to heat up, she searched the shelves again. The jars contained tea, spices, soap, and ointment, as well as an assortment of mismatched crockery. Karigan gleefully sprinkled tea leaves into a crude mug, and anticipated the boiling of the water.

She espied her old, stained shirt out of the corner of her eye where she had dropped it on the floor the previous morning. With a grim smile, she pinched a corner of the fabric between her fingers and tossed it into the fire. The rest of her clothes, except a pair of blue trousers, had been left by the roadside miles ago, deemed worthless by Jendara and Torne.

On impulse, she inspected the closet again, the scent of cedar hanging heavy and cloying in the little cabin. Within, she found more linen shirts, but only one fit reasonably well. Each shirt bore a winged horse embroidered in gold on the sleeve. Karigan glanced at her own sleeve, and sure enough, found a winged horse.

Soft hide trousers dyed in green, fur-lined greatcoats and cloaks, tall black boots, and mittens and gloves filled the closet, but only one pair of trousers fit her. She pulled out a pair of leather gloves with flaring cuffs over her hands, and liked the effect. The cuffs would hide the burns on her wrists.

"Well," she said, "everyone thinks I'm a Green Rider, so I may as well dress like one."

Everything in the closet was new and unused, and a notice tacked to the closet door requested that all items removed be reported to the quartermaster for restocking purposes. It was one more thing she would have to take care of when she reached Sacor City. If she made it.

When the water boiled, Karigan brewed some tea and set about washing herself with a cloth and honey soap. Gritting her teeth, she pried the dirt-caked dressings from her wrists. They stuck stubbornly to her skin, and the scabs broke as she pulled. Her wrists were chafed, tender, sore, and oozing, but not festering. The care of the Eletians had surpassed anything the menders in Selium could have done. She cleaned the burns, applied ointment, and dressed them with fresh bandage strips she had found in the cabinet.

A look in a dusty mirror revealed yellowing bruises on her face. She averted her gaze, Garroty's assault all too fresh in her mind.

Her stomach rumbled, and only now did she think about food. Though Torne, Jendara, and Garroty had dented her food stores, there was still some hard bread, cheese and dried meat left in the saddlebags. Further digging revealed two wrinkly apples. Karigan sat down for a feast by the crackling fire, as the warmth of the tea spread throughout her body.

It was late afternoon by the time Karigan realized she had dozed off. She stretched muscles cramped by the wooden chair, and threw a new log on the fading embers of the fire. Then she looked over the cabin's supply of books which included the fictional story, *The Journeys of Gilan Wylloland*. Karigan had read and reread it long ago, though fiction books were hard to come by. Her mother had spotted it at a fair and added it to the tiny G'ladheon library.

As a child, Karigan had pretended she was Gilan's sidekick, Blaine, traveling lands that existed only in the author's imagination. She had trooped around her father's estate brandishing a stick as her sword, and tormented the house cat as if he were the murderous dragon Viliflavo. The offended tom was named Dragon as a result.

Now Karigan was experiencing her own adventure, but it wasn't anything like *The Journeys of Gilan Wylloland*. The danger was far too real and unpleasant. Gilan and Blaine had ridden through adventure after adventure nearly unscathed. Karigan could not say the same.

Another book, titled *The Natural History of the Northern Wilderness,* had also been on the shelf of Master Ione's classroom. What possible use Green Riders would have for it, she couldn't imagine. It did not occur to her that at least one among them was interested in the wildflowers, birds, or mammals of the region. Surely Green Riders were far too busy to worry about nature.

The third and last book was bound in plain leather. It was some sort of journal. Inside, a variety of handwriting styles were scrawled across the pages, some legible, some not. She sat by the fire, absorbed by the entries.

Arrived at North waystation by dusk, wrote Pary Mantobe. *Snowshoes a must—blizzard dropping inches more of snow as I write. Am not sure I will even be able to reach the horse.*

Karigan gazed sideways at the snowshoes on the mantel. The entry was over ten years old.

Some nameless Rider wrote in another entry: *Saw a pileated woodpecker by the stream. Bear tracks in the mud of the spring. Several songbirds I couldn't identify greeted me this morning.* Karigan held the book to her chest. Bears! She hadn't even thought about them. After all her adventures thus far, they didn't seem like much of a threat by comparison.

An entry by T. Bankside read: *. . . chased by brigands all the way from North—Lt. Mapstone's knife wound festering badly. She's burning with fever—don't know if she'll live the night.* Karigan flipped the page, but the chronicler failed to mention whether or not the lieutenant had survived.

She read until dusk. Many of the entries were no more than accounts of the weather and local fauna. Some entries were set in poetry, while others were accompanied by illustrations. By the time she finished the book, she was under the impression that Green Riders were a colorful group.

Karigan left the warmth of the cabin to check on The Horse. He trotted up to the gate of the enclosure and whickered in greeting. Despite the damp weather, he seemed in good spirits.

"You deserve a break, don't you," she said. After she fed and watered him, she turned to walk back to the cabin, and walked right into a big man. She screamed and fell back, wishing herself invisible.

The man was massive, even taller than her father, with enough heft to make him appear as broad as he was tall. His face was a tangle of curly gray whiskers that hung from his face like lichen draped over spruce branches. Black eyes pierced beneath bushy brows. He was dressed in drab brown and gray, and a huge ax hung from his belt. He was a troll come to life.

He rotated slowly around, as if trying to see where she went. "Green Rider?" The voice was surprisingly gentle. "I didn't mean to frighten you. Please come back. I smelled the wood smoke and wanted to make sure all was well."

The Horse gave the giant little more than a cursory glance before sticking his nose into the grain bucket.

The weight of invisibility wore on Karigan, chafing against her like an old wound. "Who are you?" she asked, not willing just yet, to reveal herself.

The man turned in the direction of her voice, but looked through her. "I am Abram Rust, King's Forester." He moved aside his damp cloak and revealed the emblem of an evergreen embroidered on his leather vest. "I mean no harm."

Karigan dropped the invisibility and staggered against a fence post.

"You really shouldn't use your magic here," the man said, his tone matter-of-fact.

Karigan's eyes widened. Was she the last person in all of Sacoridia to know that people still used magic?

"Those who built this waystation wanted to ensure it remained hidden. They set spells around the area. Strong, old spells, I'll wager. When you use your own magic, it conflicts."

Karigan raised a brow. "How do you know all this?"

"I've known a great many Green Riders, and they've told me things. You look pale. Won't you let me help you back inside?"

Karigan clung fiercely to the fence post as he stretched out a bear paw of a hand. "Let me tell you, Forester, I've killed an evil creature from *Kanmorhan Vane,* a mercenary, and a swordmaster." The latter claim was somewhat dubious; it had been F'ryan Coblebay, using her body, who had defeated Torne, but it would serve to impress the giant.

He nodded solemnly. "I'm sure you've done a great many things, even as young as you are. Perhaps you can tell me of your adventures. It's been a while since a Green Rider has passed this way. Please let me help you in. I promise I won't harm you."

Abram's quiet voice was sincere. "Fine," Karigan said, "but I won't put up with anything. You make a wrong move, and I can't promise you'll live through the night." She wasn't sure, but Abram might have been smiling. It was hard to tell with all his whiskers, but crinkles deepened beneath his eyes. She took his hand and allowed herself to be led into the cabin.

Assured that Karigan was comfortably propped on the bed, Abram Rust sat in the chair by the fire. The chair creaked as if it might fall to pieces under his weight, but it held. Abram's bulk crowded the cabin. Silence reigned as he gazed about speculatively, every movement deliberate, as if he thought it out before he did it, even the blinking of his eyes.

"This cabin does not change, but the Riders do." His bass voice startled Karigan. "Rarely do I see the same two Riders pass through here." His whiskers drooped.

"Why is that?"

"They move on to other routes or other jobs. Many die. I visit the cabin when a Rider is present to seek news. Often they tell me that a previous occupant has died in the line of duty."

Karigan could believe it. "How long have you been coming here?"

He chuckled—it was a low throaty sound. "Years beyond count, young one. I've been roaming these woods long before the Riders decided to put a waystation here. I've roamed these woods before Zachary became king, even before his grandmother ruled. I've seen seedlings grow into mighty trees, then burn to the ground only to start the cycle anew. Through all the changes I am still Forester. I protect my domain as well as I can, though ever more it is threatened."

"Threatened?" Karigan looked around the cabin as if brigands would break through the rough-hewn log walls.

"The mills. The need to clear land to farm and settle. The need to build fleets of ships to sail the seas; and the need to warm homes during our savage winters." Abram leaned toward her, his features earnest. "There is even a growing need for paper these days. Acres of forest around here have been toppled. So far, this has been outside my domain, but they do not replant and carve ever deeper into the forest."

"But surely your job is to cut trees." Karigan looked at his ax meaningfully.

"You are correct, but this is king's land. I'm the guardian of Zachary's forests here, as I have been for three generations of his family. I am selective in my cutting. A few white pines here for ship masts, a few cedars there for shingles, and I always replant. As other forest is laid waste, my ax is used more to defend the boundaries of my domain. The folk of North are ever pressuring King Zachary to open his lands to lumbering. Some attempt it without seeking permission."

"This North is a lumber town?"

"Mostly." Abram pulled out a pipe and tobacco pouch from his cloak. He stuffed the pipe with tobacco and drew a flame on some kindling from the fire and lit it. "It began as a small settlement about a hundred years back. But with all the demands for timber nowadays, the population swelled."

Abram blew smoke rings toward the ceiling, an amused twinkle in his eyes. When the rings dissipated, the twinkle faded. "North is a lawless town now. Most of the folk descended from the original settlers left, sold their claims. Some stayed to see what wealth they could make themselves. Others opened mercantiles and inns. The fur trade is growing, too, and now I must protect the creatures within my domain, as well as the trees."

"I've never heard of North." Or had she? Something the Berry sisters had said nagged at the back of her mind.

"This must be a new route for you," Abram said. "Or maybe you are just new."

Karigan grimaced. "I'm not really a Green Rider."

Abram stood up, his head brushing the rafters. His hand went to the haft of his ax. "How can this be?" His eyes glinted dangerously. He was like a rearing bear: bristling, wrathful, and immense. His presence overpowered the room.

Frightened by this sudden transformation, Karigan tried to fade out again, but pain lanced through her head. The effort was too much.

"Who are you?" Abram demanded. "You dress like a Green Rider and use Green Rider magic. Who are you?"

"I am Karigan G'ladheon. I'm finishing a mission for a dead Green Rider."

Abram looked at her askance, then let his hand drop from the ax to his side. "It sounds an interesting story. Tell me, and I will decide." He sat again, but rigidly, his eyes still suspicious.

Karigan started with her flight from Selium and finished with her arrival to the waystation. "I am not a Green Rider," she said, "but I'm helping one."

Abram's eyes softened considerably, and he relaxed in his chair. "A long journey you've had, a brave one. I met F'ryan Coblebay once. About two years ago he passed through my domain. A lively lad, very cheerful. I'm sorry to hear of his demise. I understand now, how I mistook you for a Rider. I did think you young, though I know they will accept young people."

"I must reach Sacor City before the Mirwellians find me again."

Abram muttered something under his breath—it sounded more like a growl—and tapped his fingers on the flat of the ax head. Smoke rings drifted to the rafters one after the other. "Strange things certainly have been happening. King's men have been in the region of late, hunting out groundmites, so I understand. But a breach in the D'Yer Wall? That bodes evil. Mornhavon the Black perverted the trees of Blackveil, and they've never recovered."

"So the Eletian told me."

Abram's eyes brightened. "I'd hand over my ax to meet an Eletian. I knew in my heart they weren't legend. A sylvan folk they are, dwellers of the Elt Wood, just as I'm a dweller of this forest. And to think they were wandering through Sacoridia's Green Cloak! It's an honor."

Karigan pulled the moonstone from her pocket, certain that Abram would like to see it. The shadows of evening vanished in silver light, bringing to mind dancers in a forest clearing and moonstones glimmering on evergreen boughs.

Abram's eyes opened wide. "What is it?"

"A moonstone. A real moonstone."

"Now that I thought a legend. The Eletians gave it to you?"

"Uh, no. The Berry sisters I told you about. They gave it to me." She explained the professor's predilection for magical artifacts.

"A most unusual hobby," Abram said.

Karigan didn't hear him. Whatever it was the sisters had said about North, it was nagging her again. And then, like a bright flash of sunlight, it came to her. *East by north,* they had said. *East by north.* Karigan sat up straight.

"What is it?" Abram asked.

"I told them I didn't know how to get to Sacor City, and they said to go east by North." She had a sudden urge to giggle. When they had first told her to go east by North, she had thought it pure nonsense.

"That would make sense." Abram puffed on his pipe

as if she had said nothing unusual. "The road ends in
North. To reach Sacor City, you must travel east, and
then south. If you were traveling from Selium, you certainly went out of your way."

"The Horse refused to put one hoof on the Kingway."

"Yes, messenger horses are a strange breed. A trifle
uncanny. They've more common sense than most."

"I need to get to Sacor City. I suppose that means
going through North."

"Yes, but you best do so with utmost caution," Abram
said. "As I said, North is lawless and wild, and these are
strange times with strange folk traveling. Why, you've
already met up with brigands. I avoid North, myself."

"What kind of strange folk?" Karigan wanted to know.
"You can find brigands anywhere, even in Selium."

"There is a woman from Rhovanny, an exile, stirring
up trouble. Wants to rid all the lands of monarchs and let
the people rule." Abram stroked his beard thoughtfully.
"Anarchy, I call it. Yet there are many who follow her
and believe the rumors of new taxes on lumbering. Sup-
posedly the taxes will go toward fortifying Sacor City
and the royal house. Folks tied up in the paper and ship
building trades are infuriated.

"Other rumors circulate. The king turned down a pro-
posal to marry a princess of the Cloud Islands which
would have fostered a profitable alliance. Now the queen
of the Islands is insulted and may refuse to trade with
Sacoridia altogether. The Cloud Islands bring fruit,
spices, and whale oil.

"It is said that King Zachary still believes the old
magic should be put into use again. Most folk believe
that using magic will summon the evil of Mornhavon the
Black. When you go to North, you must be quiet about
the abilities of your brooch. The least magic will pro-
voke suspicion."

"One can only hope these rumors are isolated—" Karigan knew they would not be, however. Her own father
was suspicious of anything remotely related to magic.

"If rumors are to be believed, there have already been

assassination attempts on King Zachary. Others are calling for his brother to take the throne."

Jendara's "rightful king" was Zachary's brother, she was sure, and would explain the swordmaster's devotion as a Weapon. But what did Mirwell have to do with it?

"North is not friendly to representatives of the king, or would-be representatives." Abram thrust the poker at the logs on the fire. A flurry of sparks shot up the chimney. "As I said, I won't go there myself. Already I've been accused of being a forestry regulator."

"Is there any way to go around North?"

Abram shook his head. "If you travel east or south from here, the River Terrygood lies in your path. At this time of the year, its current runs strong and deadly. Should you attempt to ford it, even your big horse would be swept away like a leaf in a whirlpool. At midsummer or later you might ford it, but not now. The only bridge is in North."

Karigan sagged against her pillow. "Is there any good news?"

"There is. I will lead you through the woods to a point on the North Road, not far from town. In the woods, I can ensure your safety."

Karigan nodded. "That sounds encouraging. What about town itself?"

Abram grimaced, or at least his whiskers drooped. "I will not go upon the road which is beyond my boundaries. You must travel the rest of the way yourself. You should reach town by evening, and will probably wish to stay the night. Not the best of circumstances, but I know of a respectable inn that caters to the few merchants who travel this way. It is called the Fallen Tree. It is costly, but worth it. Avoid all others. When you leave North, you will find on the other end of town there is a horse track leading east and then south. It will take you partway to Sacor City. The rest will be through open countryside."

Karigan tucked her knees up to her body and wrapped her arms around them. It was beginning to sound like she was nearing the end of her journey and she grinned. "Thank you, Abram. It won't be long now before I give King Zachary his message."

"Do not let your guard down, no matter how near the king's castle you are," Abram cautioned. "It would be easy to do so, with this as the last leg of your journey. Be watchful."

"I promise."

"Good . . ." Abram tapped his pipe against the fireplace. "Then on to more pleasant topics. You told me of your adventures, so now I will tell you some of my tales."

Abram spoke long into the night. His stories took shape slowly and deliberately, his voice low and melodious. He told stories of other Green Riders who had passed through his domain:

"Disaster seemed to follow young Mayer like a crow. The shelf would fall down when he placed a book on it, or he'd trip out the door. One night he accidentally kicked a bucket of ashes on the floor and nearly set the cabin on fire." Abram pointed to a charred spot on the floor near the fireplace. "Disaster helped him on one ride, however. He was in Afton Village, which is in Coutre Province, during market. He fell right off his horse onto a fruit stand. The woman tending it, the daughter of a wealthy farmer, married him. Mayer no longer carries messages on dangerous rides, but tends blueberry barrens on his own acreage."

Abram chuckled with the memory. "There was Leon, a fierce gambler by all accounts, who came from a questionable background before he joined the messenger service. He reformed many of his ways, but never the gaming spirit, and he used to sit with me before this very fire trying to swindle the last copper from me. More often than not he succeeded. Until the very last game.

"And there was Evony, Evony with her beautiful voice who should have been at Selium for music instead of wearing the colors of the Green Riders." He shook his head sadly. "She was killed by a noble angered by the message she bore."

Abram's stories spanned more than fifty years, slowly unfolding the heritage of the Green Riders. He remembered the name of every Rider he met, along with some small detail.

"Will you remember me?" Karigan asked.

"Indeed I will. In you I see the spirit of the First Rider, she who carried the messages when Sacoridia was newly created. Even your name speaks of ancient times. *Galadeon* it would've been pronounced in the old days, not much different than today. Its meaning, however is beyond my knowledge. I expect to hear more about you in the years to come, young Karigan. This mission of yours is just a beginning."

"I just want it to be over with."

Abram shook his head. "Green Riders are always in haste. Do you know there is a legend that, during the Long War, the messenger horses of the Sacor Clans could fly? Your big red doesn't look likely to sprout wings, so I don't take the legend literally. Perhaps the horses were extraordinarily swift. Who's to say? The old days were odd and rife with magic. I imagine the legend is what inspired the winged horse insignia of the Green Riders."

Abram told tales in his melodious voice until Karigan couldn't keep her eyes open. Vaguely, she was aware of him pulling a blanket up to her shoulders and leaving as if in a cloud of smoke, the scent of tobacco lingering behind.

Green Riders trampled through Karigan's dreams. They galloped along wooded trails, horse hooves thundered over wooden bridges. A horse and Rider surged up a mountain slope, slipping and staggering on loose gravel and sand. A toothy range of snow-capped purple mountains loomed behind them.

A messenger cantered her horse along the shore, and

hooves splashed through ocean waves and sent up cascades of salty spray. The Rider laughed in pure joy. Another Green Rider rode down a cobbled city street, face grim and saber bare. The throb of hooves grew like a heartbeat.

Karigan sat astride The Horse, kicking up snow as they galloped through some winter scene. The sound of hoofbeats merged into great wingbeats as The Horse sprouted white feathered wings and flew up above the snow, above the woods and mountains, through the blue of the sky, and higher yet among the stars. Here they flew among the immortals of the heavens, past the Sword of Sevelon, past the Hunter's Belt, past the Throne of Candor the Great, and Aeryc and Aeryon smiled on them.

In time, they descended from the stars and glided through the dark of night, through the canopy of the forest to the floor. The greens and browns of the woods were intensely deep as if damp.

The beat still carried the dream, but this time it was not hooves or wings, but Abram Rust swinging his ax against the trunk of a great white pine. When he stopped, an echo continued the pulsing rhythm. He mopped his brow of sweat and turned to her. *This tree will make the mast of a ship that will carry you through the Ages.*

A winged horse was carved into the trunk. Abram Rust laughed, and with one more mighty blow, the tree crashed to its side leaving a gaping hole in the canopy to the sky. The night was coated with stars like a sprinkling of sugar.

Then the dreams dissipated, like pipe smoke.

⤳ GRAY ONE ⤴

"I've seen nothing like that," the black-smith snapped. "You had best move on. Folks here don't take kindly to your type."

Joy Overway watched in resignation as the blacksmith disappeared into the hazy dark of his shop. His was the same response she had received all day. She wondered if the good citizens of North would honestly tell her if they had seen F'ryan's horse, or the girl. Not without a hefty bribe, no doubt. She carried just enough currency to get her to Selium, then back to Sacor City, with none left over for bribes. Alas, she didn't possess Captain Mapstone's talent for seeing the truth in a person's words.

The most forthcoming citizen had been a fortune-teller in one of the inns. Joy frowned. The woman had predicted ominous and mysterious things, and had placed on the table a fortune card of a messenger fleeing arrows. "What's this?" she had asked. The fortune-teller leaned forward, her eyes wide. "You will not find what you seek if you stay on your present course," she whispered. "If you do continue down this path, your footsteps will lead you to disaster."

Joy had left in disgust. More time wasted. The fortune-teller hadn't even bothered to concoct a prediction as to where F'ryan's horse was, or where she might locate the girl. Just these vague, titillating warnings that were the common practice for the fortune-telling trade, used to draw the unsuspecting in to spend more currency for more fabricated prognostications. Strange part was, the fortune-teller hadn't even hinted at a fee for the information she did provide.

Joy mounted her horse and guided him down the muddy "main street" which flowed between ramshackle mercantiles and a seeming overabundance of pubs, and no too few brothels among them. At this peak hour in the afternoon, these places were quiet. Much of the populace was out in the woods felling trees. Soon enough however, after the sun set, the town would erupt with noise, light, and life.

When the river could be forded later in the season, most Green Riders preferred bushwhacking across the countryside in a circuitous route rather than riding directly through North. If time was of the essence, then they might gallop through town so fast that no one was the wiser. Unfortunately, Joy's mission entailed that she make inquiries in the village itself. And she had made enough of those as far as she was concerned. The people here were incredibly hostile.

She patted Red Wing's neck. "We'll spend a peaceful night at the waystation, then get as far away from this place as possible."

Red Wing bobbed his head as if in agreement. They headed south through town at a walk. Joy didn't want to give the locals the satisfaction of seeing her run.

In all, it was a strange assignment she had been sent on. Perhaps it wasn't so strange for her to look for F'ryan's horse if he still carried the message. But the girl? Someone had pull with Captain Mapstone, and that particular someone had to have a *lot* of pull. It was not in the captain's nature to involve her messengers in non-Rider affairs.

Connly had sent her a very good image of the girl. Whoever sought her must have been describing her as he sent. The girl was in her late teen years, a young woman actually, and had a well-structured face, was tall, and dressed well. An aristocrat? Connly didn't elaborate.

Joy smiled. Every contact with Connly was like a gentle caress on her mind. Every night they united this intimate way, their minds touching, sending words and pictures back and forth. It helped make their separation more bearable, though it was no substitute for being together.

She reined Red Wing around a group of people, the King-Haters, as she had taken to calling them. The Anti-Monarchy Society was just so much hoof glop. They were spreading ill rumors about King Zachary, and the people of North fell into their cause with relish.

"You are a slave, sister!" one of the people told her. "A kingless land is a free land. Monarchy is tyranny."

Joy urged Red Wing into a canter before the King-Haters could start chanting more slogans. "I wouldn't be doing this job if I didn't believe in my king," she told her horse. "I'm no slave."

Once Joy was out of town, she exhaled with relief, and pulled Red Wing to a walk. She could feel her muscles loosen as the tension lifted from her. The road was quiet except for the chorusing of peepers in the lengthening shadows. Only one other rider headed in-town. He was cloaked entirely in gray and rode at a leisurely walk. Red Wing pressed his ears back against his neck.

"What is it?" she asked him.

Red Wing snorted and sidestepped as the rider drew abreast of them. The man was cloaked and hooded, and she couldn't tell anything about him, except for a tendril of gold hair that escaped his hood. He drew his horse to a halt.

Joy nodded to him and rode on by. He did not speak to her, or even acknowledge her, and she was glad. Something about him made the back of her neck twinge. She glanced over her shoulder to see if he had ridden on. He hadn't. He was following her.

He drew a black arrow from his quiver and nocked it to his bow.

"Oh, gods," she whispered. Connly had told her how F'ryan died. Two black arrows in his back.

She had only to touch Red Wing to send him flying into a gallop. She veered off the road, crouching low in the saddle. There was nowhere to hide, though. The woods were clear cut.

Red Wing stretched his legs downslope where a boggy pond was rimmed with a thicket of trees. In the trees, bow and arrow would be next to useless. The gray rider's horse pounded after her, his hoofbeats like an echo of Red Wing's. The gray rider drew abreast of her even over the uncertain ground, plunging over snags of wood, and across slippery granite.

The gray rider dropped his reins, guiding his horse with the touch of his legs and knees. He drew his bowstring and an arrow sang.

Red Wing stumbled beneath Joy, fell away like her own footing lost. She rolled clear as he tumbled haunches over head, the air thick with his screams, his hooves flailing up toward the sky. Then he stilled. Dust drifted and settled about him where he lay dead, an arrow in his throat.

Joy hauled herself behind him, face wet with tears, and grief jammed like a fist in her throat. Her leg was twisted at the wrong angle, her thigh bone protruding through ragged muscle and skin like an ivory bull's horn. She could not feel it, but darkness hovered at the edges of her mind. She drew her saber though it would be no defense against arrows.

The gray rider sat still and silent on his steed. He nocked another arrow and aimed it at her. She heard whispers issue from his hood as if he spoke invocations over the arrow. Or maybe it was the gods calling her.

Pain exploded in Joy's chest. "Connly," she croaked. The world became gauzy around her, and she could feel life leaking away and a darkness spreading in her chest like a disease.

The gray rider sat silhouetted on his horse. He drew out yet another arrow and nocked it to the bow.

She clutched her wound and blood gouted out as if to fill her hands like cups. "Why?" She mouthed the word more than spoke it.

The gray rider drew the bow string. "You shall serve me."

His voice, she thought, was melodic.

He loosed the arrow.

Joy seemed to be looking at the night sky filled with bright pinpoints of stars where the gods awaited her. She drifted; was drawn upward. Somewhere above her, vast wings fluttered—it was Westrion come to take her soul to the heavens. Cares fell away from her as she floated light and incorporeal.

Then, as if a hand reached into her chest and clenched her heart, she felt pain all over again, and cold. She was wrenched earthward, against the forces of the heavens.

No! she cried. *Westrion!*

She was echoed by an angry screech. The flutter of wings grew more distant and soon vanished.

"You shall serve me," the melodic voice said.

Joy's feet were planted on the ground. She looked skyward, but the starry night was gone, and the air was hazy gray and dull, lifeless. The arrows projected from her chest like porcupine quills and she tried to pull them out, but only enveloped herself with pain.

"They mark you as mine. Think of them as your collar, slave." The gray rider still sat upon his horse, but he was no longer gray. His cloak and hood shimmered with the colors of the rainbow, and he almost looked as if he sat upon the air, for his horse blended in with the gray and lifeless world.

Her corpse, and Red Wing's, lay insubstantial, ghostly. Her body was splayed and broken, her blood had saturated her shirt and coat with darkness. It was not red in her vision. Only the winged horse brooch had any color. It blossomed with a cold, golden gleam. She reached for it, but her hand passed through her body.

She looked at her hands. They were flesh colored, they flexed open and closed into fists. They seemed alive. Was this what it was like to be a ghost? The living world became dead?

Joy.

Joy looked behind her, and there stood F'ryan Coblebay, more real than anything in the midst of the gray world. His green uniform was almost vibrant. *Take my hand,* he said. He stretched his gloved hand toward her.

Behind him stood a host of Green Riders dressed in uniforms from centuries gone by. They whispered and shifted like shadows. *Take his hand,* they whispered to her. Red Wing stood there with him, his mane and tail flowing in no natural wind.

Joy reached for him, the pain constricted around her chest, the darkness spread.

Come, F'ryan said. *You are one of us.*

What has happened? She gasped.

This is a between place, F'ryan said. *The Shadow Man keeps us from going beyond. His arrows, they are anchors. Take my hand.*

Take his hand, the others whispered.

"Do not listen," the gray rider said. "Or you will be tormented forever by pain. It would be worse than any hell wrought by your mythologies."

Take my hand, F'ryan said.

Joy fought the pain, her fingers touching his. They were warm, felt like real flesh. He grasped her hand and held it. The arrows seared her chest. If she went to the gray rider, she would be relieved of the pain. But it was not right for her to join him.

❖ NORTH ❖

Karigan awoke with the echo of hoofbeats fading with her dreams, and all but forgotten as she attacked her morning tasks. The Horse was promptly fed, watered, and rubbed down. Breakfast was prepared and eaten with dispatch. She took up a broom which had stood hidden in a dark corner and swept the cabin thoroughly.

She checked her packs to make sure all was in order. She found F'ryan Coblebay's love letter to Lady Estora in the message satchel. Maybe Torne and Jendara had thought any document was valuable and so saved it. Certainly they weren't being sentimental. Karigan herself had forgotten all about it. The important thing was that the message to King Zachary was still intact, the seal unbroken.

As she folded and returned the bedclothes to the cedar closet, she espied a tongue of leather sticking out between some blankets. It was a swordbelt and scabbard. A swordbelt would make it more difficult to separate her from the saber. It was a loose fit even when buckled on the last hole, but it would do. She tucked the excess leather beneath the belt, and sheathed the saber into the plain black scabbard.

In an effort not to look so much like a Green Rider in a town that would not welcome one, she dressed in her own blue trousers, and rolled up the sleeves of her new linen shirt to hide the insignia. It was warm enough anyway. She tied the greatcoat around the bedroll, but the brooch remained pinned to her shirt. It wasn't supposed to identify one as a Green Rider anyway, except to another Green Rider. It stood to reason that the tack might give her away, but she hoped nobody would look close enough to notice.

She took one last glance around the cabin and sighed. The stories it could tell . . . *I suppose I heard most of them last night from Abram.*

Gathering up the tack and packs, Karigan stepped outside into sunshine. Reluctantly she latched the door behind her and walked to the paddock, the saber slapping awkwardly against her thigh.

The path was still moist from the previous day's rain, and the air was heavy with the smells of evergreen and bayberry drying in the sun. Bayberry? She stopped in her tracks. There hadn't been a bayberry bush next to the path yesterday, had there? But there it was, next to a patch of bunchberry flowers.

"I don't believe it."

Each bunchberry flower was perfect except for one missing a petal. She plucked it and twirled it in front of her eyes. Could it be? She slipped it into her pocket and snapped off a bayberry branch just in case.

Abram awaited her in the paddock, patting The Horse on his neck. "Good morning," he said. "Your guide awaits you."

Karigan returned his greeting with a grin. She set the saddle on the paddock fence and slipped the bridle over The Horse's head. "I appreciate this. The Mirwellians won't find me in the forest."

Abram returned her smile, then helped her place the saddle on The Horse's back. "That is correct."

Abram insisted that she ride The Horse though he would be on foot—he claimed his long legs could keep up with any steed. Karigan pulled the girth tight, hoisted up her sagging swordbelt, and mounted. Abram led them out of the paddock, The Horse's hooves sinking into the mud.

Karigan ducked beneath tree limbs laden with water from the previous day's rain, but still managed to get drenched. Biters clouded in the shade, their numbers beginning to wane as the season progressed.

Sun filtered through the trees and turned droplets clinging to spiderwebs into lacy jewels. Fiddleheads unfurled into broad cinnamon ferns, and the leaves of aspen, birch, and maple trees fully budded, blotting out the sky more than ever.

Abram guided her along no visible trail. He skirted granite ledges and winter blow-downs, stepped across gurgling streams that would dry out by summer's end, and wove his way through patches of brush. Whatever path he followed, it was easy to travel. He hummed the entire way, his beard bristling as if he were smiling. Karigan wondered at his content and was surprised he did not smoke. When she remarked upon this, he replied, "I need no smoke here. Into the cities and villages, by the side of a fire, that is where I need it."

They spoke little as they traveled, though they stopped periodically so Abram could show Karigan delicate lady's slippers, bluets, and trillium, his huge hands dwarfing the blossoms. The sun changed the shapes of shadows in the woods and lifted a moist vapor from the damp ground. Pine needles scattered on the forest floor dried in the sun, and left a strong tang of balsam in the air. Somewhere a woodpecker could be heard tapping on a tree.

Abram stopped and looked up. Karigan followed his gaze and beheld the tallest white pine she had ever seen. Its girth was so wide that even Abram couldn't wrap his arms all the way around it.

"This tree is hundreds of years old," he said. "I never fail to be awed by it. See up the trunk, the scar that looks like the shape of a gull in flight?"

She squinted, barely able to discern crude wings and a body cut into the bark. The scar was dark, an old carving. "Who would bother to do such a thing?" She was familiar with the carvings made by lovers, but who would carve a gull into the trunk of a tree in the middle of the wilderness?

"One who was a forester long before me."

"But why do it in the first place?" Carving initials into a tree was a silly way to express love. Love was a bit silly, anyway. But it was also cruel if the love ended.

Abram slapped the tree trunk with his palm as if meeting an old friend. "This was a king's tree, young one. Marked to one day be the mast of some great sailing vessel. The mark is that of Clan Sealender."

"Sealender?" Karigan furrowed her brow. It was a new clan name to her.

"The bloodline that ruled Sacoridia before Hillander. When Sealender died out, Hillander battled for and won the right of succession. Both are descended from the original Sacor Clans."

"Oh." Once again, Karigan had been stumped by what was probably common knowledge. Next time, if there was a next time, she wouldn't be so neglectful of her history lessons.

"I would not cut this tree down if the king himself commanded me to do so." Abram looked up the tree trunk again, the crinkles beneath his eyes deepening with a smile.

They left the pine behind, circling around tiny spruces waiting in the shade for their chance to grow tall. The afternoon sun waned, forest shadows shifted as they walked. Abram stopped, his head stooped, listening. Blows could be heard, not the crisp *rat-a-tat* of a woodpecker, rather the chopping of an ax against wood.

"We are near the boundary," Abram said, "but that still sounds too close."

Without further comment, he bounded away, agile as any deer despite his bulk. Karigan watched after him for a shocked moment before urging The Horse to follow behind at a trot. Abram hadn't been boasting when he said his long legs could match the pace of any horse.

Two men hammered at a tree with broad axes. They had already felled one tree. Two oxen stood by chewing cud, a sledge chained to their harness to drag away timber. The two men didn't hear Abram and Karigan approach, so engrossed by their chore were they.

"Stop!" Abram bellowed.

Karigan would not have been surprised if the whole of Sacoridia stilled at his command. The very trees shivered. The two men paused in mid-strike, terror flashing across their faces when they took in Abram.

"You are on king's land." Abram fisted his hands on his hips. Sun glinted off the blade of his ax.

The two glanced at each other and raised their axes defensively. "King never cuts here," one said, and he spat. "He can't protect this forest forever."

The second man spoke more uncertainly. "Soon the demand for paper—"

"You are breaking king's law," Abram broke in without hesitation, his voice strong and sure. "Poaching the king's trees or wild beasts is punishable by death. I am commissioned to mete out the king's justice where this forest is concerned."

The first man glowered, but the second quailed. Karigan glanced at Abram in horror. His face was unreadable. Surely he wouldn't—

Abram stepped forward and the first man raised his ax, this time offensively. Abram rushed him and grabbed the handle before the ax could cut him, breaking the haft over his knee. The second man dropped his ax voluntarily.

"Karigan," Abram said heavily, "this is where we must part. North isn't far."

"What are you going to—"

"Farewell, Green Rider." He nodded his head in dismissal. "It was a good meeting."

"I—" Abram's look told her that she had better move on. "Good-bye," she said. "Thank you." But he had already turned back to the two men and did not hear.

Karigan caught the first man watching her with a dark scowl as she rode away. Surely Abram wouldn't carry out the death penalty. It wasn't in his nature to do so. But the two tree poachers didn't know it.

The trees simply ended. Karigan and The Horse were
swathed in full sunlight for the first time since their
strange journey together had begun. The Horse snorted
and sidestepped, and Karigan covered her eyes until they
adjusted to the light. She let out a low whistle. As far as
the eye could stretch, the land was a desert of tree
stumps. Only on the most distant hills, and behind her,
could she find trees.

They skirted the edge of the woods until they met the
road. Karigan cast a cautious eye before stepping onto
it. The road was a muddy gutter of cloven hoofprints,
and was rutted with gullies full of water where timber
sledges had grooved the surface. They cantered as much
to escape the devastation of the forest as to reach the
town of North by sunset. The absence of trees exposed
them to watching eyes, and left Karigan feeling very
vulnerable.

As dusk deepened, a horseman approached at a quick
trot. Karigan slowed The Horse to a jog, and patted the
hilt of her saber to ensure it still hung at her side.

It wasn't easy to distinguish the horseman from the
shadows. He was garbed in a long gray cloak with the
hood thrown over his face. A quiver of arrows was
strapped to his back, and a longbow crossed his shoulder.
His stallion was a tall gray, at least as tall as The Horse,
but more finely proportioned. The silver of his tack jin-
gled as he trotted.

The Horse clung to the right side of the road and laid
his ears back.

"What is it?" Karigan asked, tightening her grip on
the hilt of her sword. The Horse shook his head, his ears
flickered back and forth.

Karigan licked her lips nervously as the gray-cloaked
figure drew closer. It would not do to look frightened.
The more confident she appeared, the less likely she
would be attacked if the horseman was a brigand. She
released the hilt of her sword, fingers trembling, and
turned to the horseman.

"Good evening," she said.

The rider turned his hood toward her, its depths vacant of all but shadows. An inexplicable dread weighed her down as the hidden gaze raked across her, holding her for some interminable time, perhaps seconds. She sensed something fair that had been tainted, something of age, but young. Something terrible.

The horseman nodded, and the gray stallion trotted on by. Karigan sagged in relief, releasing the breath she had held during the momentary exchange.

The jingle of tack and plod of hooves paused as if the rider had stopped to gaze after her. She glanced over her shoulder, but no one was there. Karigan wilted in her saddle. There was no place for the horseman to hide, yet he was gone.

"Don't tell me I'm beginning to see other ghosts," she murmured, but the cold dread returned when she remembered F'ryan Coblebay's last words: *Beware the shadow man.*

Sunset blooded the sky behind them as she clucked The Horse into a canter, more eager than ever to reach civilization. They did not slow until they entered town, and her initial relief turned into misgiving as she took in the shamble of clapboard wooden structures with garish hand-painted signs advertising mercantiles, a smithy, inns, and pubs.

The pubs and inns were already brightly lit from within, and bodies were pressed up against the windows. Bawdy music and loud laughter drifted into the sultry dark. She passed The Prancing Lady, The Broken Tree, and The Twisted Mule, and at The Full Moon, a man staggered into the street with a woman riding piggyback. Her face was gaudily painted, she wore a corset and little else, and was covering the man's eyes with her hands.

"Ha, ha, Wilmy," he said, wobbling this way and that down the street. "You let me see now, y'hear? Y'let me, an' we'll have good fun." They disappeared down an alley. The woman's giggles echoed back out to the street, were followed by silence, then delighted squeals.

After a time, Karigan caught up to, and followed behind, a horse cart. Something large and heavy bumped on its wooden bottom as the wheels jolted over ruts in the street.

"Hey, Garl," said a man who leaned against a hitching post. "Watcha find?"

The cart driver hauled on the reins and *whoaed* his horse to a halt. "Remember that Greenie that come by the other day, asking all those questions 'bout some girl? I found her over by Millet's Pond, two arrows in 'er."

"Just as well," the hitching post man said. "We've no need for those types 'round here."

Karigan went cold. Another dead Green Rider? With two arrows in her? She rode by the cart, The Horse's head lowered as if he knew a dead Green Rider lay in it. Karigan didn't want to look, but could not avoid the glint of light from a nearby inn on the Rider's gold hair. She lay half on her side, one gauntleted hand stretched out, the fingers slightly curled. The other hand lay across her stomach. She looked as if she might be asleep, except for the two black arrows protruding from her chest. The drinking song issuing from the inn made a grotesque dirge.

Karigan urged The Horse on, and the Rider's gold-winged horse brooch shimmered in the corner of her eye. Shaken, she stared straight ahead, the conversation and laughter of the two men fading behind her. Didn't they care that a woman lay dead next to them? Didn't they know that Green Riders were brave and deserved more than being thrown into the back of some dirty horse cart?

A somber mood took Karigan. She dismounted in front of The Fallen Tree, the inn Abram had recommended. The carved sign above the door showed an ax embedded in a tree stump. No mistake about what this town was known for.

A stableboy came to claim The Horse. "Is there room for the night?" she asked.

"Yep."

"Then I'll see to my horse myself."

The boy shrugged. It wasn't what guests usually requested, but she didn't want to chance anyone seeing her gear close up. She led The Horse through an alley to the rear of the inn where a stable and small paddock stood lighted by lanterns. Karigan hitched The Horse to a railing and untacked him there. Once free, he trotted to the center of the paddock for an enthusiastic roll in the mud. Karigan chuckled despite herself.

The stableboy watched The Horse grunt and rub his neck and side into the ground. "Where'd you find the horse?" he asked.

"Huh?"

"I saw his scars. A Green Rider was asking after such a horse the other day."

Karigan had to bite her tongue to regain her composure. The Green Rider had been looking for The Horse? "Are you implying I stole a horse, boy?"

"Why—" The boy looked at her with big eyes.

"I bought that horse from a mercenary, at a fair price, too." Karigan used as stern a voice as possible, and it was working. She blessed her fast thinking. A mercenary's horse would be prone to scars, too.

"Sorry, ma'am," the boy said.

Karigan smiled. Now the boy addressed her with the proper tone of respect, and eyed the saber girded at her side with trepidation.

He thought I was some runaway, she thought. Then remembered that she was. "I don't want any slack on his grain. Give him a good rubdown, and make sure there isn't a fleck of dust on him come morning."

She fished for a coin in her pocket. Her father always insisted on tipping stableboys. He claimed they were always underpaid. It hurt to part with a copper—a night at the inn would drain her resources as it was—but she needed to put the stableboy's mind on something other than scarred horses and Green Riders. The boy received the coin enthusiastically, and reassured her that her horse would be well cared for.

Karigan caught up her gear, the bridle slung over her shoulder and the saddle over an arm, and entered the inn from a side door. She was struck by the aroma of broiled meat and fresh baked bread. Her mouth watered over a table of cooling pies and a cauldron of stew with chunks of beef, potatoes, and parsnips simmering over a hearthfire. She hadn't eaten a true meal since Seven Chimneys. Servants dashed in and out of the kitchen through a swinging door, balancing platters heaped with, or depleted of, food.

"Out-out-out!" An imposing, rotund woman brandished her ladle at Karigan. "I won't put up with horse leather in *my* kitchen."

Karigan rushed through the door, narrowly dodging a servant with a tray of empty tankards. She stepped away from the doorway to avoid further collisions.

The common room was clean and quiet—a good sign. Only a handful of tables were occupied. A woman sat by the stone fireplace reading fortune cards for a burly man, and an equally burly woman. They guffawed at whatever predictions the fortune-teller had told them. A single musician tuned his lute in a corner. It was hardly what she expected to find in North after what she had seen already.

"Do you have a request, lady?"

The musician gazed at her intently. She had seen the same expression on Estral's face often enough, and knew that minstrels missed very little.

"Uh, no. Not right now."

The man, perhaps middle-aged, bowed his head gracefully and turned his attention back to his lute. For a warm-up, he plucked a quiet song.

A skinny man with thinning red hair approached her. His fine vest and coat suggested he was either a merchant or an innkeeper. For some reason, Karigan always expected innkeepers to be a bit more rotund.

"You wish a room?" he asked.

"Yes. A single."

He raised his brow appraisingly at her trying to ascertain, she was sure, her ability to pay for a single room. His expression was doubtful, but he turned on his heel.

"This way," he said. He led her up a narrow stairway to the second floor.

The room he showed her was only slightly larger than the closet she had lived in at Selium, but it looked clean and comfortable. The mattress was feather rather than straw, and was covered with a thick quilt. An oil lamp, not lard or a candle, stood on a table next to the bed. She began to wonder what the expense of a night's stay was going to add up to, and if she was going to end up in the scullery washing dishes, or in the stable mucking stalls. Better that than spending the night in one of those other raffish inns.

"The price," the innkeeper said, "is four silvers." He held his palm out expectantly.

Karigan's mouth dropped open. *Outrageous!* Ordinarily, such an establishment would charge two silvers, and even that was considered somewhat steep. The innkeeper still stood there, hand outstretched, his expression growing more suspicious. Karigan pursed her lips and dug into her pocket. She dropped the precious silvers into the man's hand. He bowed.

"This is robbery." She hooked a lank strand of hair behind her ear. "Even the finest inns in Corsa don't charge this much."

"This is North," the innkeeper said. "The extra expense covers security. You may have dinner when you are ready." He glanced down his nose at her saber, and sniffed. "Arms are generally left in the guestrooms." Karigan self-consciously hitched the slipping swordbelt into its proper place. The innkeeper removed a key from a ring on his belt. "If you are concerned about your . . . valuables, you may use this." It was obvious he thought she didn't possess much in the way of valuables.

You'd treat me just fine if you knew I was the heir of the wealthy Clan G'ladheon, wouldn't you. "Thank you." She wanted the key, took it, and shut the door in the innkeeper's face.

She would go down to the common room for dinner in a moment, but first she was due for a cleaning in the washbowl. She splashed water on her face and contemplated the day's events. First the "tree poachers" in Abram's woods, then the strange horseman, followed by another dead Rider in a cart. Garl, the cart driver, had said she was asking about some girl. The stableboy mentioned that a Green Rider had asked after a horse. Why did the Rider search for a girl instead of F'ryan Coblebay?

Karigan's head jolted up. Water dripped from her face and splashed into the washbowl. *She couldn't have been looking for me, could she?* How would anyone know to look for her in connection to The Horse? That is, if she was the "girl" the Rider had been referring to. . . . Karigan blotted her face dry with the linen towel lying next to the bowl. No matter what the answer, she still had a message to deliver, and with the death of another Green Rider, it appeared she must be more cautious than ever.

She unwound the bandages from her wrists. The burns were healing surprisingly well, though there would be some scarring. It seemed ages since her encounter with the creature of *Kanmorhan Vane.* Would anyone believe her when she told that story? The burns could have come from anywhere, even a campfire as Torne had once suggested.

She gazed in a mirror to assess her appearance. The bruises on her face had faded some, but were still visible. There wasn't anything she could do about that. The winged horse insignia was still hidden on her rolled sleeve. She unbuckled her swordbelt and left it with the rest of her gear. There was nothing about her that suggested she was connected to the Green Riders. Satisfied with her appearance, she locked the room behind her and trotted down the stairs to put some food into her empty stomach.

A few more patrons occupied the common room. Some were dressed well enough to be merchants. Others were in either dusty traveling clothes, or the plain garb of the locals. The minstrel strummed a cheerful tune about how a chicken changed the fortune of a farmer. It was a simple tune, perfectly suited for an inn. Karigan felt the minstrel's eyes follow her as she walked across the room to a small empty table.

She dropped into a chair, only to discover that the table was an enormous tree stump coated with varnish. The number of growth rings convinced her that this tree was older than the tall white pine Abram had shown her.

"You wanting some food, missy?"

Startled, Karigan looked up at an aproned servant. "Yes. Anything that's hot."

"Thought so. You look like you haven't seen real food in a while. Drink?"

"Wine, if you have it."

"Old Ram Canoro makes blueberry wine which we sell. It's a bit rough at first, but good enough when you get used to it."

"That's fine."

The servant disappeared and Karigan settled into her chair to listen to the minstrel. Her eyes roamed the room. Most patrons were in deep discussion, a few played board games. The fortune-teller was alone now, and stared back at her unabashed. She was dressed garishly in red and blue, with colored glass beads dangling from her neck. Rings flashed on her fingers as she absently shuffled fortune cards. Without preamble, she left her table and walked over to Karigan's. She sat without greeting or permission, and adjusted her skirts about her legs, the beads of her necklaces clinking together.

Karigan shifted uncomfortably in her chair. "Something I can do for you?"

"I am Clatheas, Seer." The woman spoke with an intensity that suggested many held contempt for her title. "Perhaps I can do something for *you*."

"Sorry, I don't want my fortune told." Ordinarily, she wouldn't have minded, but she didn't possess the coin for something so frivolous.

"I won't read your fortune. These cards merely mirror one's thoughts." Clatheas spread them across the table. Colorful pictures of kings, queens, knights, merchants, seafarers, and courtiers gazed back up at Karigan. Clatheas swept them back into a deck, nimbly shuffling them as she spoke. "The cards can read nothing. They simply reflect." Her eyes, deep brown, focused on Karigan's. "I'm more interested in the ghost that shadows you."

Karigan half-stood, her chair scraping the floor. When she noticed other patrons watching, she reddened and slid back into her seat. The patrons turned their attention back to their games and conversations.

"You see—?"

"I see a young man in green. Too young to die, yet two arrows pierce his back. You know of him?"

"I—"

"He struggles to speak to you, and to me. He is speaking now, but we cannot hear. He hasn't the power now."

"Why do you tell me this?"

"Why should I not? You are more than you seem, though you try to conceal it. The ghost is warning you of something. If you know what it is, perhaps you can avoid it. If not . . ." Clatheas shrugged.

"Here you go, missy." The servant slid a bowl full of steaming stew, a platter of sliced beef and mushrooms, bread, and a goblet of wine in front of Karigan. "Now don't distract the girl from her vittles, Clatheas." The servant left humming to herself. Clatheas scowled after her.

Karigan broke off a piece of warm, moist bread and offered it to the seer. She waved it off, her necklaces jangling. Without another word, Karigan shoveled succulent stew into her mouth, sucking in air when it burned her tongue. Her stomach growled voraciously, and the seer watched her take every bite. More tables filled up, and the noise level of the common room elevated as the minstrel played foot-stomping, hand-clapping, jig-dancing, boisterous music.

When Karigan had eaten her fill, she sank in her chair with a hand on her gorged belly. More than half the food still remained on the table, but her stomach, which had grown accustomed to so little food, would accept no more. She sipped lazily at the wine. At first it was a bit sour, but after a while, she was convinced of its fruity flavor.

Clatheas shuffled her cards and leaned toward Karigan so she couldn't be overheard by others. "I find it interesting that a Green Rider should be searching for one who matches your description."

Karigan sat up, all attention now. "*My* description?"

"There are some who know seers can be helpful. They will listen to seers and believe." Clatheas frowned. "I saw only that Rider's disaster when I looked at the cards."

"She's dead."

"I warned her something terrible was going to happen. You know of her, then?"

"I saw her body."

Clatheas clucked. "I didn't learn her name, but she sought a girl and a horse. You wouldn't know what it means, would you?"

"You're the seer," Karigan said.

"You don't know either. Curious. A ghost follows you, you conceal who you are, and a Green Rider searching for someone of your description dies." She cut the deck in half and turned over a card. The picture was a rider in green, on a red steed, fleeing arrows.

Karigan's eyes widened. She had seen fortune cards before, but never this one. "How—?"

Clatheas' brown eyes were fervent. "Were I you, Green Rider who-is-not, I wouldn't linger in North. Heed the warning of the card, for it is the same one I saw when I read for that dead Rider."

⤳ KING-HATERS ⤳

Karigan sat immobilized, and it was some moments before she realized Clatheas had left her to wander among other tables to offer the telling of fortunes. More people trickled into the inn. A group sat in a tight cluster at an adjacent table. Among them was a petite, titian-haired woman. When she spoke, her eyes afire, all others leaned in closer to listen. Karigan strained to hear, too.

"Tomorrow," the woman said with a clipped Rhovan accent, "we shall hold the rally. The people will hear us and support us. It is the people who shall rule, not a man who thinks himself one among the gods."

There was a murmur of agreement. "From North to Sacor City," one man said above the others.

The woman smiled, dimples deepening on either side of her mouth, and Karigan saw how people could be magnetically drawn to her. She hushed the group. "And then the Lone Forest. We will go to the Lone Forest and answer to none but ourselves."

A babble of approval circulated among the group.

"Pie, missy?"

Karigan jumped, startled out of her observations, and wrenched her attention away from the group to the servant. "I don't think so." She smiled with regret, for the pies had looked mouth-watering. "But maybe you could tell me who that woman at the next table is."

"You thinking about joining their group?"

"I don't know what their group is."

The servant pushed a wisp of hair from her eyes.

"Why, they're the Anti-Monarchy Society." She glanced over at them, then said in a whisper, "There's some that call them the King-Haters. Their ideas are a trifle far-fetched, but they say things folks want to hear. That's Lorilie, their leader. Rumor has it that she was Rhovan aristocracy until King Thergood cast her out of the country for her beliefs. Ever since, she's been a thorn in Zachary's side. Surprises me that the Greenie wasn't looking for *her* the other day. Lorilie Dorran's considered an outlaw in Sacoridia, but seeing as most everyone else in North is an outlaw, it doesn't much matter. I'm surprised you haven't heard of her."

"I haven't heard the news of late. It's been a long while since I've traveled through a town of any size."

"I guessed. Your ribs must be bare bones beneath that shirt. Ah, well. Most aren't sure what to make of Lorilie, but they can't dispute her ideas." She collected the remains of Karigan's dinner and ambled away toward the kitchen.

Karigan glanced over at the Anti-Monarchy Society. They talked among themselves in excited voices while Lorilie Dorran watched on, somehow separate and above her companions. Then she turned as if feeling Karigan's gaze on her and smiled. With a word or two to her companions, she sauntered over.

"Are you interested in our group, sister?" she asked.

"Uh . . . I don't know what you're about, except that you don't like kings."

Lorilie pointed to the chair Clatheas had occupied earlier. "You mind?" Karigan shook her head and Lorilie sat down. "We are more than what some call us—King-Haters." She made a wry face. "Our desire is to uplift the common folk who presently slave beneath the oppressive forces of the aristocracy."

"I'm all for showing the aristocracy a thing or two," Karigan said, "but I don't understand the slave part. Slavery was banned in Sacoridia during the Second Age."

"Oh, they won't call it slavery, but that's what it is.

Landless folk breaking their backs to fill the pockets of their overlords."

"Overlords?"

"The landowners—the aristocracy. And of course it's the common folk who pay the bulk of the taxes, while the aristocrats and merchants get fatter."

"Wait a minute." Karigan sat up a little straighter. "Merchants pay taxes."

"Yes, they do, but it's not proportionate with their wealth. They should be taxed more heavily, but they are favored by the king." Lorilie leaned forward conspiratorially and put her hand on Karigan's wrist. "Look, sister, we're all in this together. Only by ousting the king and the aristocracy will we be able to raise the people to their proper level."

"Hey, Lorilie!" called one of her friends. "Skeller wants to go over tomorrow's speech."

Lorilie nodded. "One moment." Then again her intense eyes were on Karigan. "Sister, a revolution has begun, and a new order will arise." She smiled grimly, then joined her followers. She spoke softly to them, and they huddled close to her. Then, after a bout of loud laughter, they left the inn.

Karigan swallowed the last of her wine. A revolution? A new order? It was too mind-boggling for one who had been on the road so long. Although the dig about merchants annoyed her, and understandably so . . . Everyone had the opportunity to do as her father had—to gain wealth and status through backbreaking work. And would Lorilie Dorran punish her father for all his good work, and for supporting commerce in Sacoridia?

I don't even want to think about it. I've got enough problems to last nine lives of a cat.

Karigan stretched and yawned. The wine and food had made her somnolent, and the sooner to bed, the sooner to rise and leave North behind. As she strode across the common room, the minstrel's eyes followed her without his missing a note of the song he sang. She scowled at him, then realized that several of the men in the common room, many lumberjacks by the look of their wool shirts and broad shoulders, followed her with their eyes, too.

The servant met her at the bottom of the stairs. "Don't concern yourself with these lugs, missy. Innkeeper Wiles keeps order here, though he can't keep the men from looking." She rolled her eyes knowingly. "This is a respectable inn. If they want the company of a . . . woman, there are plenty of other inns in town where they can find it."

"Thanks," Karigan said. She wondered how the innkeeper enforced order in such a rough town, but was glad to hear that he did so one way or the other.

Once in her room, she changed into the oversized Green Rider shirt to wear to bed. She sank into the comfortable feather mattress anticipating a restful night, but discovered she could only toss and turn. Voices and the clatter of dishware disturbed her some, but it was the events of the day that jostled around in her mind and kept her awake.

In the small hours, when the music and chatter in the common room died down, sleep began to take her, but she suddenly jolted awake, quivering. The hairs on her arms stood on end, and her heart beat wildly, but she didn't know what had roused her. Then there it was, faint, barely perceived footfalls in the corridor outside her room. A worn floorboard creaked.

A shadow darkened the crack between the door and floor, then passed over the keyhole. The doorknob twisted one way, then the other. Karigan held her breath, stiffened, listening, afraid to move. Her sword was on the other side of the room with the brooch.

A sharp light pierced through the keyhole, searching, probing.

Karigan sat up and threw the covers aside. The cold night spread goosepimples across her body as she swung her legs over the side of the bed. She tiptoed across the icy floor, took up her saber, and waited by the door.

Strangely, the door seemed to flex and swim in her eyes. She blinked, but the door still distorted and warped in fluid motions, and she felt with a creeping certainty that it wasn't her own groggy vision that warped the door, but magic. She reached for her brooch unconsciously, and discovered it was warm to her touch. The door would give in moments, and with growing apprehension, she knew it was the Shadow Man, the rider in gray, who intended to enter her room.

The shaft of light probing through the keyhole suddenly withdrew, but before Karigan could breathe a sigh of relief, something else came through. At first it was so dark and tiny, as tiny as a fly, she could not see it, but it was even darker than the night, a small black orb that floated on the air, and her eyes fixed on it. The orb bobbed and drifted toward her, expanding as it did so.

It was oily black and radiated a halo of darkness that pushed away even the possibility of light. The orb continued to grow. Tendrils of energy flared and arched across its surface, searing and scorching. Karigan backed away, but the thing, now the size of her head, moved with her. Karigan backed until she was pressed up against the wall and could go no farther, and still it moved toward her.

Then heavy footsteps clumped outside. "Who's there?" a man asked.

The door hardened into ordinary, solid pine wood again. The orb halted, wavered uncertainly, then shrank in the blink of an eye and whisked out through the keyhole. Feet padded lightly away and Karigan closed her eyes in relief. Moments later someone tapped on her door. Holding the saber level before her, she opened the door carefully. To her surprise, the minstrel stood there, his lute in one hand and a glowing oil lamp in the other.

"May I come in?" he whispered. His face looked gaunt in the flickering light. "If the innkeeper or his guard Tarone find me here, I shall be skinned where I stand."

"Why should I allow you in my room?" Karigan demanded none too quietly.

The minstrel peered about nervously. "You are wise in your caution considering someone was trying to break into your room just now. I think I frightened him off, a stealthy fellow. You've nothing to fear from me. I am but a minstrel and carry nothing in the way of arms . . . my lute would be a clumsy weapon against your blade."

"Some minstrels are trained in the fighting arts."

"True. Especially if they were trained in Selium as I was. But I never took up a sword."

"Selium?"

"Yes. I believe that is where you've come from, too."

Karigan's mouth gaped open. She stepped aside for the minstrel to enter. She shut the door behind him, but didn't sheathe her sword.

The minstrel glanced around the room as if something might leap out of the shadows at any moment. "I am Gowen, a master of my craft. I would have sought you out sooner, but if I didn't perform as usual, someone might have gotten suspicious." What a master minstrel might be doing in a wilderness town like North, he didn't say. Without hesitation he sat on her bed. It was the only place to sit.

"What do you want?" Karigan asked. "How do you know I've traveled from Selium?"

"A Green Rider was looking for you the other day. At least, you answer her description. When she saw I was Selium trained—" he pointed to the gold master's knot on his shoulder, "—she knew she could trust me, and she knew that a master minstrel wouldn't have been placed here by mistake."

Karigan would have liked to have known what he meant by that. "I know a Green Rider was looking for me, or somebody who looked like me."

"You missed her by about a day."

"She's dead. I saw her body in a horse cart."

Gowen shook his head, bewildered. "I never thought the townsfolk would go so far as to actually kill someone from the king. Joy hadn't been a Rider long."

Karigan sat cross-legged on the floor, and rested her chin on her hands. "I'm not sure it was the townsfolk who killed her."

Gowen cocked his head, his eyes searching hers. Minstrels certainly possessed penetrating eyes. "What is it you know?"

"All I know is that others, including another Green Rider, were murdered in the same manner. Two black arrows with red fletching."

"Strange. Strange things are brewing. Poor Joy was searching for you, or your twin, but you weren't her primary concern. A messenger horse was."

"She didn't say why on either count, did she?" It was too much of a coincidence.

"No. But, young lady, of greater concern are the others who were looking for one who also matched your description. Their description wasn't as detailed as Joy's, but good enough to make a match."

Karigan bit her bottom lip. She didn't want to ask, but she did anyway. "Were they Mirwellian?"

"I see you know you're being pursued. They were here a few days ago. I'm not sure where they went after North, but they were in a hurry. I thought nothing of it till Joy described you. She didn't tell me, though, that you were a Green Rider."

"I'm not."

The minstrel blinked, his only hint of surprise. "You wear Rider insignia."

Karigan had forgotten about the winged horse embroidered on her sleeve. "I'm delivering a message for a dead Green Rider," she said.

"Killed by two black arrows."

She nodded.

"My dear young woman, you should not linger in this town. These black arrows sound like an omen to me. An omen of the dark past. No doubt it has something to do with Mornhavon the Black."

Karigan shuddered. Whether it was the cold of the evening or the name that caused her to do so, she wasn't sure. Mornhavon the Black's name had come up a lot since she had started this strange journey, even though he had been vanquished centuries ago.

"That person outside your door may not have been an ordinary brigand, either," Gowen said.

"How so?" Karigan's voice held little surprise.

"Most don't dare tamper with the guests of this inn. Keeper Wiles' man, Tarone, hasn't stopped short of killing to retain order here. Whoever wished to gain entry does not fear him."

Goosepimples broke out all over again. "Did you get a look at him?"

Gowen shook his head. "He was light of foot and disappeared into the shadows the moment he detected me. The corner of his cloak caught in my lamplight. It was gray."

A knock on the door startled them both.

"Oh, no. The innkeeper and his guard." Gowen rolled his eyes.

Karigan climbed to her feet, carefully draping a blanket over her shoulders to conceal the Rider insignia before she opened the door. The innkeeper stood in the corridor flanked by a hulking giant who was, if not as tall as Abram, at least as wide. He held an enormous club in his hand, and nothing about him suggested Abram's mild and careful nature. Now she knew how the innkeeper enforced order.

"Is everything well here?" the innkeeper asked, the corners of his mouth turned down as if to imply he didn't really care, but he had a reputation to maintain.

"Everything is fine," Karigan said. "Gowen and I were just having a conversation."

The innkeeper sniffed and cast Gowen a severe glance. "You know the rules, minstrel. No . . . associations with the guests." The guard thumped his club into his hand in emphasis. "You do your job well, but if you can't abide by the rules, I shall have to release you."

Karigan watched in fascination as Gowen affected a convincing facade of humility bordering on fear. "It's really nothing, Keeper Wiles. Really." His eyes were downcast and he bowed. "The lady and I were just making conversation. We hail from the same town. It won't happen again, I assure you, sir."

"It's truly all right," Karigan said. "He's done no harm."

Wiles grunted in disdain. "You may keep your job for now." He turned down the corridor, his guard following behind with heavy footsteps.

Gowen dropped all facade. "That man is a pompous . . . Well, you saw him. Mind what I told you, young lady. And mind whatever Clatheas told you, too. She's an accurate seer. Farewell and good luck to you!"

Karigan stood alone in her dark room. The door creaked as she closed it. She turned the key in the lock and fell back into bed. Sleep would be impossible now, and she gave some thought to leaving that very moment, but it wouldn't do to arouse any more suspicion than she needed to. Besides, the starless night was less inviting than the warm inn, and she would rather stay put than encounter the Shadow Man again in the dark.

⋙ MIRWELL ⋘

The Green Rider passed the envelope to Beryl. Beryl glanced at it front and back, then handed it to the governor.

"It bears the king's seal, my lord."

Mirwell looked the envelope over. It was addressed to *Honorable Tomastine II, Lord-Governor of Mirwell Province, Faithful Servant of Sacoridia*. The seal on the back was Zachary's, but featured his clan emblem, that of a Hillander terrier pressed into heather-colored wax, rather than the royal emblem of the firebrand and the half moon.

He slit the message open with his dagger and read the contents. Afterward, he handed it back to Beryl to read. The Greenie waited, standing statue-still with her hands clasped behind her back.

Mirwell glanced at her, then his aide. "Rider—"

"Ereal M'farthon, my lord," Beryl provided.

"Rider M'farthon, would you tell us what else you carry in your message satchel?"

The messenger's eyes grew wide, and she glanced questioningly at Beryl before her eyes fell back on the governor. "With all due respect, my lord—"

Mirwell stayed her words with his hand. "Please humor me, Rider. I ask for reasons of personal security."

Beryl nodded to her reassuringly.

Good! Sometimes it took another woman to lend support. *I am an old bear ugly enough to make anyone nervous.*

The Rider cleared her throat. "With all due respect,

my lord, while messages from His Excellency the King are matters of his own business, it's no secret that I carry another invitation to deliver to the lord-governor of Adolind.''

Mirwell nodded gravely. "Thank you, Rider M'farthon. D'rang will escort you to the kitchen for provisions to make the rest of your long journey comfortable. In the meantime, I shall craft my reply."

"Thank you, my lord." The Rider bowed out of the library, followed by a soldier in scarlet.

When she was out of earshot and the doors closed, Mirwell turned to his aide. "What do you make of it, Spence? Another Greenie trying to reach Zachary's spy?"

Beryl pulled thoughtfully at her lower lip. After a few moments she shook her head. "No, my lord."

"How can you be so sure?"

"I believe her intentions are as she says—to deliver invitations for the king's banquet and ball. It's certainly something she did not fabricate. Besides, we haven't found any spy in your household yet, and we've been very thorough."

Mirwell knew how thorough. Everyone who inhabited his keep, from the lowest servant to the highest courtier, including Prince Amilton and Beryl, had been interviewed extensively. Some to the point of torture. He had delighted in the screams of some of the courtiers he particularly disliked, and admired some of the techniques Beryl had employed to get them to "talk." The results, however, indicated that no spy existed within House Mirwell. One positive byproduct of the investigation was a reminder to his subjects of his authority. All the better if they trembled a little when he walked by.

"My feeling," Beryl said, "is that Coblebay was working on his own."

Mirwell tapped the catamount head of his armrest. "Nevertheless, I'm not willing to take chances. Bring me Taggern."

The guardsman was summoned, and clicked his boot heels to attention before his lord-governor.

"Taggern, see that Rider M'farthon doesn't come in private contact with anyone while she is being provisioned. Get a look in her message satchel if you can, then get her underway as soon as my reply to the king is prepared. Escort her out of the village. I expect a report. Do you understand?"

"Yes, my lord."

When the guardsman left, Beryl said, "I could keep an eye on the Rider myself, my lord."

"I need you to respond to Zachary for me. Your hand is fairer than mine."

She stepped over to his massive desk, a behemoth of carved cherrywood inlaid with blond oak, which sat upon legs fashioned as the talons of some enormous raptor. He never used the desk himself, and rarely even cracked a book in his library collection. These had all been acquired over the generations, mostly by a Mirwell of a more scholarly tendency. Tomastine II suspected that the province had begun to fail during that particular ancestor's reign. Still he liked the ambiance of the room with its large fireplace and hide-covered armchairs. Beryl seemed to feel right at home behind the desk. She dipped her quill into the inkwell.

"Your message, my lord?"

"Write to our esteemed king that we will accept his invitation."

"*We,* my lord?"

Mirwell smiled broadly. "Yes, *we.* Did you notice the date of the ball? Not long before the king's annual hunt."

"That's what concerns me."

"What better way to conquer than to be there to see it happen, eh?"

Beryl brought the message over for him to sign. He took the paper, and the hand that held it. He caressed her hand. The palm was well callused from using a sword, but the other side was soft and smooth, not riddled by the brown spots and tangle of green veins women his age were cursed with. She looked at him, stricken.

"As I said, you've a fair hand, my dear." He released it and looked the letter over, ignoring her as she stepped away and clasped her hands behind her back. She stared straight ahead at nothing. "We shall have a fine time in Sacor City."

"Yes, my lord." Her voice was flat.

She took the message, slipped it into an envelope, and sealed it with red wax and the imprint of the two war hammers. She left the library, a bit hastily, Mirwell thought. *We'll see what comes of a visit to Sacor City.*

He stood over his Intrigue board. He'd have to find its traveling case. Maybe he would have D'rang look for it. He picked up a red governor and a red soldier, and placed them in the court of the green king.

"I look forward to the hunt."

⋙ RALLY ⋘

Karigan stepped out into the overcast morning, leading The Horse down the alley to the main street. The stableboy watched after them wistfully, probably hoping for another copper. He deserved it, Karigan reflected. The Horse gleamed despite the dullness of the day. She just could not afford to dip into her reserves for more coins, but she had made a point of praising the boy for his fine care.

The main street was still muddy. Townsfolk walked on wooden boards lined in front of nearly every building and storefront, but the boards didn't help if one had to cross the street or veer off course. Women held their long skirts high, their faces in perpetual frowns as they trudged through the slop. Karigan grimaced herself as her foot sucked in the mud. The shine on The Horse's coat would not last long.

She mounted to let The Horse deal with the mud, and they went in search of a food vendor. Shopkeepers were just opening their doors and throwing back shutters. A blacksmith fired up his forge and the roar of flame could be heard all the way out into the street. North could have been any town awakening, but this one was without refinement. She missed the cobbled streets of Selium.

She found a shop with cluttered shelves of baked and dried goods, coarse cloth, axes, knives, rope, handsaws, blankets, lamps, flour, sugar, lard . . . everything a town of this sort could use. She dismounted and hitched The Horse to a post in front of the shop. She scraped mud off her boots on an iron rung placed outside the doorway just for that purpose.

As she stepped inside, she heard a shout on the street. She peered through a window and watched a man, encumbered by two sacks, running through the mud, making little progress. He was pursued by another man whose white shopkeeper's smock was splattered with mud.

"Come back with that, you thief!"

The shopkeeper, unencumbered, caught up with the other man, and jumped on him. The two fell into the muck, each grappling with the other. Passersby paused to watch the scene. A dagger flashed in the thief's hand, and he struck down at the shopkeeper. The shopkeeper loosed a hollow wail that Karigan felt every inch up her spine. The thief had stabbed the shopkeeper, and no one had attempted to stop him.

The thief climbed to his feet, threw the two sacks over his shoulder, and walked away. Pedestrians ignored the thief and simply walked around the shopkeeper's body as if it were no more than a rock obstructing their path.

Someone clucked his tongue behind Karigan. A burly, bald-pated man in a white smock shook his head, his jowls wobbling. "Old Mael didn't take any precautions." He patted a short sword sheathed at his side. Anywhere else, a shopkeeper wearing a sword was an unusual sight.

"Isn't anyone going to do anything?" Karigan demanded.

"Old Garl will be along to pick up his body," the shopkeeper said.

"But the thief—"

"Who's gonna run after him? You?"

Karigan blushed with shame.

"No one wants to risk their hide. I see you are sensible and carry a sword. Not common on a girl, but sensible. What can I do for you this morning?"

It took a moment for Karigan to shake off her sense of disgust at how easily the shopkeeper slid from murder to commerce. She couldn't think about it. She had to carry out her own mission, and there was no time to dwell on North's problems. She suspected that if she didn't get to Sacor City soon, more people would die.

She chose dried meat and fruit, tea, bread, and cheese from shelves, and some grain for The Horse from a hogshead. She set them on the counter in front of the shopkeeper.

"Two silvers," he said.

"Why, that's—" *Robbery* she wanted to say. She held her tongue, the price raising bile in the back of her throat. But she was, after all, a merchant's daughter, and not without bargaining skills. "Half a silver," she said.

The shopkeeper smiled in appreciation. He was a bargainer, too, and looked so smug that few probably got the better of him. "Two silvers is how it stands."

Karigan furrowed her brows together. "Half a silver is all those goods are worth, but I'll raise it to a silver. I can see it is difficult to earn a living in a town such as this."

The shopkeeper nodded. "A fine offer, but a man needs more to make a living. A silver and a half, plus a copper."

Karigan shifted her stance. The man didn't give in easily. She wondered how many people were taken by bargainers such as him. When she lowered the price to one silver, the shopkeeper scratched his bald head as if not sure how it had happened.

"One silver is still ridiculous for these goods, but I'll accept the price." She passed the precious coin across the counter. As she did so, something gold glittered in a basket of trinkets on display on the far end of the counter. "How much for the brooch?" she asked.

The shopkeeper brightened. "Why, one silver. Not so much for such a fine piece." He placed the winged horse brooch in the palm of his hand for her to look at.

"A deplorable price," Karigan said. "A cheap trinket. One copper is generous." She knew full well that the brooch was just as much pure gold as her own, but chances were that the shopkeeper saw it as a gaudy piece of costume jewelry, as had Torne and Jendara seen hers.

The shopkeeper raised his brows. "That ring you're wearing . . . A clan ring?"

Karigan had forgotten about her mother's troth ring. It probably wasn't something she should wear openly, with its gold and diamond, in a town such as North. She sensed, however, that the shopkeeper was suddenly intimidated. Rarely did she ever use the traditional clan bow, but she did so now. She placed her hand on her heart and dipped low. "Clan G'ladheon at your service."

"Merchant clan?"

"Yes."

"I should have known. I wondered how you managed to outbargain me." He chuckled good-naturedly. "A copper it is, for the brooch."

Karigan couldn't believe her good fortune. She thought she would end up having to pay at least half a silver. She pushed the copper across the counter and took the brooch. It was heavy and cold in her hand. All of the blood hadn't been polished off. The folk here were no better than Torne and Jendara, picking valuables off the dead. She dropped the brooch into her pocket, collected her goods, and left just as a bewhiskered man dressed in buckskin strode in, beaver, fox, and mink pelts swaying over his shoulder.

The body of the shopkeeper had been removed. Farther down the street, a crowd assembled. Most folk were garbed in the colorless textiles or buckskin of the town. A few merchant types added a splash of color. Karigan loaded the saddlebags with her newly purchased goods, and mounted The Horse. The sooner they left town, the better.

They plodded carefully toward the assembly. Members of the Anti-Monarchy Society formed a barrier around Lorilie Dorran who stood atop an overturned apple crate addressing the crowd. *Not everyone likes Lorilie's ideas,* Karigan thought idly. *Or they just don't like Lorilie.*

"You say the king protects you?" Lorilie demanded.

A man shifted uncomfortably in the crowd. "That's right."

The crowd jeered him. He was well dressed, perhaps a merchant, and definitely not local.

Lorilie held her hands up to quiet the crowd. "I suppose the king does protect and favor the *wealthy*. The *wealthy* can afford it. Your merchant's guild is as bad as the governors' council, trying to control entire villages with your trade, and your rules.

"But what of the folk here in North?" Lorilie's eyes seared those of her audience. "A man was killed this morning in the street. No one was here to prevent the crime. The king didn't protect him. The king won't fund a constable to keep order in this town. He will fund constables to guard the warehouses of rich merchants in Corsa." Her hands flew as she spoke. "The only time *we* see a representative of the king is at tax time."

A low grumble circulated among the gathered. Karigan tried to guide The Horse around the fringes of the crowd without drawing attention to herself, but people blocked the entire street, and were too transfixed by Lorilie to move out of the way.

Lorilie drew herself to her full height, which was not considerable, but seemed impressive nonetheless. "Will raising taxes on lumber products protect the folk of North, or other small villages like it? No! It will cast more beggars into the street. More families will go hungry. Despair, my sisters and brothers, will consume them."

"The king uses the taxes to fortify the country," the merchant shouted. "I call that protection, what with all the groundmites lurking about the borders these days."

The crowd cast questioning eyes on Lorilie, but she didn't hesitate with her response. "Yes, King Zachary is putting the taxes to good use. He is refortifying the wall around Sacor City. He is strengthening the defenses of the castle. This will surely protect the people in the rest of Sacoridia from groundmites."

This had to be only half the story, Karigan thought,

but what if it wasn't? Maybe the Mirwellians were right. Maybe Sacoridia did need a new king. But Lorilie Dorran did not want a king at all. What would she put in his stead? Herself? Karigan shifted in the saddle, guiding The Horse toward a sudden opening between some clumps of people. She wasn't ready to side with the Mirwellians or Lorilie Dorran.

"King's folk will protect Sacoridians!" shouted another man.

Lorilie met his outburst with laughter. "Like they protected the families on the borders? A whole unit of soldiers was slain down the North Road. Is that protection?"

The arguments went back and forth for some time, and Lorilie churned the emotions of the audience. She pounded her fist into her hand to add emphasis. She used facial expressions to affect sadness or anger, her voice alternately beseeching and persuasive. She derided all forms of kingdomship, including those who served the king, such as Green Riders, and accused the wealthy class of supporting the tyranny of the king. The merchants walked away amidst jeers. Lorilie was a master performer, and soon she had the crowd waving their fists above their heads and chanting, "A kingless land is a free land! Monarchy is tyranny!"

Karigan tried to work the horse through the log jam of people and was cursed at for getting in the way. "Well, if you let me through," she said, "I'll get out of your way." In the distance she espied the wooden bridge that spanned the River Terrygood, which upon crossing, would free her from the main portion of the town of North.

Then, above the chanting, one voice rang out, *"She's a Green Rider!"*

Karigan froze. Two men pushed through the crowd and pointed in her direction. Abram's tree poachers. An angry murmur swelled through the crowd though they couldn't quite figure out who the lumberjacks were pointing at. There was no one dressed in green.

Karigan had to act fast before the anger of the mob, for mob it was now, turned on her. If they realized who the lumberjacks were pointing at, they would tear her apart. She glanced ahead and saw a woman wearing a light green tunic. It was the burly woman she had seen Clatheas giving a card reading to the previous night at The Fallen Tree. Karigan pointed at her and yelled, "There she is! There's the Greenie!"

An expression of bewilderment, then fear, took over the woman's face. As the crowd surged toward her, Karigan meandered through the angry people until someone grabbed her boot and tried to pull her from the saddle. It was the two lumberjacks.

"You're the Greenie," one yelled at her. Fortunately, no one else could hear over the roar of the crowd. "I heard that troll call you a Green Rider."

Karigan clung desperately to The Horse's mane, and gasped as she was pulled inch by inch out of the saddle. A well-placed kick from The Horse, however, quickly ended the struggle, and one of the lumberjacks fell with a howl beneath the feet of the crowd.

Karigan urged The Horse on toward the bridge, heedless of people who got in her way. The Horse did not trample them, but rather pushed them aside like the prow of a boat on the water. When she was clear of the mob, she galloped the horse over the bridge, his hooves clattering on the wooden deck, the river churning frothy and turbulent below and sending up mist and spray that dampened her face. When finally she was across, and thus free of the town except for a few ramshackle shops and a tavern on this bank, she reined the horse in and looked back.

It was impossible to discern exactly what was happening—the mob had become a single moving mass. She wondered what had become of the woman she had "accused" of being a Green Rider. She had done it not out of mischief, but to save herself.

A mounted figure stood amidst the mob, a gray figure

fixed like a statue in the middle of a swift-running, roiling stream, unable to move forward or backward. Karigan felt cold, knowing with some certainty that he watched her from beneath his gray hood.

❧ WILD RIDE ❧

Karigan rode for two days, snatching moments of rest when she could no longer keep her eyes open. The landscape varied little—tree stumps interspersed with staghorn sumac and tiny birches and maples growing up where a vast spruce forest once stood. Many of the useless trees had been toppled to allow easier access to the more profitable ones. Their skeletons lay on the ground, bleached gray and dry by the sun.

Karigan's skin burned, and she felt bleached and dry herself in the intense sunlight without sheltering trees to offer shade. The scolding of squirrels and the spring songs of birds were eerily absent.

She spent much of her time scanning the land. The horse track offered no concealment and anyone could be seen from a long way off. She tried to think of this as an advantage. Without concealment, a trap could not be set for her. She would be able to see her foes from far away.

There was no telling how far it was to Sacor City. They came upon an ancient stone marker so weathered and splotched by lichen that it was impossible to read the inscription.

They passed several teams of oxen hauling sledges piled high with logs, leaving plumes of dust in their wake, which could be seen miles away. Karigan coughed and gasped behind them, wishing she had a scarf to tie around her nose and mouth. The cargo masters paid her no heed, intent on the track ahead.

She spent sleepless nights, huddled beneath the great-coat, the saber drawn and ready. There was no sign of pursuit, and this was somehow more disquieting. Did other Green Riders spend sleepless nights, too? Or were they used to the dangers of the road?

On the third morning out of North, logged forests gave way to farmland. Fields checkered in spring green and deep brown loam rolled away in each direction. The air freshened and was less arid. Here, birds sang in hedge-rows and the occasional trees, but the land still offered no cover. Farmers plowed on distant hills with their teams in plain view. Karigan continued her rigid pace, pausing long enough only for The Horse to recover for another run.

They found an abandoned barn netted by clinging grapevine and thorns to spend the night in. The barn leaned to one side in an attitude of collapse, but the grapevine, Karigan thought, ought to hold it up for at least one more night.

Under cover and out of sight, she slept soundly, not even flinching when bats left their roosts above where she lay curled up in her bedroll. She didn't awaken when they returned from their hunt, or to the yips of coyotes ranging the countryside. The night world moved about her, but did not disturb her.

In the morning, sunlight thrust between boards and broken windows like bright spears. Motes of dust drifted upwards in the light as she slipped tack and packs on The Horse. Both messenger and messenger horse were better for their night of rest.

Karigan peered through the old barn windows before stepping outside. If it had occurred to her that the barn was the only place that offered concealment in the area, and she had been in a less exhausted state, she would have abandoned it as too obvious. What was done was done, and no harm had come of it. No one was in sight except crows which launched into flight as she led The Horse from the barn. She mounted, and the race went on.

That afternoon, a wood came into view. It wasn't the deep forest of the Green Cloak, but a young forest of slender birches, oaks, and maples. They had grown up in what had once been a farmer's field—a wall of fieldstones skirted the horse track and disappeared into the wood.

Karigan approached it with both relief and apprehension. The wood offered cover, but also offered concealment for foes, the opposite of her previous problem. A breeze rustled leaves which whispered secrets among themselves.

A figure in green appeared ahead, and she stiffened. He merged with the vegetation, and disappeared. F'ryan Coblebay? When he appeared, dire things tended to happen. Karigan licked her dry, cracked lips.

The sun was high and bright, glistening on leaves, turning them into emerald jewels. The shade within the wood beckoned her out of the hot sun, would soothe the sunburn that had afflicted her since leaving North. She could think of no place less sinister than the wood. She took a deep breath and plunged in.

The shade cooled her down. It was like stepping into her father's wine cellar on the hottest of summer afternoons. A bee droned past her ear, and she inhaled the woody scents of decayed leaf litter and earth, much different than the evergreen scent of the northern forest she had left behind.

Leaves thrashed like the sound of a bear charging through the woods. Karigan grabbed the hilt of her sword and looked wildly about. When she saw the source of the disturbance, she laughed nervously. A red squirrel! A squirrel stirring up the leaf litter!

Her imagination was getting the better of her, but what was upsetting The Horse? He sidestepped, his ears flopping back and forth.

"What's wrong?" She had long since learned to trust his signals.

"Hello, Greenie."

Karigan twisted around. Sitting motionless on their

horses were Immerez and the gray cloaked rider. She screamed inside.

Immerez uncoiled his whip. Karigan reined The Horse around to flee, but two mounted figures rode from the woods and blocked her path. Sarge and Thursgad! Where had they come from? Immerez leaned toward the gray-cloaked rider, the Shadow Man, listening as something was whispered to him. His one eye was anchored on Karigan, and his hands worked the whip as he listened. Karigan's hand went to her saber, but not soon enough.

"Drive her into the sunlight, boys!" Immerez shouted.

The soldiers charged her in a flurry of Mirwellian scarlet, their swords drawn. Their steeds rammed into The Horse, biting and pushing. Karigan fought to stay mounted as he half-reared and bucked, but the mere force of two against one was too much, and she found herself squinting in the sun. She reached for her brooch and wished for invisibility. The bright world became dull and heavy, and the Shadow Man faded from sight.

Immerez laughed. "I see the Greenie magic doesn't work so well in the bright light of day."

Karigan gasped as she looked down at herself and The Horse. They were too solid. And somehow Immerez and the Shadow Man had known this would happen. She dropped the invisibility—maintaining it would only exhaust her. The Shadow Man reappeared. What did it mean?

She veered The Horse around, but Immerez and his men crowded her. The Shadow Man stayed aloof, watching from the depths of his hood.

Bunchberry flower. Someone would come in need— Before she could even complete the thought, Immerez's thong snarled past her face and lashed around her chest and shoulders, gashing her left arm. She cried out. The leather thong tightened, and Immerez dug his spurs into the sides of his stallion. It leaped backward, and Karigan was hauled from her saddle. When she hit the ground, all the air whooshed from her lungs. She struggled dazedly against the binding thong, fighting waves of pain from the jarring impact of her fall. The whip held her fast.

"Get the message satchel, boys."

Sarge and Thursgad hurried to obey their captain's command, but The Horse wouldn't let them near. He kicked Thursgad's steed squarely in the chest. The unfortunate horse grunted and shied away. The Horse backed from Sarge as if to flee, then swerved around and lunged at him in a rear.

"Damn the beast!" Sarge pulled away unsuccessfully as the hooves of The Horse collided with the shoulder of his bay, leaving behind shiny streaks of blood.

"Hamstring him, or cut his throat," the captain said. "I don't care. Just get that message satchel."

"I'll help ya, Sarge." Thursgad kicked his horse, but it would only step backward. Sarge's horse now shied from The Horse who, with teeth bared, snorted aggressively.

"Proud cut, I'll warrant," Sarge grumbled.

Karigan shook her head to clear her thoughts—not an easy task with hooves flying just inches from her. The hilt of her sword was lodged beneath her hip. She wasn't disarmed yet. The Horse would occupy Sarge and Thursgad, but she would have to deal with Immerez and the Shadow Man by herself. The Horse lunged at Sarge again, and she was showered by clods of dirt and pebbles.

The Shadow Man made a sweeping gesture with his hand. It was a white hand, perfectly proportioned, not the skeletal hand she had somehow imagined. *Someone* living and breathing was concealed beneath that hood.

Immerez nodded in response to the gesture, and clucked his horse backward. Karigan grit her teeth as the whip tightened around her, strangled her, cut into her flesh. He dragged her several yards across rocks and tall grasses away from sharp horse hooves. He dismounted, and keeping the whip taut, stood above her. The sun glared behind him, and Karigan had to squint to see him.

"I don't know what kind of training you give your Greenie horses, but my men will have him down shortly. No doubt about it." His green eye flicked over at the action, then planted on Karigan again. "What do you know about a spy in House Mirwell?"

Karigan struggled to sit up, but he drove his boot heel into her shoulder and slammed her back into the ground. Her shoulder flashed with pain.

"Mirwellians," she gasped. "Nothing but cutthroats."

There was no reply for a moment. "I asked you a question."

Karigan craned her neck upward. "I don't even know what the message is about. I don't know anything about anything. You understand?" She was surprised by her own vehemence. Her voice did not sound high-pitched and frightened.

Immerez squatted down out of the glare, which shifted the shadows on his face. Sweat gleamed on his bald head. "I don't know how it is F'ryan Coblebay passed his mission to you, but he did. You do know the information."

"I do not."

Immerez peered over his shoulder, and to the Shadow Man he said, "I don't wish to play this game anymore." There was no response. Only Sarge's curses could be heard down the track. When Immerez gazed back at Karigan, his features were tight. "You could tell me about the spy now and spare yourself some trouble."

"Does your statue friend make you do all his work?"

Immerez grinned humorlessly. "He is no friend of mine."

"Then *why?* What's so important?" Karigan wriggled her hand pinned beneath her body, reaching for the hilt of her sword. No one was here to help her. No eagle, no Abram, no Berry sisters, no Eletian, no ghost. Curious that F'ryan Coblebay wasn't here to help, or at least to communicate. Perhaps his time walking the earth had expired.

Immerez seemed perplexed by Karigan's questions. "What do you mean *why?* I'll wager you're trying to throw us off the track."

Sand and grit abraded Karigan's hand as she burrowed it beneath her body. She fixed her gaze on Immerez, so not to give away her intent. "I'm not really a Green Rider. I don't care what's important to you, or what's important to King Zachary. I found the messenger dead and took his horse. I'm just trying to get home, nothing more. You can have the message if you want."

Immerez laughed and slapped his thigh. He looked over his shoulder at the Shadow Man. "Did you hear that? She says we can have the message if we want!" The laughter stopped cold and he gazed down at her. "If that is so, call off the horse."

Karigan shrugged as best she could in the confines of the whip. Her fingertips touched cold metal—the pommel! "He doesn't listen to me."

"I thought so. If you're no Green Rider, you certainly look like one."

Karigan had slipped on the green trousers that morning. "The clothes . . . they were in the messenger's pack." Her fingers worked down the hilt, slowly tugging the sword from the sheath. A drop of sweat glided down to the tip of her nose and hung there.

Immerez seized her by the jaw, and lifted her from the ground to look her in the eye. "No more lies," he hissed. "Admit that you know of the Mirwellian involvement. Tell us about the spy."

He released her jaw, and she fell to the ground with a solid thud, her grip on the saber lost. "I know nothing about F'ryan Coblebay or what he did. *I'm not a Green Rider.* Mirwell is a province of idiots anyway!" It sounded childish, and as the fury grew on Immerez's face, she was sure he would kill her.

"I don't care how young you look, Greenie," he said calmly. There was no explosion, but somehow this was worse. "You shall be bound to a tree and my whip will extract the information from you."

Alone. I'm alone.

The Horse was tiring, and even now Sarge reached for his reins.

Immerez towered over Karigan. "Stand up, Greenie." *Now. Now, or I won't have another chance.*

She climbed to her feet, gripping the hilt of her sword as she did so. Immerez gasped in surprise, tightening the whip too late. The leather thong unraveled from her shoulders and she jumped to the attack.

She was too close for Immerez to draw his own sword, but he ducked as she swung the saber at him, and double fisted his hands into her stomach. She crouched over, holding her stomach and retching.

"Foolish. Very foolish." Immerez lashed his whip as slowly and deliberately as a cat would its tail. "Drop the sword."

Karigan's lungs ached for air. Blood thrummed through her ears. It was rhythmic, like the galloping of hooves.

"You won't drop the sword, then?" Immerez flung the whip at her. It coiled around her ankle, and he jerked her foot out from under her. She crashed back to the ground.

Karigan cried out. It was the same ankle the creature of *Kanmorhan Vane* had clenched in its claw. The sense of complete helplessness rushed back to her, and the memory of how she had overcome it to defeat the creature and its offspring. She chopped at the leather thong, but it was too thick to be severed completely through. Immerez threw back his head and laughed at her futile attempts. He loosened the whip, drew it away, and gathered it for another lash.

I killed the creature of Kanmorhan Vane, Karigan thought. *But I had help.* . . . Yet she would not allow Immerez to use the whip again. The crescendo of hoofbeats. . . . Heartbeats thundered in her ears. She sprang to her feet with a growl, and this time she didn't hack at the whip, but at the hand that held the whip.

She stopped, staring stupidly at the saber dripping blood, at Immerez groveling on the ground. His hand was several feet away just like in the vision she had through Professor Berry's telescope. The hoofbeats in her head drowned out his screams.

"Horse!" she cried, but he was already beside her, quivering with energy she did not understand. Sarge's and Thursgad's horses spooked at the air. Even the Shadow Man's mount pawed the ground, his neck foamy with sweat. Immerez's stallion had run away.

Mount. The voice pierced through the hoofbeats drumming in her ears. She obeyed, and the world reeled out of balance.

Thursgad and Sarge and their horses turned slowly, each movement prolonged and exaggerated, removed from real time. Everything blurred in Karigan's vision except herself and The Horse . . . and the Shadow Man.

The Shadow Man sat serenely on his stallion. A bow appeared in his hands where there had been none before. He removed two arrows from his quiver, each black-shafted with red fletching. He nocked one to the bow string.

Ride! the voice commanded.

Karigan dared not disobey. She squeezed The Horse's sides just as the first arrow was loosed. The Horse leaped into a gallop. Blue of sky, green and brown of wood, rushed by in streaks. The buildings of a village were a smear they left behind. Two arrows, she knew, sang behind her and would not stop till they found their mark.

Wind buffeted her, loosened the braid in her hair. The rhythm of The Horse's hooves pounded through her body, but for all she knew, they flew.

There were other pounding hooves, other riders abreast of her, filmy white and transparent. Trees and buildings did not hinder them, they traveled right through. They called to her with far off voices in what was like a battle cry: *Ride, Greenie, Ride! It's the Wild Ride!*

Cold arms slipped around her waist from behind. *Ride,* F'ryan Coblebay whispered. *It's the Wild Ride.*

The more the landscape grew indistinct, the more the riders clarified. Men and women in greatcoats or tunics striding alongside, some in light armor of war astride battle steeds, and some in uniforms of archaic vintage riding lean messenger horses. All traveled at the same unnatural speed as she and The Horse. All of them were

Green Riders from times past, all of them dead. What stake did ghosts have in her survival?

Ride, Greenie, Ride!

Their chant spun the world faster, and still The Horse surged blindly ahead. Their pale faces were young, few were old. Some Riders thrust their sabers above their heads, others shook their fists, their shouts echoed to her from someplace far away. A cold sweat blanketed her body as she charged along with the ghostly cavalry.

The arrows still followed behind with the same momentum, she knew. She could hear them whining through the air. How long could this Wild Ride last?

Ride, Greenie, Ride! It's the Wild Ride!

The chant kept time with the rhythm of pounding hooves, of her heartbeat, of the blood pumping through her ears.

They burn.

At first Karigan didn't know what F'ryan meant. Did the spirits burn?

The arrows burn.

Karigan glanced over her shoulder, disconcerted at looking through F'ryan's gauzy form. Indeed the arrows were aflame and falling behind. A shout of victory, like a rush of wind, arose from the spirit riders. They pulled their horses to a halt, The Horse slackening his gait without direction. Though all were stopped, the world still hastened by, as if they were being swept away on some spectral current.

"Why?" Karigan asked.

F'ryan Coblebay slipped off The Horse and backed away, melting into the others. *I cannot rest till you complete the mission.* His voice faded. *It was a good Ride.*

"Why?" Karigan demanded, the reins bunched in her fist. "Why did you intervene?"

A lone Rider broke away from the group, her long hair drifting in an unearthly breeze. Two arrows protruded from her chest. The Rider Karigan had seen dead in North. Joy.

If this did not go beyond earthly matters, we would not

have intervened. There is much you might accomplish to thwart the plans of an old evil. May we Ride together again some day, Green Rider.

Joy turned her horse back among the other ghosts. The mass merged into itself, then lifted and dissipated like a fog carried off on a breeze to the heavens. Still, the rhythm of the Wild Ride pulsed in Karigan's ears.

⋙ RIDE'S END ⋘

The world slowed down, though colors still smeared like water on paint. A massive stone structure of towers and parapets and crenelated walls loomed ahead with colorful pennants streaming from its loftiest heights.

An arched entryway flanked by rounded turrets gaped before her.

Behind her stood the guardhouses, the portcullis suspended between them, ready to cut off an invasion should an army attempt to swarm across the narrow drawbridge spanning the moat and assault the castle. A wall encircled the castle and its grounds. Somehow, the ghosts had carried her miles in just moments to the courtyard where she now stood before the castle of King Zachary.

The Horse's hooves crunched on gravel. She dismounted and, hands shaking, unbuckled the message satchel from the saddle. She left The Horse standing there, no worse from his strange run.

Time lagged again, and Karigan swayed as if the ground moved beneath her feet. The pennants, each representing the provinces, snapped into definition. Though their lines were no longer blurred, their motion was jerky and slow.

When her footing grew solid again, she proceeded to walk the distance across the courtyard to the castle entrance. Guards in black and silver stepped forward with halting movements to intercept her. They had not man-

aged two steps by the time she was far beyond their
reach.

As she walked beneath the arched entryway, more soldiers attempted unsuccessfully to stop her in jerk-and-
stagger movements. They were too slow, she was too
fast. Their voices were muffled, the words drawn out in
a moronic drone.

She strode through a great corridor past guards and
courtiers stalled in time. Most did not note her passage.
Lamps lit along the walls flickered absurdly slow, casting
a wash of strange tones of bronze and gold along the
corridor. The corridor, she hoped, led to King Zachary's throne.

Coats of arms and weavings adorned the walls, and
these remained static and clearly defined. She focused on
these things rather than the unnatural, disorienting motions of the people around her.

Two doors appeared ahead of her, open. Some huge
oak tree had been felled to create them. The firebrand
was carved into one, and the crescent moon in the other.
Two guards clad entirely in black were posted beside the
doors. They were Weapons, but even they weren't im-
mune to the time anomaly.

She swept past them and through the doors into a
vast chamber. Sunlight lanced through tall and narrow
windows at cross slants. Voices echoed off the vaulted
ceiling in a weird and long drawn out babble. Black-clad
guards stood like pillars in shadowy recesses.

A tapestry of Zachary's family crest, a white Hillander
terrier against a field of heather, occupied the space behind the throne. It was said that the brave little dogs had
rooted groundmites out of their earthen burrows during
the Long War.

Below the tapestry stood two men and a woman attending a man who sat in an ornate chair. A white terrier
sat up from where it had been lying at the seated man's
feet. Before it was on its feet, Karigan had crossed the
cavernous room. The three people and the king were just
beginning to look up at her.

Slam!

Like walking into a wall, like the ground being pulled out from beneath her feet, the force rocked through her body and she fell away piece by piece, like feathers from a burst pillow cascading in a soft flurry.

She lay in a field immersed in sunlight. Sunlight leaked through her closed eyes. Asters and goldenrod droned with bees lighting from one blossom to another. A swallow chirped somewhere above her. She felt warm and drowsy. The light, the light . . . Something cool and wet ran along her cheek . . .

Time and motion snicked into place, like the latching of a door. Karigan shook her head, willing the stinging drone of bees and shock of light to leave her. She sighed, closed her eyes, and settled down to continue her nap, but the cool, wet something now licked her hand. She cracked open an eye. A pair of brown eyes gazed back at her from beneath a clump of white fur. The terrier panted and looked at her with a grin.

Karigan widened her eyes. *Dog! Castle! Zachary!* She sat up too fast, and spiraled back down to the woolen runner in front of the king's dais. The buzz filled her head again, but it might have been the voices of people around her. This time when she looked up, four blades wielded by black-clad Weapons were pointed at her chest.

"This is no Green Rider I've ever seen before." A man's voice with a hard edge to it.

"Could it be another assassin?" the woman asked.

"Her coming here smells of magic," said a second man with a sniff.

Karigan had fallen on the message satchel. She rolled to her side to unwedge it, and the Weapons pressed the tips of their blades against her chest.

"Message." Karigan's mouth felt too full of tongue. "Message for the king."

"Let us see it," said the first man.

Karigan took the paper from the satchel and handed it to a Weapon who in turn passed it to someone she

could not see. Indistinct murmurings echoed off the walls
of the cavernous room, which seemed, rather, like whispers issuing from the fresco-painted figures on the ceiling. The age-cracked figures of kings, queens, knights,
and the god, Aeryc, riding the sickle moon, and the goddess, Aeryon, haloed by the sun and peering from behind
a cloud, all looked down on her. Among them, and at
the center, was a great black horse whose arched neck
and flanks rippled with motion.

"—spy," a queen seemed to say from above.

"This message is from F'ryan Coblebay, but this is—"
said the king.

"—unimportant and irrelevant. It's the magic I'm—"

"Too young to be—"

"Should be confined and interrogated—"

"—unimportant."

Karigan drifted away again in search of the sunlit field,
but she was not able to find it. The Weapons seized
her roughly under her arms and hauled her to her feet.
Someone took away the saber. She protested weakly, but
no one heard.

"Lock her up until we decide."

"Not in a prison cell," said a gentler voice Karigan
hadn't heard before. The Weapons blocked her view with
their broad shoulders and she could not see who spoke.
"Choose a guest room and guard it."

"But, Majesty," said the harsh voice, "you may be
endangering yourself. This one uses magic like we've
never seen before."

"And all the prison cells in the world would not hold
her if she did anyway. A guest room. Does she look
threatening to you in her present condition, Crowe?"

"Majesty, begging your pardon, but she may just want
it to look that way."

"Of all the idiotic ideas I've ever heard, that is the
worst," said a new voice from the direction of the entryway. It belonged to a woman accustomed to authority.
The Weapons still blocked Karigan's view, but she heard
the purposeful click of boots on the flagstone floor as

the woman approached. She passed by, and the clicking ceased. "Your Majesty."

"Captain, your intrusion speaks of—"

"Disrespect, Castellan Crowe? Is that what you wish to say?"

"I will not have this bickering," said the king. "Captain Mapstone, do you have anything you wish to say? Do you know this girl? She dresses as a Green Rider."

"I've never laid eyes on her before, but I think I can tell you who she is."

The woman stood on tiptoes and peered over the shoulders of the Weapons. Karigan received a fleeting impression of hazel eyes and reddish hair.

"I can also tell you that she is a Green Rider."

"No," Karigan whispered, but no one was listening.

"I can't say I understand, Captain," Crowe said.

"Your Majesty, have her taken to Rider barracks. She will do you no harm, and if I'm not mistaken, the message you hold in your hands is of great import."

"We have our doubts about that," the king said.

"Then what of this?"

The captain held aloft two black arrows. Karigan groaned and lurched to her side, and would have fallen if not for the support of the Weapons.

The two Weapons led her away from the throne, each stony-faced and silent. They passed through alternating shafts of dazzling sunlight and shadow as they walked to the far end of the throne room. Had Torne and Jendara once been this way? Stern and silent? Courtiers, servants, and soldiers who walked the corridors spared her a glance not at all.

They left the castle by a different entrance than she had come in, and passed through a courtyard, skirting the castle. The Weapons gripped her elbows, practically lifting her from the ground, as they escorted her past curious onlookers. They brought her to a whitewashed wooden building, the unmistakable odor of horse manure permeating from a not-too-distant source. The people

here were all dressed in green and they were very curious. They stared at her.

"Where am I?" she asked.

"Rider barracks," the Weapon to her left said, and
that was all.

They entered the building, floorboards creaking beneath their feet, and a hint of leather in the air. It was
far more appealing than the stone castle. Abruptly they
stopped and the Weapon to her right threw open a door.
They shuffled her into a room sparsely furnished with a
bed, table, washstand, stove, and chair. Sunlight poured
through a window, warming the place.

"You will empty your pockets," said the Weapon who
had been at her right. The other stepped out of the room
and posted himself by the door.

"I will *what?*"

"Empty your pockets." The man lacked any hint of
emotion.

Karigan tossed the message satchel on the table—
somehow she had managed to hold onto it—and dug into
her pockets. She produced the moonstone, some coppers
and one silver, the bunchberry flower with its missing
petal, the sprig of bayberry, and Joy's winged horse
brooch. The Weapon gathered her things up into one
large hand.

"The ring," he said.

"The—No. You can't have it." She covered it
protectively.

The Weapon stepped forward. "The ring. Until your
identity and purpose is ascertained, we will hold these
things."

"No. Not the ring. All of these things, all except the
brooch, were gifts. This ring was my mother's. I won't
give it to you."

The Weapon took another step toward her, his face
implacable.

Karigan stooped into a defensive crouch. "The gods
help you if you take a step closer. I've about had it. All
I've done is deliver a message to the king, yet all I get

in thanks is trouble. Well I'll tell you, granite face, I've killed one of your kind, and if you take another step, I'll do my utmost to damage you."

That stopped him, though the threat didn't seriously concern him. He didn't even bother to draw his blade. "I doubt you could hurt any of us. If so, who was it?"

In a measured breath, she said, "His name was Torne."

The Weapon's brows knit together and his eyes flashed angrily. "Torne! A traitor of Saverill's ilk. A deserter. Keep your ring, then. These other objects will be returned to you if it is found you are not lying." With that, he turned crisply on his heel and glided out of the room, closing the door behind him.

Karigan supported herself against the table, her knees ready to buckle. What possessed her to challenge a Weapon? When she had killed Torne, F'ryan was in control of her body. She staggered across the small room to the bed and collapsed. Straw poked through the mattress ticking, but it felt, for all the world, like a feather bed to her overtaxed body.

A noise awakened Karigan. Someone was in the room bending over her bed, and it was too dark to see who. She reached out into the gloom and grabbed a handful of hair. Her assailant squeaked.

Karigan tugged harder.

"Ow! Stop it!" a girl cried out. "I'd like to keep my hair if you don't mind."

Karigan shook her head. The room was dimly lit by an oil lamp at lowest glow. Orange flickered around the edges of the stove door, and the room, she noticed, was quite cozy. She had slept well into the night. Her "assailant" was a girl of about twelve years old, dressed in messenger green. Her hands were on her hips, and her feet were spread apart, and to Karigan, it was like facing one of her own strong-willed aunts. *You won't finish dinner, eh?* she remembered. Aunt Stace wouldn't let her eat dinner for the next two nights.

"Uh, sorry," Karigan said. She let a handful of brown hair drift to the floor.

The girl's stance relaxed. "I'll accept your apology. Most Riders are jumpy anyway."

The girl's name, Karigan found out, was Melry Exiter, and she had been in the midst of checking on Karigan's condition.

"The nitwits around here don't have the head to take care of anything." Melry cleaned and bandaged the whip wound Immerez had inflicted on Karigan's shoulder. "*Look in on her,* says the captain. Well, what a mess I did find. You look like Condor dragged you all the way from Selium. Are you sure you were in the saddle?"

"Condor?"

"Yeah, F'ryan's horse."

Karigan had grown so used to calling him The Horse that she had forgotten he might answer to another name. Condor fit, though. Condors were not the most beautiful of birds, but they had the capacity for elegant flight. Karigan looked up at Melry's face and was surprised to see tears trickling down her cheeks. "What's wrong?"

"F'ryan's dead, isn't he? That's why you came on Condor, right?"

Karigan nodded. "Yes, he asked me to carry on his mission."

Melry wiped her nose with the back of her sleeve and sat in the chair. "They told me, but I couldn't believe it till I saw Condor. F'ryan's the closest thing I ever had to a brother. He played games with me, kept an eye on me, let me tag after him around the castle."

"I'm sorry," Karigan said. She knew it was inadequate, but it was what everyone had said when her mother died.

"Yeah. I knew it might happen sometime. I try not to get real close to the people 'round here 'cause they die. It hurts. Captain and F'ryan are the only ones I got close to."

They sat in silence for some time. "Aren't you a little young to be a Green Rider?" Karigan asked. Everyone seemed to think she was too young, and this girl was even younger.

Melry laughed, the tears miraculously drying. "I'm too young? You're too young! I was raised here."

"Here?" Karigan crooked a brow, disbelieving.

"Yeah, here. Captain found me in the stable. I was newborn, all wrapped in a blanket. Someone, my real mother, left me in the stable." Melry shrugged at the illogic of such an act. "They think my father was a Rider who got killed months before. He had a reputation with women. . . . Captain took me in, named me after her grandmother, and she and the other Riders raised me. I'm not a proper Green Rider, I just help out at the stable, and sometimes I run messages for the Green Foot."

"The Green Foot?"

"Yeah. We run messages around the castle. Gives me a few coppers for fair days and Master Gruntler's Sugary. But I imagine I'll be a Green Rider when I get older."

What would it be like to know one's destiny? Karigan had always thought she would be a merchant like her father, but was now certain that she had never really known. "I'm sure you know what it's like to be a Green Rider."

Melry gave her a sideways look. "I'm sure you do, too."

"What?"

"Are you hungry? You're kinda pale."

"What do you mean I'd know what it's like to be a Green Rider?"

"You have a brooch, don't you? I can't see it proper because I'm not a Rider yet, but you have a brooch. That makes you a Green Rider."

"A brooch doesn't make me anything."

"Whatever you say. You want some food? After that, it's off to the baths for you."

Karigan perked up. "Bath?"

Melry chuckled and slipped out of the room. Shortly she returned, bearing a platter of steaming meat and potatoes, cheese, and bread. In her other hand she carried a mug of fresh milk. She watched in amazement as Karigan all but licked the platter.

"Your color's coming back," she said.

Karigan swallowed the last of the milk and wiped the milk mustache off with her sleeve. "Today drained me."

Melry leaned forward with an expression of deadly seriousness that only near-teenagers can achieve. "There have been rumors flying around all day about you, like you did something today that no one's done in a million years. Or was it a thousand?" Melry screwed up her face. "I'm not real good with numbers. Frustrates the captain a lot. Is it true?"

"I've no idea," Karigan said. "But I did have a strange day."

"What happened?"

How could she tell this girl that she had ridden with the ghost of her friend, F'ryan Coblebay, not to mention ghosts who were among the first to be Green Riders? "I—I don't feel up to discussing it."

Melry's face crumbled in disappointment. "Well, they said you traveled fast, whatever that means. Condor is fast, but not the fastest. That would be Ereal's Crane. Anyway, it's off to the baths for you."

Karigan followed Melry out of the room. A Weapon whom she hadn't seen before fell in step behind them. Melry rolled her eyes. The few Riders they encountered in the corridor goggled at Karigan as if she were some unknown creature from another land, but said nothing. One young man, with sandy hair, actually smiled at her and said, "Welcome, Rider."

"That was Alton," Melry said after he passed by. "He's always full of himself—aristocratic blood, y'know, but not a bad sort."

A steaming hip bath awaited Karigan in the bathing room. Several other baths were partitioned off by curtains, but the room was empty of other people. She stepped toward the bath, then hesitated, glancing at the Weapon.

Melry followed her eyes, and put her hands on her hips. "You mind watching things from outside, Fastion? Give Karigan a little privacy, will you? If you want to see a naked woman, go downtown."

Karigan's eyes widened that Melry would speak to a Weapon so, but Fastion's expression did not alter as he stepped outside of the room.

"I haven't decided whether or not Weapons are a natural phenomenon," Melry said, pronouncing the last word with special care. "The captain says that a lot."

Karigan smiled, something her facial muscles were no longer used to. "Thanks, Melry."

"Only the captain calls me Melry. You can call me Mel, if you like." She left the bathing chamber, whistling.

Karigan sank into the tub, her battered and bruised body easing in the heat. She nodded off, and woke up with a snort to discover she had dozed long enough for the water to become tepid. With a shiver, she stepped out of the bath, toweled herself dry and dressed. Tentatively she opened the door and found Fastion waiting patiently for her outside.

"I'm done."

He nodded, and they headed down the corridor. They arrived at the room simultaneously with Mel who could hardly see over an armload of green clothes.

"Thought you might need a change of clothes," she said, "so I stopped at the quartermaster's. He wasn't happy about being woke up so late, nor about giving up good uniforms."

Fastion took up his post outside, and Melry dumped the load on Karigan's bed. "Hope it fits, and I hope you don't mind green."

Karigan sighed, lamenting her wardrobe left in Selium so long ago. "I'm getting used to it." She held a familiar linen shirt to her shoulders for size. "I think this will work. I borrowed some things from the waystation near North."

Mel's eyes grew large. "You were there? That's wild territory."

Karigan nodded. "I read a notice that the quartermaster was to be informed when things are taken."

Mel listened attentively while Karigan listed the uniform pieces she had removed from the waystation. When Karigan finished, Mel yawned. "I'll take care of it in the morning. Quartermaster'll skin me if I wake him up again. I'm about done in myself, anyway. Have to get up early to feed the horses."

Karigan's eyes fell on the message satchel still lying on her table. "One more thing," she said. "F'ryan Coblebay wrote a letter to a Lady Estora. Would you mind delivering it to her?"

Mel's eyes nearly bugged out of her head. "Oh, no! Estora—she doesn't know about F'ryan yet."

"Then best she hears it from you and not a total stranger like me." Karigan took the letter from the satchel and passed it to Mel, feeling a great deal of self-satisfaction: she had achieved her mission, had delivered the king his message, and even the love letter. And she was still alive.

"I'll take it." Tears threatened to spill down Mel's cheeks again. "You're right. Best she hears it from me."

Mel left, and Karigan sagged in exhaustion to the bed. She kicked off her boots and wrapped a blanket around herself, and fell asleep as soon as her head touched the pillow.

❖ STEVIC G'LADHEON ❖

"Like old times, isn't it?" Stevic G'ladheon poked a stick at the crackling campfire. "Just the two of us on the road without an inn in sight."

Sevano grunted from where he lay on his bedroll with his hands folded across his belly. "Aye, well, you ought to be home looking over accounts, or at the very least, leading one of your caravans."

The night was thick in this unpopulated countryside, and the piercing glimmer of stars above cold and distant. To the gods watching from above, would their little campfire appear as a point of light like a star? Not even a farmer's cot could be found for miles along this forsaken stretch of road, denying them even the homey glow of a candle in a window. They were alone, he and Sevano, with the night and the gods.

Stevic rested his arms on his knees. "Do you suppose she has spent many nights like this?"

Sevano grunted again. He knew to whom his chief referred without asking. "Kari is a bold lass. A little dark is nothing to her."

Stevic pulled his cloak over his shoulders and remained silent for a while, listening to the hiss and pop of the fire. He allowed the dancing tongues of flame to draw his gaze inward. He said, "I can't just sit at home reviewing accounts, you know. Nor can I lead a caravan. How do you expect me to do that?"

Sevano sighed. "I don't, but this delay will cost you profit."

"What is a loss of profit compared to my daughter?"

"Nothing," Sevano said. "If it were, you would not be you, and I would not follow you."

Stevic chuckled. "Old fool, old friend. More than a cargo master you are to me."

"If anyone can find Kari, it will be you."

When they had reached Corsa after their trip to Selium, Stevic learned the disquieting news that no one had seen Karigan and that she hadn't come home before them. He commenced to spread the word among his people that Karigan was missing, and he bade them keep watch for her on the road while they set out on trading missions. The word was spread among other merchants and their staffs as well. It was not long before all of Corsa had heard that the heir to the great G'ladheon fortune was missing. Rumors spoke of kidnappers, and some mean-spirted persons had even sent letters demanding ransom for her return. Stevic had followed up on each, but discovered them all to be lies. All lies that delayed him from finding his daughter.

Eventually Stevic and Sevano discarded the rumors as speculation, and left Corsa abuzz. They set out for Sacor City and would look for Karigan along the way. When they reached the city, they would look up Captain Mapstone and see if she had any news of Karigan.

Stevic left the fire and stretched out on his own bedroll. "We've a few more days on the road," he said. Oddly, he looked forward to reaching Sacor City, and dreaded it at the same time. He looked forward to sparring with that fiery Captain Mapstone. Quick she was. Quick to anger, quick of wit. She had a bright burning intelligence he found intriguing.

He dreaded reaching Sacor City because of the news he might find there, the news he most feared. He feared he might find that Karigan was still missing, or worse, if found, was dead.

Sevano snored softly on the other side of the campfire. Stevic could not sleep. Instead, he gazed long and hard at the distant stars and wondered about the capricious gods who inhabited them. If the gods existed, why was his daughter missing?

⊰ VISITOR TO THE REALM ⊱

Laren Mapstone sat at the base of the king's dais with his advisors, the Honorable Counselors Sperren and Devon, and Castellan Crowe. The crusty Sperren jabbered aimlessly about supposed civilians who disguised themselves as Green Riders and foolishly risked their lives to deliver unimportant messages to the king.

The discussions had been grinding round in circles for hours now, and night coated the tall windows like black enamel. Pages had come by an hour ago to light wall lamps and candles ensconced in wooden chandeliers. In the flickering light, the figures painted on the ceiling appeared alive, their expressions severely disapproving of those down below them. They were like ghosts who watched.

Finder, fast asleep at his master's feet, yipped and pedaled his paws in some doggie dream of chasing hares. At least he'd had some dinner and a good stiff walk. The kennel master had seen to that. Laren's stomach growled—even Finder's raw horse meat began to sound appetizing, and she would pay with a rotten backache for sitting in this Second Age-stiff chair probably created specifically to torture advisors.

"We can't just have civilians dressing up," Sperren droned on, "as servants of the realm."

Blah, blah, blah, Laren thought.

The king sat preoccupied in his chair, his brown eyes

distant, one leg across the other, his chin on his hand. He was crowned by a delicate silver fillet which he regarded, she knew, as more of a collar than a symbol of his kingship. His beard made him appear older, wiser, but Laren knew a tired young man was behind the beard. Crumpled in his lap lay the all-important message. At least, it should have been important.

Laren wondered what world the king's mind traveled in, for he seemed disinclined to participate in the discussion—rather, the bickering—of his advisors. He was probably walking the hills of his ancestral land with his dogs capering about him, where he could hear the rumble of the sea and the cries of gulls, and feel the free wind on his face. That was where he would be now if his father had not astounded all by naming him heir to the realm.

Zachary had protested exhaustively, had planned to govern Hillander Province and raise dogs, while his brother did the dirty work of managing the realm. In the end, King Amigast had seen through Prince Amilton, however. He had seen how the spoiled child had grown into a spoiled man who possessed not a single iota of leadership. The prince's mercurial temper was reflected in bruised servants, abused bed partners, and too many fine horses that had to be put down. Zachary wouldn't let his brother near the dogs. Everyone knew Amilton's nature, but said nothing, for his father saw only the charming side of his son. And Prince Amilton could be charming indeed.

Then, a delegation from the Cloud Islands had come to Sacoridia to negotiate trade agreements. The relationship between the two countries had never been very secure, and King Amigast sought friendship with the Islands knowing it would make Sacoridia a leader in commerce. Prince Amilton raped the daughter of one of the delegates, a girl hardly in her teens.

When Prince Amilton's act was discovered, the trade negotiations fell into shambles. The king finally listened to the whisperings around him, the whisperings of his son's indiscretions. Horrified that one of his own flesh was capable of such abuse, he began to look to his other son, Prince Zachary the workhorse, the son who, while his father was occupied fruitlessly teaching Prince Amilton the principles of kingship, excelled at his studies, learned about managing a province, and traveled to familiarize himself with the countryside and its people. When King Amigast chose Zachary to be his heir, everyone breathed a sigh of relief. Almost everyone.

Prince Amilton, soured and seething hate after the loss of the throne, had returned to Hillander Province as governor. But his indiscretions continued, the clan's wealth dwindled, and the province suffered. Zachary, now king, exiled his brother from the province and the country. No one knew where he had ended up. Laren had her own ideas about that, and had hoped the message would confirm her suspicions.

"Captain?"

"Hmmm?"

"*Captain.*"

Laren blinked. All of the advisors gazed at her. She straightened in her chair and cleared her throat, embarrassed to have been caught daydreaming. "Yes?"

"What is the story behind this girl?" Sperren asked. "Would you care to explain?"

Finally, a flicker of interest lit in the king's eyes.

"Karigan G'ladheon is a runaway from the school at Selium. Her father is a merchant in Corsa." Laren described her chance meeting with Stevic G'ladheon, and his request for her Riders to search for his daughter.

"And how did she contrive to get hold of F'ryan Coblebay's message?" Castellan Crowe asked in that snide tone of his.

Laren tried to conceal the annoyance in her voice. "I'm aware of the holes in my story, but I don't believe that *contrive* is an appropriate term. I can only speculate about how and why Karigan G'ladheon came into possession of F'ryan's message, and what happened thereafter." Undoubtedly the brooch had called her, but this she wouldn't tell the advisors. Let them believe it was pure coincidence.

"Then why don't we have her here for questioning?" Crowe had been a law speaker before coming to serve King Amigast, and often insisted on cross-examining people.

Counselor Devon echoed Crowe. "Yes, why isn't she here?" Devon was half blind with age, but immeasurably sharp. Often she was an excellent resource for how situations had been dealt with in the past. She had first served as Queen Isen's personal Weapon, then instructed a generation of Weapons in the way of the Black Shields. She slid into the advisor's position when her slowing reflexes and poor eyesight demanded she retire from the sword. As advisor, she oversaw the administrative activities of the Weapons, and so was not completely sundered from the profession that had once consumed her life.

Laren rubbed the brown scar on her neck. "She isn't in any condition for an *interrogation*." Crowe perked up at the word. "Perhaps you didn't notice, but she couldn't even support her own weight when she arrived."

"Yes, but if she's a threat—"

"She isn't a threat," Laren snapped.

"She used magic," Crowe said.

"Magic isn't necessarily a threat. Look, this girl isn't what we have to fear. She brought a message through who knows how many perils, and we should be thanking her rather than hurling suspicions at her like rocks."

"The message says nothing," Sperren said. He had been steward-governor of Hillander Province since Amigast had been a boy, only to be brought to Sacor City by the late king to advise him. Laren wondered who held that position now. "We've known about Lorilie Dorran living in North for months, and the king has tolerated her presence. And the two assassination attempts? Easily thwarted by Weapons."

"F'ryan Coblebay died because of this message." This time Laren did not bother to conceal her annoyance. "And F'ryan was known to write important messages in code so they would remain uncoded by any enemy who captured them. I request that I be permitted to take the message, Excellency, so I might determine whether or not it is in code."

Zachary nodded and passed it to her.

"What we should fear," Laren said, "are these." She held up the two black arrows which had lain on the floor beside her chair. She loathed touching them. They felt tainted and thirsty as if they could eat into her flesh.

"Yes, Captain," Crowe said. "You came in waving those arrows about this afternoon as if you knew the answers to Bovian's Seven Secrets. Please do explain."

"I won't pretend to know the answers to the Seven Secrets." She smiled grimly. "But I have a good inkling about these arrows. I found them in Selium . . . in F'ryan Coblebay's back. I spoke with a historian there, Master Galwin, who has an interest in relics of the ancient past."

"Those hardly look ancient," Devon said. It was amazing she could see them at all.

"I suspect they were very recently made, but in an ancient way. Master Galwin suggested that, by the way they were used to kill F'ryan—two arrows of a certain wood—that they are soul stealers."

"Oh, come now, Captain." Devon waved her hand dismissively. "Don't waste our time with mystical fancies. There is no magic of that dimension anymore, and no one can steal souls. I'm sorry for the loss of Rider Coblebay, for he was a good man, but I doubt his soul is anywhere but with the gods."

If Devon only knew. Oh, all the counselors knew that Green Riders had "talents," that they could do certain tricks, but if they all even knew to what extent magic was still used . . . Green Rider magic was *true* magic, not just something to perform after dinner for guests. Their magic was so taken for granted by the counselors that they forgot it was magic. At least the king was aware of the capabilities of his Green Riders, capabilities he utilized often—and exhaustively.

"Such weapons were used by Mornhavon the Black's

forces during the Long War," King Zachary said. His aides looked at him aghast, as if he had suddenly arisen from the dead. Finder lifted his head at the sound of his master's voice, and when he realized he wasn't the center of his master's attention, he dropped it down on his fore-paws again.

It's about time he spoke up, Laren thought. *My credi-bility has been sinking on a fast boat.*

"Soul-stealing weapons," the king continued, "were usually arrows, but could also be spears, so long as the shaft was made of wood from Blackveil Forest." The light flickered, as if simply naming the legendary forest held the power of the dark. Zachary combed his fingers through his beard, his eyes had grown distant again. "Strange, but I haven't thought about Blackveil in a very long time."

"Your Majesty," Devon said, "with all due respect, the Long War was nearly a thousand years ago. For all we know, the old forest has withered and died. Or a thriving green forest exists there. Who really knows what is on the other side of the wall?"

"Who knows, indeed?" The king shrugged. "But I doubt a green, living forest has supplanted the evil heart of the old. I shouldn't be so hasty to dismiss magic, Counselor. The potential for such powers never left the earth, though most of those who wielded them have. May I see the arrows?"

Laren handed them over, and the king scrutinized them, eyes squinted as if trying to make out some fine detail. Then he glanced at Laren.

"Captain, were you aware there were markings on these shafts?"

"Yes, Excellency. Master Galwin looked them over with a reading glass, but he didn't know what to make of them."

"They've the feel of Eltish script, but not. They are foul, not fair, and burn the eyes even as I try to read them. Probably some spells carved to ensure the arrows hit their mark, and to possess the soul. If they are soul stealers." The king shuddered visibly, and gave the arrows back. "I hate to contemplate how this wood came here, and who made the arrows."

The counselors fell into a thoughtful silence as they considered the ramifications of the king's words. Before any one of them could speak again, however, a low growl issued from Finder's throat, then a commotion broke out beyond the throne room doors. Excited voices drifted to them from the entryway.

"What is it this time?" Crowe muttered. "Another whirlwind?"

The king's herald ran full tilt down the runner, his cheeks flushed red. He skidded to a halt before the king, and gave a cursory bow.

"Neff?" the king asked.

The herald straightened to attention, and a stray tuft of yellow hair fell into his face. "Your Excellency." Neff drew his ceremonial trumpet to his lips, panted, and blasted five off-key notes. The brassy notes ricocheted around the chamber for some moments before Neff could continue with his breathless introduction. "May I present—"

The visitor was already striding down the runner. The advisors stood to their feet. Finder sat up with ears and head cocked.

"—his Lordship—"

The visitor glided as if on air, his cloak of many colors shimmered and floated behind him. A cowl concealed his face. The captain felt a certain thrill surge through her, a sense that something momentous was about to happen.

The visitor halted before them, and held his perfect hand up to stay Neff's introduction. He dipped in a graceful bow, then eased the hood away from his face and head.

Laren was struck at once by the radiant gold of his hair sweeping his shoulders. If his hair was the sun, his eyes were full of sky, like a clear crisp winter day. With regal and fair bearing, yet a bearing of ease, the visitor gazed at the king and his advisors with a smile.

"I greet you, King Zachary, son of Amigast. It is long since I last passed within Sacoridia's borders, but I find it fair as ever."

Laren heard his melodious voice, but also reached out with her mind to see what she could read within him, this stranger. But he blocked her, and all she could discover about him was that he was well-shielded.

"Who are you?" Devon asked. Her voice, compared to the visitor's, was as brassy as Neff's trumpet.

"I am Shawdell of Eletia." He waited for the astonished gasps to circulate around the advisors. Only King Zachary remained composed, and it was upon him that the Eletian cast his brilliant blue gaze, as if to exclude all others. "We've many things to discuss."

Karigan's sleep was dreamless and long. She was half aware of nighttime dark softening to dusky gray; vaguely she knew someone occasionally checked in on her and left trays of food. She merely rolled over and continued to slumber.

When her body felt restless and no longer able to contain itself, she swung her legs over the bed and stretched. She pulled the curtains away from the window, and dropped them with the shock of light. Then, slowly this time, she peeled the curtains away and allowed her eyes to adjust.

The barracks sat on a slight rise. The ground slanted away to a pasture where horses grazed on lush spring grasses, and flicked their tails at flies. Beyond the field was a line of trees which softened a high stone wall behind it.

In the shrubbery outside her window, chickadees and white-throated sparrows called out. She opened the window to listen, and was startled by a movement in the shadows of the barracks. Another Weapon. One to guard her from the inside, the other to guard her from the outside.

Karigan turned her back to the window, letting the curtains fall back into place. With a sigh, she attended to washing up and eating some of the food that had been left on the table. Eventually, someone would come to question her.

It was another hour or so before Karigan found herself pacing the tiny room, wishing for Mel or any company at all. The remnants of her meal had been swept away by a servant who was in too much of a hurry to say much more than she was sorry for the intrusion.

Another half hour passed and Karigan stared out the window at the horses, wishing she were one of them. The life of a horse must surely be less complicated.

Finally, a knock on the door drew her from the window. A Rider, whom she guessed to be Captain Mapstone for her red hair and hazel eyes, stepped through the doorway. She sniffed as she took in Karigan and the room, and said, "How depressing, but it would have been worse in the castle, guestroom or not." The captain appraised Karigan without expression, her hands clasped behind her back. "You ready to talk?"

Karigan was tired of the cramped room, tired of having nothing to do but stare out the window. "Not until I see The Horse."

The captain blinked. "The horse? What horse?"

"The—Condor."

"I can assure you that Condor has been well cared for. Melry has taken him under her wing, herself. It's important that we—"

"I won't talk till I've seen Condor."

Captain Mapstone raised a single brow. Without another word, she opened the door and gestured for Karigan to follow. Surprised the captain relented so easily, and a little embarrassed, Karigan stepped out into the corridor. Stone-faced Fastion blocked her way.

"Stand off, Weapon," the captain said. "This young

woman and I are just going out to have a talk and check on her horse."

"Sorry, Captain, but I can't sanction—"

"This is Rider business. If you feel compelled to protect the realm from a weaponless girl, then you may follow. This room has too much the feel of a cage, and she is not a prisoner."

There was a turning down of the thin line that was Fastion's mouth, but he didn't argue. Rather, he followed them down the corridor at a discreet distance.

The captain leaned so her words could be heard by Karigan only. "Sometimes I'm not sure if Weapons are a natural phenomenon or not."

Karigan chuckled, remembering what Mel said the previous night.

"We were a little concerned," the captain said. "You didn't awaken for some time. I even had a mender check on you."

"What time is it?"

"Near eight in the evening."

Karigan's mouth dropped open. When they stepped outside, the sun was low and the grass was wet with dew. "At first I thought it was morning when I looked out the window, then I knew it must be afternoon at least. But evening?" The Wild Ride must have been more taxing than she could have known.

The captain nodded, and left the path to walk down the slope behind the barracks to the pasture. She leaned against the fence, scanning the pasture as a sea captain might the horizon.

"He's in the far corner, if my sight isn't failing me."

Karigan squinted her eyes. In the deepening dusk, she made out his familiar gawky figure in the distance.

"Call him," Captain Mapstone said.

"What?"

"Call him. He'll come."

Karigan cupped her hands around her mouth. "HORSE!"

He lifted his head, his ears perked forward. He cantered across the field with his tail held high, and when he reached them, Karigan slipped between the fence rails and flung her arms around his neck. He rubbed his head against her shoulder almost knocking her over.

"You crazy horse," she said, grinning. "Mel sure shined you up."

"Yesterday, he was nearly as gray as you," Captain Mapstone said. "That's why we didn't question you sooner. We wanted to make sure you were well. But now we must talk." At Karigan's crestfallen look, she added, "We can talk here. You are fortunate the counselors and king are preoccupied, or they would've exhausted you with hours of meaningless questions."

They sat on the top rail of the fence as Condor grazed nearby.

"You are Karigan G'ladheon," the captain said.

"Did I tell you that?"

"No, but your father's description was most complete, and the ring on your finger matches his." At Karigan's look of astonishment, she explained how she met Stevic G'ladheon in Selium, and the events that followed. "We've a Rider named Connly who has the ability to send messages in a most unusual way. He sends them with his thoughts."

Before Karigan's adventures, she would have thought the captain's statement absurd. But not now. She hooked a strand of hair behind her ear. "He sent a message about me to other Riders?"

"Not exactly. He could send to only one other Rider. Joy Overway."

That explained why Joy had been searching for someone in North who answered Karigan's description. "I saw Joy . . . dead."

"We knew, or Connly knew, exactly when she died. Joy's talent was similar to Connly's, only she *received* thought messages. They were partners, you see, who were intimately bound by their abilities even though it was those abilities that often separated them by great distances. There is no use having a sender and receiver in the same town. Despite the distances that separated them, they were closer than any couple I have ever known. I can't tell you what it was like to experience Connly's grief."

Bats, drawn to the insects hovering above their heads, careened in the air around them.

"I brought Joy's brooch with me."

"Yes. The brooches do have a way of finding their way home." Captain Mapstone rubbed the dark scar on her throat. "You brought it here among other things, including a very curious crystal. Tell me Karigan G'ladheon, how a schoolgirl managed to get herself involved in Green Rider affairs. I don't want any omissions."

Karigan sighed, but The Horse, *Condor,* she had to remind herself, nuzzled her knee in encouragement. She started with the beginning, all the way back to the fight with Timas Mirwell and the private sessions with Arms Master Rendle.

"I met Rendle," Captain Mapstone said. "Before I left Selium, he spoke with me—at your father's behest—to urge me to do my utmost to find you." The captain smiled briefly. "Your father had already persuaded me to do so, but I guess he thought that adding Master Rendle's voice to the cause would ensure my cooperation without a doubt."

Karigan smiled faintly in return, knowing just how persuasive her father could be.

"Rendle was very concerned about you," the captain continued. "Said you were the brightest student he had had in a long time. You would do well to continue lessons with him. He also believed you were innocent of mischief in that swordfight with young Mirwell, and has since been trying to clear your name."

Karigan was surprised and touched by this, wishing suddenly to be sitting in Selium's field house, sewing together pieces of worn fighting gear, and listening to Master Rendle's advice and tales.

She continued her own narrative, jumping on the ground when the railing grew too uncomfortable to sit on. Captain Mapstone sat silhouetted against the night sky, as unmoving as a Weapon, and watching her with an intensity that was disquieting. Every so often she touched her winged horse brooch, and Karigan had the feeling of being tested, especially when she told of communicating with the ghost of F'ryan Coblebay. She described the Berry sisters, and recounted her fight with the creature of *Kanmorhan Vane,* and the help provided by the gray eagle Softfeather and the Eletian, Somial.

"Curious you should mention an Eletian," the captain murmured. Then she motioned for Karigan to continue.

She told of Immerez, and Jendara and Torne, and of her flight to the waystation in North. She paused and stared at the captain. "You're alive! You're the Mapstone mentioned in the book at the waystation. You survived."

"I'm no ghost, if that's what you mean." The captain actually chuckled. "Close calls come to all Green Riders. So far in your story, you've had as many as some."

Karigan spoke of Abram Rust, the forest, Joy's body in a horse cart, Lorilie Dorran, the gray-cloaked Shadow Man, and the Wild Ride.

"The Wild Ride," the captain said. "They—the guards and the counselors—didn't know what you were when you arrived. A blur, a twist of wind, they said. Sacoridia has not heard the like of it for a thousand years. How did you do it?"

"I—I didn't do it," Karigan said.

"Are you so sure?"

"The ghosts—"

"Ghosts. I don't know."

The scent of grass was heavy in the damp air, crickets chirruped in the distance, and fireflies left behind tiny blind spots in Karigan's eyes.

"Yes," Captain Mapstone said as if to herself. "You are fortunate the king and his counselors are busy with their guest. Let me see your wrists, Karigan."

They had healed so quickly that she hadn't needed to

dress them the last few nights, but the burns had left scars of melted flesh that shined in the moonlight.

"The burns were from the blood of a creature from *Kanmorhan Vane?*" Captain Mapstone asked.

Karigan nodded.

"Interesting. Those black arrows were made with wood from *Kanmorhan Vane.* Your Shadow Man works with very old and evil magic. I can only guess what torment they caused F'ryan and Joy."

"I think they're still in pain," Karigan said. *Two black-shafted arrows protrude from a blood-dampened back that will not dry,* Miss Bunchberry had said.

"I fear that our troubles are greater than I already thought," Captain Mapstone said. "I begin to wonder how this gray-cloaked character is connected to Mirwell." Then she looked at Karigan with a grim smile. "You outran two black arrows on the Wild Ride. Karigan, you are no ordinary schoolgirl."

Karigan did not know whether or not to take it as a compliment. This Captain Mapstone was difficult to read, an admirable trait in a merchant, but otherwise frustrating. "What now?" she asked.

The captain jumped from the fence to her feet, and slowly stretched her back with a grimace. "This damp is getting to my bones," she said. "What now, indeed. The counselors have dismissed the message you carried through such peril."

"What?" It was unthinkable! "People tried to kill me . . . The Mirwellians . . ."

Captain Mapstone nodded. "The message speaks of events that have long since passed. The counselors refuse to take it seriously. Gods be cursed!" She pounded her fist into her other hand. "I expected the message to bear news of some Mirwellian plot and the whereabouts of Prince Amilton. From your story, it sounds as if my suspicions are on track, but I've nothing to back it up with. The counselors must hear how the Mirwellians were so intent to stop you. F'ryan and Joy were effectively stopped. There is much to indicate a plot, but they won't listen to me now that their attention is focused on their visitor. I've some Riders working on the message to see if it's in code. It seems straightforward, however."

Dumbstruck, Karigan hardly heard the captain. "I can't believe the message said nothing important."

Captain Mapstone sighed deeply and slapped Condor on the neck. "Some Riders never see, in the duration of their careers, as much as you did in one ride. Your courage to carry F'ryan's message, essential in content or not, is more than admirable. Karigan, I've believed every word you told me of your incredible story because my talent is detecting honesty." She touched her winged horse brooch. "I want you to talk with the king. I want you to tell him your story—he will be interested in hearing about Immerez. And I think he trusts me enough that he will grant you an audience without his advisors present."

Me? Karigan cried from inside.

"Oh, Fastion," the captain called out sweetly. "You can come out from whatever shadow you've been lurking in. We're done now."

Karigan perceived a great weariness in the captain as they bade Condor good night. The captain moved stiffly, and her features seemed pulled back in some sort of pain.

The brooch? Karigan wondered.

◈ INTRIGUE AND INVITATION ◈

Karigan did not hear from the captain again the next day, or the day after that. Mel, however, provided her with companionship, a friend amidst stony-faced Weapons who guarded her door. Eventually she was allowed to accompany Mel to the stable to help with chores and visit Condor, but always with a Weapon in tow. The normalcy of the activity, the drone of flies, stomp of hooves, familiar smells of leather and manure, and Mel's earthy personality, helped ease her nerves despite those who shadowed her.

Mel pitched muck out of a stall into an overflowing barrow, and Karigan propped her elbows on the stall door. "I must say," Mel said, "the castle folk are abuzz about that visitor. I'm certain they've forgotten all about you."

"What visitor? Captain Mapstone mentioned something the other night."

Mel leaned on her pitchfork and raised her brows. "You haven't heard? But then again I don't expect you would have. The day after you arrived, one of those Eletians rode right up to the castle."

"An Eletian?" Karigan asked incredulously.

"Yeah, like the old stories. Have you heard those?"

"I have. What's an Eletian doing here?"

Mel paused to wave away a phalanx of flies buzzing around her face. "Well, that's what I would like to know. Captain says no one's seen one for so long, no one knew if they were still real. And all of a sudden one comes looking for King Zachary."

"I met an Eletian," Karigan said.

"Oh, go on."

"It's true. But I was sick at the time and didn't notice much. If you don't believe me, ask the captain."

Mel let out a low whistle. "She'd know if you were lying or not. Say, I wonder if this is the same one."

"Did he give a name?"

Mel scratched her head and thought for a moment. "Shaw . . . Shawsomething, Shawdale. No, wait a moment. Shawdell. That's it."

Karigan shook her head in disappointment. "No, not the same one."

"Captain said she's never seen hair like his before. Like spun gold, she said. And she can't read him, you know, for honesty. She says he knows how to shield his thoughts."

"Eletians are different," Karigan said, and she could almost catch the rhythm of the soundless song she heard long ago in a clearing she would never find again. "Childlike, ancient, magical, and beautiful all at once. Of course, I only really saw the one and who knows what the rest are like. Just like there are good Sacoridians and bad Sacoridians." Immerez, for one, came to mind. She shrugged. "How strange one would come here, though, after all this time."

"He wants to reestablish ties with Sacordia." The Rider Alton D'Yer stood silhouetted between the great sliding doors of the stable entrance. Then he strode toward them, his features defining as he walked into the shadows of the stable. His shoulders were thrown back in a confident way. Gauntlets hung neatly folded over his belt, and not a speck of dust deigned to settle on his boots. Nor did he exhibit any outward signs of past injury as so many Riders seemed to.

He was the only Rider who dared approach Karigan and speak to her directly, unintimidated by the Weapons, or rumors of her strange arrival. At least, she hoped it was the Weapons who caused the others to keep their distance and not something about herself.

He touched his forehead and bowed gracefully. "Alton D'Yer at your service."

Karigan raised her eyebrow. A formal greeting. She put her hand to her heart and bowed in return. "Karigan G'ladheon of Clan G'ladheon at yours."

"Ah," he said, "a merchant clan."

Karigan nodded, expecting the usual sarcasm, but none was forthcoming. He was a D'Yer, a very old family, a bloodline directly descended from the original Sacor Clans. If the Hillander Clan died out, the other old lines would vie for the throne, marking Alton as a possible heir. It was surprising his family allowed him to be a Green Rider, especially with the danger the occupation entailed.

"I see you keep stern company," he said.

"My shadow." Karigan glanced over her shoulder at the Weapon who stood planted in a dark cobwebby corner, her back ramrod straight, and her arms crossed. She did not so much as blink an eye or shift her weight, her mouth a tight, grim line.

"The Eletian," Karigan prompted him.

Alton shrugged. "I saw him from a distance, but I've heard that the Eletians are planning to leave their seclusion. With all the groundmite activity, I'm not surprised."

Karigan sucked on a piece of straw. The dusty haze of the stable softened Alton's features. "But why come to Sacoridia and not, say, Rhovanny?"

"Why not?" Alton countered.

Why not. Karigan considered, but she could find no reason why the Eletian would have chosen one kingdom over the other, except that Sacoridia was directly south of the mysterious Elt Wood. Whatever the case, the Eletian's arrival had taken the focus off her. Maybe they would forget about her completely and she could go home.

A bell clanged, cutting off further discussion.

"Rider coming!" Mel dropped her pitchfork and

sprinted from the dark stable, Alton on her heels. Karigan followed more slowly.

A stablehand rang the bell which was mounted on the outside of the building. A Rider galloped up the hill trailing a cloud of dust, and dismounted as his horse skidded to a halt. Alton grabbed the horse's reins, and without a word, the Green Rider strode away toward the castle with message satchel in hand.

"Got to fetch a fresh horse," the stablehand said, "in case he's gotta go out again."

Alton and the stablehand ducked inside to tack another horse. Mel loosened the girth on the messenger's puffing horse, and proceeded to walk him in a large circle to help cool him down.

"I wonder what's so important," Karigan said, keeping step with Mel.

"Not much, I'd say," the girl replied. "If it was real important, he would have ridden right up to the castle. Also, he walked fast, but didn't run toward the castle."

"Oh."

"I'm real used to how things work here," Mel said. "So is Alton."

"When does he ride?"

Mel slapped the neck of the sweaty horse and whispered something to his flickering ears. "He doesn't."

"What?"

"Alton doesn't. His parents won't permit it. Pure D'Yer blood, you know. Rubs him like a saddle sore to see everyone else ride while he sits here."

"But why is he a Rider in the first place?"

"The brooch accepted him."

"Accepted him?"

"Yep. The brooches are attracted to people who will be able to use them. People who have talents." Here Mel faltered, as if she was not sure how it worked herself.

Karigan nodded slowly, recalling a conversation in the parlor of the Berry sisters. *The brooch has accepted you,* Miss Bay had said. *It wouldn't permit you to wear it if it didn't perceive you as a Green Rider.*

"And what talent does Alton have?"

"No one knows. He's never been on a ride, so he hasn't found out."

Karigan fingered her brooch. Had the brooch accepted her for her talents, or by default because its previous owner had died and willed it to accept her? Maybe it was because she was the only one around stupid enough to take it.

"Karigan?" Captain Mapstone had walked up to the stable as quiet as a Weapon. She stood in the entrance, leaning against the doorway. "The king will see you now."

The captain insisted that she change immediately, saying that what she presently wore was covered with too much horse dust, and that would not be acceptable in front of the king. Karigan dressed in the full uniform of a Green Rider, her black boots highly polished, collar stiffened and wrapped with a black stock, and gauntlets folded over her belt. The winged horse brooch was clasped to her shortcoat, no matter that the king wouldn't even be able to see it. All that was missing from her ensemble was the saber.

The uniform was pressed with razor-sharp creases, and formally cut. Captain Mapstone, Karigan decided, must be trying to make some sort of point by having her wear it. It was painfully uncomfortable, not in the way it felt on her, but in the way she was certain everyone who looked at her would see through her, as if she tried to pass herself off as someone she was not. A fraud. Of course, she had worn the field uniform before, but that was different. All of her clothes were rags, and it was either wear green, or wear nothing at all.

"I don't see why I have to wear this," Karigan said. She followed slightly behind the captain as they passed through the castle courtyard. She avoided the glances of other folk, though in truth, most did not notice her. She was one uniformed commoner in the midst of many. A few Green Riders hastening to and fro, however, caught her eye and smiled encouragingly.

"Appearance is nearly everything in court," Captain Mapstone said. "The first time the king saw you, you had just arrived under remarkable circumstances which prevented you from appearing polished. Of course, he expects that when a message is being delivered, but at other times, a professional appearance is in order."

Karigan wanted to protest that she was not a professional Green Rider, but already they were in the throne room and she was looking down the chamber where a solitary man sat in an ornate chair, a dog at his feet. No counselors were in attendance, as the captain had desired, though the everpresent Weapons hugged the shadows.

As she started toward the king, the captain at her side, the white Hillander terrier trotted down the runner wagging his short tail. He jumped up on Karigan in greeting, and forgetting where she was, she bent down to pat him on the head. The captain nudged her and they proceeded forward, passing through columns of sunlight that streamed through the west side windows. The dog ran alongside them.

Karigan copied the captain's bow, rather plain and straightforward in her mind, compared to the traditional bows of the clans. The king was young for a king, or at least for what Karigan thought a king should be. He was no more than ten or fifteen years older than herself, though an amber beard made him appear more mature. He reminded her of a younger version of someone she had once seen, but could not place who or where.

And his eyes. The almond-shaped brown eyes of the Hillander region where one could look out to sea, look out to the horizon and find nothing between land and sky but the constant undulations of waves. It was said that the folk of Hillander bore more saltwater in their veins than blood. And here the king sat trapped in his stone castle, in the stifling static air. He had the look of a young shipmaster stranded inland, brooding under heavy weather, yearning for free air and the open expanse of water, the rhythmic curl of waves on the shore.

The king sat slumped and tired on his throne chair, his head propped on his hand. His lids hung low over his eyes as he listened to Captain Mapstone begin an introduction.

"Dismissed, Captain."

The captain stopped in mid-sentence, her mouth hanging open until she remembered to close it. "Yes, Sire." She flicked a warning look in Karigan's direction, bowed, and left the throne. The terrier began to follow her out.

"Finder!" the king snapped, and the dog reluctantly stopped in his tracks, tail wagging, and watched the captain's retreating back for a moment before curling up at Zachary's feet.

What had been in the captain's warning look? And now the king gazed at her. Boredly? Expectantly? She fidgeted and cast her eyes to the floor.

"Clan G'ladheon?" he asked. The abruptness of it caused Karigan's heart to leap. "A bought clanship if I've been informed correctly."

Karigan's cheeks heated. "A clanship your grandmother sanctioned." She nearly bit her tongue. It was just like her to speak without thinking.

Zachary blinked like a somnolent lion. "Captain Mapstone has told me something of your journey. Of course, my counselors and I witnessed your unusual entrance." He paused, stroking his beard. "But, that's all irrelevant at the moment. Do you play Intrigue, Karigan G'ladheon?"

"I, uh . . . ." The change in topic caused her tongue to stumble. What did he mean her journey was irrelevant? "I've played Intrigue."

"Good."

The king clapped for a servant. A chair was brought for Karigan, and a table was set between them, the game placed on top.

"It's not as good without a Triad," the king said. "Perhaps I should have had the captain stay, but this will do. I've not played for some time."

"But—"

"Green or blue pieces?"

"Green, but—"

The king chuckled gleefully. "Perfect."

Karigan then realized what color she had chosen and groaned. Why did the king want to play a game? Why was her journey irrelevent? He actually stepped down from his throne chair and sat on the bottom step of the dais, and set up the game for two players. The pieces were little wooden figures. Karigan thought the king would possess a game made of silver and gold and jewels, but his set was far cruder than any she would have imagined.

"Now roll the dice, and we will see who possesses the stronger strategy."

The sleeping lion came to life as the game progressed. The king managed to counter any move Karigan made. Her pieces were pushed back, captured, and "killed." He lured her spies into fatal traps and goaded her knights into fights they could not possibly win.

The fresco paintings of Zachary's ancestors glared down at Karigan from the ceiling. She clasped and unclasped her hands under Zachary's relentless attack, as each of her knights was killed by common infantrymen. Her mind screamed that this was not what the king should be doing, that he must be insane to want to play games rather than hear of her journey. And yet there they sat, he on the dais step, she on the chair, each the reflection of the other as they concentrated on the game, as the sunlight penetrated the throne room at a greater slant, then began to recede like a blade withdrawn.

After two hours, Karigan sat limp in her chair. Zachary knocked her king off the board with a flick of his forefinger, and frowned at her. "You told me you've played Intrigue before."

"I have."

"That was one of the sloppiest games I've ever seen. You had messengers. Green Riders use special talents. Why didn't you give your messengers special talents?"

"It's a game. You can't just give pieces special abilities. I mean, the rules—"

"Listen to me, Karigan G'ladheon." The king bent forward, his face just inches from hers. "You can't play at Intrigue and expect to win by adhering to the rules. Use what is available to you. If I did not," he added in a whisper, "my portrait would have been painted on the ceiling long ago. Do you see the space there behind the late king, my father?"

Karigan followed his gaze toward the ceiling where King Amigast was painted beside Queen Isen. His eyes were solemn, and almond-shaped like Zachary's. A long blue robe fell to his feet, and while most of the other figures on the ceiling held weapons or scepters, King Amigast held an open book. On his other side was nothing but empty ceiling, a blank canvas. A chill tingled in Karigan's spine.

"That space," Zachary said, "is for me."

He removed a velveteen pouch from beneath his heather mantle of state, and handed it to her. She loosed the drawstrings, and the scent of bayberry drifted to her. Inside, she discovered with joy, were the items the Weapon had confiscated from her, except for Joy Overway's brooch. She removed the moonstone which ignited in a silver blaze at her touch.

Zachary squinted through the intense light. "Curious. That stone would not light for anyone else, not even the Eletian."

Karigan dropped it into the velveteen pouch and reluctantly passed it back, but the king shook his head.

"You are to keep those things, they are yours. Captain Mapstone says your stories are true, and by the special nature of her ability, I believe her. Your trinkets are your tools. Use what is available to you. I see no threat to me from you."

Karigan relaxed and clasped the pouch in both hands. "Thank you," she said with a relieved breath.

Zachary nodded, and patted his knee. Finder jumped into his lap, tail wagging furiously. The king absently stroked Finder and gazed at nothing, his eyes unfocused. Eventually he said, "The sequence of events that have led you here are quite remarkable. A schoolgirl who can't even play a decent game of Intrigue. The daughter of a wealthy merchant . . ."

Karigan stiffened again, anger prickling inside. "Sire, for one thing, I don't know exactly how you get your information except from people who risk their lives to deliver it to you. By chance, I was one of those people. Yes, a schoolgirl. Yes, a merchant's daughter. My life was threatened, I was held captive, and I went through a lot to get here. I am tired of being treated like some criminal for doing my best for Sacoridia.

"I might suggest, Excellency, that you leave behind your stone walls and see those whom you rule. Take a look at your realm. The North Road is in terrible condition. How do you expect healthy commerce up north when merchant trains can hardly make it down the road? And what about the outlaws who attack caravans, homesteads, and the village of North?

"Take a look at the people who live in the borderlands in fear of groundmites, not to mention any strange creatures that might come from Blackveil Forest. The eagle, Softfeather, told me to tell you there is a breach in the D'Yer Wall. Your people, Excellency, are crying out for protection from you, and fewer taxes, and—" Karigan stopped and swallowed. Speaking her mind to Dean Geyer was one thing, but speaking it to a king was another. The dean could suspend her, but the king could do much worse.

Zachary laughed. *He laughed!* Finder sat up and barked. A light ignited in the king's eyes. "Many people hate me and my policies," he said. "It is refreshing to hear a new voice, though. You will make a fine Green Rider."

"I'm not—"

"Dismissed."

"But—"

"Dismissed until tomorrow night's ball. I expect you to be there. In fact, I command it."

Karigan opened her mouth to protest again, but the firm hand of a Weapon on her shoulder prompted her to clamp her mouth shut. She stood up on shaky legs and bowed awkwardly, but she wasn't sure the king even knew she was still there. He continued to stroke Finder's back, his thoughts haunting some faraway place.

Karigan left the throne room as fast as possible without running. When she cleared the huge double doors, she brushed into some crusty old man wearing a bear pelt. She mumbled an apology, and rushed away, intent on leaving the king far behind.

Karigan burst into her room, and caught Captain Mapstone in mid-pace. "Finally," the older woman said. "Tell me what happened."

Exhausted by her afternoon with the king, Karigan dropped down on her bed and groaned.

"I see I won't get anything from you until you're nourished with some food and drink." She tracked down the food herself, bringing it to Karigan faster than anyone else could have.

Between mouthfuls of pastry and sausage washed down with cold cider, Karigan told all that transpired in the throne room. By the time she finished, the captain was pacing again.

"Tell me again what you said to the king about his policies."

Karigan heaved a tired sigh and repeated that part of the story. Captain Mapstone paused, her expression bemused. She rubbed her chin, and smiling, said, "You told him to . . . You told him to . . ." Tickled by the thought of some common girl standing up to the king, she fell into convulsive laughter.

Karigan scowled. It wasn't unlike the king's own response, and one she hardly expected from Captain Mapstone.

Captain Mapstone wiped tears from her eyes. "You've got spunk, girl. I wouldn't be surprised if you made it to Sacor City in one piece on pure spunk alone." She scraped the chair out from under the table and dropped wearily into it. Her expression turned stern again, yet her eyes still danced in amusement. "I haven't laughed like that in a hundred years. And don't you let on to the others that I did either." She sighed. "It wouldn't fit their image of me."

Karigan crossed her arms. "I don't find it particularly funny."

Captain Mapstone gazed at her levelly. "Considering the king didn't lop your head off himself, you shouldn't complain. I'm not sure I comprehend his behavior either, though I've known him since he was a boy. I was certain he would want to hear more from you. Why play Intrigue?"

"Does this mean I can go home now?"

Captain Mapstone shook her head. "The king expects you to attend the ball tomorrow evening. That's another curious thing. Why invite *you?*"

Karigan glowered. "I don't care. I just want to get out of these green clothes and go home. I've done enough here. You can't hold me here against my will."

The captain's face grew unreadable. "There are a few things you must understand, Karigan. First of all, you are not being held here. At least, not anymore. The king requested that you attend his ball—quite an honor and one that few Green Riders experience. Secondly, you carried F'ryan Coblebay's message here in a way no Green Rider will ever forget. We may not understand why such a message, seemingly unimportant, was so pursued by the Mirwellians and the Shadow Man, but it doesn't lessen your deed. Thirdly, we would like you to stay with us for a while so we can understand the Wild Ride." Then she added very quietly, "And you've the brooch."

Karigan stood up, the wooden floor groaning beneath her feet. She peered out the window. The last rays of sun caressed the pasture where Mel was out banging on a bucket of grain to lure the horses in for the night. "I don't care about the brooch. You can keep it."

"I'm afraid that's not possible. It has accepted you."

Karigan turned on the captain. "Everyone keeps referring to me as a Green Rider. I am not a Green Rider and I don't want to be a Green Rider. I just want to go home. My father probably assumes I'm dead by now."

"I dispatched a Rider upon your arrival to inform him otherwise." Captain Mapstone rubbed her neck scar. "Whether you act as a Green Rider or not is up to you, but I'll warn you now, that you will always hear the rhythm of hoofbeats in your dreams." She stood brusquely to her feet. "I recommend you appear at the king's ball as a Green Rider. Then, Karigan G'ladheon, you may go home as you will." Without another word, she left.

Karigan looked out the window with a sigh. She would never get home at this rate, and things were only getting worse rather than better. She caught some movement near a tree about a hundred paces from her window. *Weapon,* she thought, but F'ryan Coblebay looked back at her, his features pained. Without movement, or the flick of an eyelash, he disappeared.

F'ryan Coblebay's message had been delivered. Why did his ghost still follow her?

⊰ MIRWELL ⊱

"Let go of my arm." Mirwell batted Beryl's hands away. Normally he would enjoy her touch, but not now, and not here at the entrance to King Zachary's throne chamber. Imagine that Greenie nearly knocking him over as if he were no more than a common servant! They had no respect for their betters. "I can make it on my own two feet," he grumbled to his aide. It was bad enough having to lean on her for support all the way from the courtyard, down the long castle corridors, until they finally reached the great oak doors of the firebrand and crescent moon.

The herald was bearing the standard of Mirwell down the runner, announcing in high-pitched tones the arrival of Lord-Governor Tomastine II.

Mirwell laughed gruffly.

"What is it, my lord?" Beryl asked, stoic as ever.

"Look to the king, my dear. Either my vision has deteriorated greatly, or for the first time since His Excellency's ascension to the throne, the bit—" He swallowed suddenly and amended, "Captain Mapstone isn't by his side in my presence." Mirwell glanced at the Weapons by the door to assess whether or not they had caught his near indiscretion, but they stood mute and glassy-eyed like wax figures in a diorama at the Sacor City War Museum. "Unnatural," he muttered.

Beryl cast questioning eyes on him.

"The captain," he said, "do you see her?"

"No, my lord. Your eyes haven't failed you."

"I thought not! Can't get around as well as I used to, but I can see as well as any old owl."

A shrill trumpet blast was their cue to make their way down the runner to the king's throne.

Mirwell straightened his shoulders despite a back that protested after days of arduous travel, and cleared his throat. "Now remember," he whispered to Beryl, "keep just a pace behind me, no slower, no faster. We'll make it look natural, right? Make him wait some." Mirwell adjusted the bear pelt on his shoulders, which he wore for state occasions no matter what the heat. It reminded all that he, Tomastine II, though he be old, was still the same man, the strong man, who with only a dagger, had slain a bear that would have killed a lesser man.

Mirwell made his way down the runner, slow and deliberately, as if carrying his weight with great dignity. He ignored the gravelly pain in his knee that intensified with each step, and he concealed the limp as best he could. The effort, combined with the heavy pelt, caused sweat to trickle down his temples.

Beryl, true to his command, remained precisely a pace behind him. He imagined her shoulders thrown back, the erectness of her spine, and the tilt of her chin all communicating: *I am of Mirwell and I serve with pride.* The very thought made his heart swell and a tear fill his eye, the same way the Arms Parade did on his birthday—Mirwell's own provincial holiday. Oh, there were few sights so exhilarating as hundreds of columns of soldiers and horsemen with shining helms, marching and riding in precise formation down Mirwellton's main thoroughfare.

The herald stood at attention catty-corner to the king's throne, trumpet tucked under one arm, and the Mirwell banner supported on its ceremonial pike leaning against the other. Mirwell noted, with some surprise, a chair recently vacated, and a game of Intrigue set before the king.

"Your Excellency." He touched his forehead and strained his back in a deep bow.

"Welcome, War Hammer." The king used the traditional greeting and Mirwell was pleased. "Won't you be seated? It will be easier for us to speak eye to eye."

"As you wish." It wasn't true, of course. Mirwell would have to crane his neck to look at the king up on his dais, but it was better than having his knee suddenly buckle beneath him and send him sprawling on the floor. He suspected Zachary was well aware of his infirmity, whether he learned it from that mind-reading woman Mapstone, or deduced it from his own keen observations was another question, but the king's craftiness impressed Mirwell. The excuse allowed him to rest while retaining his dignity.

The two exchanged the usual civilities: weather, travel, health, the state of the province. Zachary's dog jumped from his lap and sniffed the hem of Mirwell's bear pelt. It wheezed, then rejoined its master. It was beyond Mirwell how these little terriers had been such a menace to the groundmites during the Long War. He doubted they could even tree a bear, or retrieve a duck from a pond, but they probably had their uses.

"My aide, Major Spencer," Mirwell said in introduction. He could almost feel the heat of her presence through the back of his chair. "She is new since last we met. Old Haryo at long last met his soldier's final rest." A good solid friend, Haryo. And more loyal than a dog. Mirwell had seen to it that his friend had received a most impressive funeral.

The king barely flicked an eyelash at Beryl. "I trust you will join us for the annual ball and hunt?" the king said.

"I wouldn't think to miss it. About the only time I see Sacor City is at the King's Spring Hunt, Excellency." He would not miss it, indeed. After the hunt—or was massacre a better term?—Amilton would take the throne as king. Did Zachary suspect? His demeanor was as cool and distant as ever, and Mirwell's own court spy had informed him that, though the message had gotten through, it said nothing about the assassination plans, and in fact, nothing to implicate Mirwell or Amilton, and no one was paying attention to the Greenie who had carried the message. A waste of time and effort, the pursuit of that Greenie, but better to be on the safe side.

But who knew what went on behind the king's closed features? He had a card player's face, even better than his father's, and loads better than his brother's. Amilton was as subtle as a herd of horses, but he would be all the easier to control. Mirwell bent over and picked up the game piece of the green king from the floor. Other pieces still stood in formation on the Intrigue board.

"Are you an Intrigue player?" the king asked.

Mirwell chuckled. "You see my interest! Well, yes, I admit the competitive streak runs through me. When the long winter runs dull, a game of Intrigue is in order. I see you soundly defeated your opponent in this game."

Zachary bent down and scratched the dog behind its ear. "An unskilled opponent . . . No, rather, an uncommitted player."

Mirwell grunted. "When you aren't committed to the outcome of the game, there is no way you can win. It must have been a very disappointing match."

"In some ways it was, but in other ways it was quite rewarding."

Mirwell wondered at the king's expression, for suddenly the card player's facade fell away, and he saw a man who seemed amused and preoccupied about something. Whoever his opponent had been, he had caught the king's interest. He set the green king on the board, on its side in the dead position, the way it should be.

"Tomorrow," the king said, "I'm calling a council of governors. All but Adolind are here, the governor still mourns his daughter."

"Ah, yes. Killed in the groundmite massacre with those other schoolchildren." Mirwell shook his head as if he had not been the one who engineered it. "A pity. I am thankful to the gods my Timas was not among them."

"A great loss," Zachary said grimly. "Those children were part of Sacoridia's future. Despite the loss among your other counterparts, they deemed themselves able to attend. We've a visitor in the city the likes of whom we have not seen for hundreds of years."

"Truly?"

"Yes. I should like you to meet him, and judge him as you may. In the meantime, your suites in the east wing have been readied for you and your staff. I hope you will be comfortable."

Mirwell stood up to bow, thinking that he would like Zachary well enough if he wouldn't impede his acquisition of power and lands. "It is always comfortable, Excellency."

With the formalities concluded, he hastened out of the throne room at a rate at which he surprised himself. But once he was through the doors, he clamped his hands around Beryl's arm.

"We shall go to our suites, my dear," he said. "You will have a much different perspective of the place than when you were with the regular militia."

"I already have," she said.

Mirwell scrunched his brows together. "Already?" Ah, well. He would experience every moment with her. He wouldn't let her out of his sight.

↫ KARIGAN ATTENDS THE KING'S BALL ↬

Karigan approached the grand entrance to the ballroom from a walkway that wound through the rose gardens of the east courtyard. The cloying scent of red and pink blossoms almost overpowered the still night. Luminiers flickered along the walkway with a festive radiance that might have put her in a celebratory mood if not for the choking collar of her Green Rider uniform. Once again, Captain Mapstone had seen her into the formal uniform, this time with the addition of a gold sash about her waist.

Music and gold light, conversation and laughter, and orchestral music drifted from the open doors into the warm evening to mingle with the chirping choruses of crickets. Guests in colorful finery clustered around the entrance and Karigan wondered again what she was doing here. Like her father, she was not fond of the aristocracy and here she would be surrounded by it.

She stood in line, tugging at her collar, waiting while two guards in king's livery checked invitations. Her palms sweated because she had not been given one, and had nothing to show the guards. She was about to turn back, to return to the sanctuary of Rider barracks, but was just then noticed by a guard.

"Hey, Greenie," he said.

Karigan swallowed and stepped forward.

"You have an invitation?"

"I, uh . . ."

The other guard laughed. "Greenie's trying to break in on the ball without an invitation."

Karigan furrowed her brows. "I was invited. Rather, I was commanded here by the king himself."

The first guard broke out laughing. "Commanded! That's a new one. Commanded by the king to attend a ball."

"Greenies never pull their weight," the second said. "King's a magic-lover if you were invited."

"Begone, girl. We've lords and ladies to attend to."

Karigan put her hands on her hips. This sort of treatment she expected from aristocrats, not from fellow commoners. "Now you listen here—"

"Is there a problem?"

Karigan almost did not recognize Alton D'Yer. He stood resplendent in a gold silk waistcoat and a long red coat. A gold medallion, undoubtedly a family heirloom, hung from his neck, and a royal blue sash was tied about his waist. He definitely was not attired in green, though his gold-winged horse brooch was pinned to his lapel. Thunderstruck by the transformation, Karigan almost missed the two guards bowing.

"There is no problem, my lord," the first guard said. "This Green Rider has no invitation, therefore she cannot be admitted."

"Oh," Alton said. "It has nothing to do with the king being a magic-lover, then?"

Both guards blanched. "N-no, of course not, my lord. I mean, we didn't mean to say . . ."

Alton's face grew stern. "Enough. This Green Rider is with me." He handed the invitation to the guard and steered Karigan into the ballroom.

As soon as they were through the entrance, Karigan quailed. She wanted to turn back and run, no matter what the guards would think. The ballroom exceeded the size of any great hall she had ever seen. It possessed vaulted ceilings like that of the king's throne room, supported by carved granite pillars. The floor was checkered with exquisite tile illustrated with scenes from the legend of Hiroque, Son of the Clans. Large doors opened up to balconies and the night air.

Dancers swirled around the ballroom in brilliant colors, the long dresses of ladies sweeping the floor and their jewelry sparking in the light of crystal chandeliers. The formal coats of men twirled as they swung their partners around the dance floor. Everything seemed to sparkle and shimmer, and Karigan felt very small and plain in her Green Rider uniform.

"Oh, look," Alton said, smiling. "Someone dug out all the old tapestries."

Tapestries representing each province billowed on the walls. Faded and worn tapestries of original Sacor Clans, clans that had long ago disappeared, had also been hung.

"I suppose the king wants to remind us all of the days when the Eletians were not strangers to the Sacoridians," Alton said. "There's D'Yer's."

Its field was gold like his waistcoat, the crest a simple sword crossed by a hammer, and bordered by a stone wall design. It matched the design etched on his medallion. The tapestry was too far away for Karigan to read the words stitched beneath the emblem.

"*The hammer of D'Yer shall break stone,*" Alton quoted, as if reading her mind, "*but no other shall break stone walls built by D'Yer.* It is said my ancestors learned the craft of stonework from Kmaernians, and though they mastered it, they were never able to achieve what the Kmaernians had. Even so, D'Yer stonework was considered the best outside of Kmaern. The castle is built of it, and so is the D'Yer Wall. But if I've heard correctly, the D'Yer Wall has been breached."

Karigan caught herself pulling at her collar again, thinking that if her father had designed the uniforms, they would be far more comfortable. She cleared her throat when she noticed Alton gazing hard at her. Did he know she was the one who had reported the breach of the D'Yer Wall? Or, was there something else in his expression? Perspiration slid down her temple.

"If I didn't know any better," Alton said, his voice

barely heard above the orchestra, "I'd say that you were
a bit shy of crowds."

"I—I—" She blushed, confirming Alton's suspicions.
"Aristocrats," she blurted.

"Ah, you are allergic to us."

Karigan crossed her arms, wishing away Alton's pa-
tronizing smile. He wasn't the usual aristocrat, perhaps
because of his connection to the Green Riders, but there
were moments. . . .

"Look, the Eletian." Alton pointed across the room,
and there, flickering between the blur of swirling dancers,
Zachary sat on a smaller replica of his throne chair, conversing with another. Karigan's impression of the Eletian
was simply of gold hair—gold hair such as she had never
seen before.

"Shall we go meet him?"

Karigan was horrified by the very idea, especially since
it would bring her in proximity to the king. "Uh, no. I'd
rather stay here." "Here" was just inside the entranceway hidden by shadows.

"How will the king know you're here, then?"

Karigan gave Alton a cockeyed glance. "Are you now
my keeper?"

"No, the captain asked me to look after you."

Well, that explained it. Leave it to Captain Mapstone
to make sure that Karigan had someone watching out
for her own interests. "I have no wish to see the king or
to be seen by him."

Alton shrugged. "Do you want to dance, then?"

"Dance?"

"It is what people do." His eyes seemed to laugh at
her though his expression was perfectly sober.

"No." Karigan didn't mind dancing in a family setting,
but this was far different.

"I'm off to the refreshment table, then. Skulk in the
shadows if you wish, but watch out for Weapons." He
strode off along the edge of the dance floor, weaving in
and among people, pausing to greet a few. Karigan stood
alone, an island in the midst of a sea of strangers. She

took a deep breath, then plunged after him. He handed her a goblet of wine, and a single sniff told her it was Rhovan White. "Good," he said. "I see you've decided to join the festivities."

Karigan held the goblet tightly, her hand shaking. The entrance was now many lengths away. Aristocrats fairly jammed the place, and over the scent of her own wine, she could smell their perfumed bodies as well as the underlying sweat. A breeze tickled her as the dancers swept by. Their long gowns brushed against her. Excited voices chatted over the orchestra, their words an indistinct babble. The colors of different clans sprinkled the crowd. More gold of D'Yer, the purple of L'Petrie, the cobalt of Coutre. The scarlet of Mirwell. She started, spilling wine on her hand.

Alton passed her a cloth napkin. "On nights like this," he whispered in her ear, "there are no enemies. It is part of the intrigue."

Karigan shivered despite the close heat of the room. She did not recognize any of the Mirwellians present.

The orchestra music ceased, as did the dancing, as if only the music controlled the motion on the ballroom floor. The dancers, some panting, some fanning themselves, laughed and clapped with gloved hands before converging on the refreshment table. Karigan watched with wide eyes at the tide of people descending upon her, and was edged toward the dance floor by Alton.

She nearly panicked in the crush of swarming, moving bodies which flowed by her like the torrent of a river. She turned round and round and bumped into a stout old man. The beard looked vaguely familiar. Then it dawned on her: the old man with the bear pelt at the throne room entrance the other day, only now he wore . . .

Karigan jabbered something unintelligible, and the old man glared at her. "Humph. Manners lacking, eh?" he said. "I don't know what kind of training they give you messengers these days. Spence! This person has spilled wine on me."

A woman in the uniform of Mirwell Province was instantly at the man's side, dabbing his scarlet surcoat with a cloth. The woman was tall and attractive, but expressionless. Then her winged horse brooch caught the light. Karigan opened her mouth in exclamation, but a subtle shake of the woman's head stopped her short.

"S-sorry," Karigan mumbled.

"You will be sorry," the old man said, "if you bump into me again." He sniffed. "At least you have good taste in wine."

Alton reappeared, and before she could consider the significance of a Mirwellian wearing a Rider brooch, he grabbed her by the sleeve and hauled her onto the dance floor. The music piped up again, and a mischievous look crossed his face. He took her goblet and placed it on the tray of a passing servant. He held both of her hands in his and steered her around and around the floor at a breathless rate, magically synchronized with the music and other dancers. Karigan stumbled, but Alton helped her find her footing.

The dance was similar to the reels she knew from clan celebrations—the music was just fancier here. Her stomach muscles loosened, the dance releasing some of her nervous tension. She fell into the rhythm of the dance, the surroundings all a blur like the Wild Ride, so dizzying that she thought she might lose her bearings and fly across the room.

"Look at me," Alton said, "and you won't get so dizzy." He grinned at her as he led her through the circular motion of the dance.

Instead, Karigan closed her eyes and imagined herself on horseback, the swishing of long gowns sounding of wind, her heartbeat the rhythm of hoofbeats. The *hoofbeats*. She shook her head, yet she could not rid herself of the rhythm which meshed with the dance, speeding ever faster.

Alton released her hands, and she spun to another partner. She found herself face-to-face with the Eletian.

He nodded to her with a smile as if he knew something she did not, and carried on the rhythm of the dance.

Karigan's heart pounded harder, hard enough, she was sure, that everyone else could hear it, especially the Eletian. His pale blue eyes, eyes like the winter sky, met hers only briefly before turning elsewhere, taking his secret with his gaze.

The music ended, and he dropped her hands. She watched breathlessly as he bowed away, the spectators watching both of them, the women with envy. Karigan's cheeks burned as she strode quickly off the dance floor in as dignified a manner as possible. She followed a current of fresh air to a balcony. No one else was there, and she walked directly onto the parapet, her hand over her thrumming heart, willing it to slow down.

The moon sat in the sky like a fat silver coin with a halo radiating around it. In one corner of the balcony, a brass telescope sat propped on a tripod, pointed toward the moon. She placed her hands on the balustrade and ran them along the smooth granite craft of Clan D'Yer.

"You dance well." Alton stood behind her.

"I didn't hear you come out," she said.

"The music is starting again. Do you want to dance?"

"I've had enough for one night."

"Karigan, the Eletian . . ."

"I—I don't want to talk about him." She shivered remembering those cool hands and whatever secret his blue eyes held.

"All right." Alton's expression clearly said that he did not understand, but he would not press her. The two stood at length, not speaking. After a time, Alton cleared his throat. "I'm sorry I pulled you into the dance like that."

"The dancing was fine," she replied. "It's the aristocrats I don't—" She stopped, remembering who she was talking to. "I've got to leave."

Alton caught her arm. "I uh . . . was . . . I would . . . What I want to say is . . ."

Karigan raised a brow as blood flooded Alton's cheeks.

Suave Lord Alton had turned into a fumbling schoolboy, and it served him right, too, for dragging her into the dance. "What is it you want to say?"

"I . . ." Now Alton pulled at *his* collar. "Would you consider . . . Would you . . . I mean—"

"Lord Alton, how good to see you."

They both turned as King Zachary strolled onto the balcony, his hands clasped behind his back.

Alton released Karigan's arm and bowed hastily. "Sire, how may I be of service?"

"By allowing me to have a private conversation with Rider G'ladheon."

With a crestfallen look, Alton bowed again and returned to the ballroom. Karigan had a time holding her tongue. Imagine the king presuming to call her *Rider* G'ladheon!

"My apologies for interrupting your conversation with Alton," the king said, misinterpreting her expression. When no response was forthcoming, he added, "I am pleased you made it to my ball."

"It has been very nice, and I'll thank you now, but I must be off."

"Hold one moment if you please. Could we talk for a bit?"

Karigan couldn't exactly turn down the King of Sacoridia no matter how much she wished to flee, could she?

He stepped up to the balustrade beside her, and gazed at the moon. "It is a night an Eletian would appreciate, don't you think? A silver moon out of legend, yet our fine guest lingers within the stone walls of the castle."

In the ballroom, where the gold light glared, the orchestra was on break, the courtiers surrounding the Eletian. He spoke and nodded to his admirers, his smile most charming. Karigan had imagined all Eletians, especially after meeting Somial, to be above such earthly concerns. It was a night to walk beneath the moon, a night to chase silver moonbeams.

Zachary clenched and unclenched his hands. "He offers us ties with Eletia, something that faded shortly after the Long War. And he offers me . . . great things. Powers that have not been seen since the First Age or the beginning of the Second. Powers, he says, that I can use to keep order in unruly towns like North, or to prevent folk in Adolind from starving the next time winter lasts longer than their food stores. Can you imagine? He offers me powers that would make your Green Rider brooches look like no more than trinkets."

"Do such great powers still exist?" Karigan asked.

"He says that strong powers emanate from Blackveil Forest, and if Sacoridia keeps the breach in the D'Yer Wall open, Eletia will filter and purify them using its own powers." Zachary removed the silver fillet from his brow and began to comb his fingers through his hair. For a moment, years fell away from him, and he appeared a youth not yet hardened by rule: young, afraid, and alone. Vulnerable.

"He offers me much," Zachary said. "Too much, I think, though it has not been my experience to know what Eletians are like."

"So you have to figure it out for yourself."

Zachary smiled grimly. "One is used to listening to advisors. All of my court counselors are entirely charmed by Shawdell the Eletian. I suppose I should be, too." He drummed his fingers on the granite surface of the balustrade. "Here I am assured no one listens, and I've posted Weapons by the doorway so that no one drifts out here. I fear that in my own throne room others can somehow hear what I say, though it appears the room is secure. Thus, the game of Intrigue yesterday. You must have found it quite strange."

Karigan nodded, relaxing a little. "You thought that if I had something important to say, it would be overheard by the wrong people."

"Yes. I am particularly concerned about the Mirwellian aspect of your journey. Do you have a few moments to share that with me?"

Karigan told him everything she could remember, including Torne's and Jendara's references to the king's brother. This time she found an absorbed, avid listener, rather than the unpredictable and nonchalant Intrigue player.

"Why were they after Coblebay?" he mused. "His message was worthless."

Karigan shrugged, her opinion of the king now bending toward pity. She had no brothers of her own and so couldn't fathom the betrayal he must feel.

"I trust you will be in the city for a few more days," he said.

"No, actually I plan to leave—"

"I see. When will you be returning?"

Karigan gaped. "Excellency, I don't plan to return. I'm going home to my family. My father is a merchant. It's spring, and he will need me."

The king's expression froze, and she wondered what he did not want her to read. As a king, he must be a master at masking his expressions, or otherwise possess no political leverage, just as a merchant must maintain a neutral gaze during a transaction.

"Are you sure?" he asked her. "After all, you are a Green Rider now. At least in name if not legally sworn in."

"I'm not a Green Rider," Karigan said, maintaining her self-control admirably, she thought.

"I could command you to sign papers to become a Green Rider, to work in my service, but I don't think that will be necessary, and I can only guess how much you would resent it. Coercion is not my usual tactic. Laren—Captain Mapstone—informs me that being a Green Rider is more a matter of spirit than desire, a compulsion, if you will. Something about hoofbeats." Zachary strode across the balcony to the telescope and bent down to peer up at the moon. He pulled back, blinking. "It's bright."

Karigan blinked, too, as if struck. King Zachary had reminded her of someone, the someone she had seen in the brass telescope of the Berry sisters. Images she had seen, of a man much like Zachary, with brown almond-

shaped eyes, but slightly older with careworn lines on his
brow, imploring her not to . . . not to go away; that he
needed her and could not bear to lose her. Karigan trembled. A future vision? Blood drained from her head and
she wobbled.

The king steadied her. "Are you all right?"

"No! Yes. Please, just stay away. I'm leaving. I'm not
a Green Rider and never will be."

Driven by a fear that the future might happen if she
stayed there with him, with his hands on her arms, she
ran from the balcony without bowing, ran past the
Weapon Fastion who stood in the doorway, his usual
stoic expression scandalized. When she erupted into the
glare of the ballroom, a few heads turned to look, then
resumed conversation and sipping wine. The orchestra
tuned up, and the sound of off-key notes clamored in
her ears.

Alton D'Yer tugged at her sleeve. "Karigan, are
you—?"

She yanked her sleeve away from his grasp and pushed
unapologetically through the guests in desperation to
leave. She broke free near the entrance and looked back
over her shoulder. King Zachary stood by the balcony
doorway watching her with a bemused expression, Alton
D'Yer was lost in the swarm of aristocrats, and the Eletian, though in the midst of a group, seemed to stand
apart, almost godlike with his golden hair and perfect
features. He caught her eyes and smiled. That smile of
secrets! She was not warmed by it, and without looking
back, she darted into the darkness of night.

King Zachary, indeed! she fumed. *Needs me, does he?
Humph!* Yet, inside, she shook. The thought of it, the
king needing her, overwhelmed her. It terrified her.

She stalked down the corridor to her room. The silver
moon spread shadow bars across the floor from the

many-paned window. All else was submerged in darkness. From her pocket she pulled the moonstone, which illumined the room to the darkest floor cracks, seeming to draw moonlight from outside until all was cast in silver. Karigan watched in wonder until a tiny gasp from behind startled her.

Sitting in the chair by the table, was a woman cloaked and hooded in black. A length of black silk veiled all but her eyes, and she looked like one of the wives of some lord of the Under Kingdoms. Were there tattoos under the veil? Karigan reached for a sword that was not there, and considered hurling the moonstone at the intruder.

As if guessing her thoughts, the intruder raised her black-gloved hands defensively. "Please, I am no enemy." The accent wasn't of the Under Kingdoms, but of some eastern province. Coutre, perhaps? When Karigan did not respond, she added, "I am Estora. You delivered the last letter from my lover, F'ryan Coblebay."

Karigan blinked, but did not relax her tense body. "Then why do you come at this hour? Why do you hide your face?"

The woman's green eyes glanced down, and she shuddered with a sigh. "My family would never permit a liaison with a commoner such as F'ryan. Our affair was a secret one. I hide myself even now. Should my family ever find out that I loved F'ryan Coblebay, they would be shamed and cast me out."

That was no way to live, Karigan thought, her own revelation about King Zachary as the image in Professor Berry's telescope set aside. She relaxed and sat lightly on her bed, her hand passing over a woolen coverlet. "I'm sorry," she said, not sure whether she meant F'ryan's death or her family's restriction.

Lady Estora looked far away. "The Riders always helped. They brought me in secretly to see F'ryan. When asked, they knew nothing of us. And here you have helped again, by bringing this letter." She drew a crumpled piece of paper from her cloak. "Mel tells me you were the last to see F'ryan alive."

"Yes." Karigan had no wish to elaborate she had seen him after death, too. "He died bravely." What else could she say? *She died bravely,* her aunts had said of her mother.

"As I knew he would. Often I believed he was half crazy and too daring. Many times he risked death to visit me in my family's house. It was reckless, but I loved him for it." The woman's eyes welled with tears, the veil darkening above her cheeks. "I've cried often, but could share my sorrow with no one. I just wanted to thank you for bringing this letter to me, and for finishing F'ryan's mission. But . . ."

Karigan cocked her head, waiting.

"I don't understand why he wrote this letter if he planned to see me upon its delivery."

"Maybe he knew he might not survive this last mission," Karigan suggested.

Estora's thin brows were bunched together, her eyes troubled. "Yes, that could be, but still, F'ryan wasn't one for writing letters. If ever one was intercepted by the wrong person, it would mean the end of all we had together. There are also certain details in the letter that aren't quite right."

Estora stood up and paced the floor, her long black skirts flickering in the silver light. "I don't have dark amber hair," she said. "F'ryan knew that well. He spoke no end of my gold hair, of passing his hands through it." She stopped abruptly and a blush spread just above the veil. "A summer wedding! He mentioned a summer wedding. We had planned no such thing, impossible as it was. We talked in whimsy, of course. He also mentioned a brother. F'ryan has no brother. There are other details of similar type. It is strange."

Karigan scratched her head. "Perhaps he was distressed when he wrote it."

"I do not think so. Very little distressed him." Estora paused by the window with a sad sigh.

Karigan straightened in inspiration. What was it Captain Mapstone had said about F'ryan bearing messages in code? "Are . . . are you sure the letter was meant for you?"

Estora looked at Karigan as if she had suddenly sprouted horns. "Of course it was. Why, for all the mistakes, he does mention things that were known only between the two of us."

"There could be more in that letter." Did F'ryan hide the real message in the form of a love letter and use the other message as a decoy? "May I have the letter?"

Estora clutched it to her breast. "Whatever for?"

"I would like to show it to Captain Mapstone. I think there's more to it."

"I told you my family would cast me out if ever my relationship with F'ryan was discovered."

"You said yourself that no Green Rider ever revealed the two of you, didn't you?"

"Yes."

"I promise this won't go beyond Captain Mapstone. I think it's important."

Estora still held the letter to her. As she hesitated, F'ryan Coblebay appeared dimly beside his beloved. Estora did not detect him, and Karigan thought that of anyone, she should be the one to see him. F'ryan looked at Karigan with his somber expression, the arrows stiff in his back. He turned to Estora and whispered in her ear.

Estora shuddered as if suddenly remembering where she was. "If you can return this to me when you are done with it," she said, "I would like it back. It is all I have left of him." As she handed the letter to Karigan, F'ryan's hand merged with hers as if to help her. "Odd," Estora said, "but I think F'ryan would have wanted me to do this."

The ghost cast Karigan another penetrating look, then faded out. "Thank you," she said a bit breathlessly. "As I told you, this will not go beyond Captain Mapstone."

Karigan didn't wait for Estora to leave. Rather, she flung the door open and strode down the corridor, out of the building, and across the courtyard where the officers' quarters stood. Unlike the long wooden Rider barracks, the officers quarters was a squat stone structure made to house only a handful of people. The stone walls protected those within from fire arrows and catapulted coals. The windows were mere slits through which defenders on the inside could shoot arrows. Even so, Karigan was glad she was housed at the barracks with the large window that overlooked the pasture.

The narrow windows were black. The captain was the only officer in residence, or so Mel had intimated. Karigan knocked hard on the thick green door. When no one answered, she knocked again. This time, light flickered to life in the windows, and a few moments later, the door groaned open on ancient hinges.

"What is it?" Captain Mapstone squinted at her, a lamp in one hand, her unsheathed sword in the other. She stood barefoot, a flannel sleeping gown fluttering in a breeze. Her hair, the color of new copper in the silver moon, flowed unbound and loose down her back. When Karigan did not answer immediately, she snapped, "Well, don't just stand there, girl. I was sound asleep. What do you want?"

"I, uh . . . have this letter." It was rather disconcerting to see the captain bleary-eyed and dressed in anything other than her smart green uniform. And the brown scar didn't stop at the collar line, but continued in a ragged line down beneath the low neckline of the nightgown. Karigan licked her lips. "It belongs to Lady Estora. It was from F'ryan Coblebay. I found it in the pocket of his greatcoat after he died."

"Repeat that." When Karigan did, the captain's eyes seemed to pop open one at a time. "You mean you knew about this letter all along and you never mentioned it?"

"It was a love letter. I never thought anything of it."

Captain Mapstone was now fully awake. "You had better come in and explain this to me."

Karigan followed her down a short corridor to her room. It was nearly as sparsely furnished as the barracks.

A small bed, blankets rumpled and the pillow still depressed from the captain's head, stood against one wall. The captain sheathed her saber and they sat in chairs beside a blackened fireplace.

"Now tell me."

Karigan handed her the crumpled paper and watched as the captain read it. She explained how she had originally found it and vowed to deliver it to Lady Estora when she reached Sacor City. "I just left Lady Estora in my chamber. She told me there were peculiarities about the letter." Karigan repeated their conversation. "I remembered that you said F'ryan Coblebay sometimes put his messages in code."

Captain Mapstone rubbed absently at her scar. "This must be examined immediately. It wouldn't be unlike F'ryan to do this."

"I promised Lady Estora that there would be no connection made between her and F'ryan."

"Yes, yes, yes. I know all about that. You may leave now."

A little piqued at the brusque dismissal, Karigan left the chamber. As she stepped through the doorway, the captain was already removing her uniform from her wardrobe. What would the message reveal if the love letter was truly a message in disguise?

Karigan walked into the wash of the silver moon, hands in pockets, tall dewy grass wetting her trousers. The ball should be about over. Hopefully it was the last such engagement she would have to attend.

Across the pasture, a solitary figure waded through the tall grass. He was a dark shadow, even in the moonlight, darkness hovering over him like a shield. In fact, he seemed to repel the moonlight.

Shawdell the Eletian's lithe movements were unmistakable, his golden hair vibrant despite the shadow that shrouded him. He was doing what Karigan imagined all Eletians must do—walk in the moonlight, but she felt cold, wondering about his purposeful pace. She hurried to Rider barracks to escape the night.

⇒ A SILVER MOON NIGHT ⇐

"Pssst, Green Rider!"
Karigan paused in the doorway and looked wildly about. At first she could discern only the shadowy bulk of shrubbery near the barracks building, then from one of these, a woman stepped forward into the glow of the door lamp, revealing the fine oval face of the Mirwellian with the Green Rider brooch.

She stiffened. Brooch or not, the woman was Mirwellian, and Mirwellians had only caused her trouble and pain. "Something I can do for you?" she asked warily.

The woman glanced about as if someone was about to leap out of the shrubbery. It had been a strange night thus far, with a silver moon to boot, and Karigan supposed anything was possible.

"Please," the Mirwellian said, "I've a message that needs delivering to—"

"Look," Karigan said. "I'm not a Green Rider. I'm not a messenger."

The woman snorted haughtily. "That is what you say now. Look at yourself. You wear the brooch."

"So do you."

The woman pursed her lips and folded her arms. It was unlikely she was used to such impertinence. Karigan was not schooled in the meanings of military insignia, and thus did not know what rank the epaulets on the woman's shoulders signified.

The woman took a step closer. "Listen, I don't have time for games. I need your help. I—"

"Major!"

The Mirwellian's eyes widened with fear for a moment. Then she mastered herself; her expression cooled. She turned to watch the approach of two Mirwellian soldiers. Karigan concealed herself within the doorway, hoping she had not been seen.

The Mirwellian woman placed her fists on her hips and drew herself up into a forbidding posture. "What is it D'rang?"

"The governor. He needs you."

"He always needs me. What is it now? Does he need someone to draw his bath?"

"It's urgent, Major."

"Very well."

Karigan peered around the doorway as the woman hastened away flanked by the two soldiers. She scratched her head. *Now what was that all about?*

Mirwell sloshed out of the tub with the help of a wide-eyed servant. The tub was a behemoth of porcelain with brass beast's feet. Very homey, but nothing compared to the sulfur water and plumbing of Selium. In time, he would acquire that place, too. It was far milder during the winter there than the far reaches of Mirwellton, and the hot springs couldn't be surpassed for relieving old creaky muscles.

"A-anything else I can do for y-you, my lord?"

Mirwell chortled. The boy had gotten a good look at the ivory claw marks that crisscrossed his body and stood out especially well against skin flushed red by the hot bath. "Fetch me a towel before I die of the cold, boy."

"Y-yes, my lord." The boy scurried across the private bathing chamber and returned with a sheet-sized, plush towel.

"Now dry me, boy, and don't rub my skin off."

"Yes, my lord."

The boy dabbed so softly he barely touched Mirwell's skin.

"I'll never get dry that way, boy. I'll die of old age first. Now firm up, my lad. I'm not going to eat you."

"Yes, my lord."

The blotting grew more assured, but stayed gentle. Mirwell was used to the intimate ministrations on his body by others. He had grown up with servants attending to his every need, including cleanliness. Only, he had hoped that Beryl would attend him tonight, though she technically was not a servant. His personal servant's slight illness had been a serendipitous excuse. And he supposed that, if Beryl were a man, or not even half as beautiful, he wouldn't have even thought of it.

The boy helped him shrug into his robe. Where was Beryl? She had escorted him back to chambers after the ball, but had slipped out during a moment of inattention. Here he had hoped they could spend a little time together, to let her get to know him in a different way other than "lord-governor."

"Slippers, boy, my feet are freezing."

"Yes, my lord."

The boy scuttled after the fur-lined slippers and set them by Mirwell's feet.

"Dry the bottom of my feet first."

"Yes, my lord."

Mirwell put a hand on the boy's head to balance himself while the boy dried one foot, then the other. "Do you know how to say anything other than, *yes, my lord?*"

The boy licked his lips. "Er, yes, my lord."

"What would you have to say that would interest me anyway?"

"Nothing, my lord."

Mirwell laughed then, a surprising belly laugh. He took his hand from the boy's head and allowed him to stand. "You would make a fine politician, my boy."

"Yes, my lord."

Mirwell dismissed the boy. With any luck, Beryl would be back and she could help him dress. He draped his towel about his neck and sauntered out of the bathing room and into the parlor. Beryl *was* back! But all fantasies of her dressing him were dashed.

She sat in a straight back chair, and D'rang and that other soldier, what's-his-name, pressed down on her shoulders so she could not rise. Beryl's face was as cool and unreadable as usual.

"D'rang?" Mirwell queried. "Why are you restraining your superior officer?"

D'rang glanced at the other soldier, and then back at Mirwell. But before he could speak, the Gray One stepped from the stone wall as if he had been a part of it. Mirwell shuddered involuntarily. For all he knew, the Gray One had done just that.

"Do you still seek a spy?" the Gray One asked in his melodious voice, a beautiful voice that disguised something ugly.

Mirwell felt his scrutiny from beneath the hood. He slid into the cushioned chair across from Beryl, next to a little table that held his game of Intrigue. He had set the pieces exactly the way they had been before they left his keep. "Of course I still seek the spy."

The hood turned toward Beryl.

"Spence? You must jest, Master Gray One. She's my most trusted aide."

"Who else better to betray you?"

Mirwell's eyes shot to his aide. "Spence?"

"I'm no spy," she said. Her features remained neutral.

Then, in a swift sudden move, the Gray One swooped upon her and tore something from her surcoat. She jerked back with a stifled scream which sounded more like a snarl. The Gray One held out whatever he had snatched to Mirwell.

"What do you see?" he hissed.

"Why her medal of valor, for when she served in the king's militia."

"Look more closely."

Mirwell squinted his eyes. The medal, a gold oval imprinted with the firebrand and the crescent moon, wavered in his vision for a moment, as if suddenly transformed, and then resolidified into its usual composition. *My eyes,* he thought. "I see nothing unusual."

"It is a Green Rider brooch," the Gray One said. "Mundanes cannot see them properly, but I can. This spy had it well-shielded just so I would not, but my magic is stronger, far stronger, and eventually I saw it for what it was. I expect, through questioning, you will find I speak the truth."

Mirwell ran his fingers through his beard completely aware of what kind of questioning the Gray One meant. "I-I don't know."

"My lord," D'rang said, "we found her over by the Greenie barracks talking to someone."

The Gray One slapped the medal down on a table. "She is a spy. There is no question of it. If you wish to see your plans through, kill her. If there is a question in your mind, torture her. Find out the truth."

I've become a doting old fool, Mirwell thought. *I've allowed this woman to get to me. I've grown weak.* Perhaps he had known the truth all along. "We will not kill her, nor will we torture her."

An expression of triumph flashed across Beryl's face before it turned neutral again.

Mirwell picked up the green spy from his game board and shook it in his hand as if he were about to roll dice. "Tie her up," he said with a heavy sigh.

Now Beryl frowned.

D'rang found some lengths of cord and proceeded to truss her up and gag her. Beryl took it all silently.

"I want all to appear as normal," Mirwell said, "so the king doesn't suspect anything. She will attend me at every moment, just as the king would expect."

"My lord," said D'rang, "what if she should try to pass word on to the king's folk?"

"That is a consideration," Mirwell said.

The Gray One bent over Beryl, and she shrank in her chair. "I believe I know a way," he said. "I shall teach you some words which will give you power over her."

Mirwell tipped the green spy in the red court onto its

side. "D'rang, go find the castellan and ask if he has heard anything about our plans. That is the simplest way, I think, to find out if Spence has betrayed us."

The Gray One placed his hands on either side of Beryl's head. She rammed her back into the chair and squirmed.

"By all means," the Gray One said, "seek Crowe out. But this one is still a liability."

Beryl screamed, and though it was muffled by the gag, Mirwell could feel it down to his toes.

Bright silver moonlight fell through the close network of interlacing branches of the forest canopy, dappling the overgrown track—once a woods road—with strange and moving patterns. The moonlight served not as an omen, but as a suitable light source for Prince Amilton Hillander and his host of soldiers.

They were Mirwellton regulars, scruffy mercs, conscripted peasants, and no few thieves and scoundrels among them looking for opportunity. They were a rogue army, and Amilton rode at their head. The notion of a rogue army appealed to him. He was, after all, a rogue prince. Hadn't his brother stripped him of his titles, his lands, his *destiny?* Yet here he was, about to grab the highest seat in the land, and there would be even more beyond that according to the Gray One.

Amilton ground his teeth together. His forces would prevail and Zachary would burn. He dreamed a hundred torments for his brother and how he would delight in his brother's screams. Such thoughts warmed his belly as he and the rogue army, some five hundred soldiers, plodded along.

The isolated track would lead them to Sacor City with little notice. All they encountered along the way were killed so they would not spread the word and alert Zachary's minions of their approach. So far, only a few hunters had perished, their bodies far behind, bristling with Mirwellian arrows.

Mounted warriors rode up front, followed by draft horses straining at their collars to haul siege engines and supplies. Infantry toiled through the churned earth at the very end. The plan was not so much to hold siege, but to create a show of force at the sleeping city. It was also a precaution should Mirwell's man in Zachary's court not have the gates open to welcome them as planned.

Amilton's forces would ride right up to the castle gates, enter, and secure it. Then Mirwell would bring him his brother, dead or alive. If dead, he would bring Zachary's head. The rightful king would then take his place on the throne.

Five hundred was not a great number of soldiers, but it was far more than the one hundred and fifty to two hundred garrisoned at the castle.

"You think of your throne, my prince?" the Mirwellian captain who rode with him asked.

"Just so," Amilton said. He clasped the black stone that hung from his neck on a gold chain. It had been a gift, a great gift, from the Gray One. It was a gift of power. The Gray One said it would strengthen them both. The more he used it, the stronger they would become. "It will not be long before you address me as your king," he told the captain.

The captain inclined his head. "With pleasure, Sire."

The man was an ingrate, Amilton thought. Already he sought favor with the new king.

Two riders appeared down the track—a Mirwellian scout and someone mounted on a big battle horse. Amilton held his hand up to stay the army. The order was shouted down the length of the host. The captain rode forward to meet the scout as the thud of hoof, clack of armor, and grind of wagon wheels drew to a halt. Quiet settled over the army, interspersed by the shift of horses, ring of harness, and the occasional cough.

The captain rode back at a canter and halted before

the prince. "The scout has found someone, my lord," he said.

"Why isn't he dead?"

"*She* says she knows you. She rides a battle horse branded with the mark of the Talon company."

Amilton raised his brow. "Interesting." Mirwell had hired a squad of Talon mercs to supplement the infantry. Perhaps this rider carried a message. "Bring her here."

The captain rode back to the scout and the mystery woman. After a moment, they approached at a slow jog. When they were just two horse lengths away, the stranger swung off her horse and fell to her knees before the prince.

"My lord," she said, keeping her face turned to the ground.

Amilton started in surprise. He dismounted and threw his reins to the captain. Placing his fingers beneath the woman's chin, he tilted her face upward. Moonlight splayed across a swollen and off-center nose. Dried blood was crusted near her hairline though it looked as if she had tried to scrub it away. Her face was thin, but it was unmistakable.

"Jendara," he whispered.

"Yes, my lord."

He caressed her face, his fingers trailing against her sharp cheekbones. "I've missed you more than you know. What has happened? Where is Torne?"

"Dead. The Greenie, my lord. We had the Greenie, but there was more to her than we knew. . . . She escaped. We have failed you."

He moved his hand as if to comb it through her lush hair, but instead he grabbed a handful and yanked her to her feet.

"Failed? Do you know what your failure may cost me?"

"Yes, my lord," she whispered.

He struck her hard across the face, and struck her again. His blows fell repeatedly, and blow after blow she stood mute, never crying out, never pleading for him to stop. She did not run away or resist. She simply accepted the pummeling, her body knocked this way and that from the blows. The smack of his fist against her face punctuated the relative quiet of the forest.

Amilton paused. She still stood, though barely, when such a beating would have rendered any ordinary woman or man unconscious. She wobbled from side to side as if she might drop at any moment, but never fell. Blood flowed freely from her nose and a split lip. The flesh around her eyes purpled and swelled.

Amilton wiped Jendara's blood off his knuckles with a cloth handed to him by his squire.

Why this violence, he wondered, when he could test his gift from the Gray One? He shut his eyes and touched the cold stone. His thoughts delved into dark regions as the Gray One had instructed him. He searched, reached, and called upon the power of *Kanmorhan Vane*. It surged through him with a cold, sinuous tingle. When he opened his eyes, currents of black energy licked his hands.

He grasped Jendara's shoulders and the energies bore into her. Jendara's scream rang through the woods, and she dropped to her knees.

Amilton removed his hands from her and watched in fascination as the currents of energy crackled on his palms and around his fingers. He let the magic dissipate, then his hands fell to his sides.

"What now, my lord?" the captain asked. All blood had drained from his face.

"We go on."

"But what if the Greenie has alerted the king? What if we march into a trap?"

"Immerez may have stopped the Greenie. Even if he has not, we go on. We are equipped for a siege if need be." The prince turned to the captain, and in an uncompromising tone he said, "No matter what, we shall proceed. It is all I have left, and I shall take it. If I hear one murmur of dissent, we will have an immediate execution. Do I make myself clear?"

The captain bowed his head hastily. "Yes, my lord."

Amilton placed his hands on Jendara's shoulders again, and she shrank from him though he did not call on the magic. He pulled her close. "I am glad you have returned to me." He kissed her with greatest tenderness on her swollen cheek. "Now you will ride beside me and protect me as you have sworn."

"As I have sworn," she whispered through her broken mouth.

"Then take your place beside me."

She staggered to her feet and stumbled to the battle horse's side as if in a daze. She tried several times before her toe found the stirrup and she dragged herself into the saddle. She reined her horse beside Amilton's. Hunched over the saddle horn, she whispered to him, "I serve with my life."

⊰ THE HUNTING ⊱

A day slipped by, and another, and still Karigan heard nothing about the letter, nor did she see Captain Mapstone at all. In fact, no one in particular, not even a single Weapon, paid her any attention except for Alton, who had nothing else to do, and Mel, who was as cheerful as ever, but for once couldn't shed any light on the situation.

"Just as I told you before, I haven't seen the captain since the night before last," Mel said, plopping on Karigan's bed.

Karigan secured her bedroll to her pack which the kitchen servants had filled with food. She slung the pack over one shoulder and a water skin over the other. "I'm out of it, then. I've done my part, and I'm going home."

"Do you have to?" Mel's eyes looked sad. "I haven't had another girl to talk to in so long."

How lonely it must be for her to live in a world of adults who possessed adult problems and no imaginations whatsoever. "I have to go home. My father will be expecting me. Maybe . . . maybe he will come trading here in the fall and I can come with him."

"Maybe the captain will let me visit you." There was the sound of hope in Mel's voice.

"I don't see why not." Such an excursion would be good for her. Maybe Mel hadn't even been outside of the city walls before. "Guess I'm ready."

Karigan walked down the main corridor of the barracks, Mel in tow behind her. The corridor was empty;

Green Riders were scattered across the countryside on messenger errands.

They emerged outdoors, the sun falling warmly on their shoulders more like summer than spring. Karigan walked along the railing that lined the horse pasture, squinting her eyes to pick out a familiar friend, to say good-bye.

"What are you looking for?" Mel asked.

"The Horse. All of the others seem to be out, but not him."

"Condor? He's in the stable."

Karigan wondered about that, and about the mischievous smile on Mel's face. They walked on into the stable, blinking until their eyes adjusted to the sudden dark. Alton D'Yer stood in the aisle between the stalls, holding the reins of his tall black gelding, who, with white socks and a white blaze down his nose, had earned the name Night Hawk. As always, Alton looked immaculate, as did his horse and gear. He gave her a lopsided grin and patted Night Hawk's neck. "Where are you going?" he asked.

Karigan frowned. Corsa, of course. She had told him time and again. "Home."

"Must be a long walk."

Karigan placed her hands on her hips in annoyance. "I'll catch a ferry down on the river."

"But you have a Green Rider uniform on. It wouldn't look right for you to be traveling on foot."

"What do you want me to do? Go in the nude?" Alton snickered at that, but Karigan ignored it. "I suppose I have enough currency left to buy something so I can get rid of this green outfit."

"Green is your color." This time Alton was not joking. "Why not ride instead?"

"I can't afford a horse."

"I don't know what Condor would say to that."

Mel had disappeared into an adjacent section of the stable, only to return with a tacked and groomed Condor.

He whickered in greeting. "He's all set to go to Corsa," Mel said.

"What?" Karigan looked at Mel, then at Alton, her mouth hanging open. "But he's not mine."

Alton said, "These messenger horses are particular about their Riders. You are Condor's Rider, whether you choose to join the messenger service or not. Captain Mapstone said giving him to you was the least we could do to thank you for delivering F'ryan's message."

Karigan took the reins from Mel and looked up at Condor. "So you think you can put up with me?"

Condor snorted and shook his head, the bridle jingling.

Karigan smiled broadly. "I guess he will." A mount would make her journey far easier. She would still find a way to get rid of the green uniform, though.

"Karigan," Alton said, "I would . . . I . . . well, it would please me . . . What I want to say . . ."

One moment he was speaking as a polished aristocrat should, the next he couldn't speak at all. She wished he would just blurt out what it was he wanted.

Mel rolled her eyes, apparently wishing the same thing. "He wants to ride down to the river with you."

Alton blushed.

"Oh!" It would be the last time she got to see him, and it would be pleasant to have company—to have *him*—along the way. "I don't see why not."

Alton exhaled in relief. "Very good," he said, taking on a confident air again.

Karigan thought she heard Mel mutter something about "males." The two girls said their good-byes, and Karigan left Mel standing forlornly in the shadows of the stable, the drone of flies filling the air.

At first Alton and Karigan rode in silence, he glancing at her covertly. They passed beneath the portcullis and through the castle gates. The horses' hooves clunked on the wooden drawbridge. Two guards on duty watched them sourly as they passed through. Relations between the militia and messenger service, she learned, were

strained by the misconception of the soldiers that Green
Riders led uncomplicated lives.

Part of the castle wall that faced outward into the city
was scaffolded. Workers on break sat idly on the wood
scaffolding and passed around a jug. Alton scowled.

"What's wrong?" Karigan asked.

"There is nothing wrong with that wall."

"Then what are they doing?"

"Supposedy reinforcing it. Hah! That wall has survived
since the Long War, and not a nick in it. D'Yers built it."

"The king seems to think it needs reinforcing."

"Evidently. I don't know what he expects is going to
happen. It wouldn't be so bad if their work wasn't so
sloppy. He could have used D'Yers if he wanted the job
done correctly. Granted, we've lost some of our skill
since the castle was built, but Clan D'Yer still has the
finest stone workers in all of Sacoridia." He sighed. "I
suppose the king wanted to generate local work."

From the gates they followed the cobble-paved road
that led from the castle into Sacor City. The cobbles,
stones rounded for a millennium by the ocean, were harvested from the shores of King Zachary's own province
of Hillander.

As they descended the sloping road, Karigan looked
over her shoulder, and for the first time, truly saw the
castle as a whole, a view she had been denied during the
Wild Ride. It stood high on a rounded hillock, turrets
casting solid shadows across its gray granite facade.
Blocky walls anchored the castle to the earth. It looked
indestructible, unmovable, almost as if it had been hewn
from the raw earth itself.

Tiers of courtyards, gardens, and the pasture softened
the blunt effect of the castle. Smaller buildings, the barracks of the regular militia and the Green Riders, stables,
and other structures, clustered at its base like children at
their mother's knee.

Karigan thought about the fragile people who dwelled
within the forbidding fortress. She thought of stern Captain Mapstone scouring a love letter for hints to some

Mirwellian conspiracy. She thought of poor Mel, young and alone, trapped inside those cold, stone walls. King Zachary was trapped, too, and he was just as alone as Mel, doing a job he never wanted to do. Caught by circumstance as she had been.

She felt regret on her own part for leaving these people who had been kind to her, but they were caught up in great things, and she felt tired, so tired. She had had enough intrigue and danger to last generations, and it was time for more capable hands to pick up where she had left off. *When I get home, everything will be all right.* She felt regret at leaving, but also relief.

Karigan and Alton continued downward, the castle and grounds soon lost from view behind the protective, encircling wall. Below them, houses and shops with cedar-shingled roofs jutted in jagged, descending disorder. Two more walls spread outward like growth rings. As the city had grown, new walls were built to surround it and protect it.

They rode through the second wall which led into the old part of the city. Peddlers hawking their wares filled the street. Musicians played on street corners for coins thrown by those who stopped to listen. Folk of all stations roamed the streets on horseback or in buckboards and carriages, and they yanked on rope leads to coax oxen to follow them. Shoppers paused at booths and ducked into well-stocked emporiums.

A small knot of people huddled up to a building where a woman stood on a hogshead. Karigan started in surprise, for it was the leader of the Anti-Monarchy Society, Lorilie Dorran. The woman's eyes were wide as she took in the commotion of the city, and despite the meager group that had collected to listen to her, she spoke fervently, waving her fist this way and that in the air. Karigan heard nothing of the speech except an occasional "tyranny" or "taxes." Lorilie's supporters worked the crowds, passing out leaflets. A young man thrust one into Alton's face.

Alton looked it over and scowled. "A waste of good paper, this." He crumpled it in his fist.

"What did it say?" Karigan asked.

"It listed King Zachary's crimes against the people of Sacoridia."

It was not long before Lorilie Dorran and her supporters were lost in the moving throng, and Alton pointed across the thoroughfare to a Green Rider maneuvering her horse uphill and against the flow of traffic. She wove between wagons overloaded with wine casks, around children playing in the street, and a merchant burdened with numerous packages. She used her reins one-handed to guide her horse, tapping the gelding's flanks with her heels.

"That's Patrici," Alton said, "Captain Mapstone's aide. She comes from the borderlands where her clan raises horses. See how she handles Plover? Horses are in her blood."

Patrici guided her horse into any available opening, picking up speed when possible. Not many in the crowd were inclined to get out of her way.

"She's in a hurry," Alton said. "I wonder what message she's carrying. Must be important. This press can be a real aggravation when you have to get to the castle in a hurry." Again, he frowned.

"Now what?" Karigan asked.

"The city has been filling up with commoners of late."

Karigan halted Condor, unmindful of the traffic that jammed behind her. Alton turned Night Hawk about to see what the problem was.

"Are you going to start telling me they don't belong here in your opinion?" she asked. "Because if you are, I'll go the rest of the way on my own."

Alton blushed. "I-I didn't mean to offend. I was just making an observation. Truly."

"I hope so," Karigan said. "Those folk have been subject to groundmites and thieves taking advantage of them. Don't you think they have a right to seek safety within the king's walls?"

"Well, yes, I suppose. But there are so many of them."

Karigan shook her head and urged Condor right past Alton. Night Hawk nosed up alongside her.

"I'm sorry," Alton said. "I just can't seem to say the right things around you."

Alton would have fit in admirably at Selium, Karigan thought. The aristocratic girls who were her classmates would have talked of nothing else other than handsome Alton D'Yer with his square chin and radiant smile. She shook her head.

"I understand your father's wealth is worth more than that of many lords," Alton said. "He could probably purchase whole provinces."

Karigan glared at him. "It wasn't always that way. My father earned everything he has. He wasn't born to it." She tossed her head and concentrated on the road, but did not miss Alton's stung expression. Of course, she had been too little to remember how her parents had struggled, but she had heard enough stories.

The scent of freshly baked bread drifted to her from the stall of some vendor along the street. Strains of a well-known tune reached her from a busker playing a lute.

"Perhaps we shall see the king," Alton said in a ploy to change the subject. It worked, for Karigan's attention suddenly focused on him.

"The king? What do you mean? We're heading out of Sacor City, not in."

Alton fussed with Night Hawk's reins. "The king has gone hunting. For hare, mostly . . . with his dogs. I was invited along with some other nobles, but I opted to ride with you."

That was interesting. Most aristocrats would seek the king's favor whenever possible, and yet here he was, riding with *her,* the daughter of a merchant. She couldn't help but be disarmed, and she flashed a smile at him.

Before they passed through the last wall, Karigan ducked into the shop of a likely clothier. It was not long before she exited the shop frowning.

"What's wrong?" Alton asked.

"I haven't the coin to purchase even a plain shirt."

"Things are more expensive in the city. I could help if—"

"No thanks. I'll check elsewhere." They stopped at several shops, but the problem was the same. Karigan did not have enough currency.

"As I said before," Alton remarked, "green is your color."

Karigan did not reply.

They left Sacor City and the crowds behind and were soon surrounded by meadows and cultivated fields. The cobble streets transformed into dusty, meandering dirt roads, not much better than the North Road. Uplands curved to the east, their ridges crowned by a mix of evergreens and deciduous trees. The road itself began to rise on an upland so that a valley formed between two ridges.

"The Lost Lake," Alton said. "Before the Long War, a lake existed here. It is said that if one pure of heart looked into it on a full moon night when the stars shone bright, they could see straight into the heavens and speak with the gods. *Indura Luin* is its old name, Mirror of the Moon."

Karigan cocked her head skeptically. "By looking into a lake? At night?" She did not believe in myths. "What happened to the lake?"

"It is said Mornhavon the Black drained it, for it gave too many answers to his enemies."

In the valley, the grasses were lush amidst stalks of purple lupine. A narrow stream gurgled through the valley basin. She could almost believe the part about Mornhavon the Black. Her experiences since she had left Selium convinced her that magic did exist, but could one possess enough to drain an entire lake?

Laren Mapstone paced before the empty throne chair, feet echoing hollowly on the stone floor. With the king absent, only two silver-and-black-clad guards stood at the throne room entrance. She prayed that wherever the king was, he had taken all of his Weapons with him.

Where was Crowe?

Hours upon hours had been spent deciphering F'ryan Coblebay's letter to Lady Estora. A message hidden within the message. The king was in grave danger and they might already be too late to prevent an assassination attempt. She had instructed the Chief Rider to assemble as many Riders as possible, to find everyone that was in the city who wasn't on a run. If they were about to head out on a run, he was to delay them, and get every Rider mounted, armed, and ready to move. However, it did not look too hopeful that many would be available.

The clearing of a throat broke into her thoughts. "Captain, you wished to see me?"

Laren turned on Crowe. He leaned on his staff of office, long, cobalt robes brushing the floor. His piercing black eyes, and the way he cocked his head were decidedly crowlike.

"Castellan, thank you for meeting with me on such short notice."

"Short notice, indeed. The king gave me today as a holiday."

Crowe must think her an idiot if he believed she called him here for some trivial matter. "This concerns the king. I fear for his safety."

"We all do. Every day."

Laren felt the sudden urge to grab him by his robes and shake him. "I have evidence that the king now faces a specific danger *today*."

"What sort of evidence?"

"Karigan G'ladheon carried with her not one message, but two. The second was written in the guise of a letter to a friend of F'ryan Coblebay's."

"Karigan who?"

"The girl from Selium who—"

"Oh, that one. Yes, proceed."

Laren screamed inside at the delay. "The letter spoke

of trouble from the king's brother, that he was planning to take the throne by force, with help from Mirwell, on the day of the king's annual spring hunt. It spoke also of an Eletian who could not be trusted."

Crowe gazed impassively at her. "Where is this letter? Could I see it, please?"

"No. I can't give you the letter. It was entrusted to me by F'ryan Coblebay's friend who wishes anonymity."

"Then why should I trust your information?"

Laren counted to ten before she spoke, but there was still an edge to her voice. "Why shouldn't you trust the information? We are talking about one of the most trustworthy Riders I knew. He died trying to deliver this message. You've never questioned me before, and you know I can see the truth in the message."

"Ah." Crowe squinted his eyes and nodded.

"Where is the king, Crowe? Where did he take the hunt?"

"He wished that I tell no one this information."

Why was Crowe being so evasive? Her fingers brushed her brooch. He was telling her the truth, the king had certainly told him to keep quiet about the hunt's destination, but it was as if he was trying to hide something from her. "Castellan, I think the king would certainly understand. This is an emergency, after all. His life is at stake."

"I follow the king's command," he growled, "not that of some Greenie."

Laren clenched the hilt of her saber with her gauntleted hand. She was so very tired. Tired from the lack of sleep as she and two others pored over F'ryan Coblebay's puzzle of a letter. Tired, tired, tired of Crowe and his petulant words. Tired of the way everyone viewed Green Riders as useless and lazy, of some lower caste incapable of anything but riding a horse to carry a message. And Crowe was delaying her, and she had no idea why.

"The Eletian. Is he here?"

"I don't know. I don't follow his every move."

Lie!

"Captain, might I suggest that you are overreacting?"

Laren opened her mouth with a retort, but he was just trying to delay her again, this time in argument. "Castellan, what are you hiding? You know it is foolish to lie to me."

Crowe made the sign of the crescent moon, fingers formed into a C, the sign of the god Aeryc. "Phaw! Don't use your dirty magic on me. I have nothing to hide."

Oh, yes, he did, and he was attempting to delay her again. The sound of footsteps running down the length of the throne room stopped an angry response in her throat. Her aide, Patrici, dusty from the road, halted before them.

"Captain, Castellan," she said panting. "The king—where is he?"

"I don't know," Laren said. "Do you carry an important message?"

"The message isn't important. What I saw is: groundmites. Groundmites east of the Lost Lake."

Groundmites? So far inside Sacoridia's borders? Impossible! "Crowe," Laren said, her voice that of a captain in command. "One last time. Where is the king? If you do not tell me, I'll make sure that he is made aware of your efforts to delay me."

Crowe's knuckles whitened as he clenched his staff. Something flickered behind his eyes as if some inward struggle was going on. "Lost Lake," he said. "King Zachary is hunting at the Lost Lake."

Laren turned on her heel, no time to lose. "Patrici, are you up for another ride?"

"Absolutely."

Laren fleetingly wished for the energy of youth, to not feel any pain, like the pain that racked her body every time she rode or used the brooch too much. She glanced behind her. Crowe watched them leave, his eyes like black darts. They passed through the big double doors of the throne room and found the two guards throwing dice. She shook her head in disgust.

"Sergeant," she said, "put away your dice and take up your sword. An armed contingent may try to enter the castle and claim the throne."

"I don't take orders from any Greenie," he said, and spat tobacco just short of her boots.

Laren drew herself up and closed in on him, the tips of her boots nearly touching his, her hawklike nose inches from his. "You will take orders from any officer who outranks you, worm. My good friend, Captain Able of the guard, will not be pleased to hear of your unwillingness to take orders."

The sergeant straightened up. "An armed contingent, you say? Claiming the throne?"

"To arms, Sergeant," she said, and stalked away, Patrici trotting alongside.

"Ingrate," Patrici said.

"Patrici, I need you to send a runner to both Captain Able, and to Horse Marshal Martel. There won't be enough of us Riders to take on those groundmites by ourselves. Have the runner tell Marshal Martel that we need as many mounted soldiers, ready for combat, as possible, and to meet us at the Lost Lake. He will need to know this may mean life or death for King Zachary."

"Right."

"One more thing, Patrici, do you still keep that old horn with you?" It was an old battered thing she had picked up secondhand from a bargain shop, and carried in memory of the First Rider, Lilieth Ambrioth, whose horn, it was said, could be heard clear across Sacoridia by any Green Rider. They had all laughed when they first saw Patrici carrying it, and she had been much offended.

"It's in my room," Patrici said, with a quizzical expression.

"I'll need you to play the Rider Call as we ride through the city. Think you can manage that?"

Again, with the confidence of the young, she replied, "Absolutely. I'll rouse the First Rider if necessary."

Laren strode toward the stable. If only the First Rider

really could raise herself from the ashes of Ages past to ride again.

Alton and Karigan stopped under the shade of a beech tree for a leisurely midday meal. Alton unpacked food obviously meant for a picnic, not extended travel. Freshly baked bread with honey to dip it in, and cake, meat rolls and spiced wine, peaches and plums. It was as good as any picnic Karigan had ever been on. The tension of the morning faded as they made small talk while robins chirped on a branch above. The horses cropped grass nearby.

Alton asked, "When you return to Corsa, what will you do then?"

Karigan caught a drop of peach juice running down her chin. Remembering it was not exactly polite to use her sleeve, she dabbed the corners of her mouth with a napkin. She had spent too many days on the road by herself, and such niceties had become less important.

"I will assist my father with the summer trade season."

Alton lay on his side in the fragrant grass, propped on an elbow, considering the golden peach he rotated in his hand. His hands were large and thick. "You are so certain? You won't return to Selium or join the Green Riders?"

"I was wrongly cast out of school," she told him.

"And the messenger service?"

"As for that," Karigan said, "I've told you and the others that I am not a Green Rider, and I never will be."

Alton shrugged and bit into his peach, and both fell silent again for a time. After a while he said, "I don't feel much like a Green Rider. My family won't permit me to ride, but I feel as if I *must*. I hear hoofbeats in my dreams sometimes, and I wake up in a sweat as if I must go, but I don't know where. It twists my stomach every time someone else goes out, and all I can do is watch them ride off. I can hardly look the others in the eye. Especially when one of them gets hurt. Or dies."

Karigan was surprised Alton chose to share his feelings with her, and she was even more surprised by the intensity with which he spoke. She supposed he did not have anyone else to confide in, not even Riders who might not understand the limitations of his status. He would be viewed as shirking his duties or, worse, receiving special treatment. His family certainly wouldn't be sympathetic to his feelings since they forbade him to ride. Maybe he could talk to Karigan because she was resisting the impulse to be a Green Rider, and she also knew what it was like to hear those hoofbeats.

"What would your family have you do?"

"They would have me ornament courts filled with eligible noblewomen." He grinned wryly. "I still have to do that on occasion, as at the ball the other night. If my family knew I had spent time with another Green . . . commoner . . . young woman . . ." He stumbled along, not quite sure how to say it without offending her. "They would haul me back to the manor house to teach me more stone craft."

Now he looked at his big hands, fingers splayed out, palms up. "It might surprise you to know that I possess calluses on these hands. From a young age, I had to learn to cut stone. It's a family tradition. You wouldn't believe the hours I spent hammering on granite, my knuckles bleeding until I became proficient enough to hit the drill dead on." He sighed. "The breach in the D'Yer Wall is a disgrace to my family."

She took his hand in hers, feeling the calluses herself, and the strength of his grip. They smiled at one another. Karigan released his hand. "But the wall was built a thousand years ago," she said. "Stone walls crumble with time."

Alton shook his head. "This wall shouldn't have. It was built of the finest craft we possessed, the rock magically bound in ways that are lost today. The wall had to be strong to keep at bay the evils of Blackveil Forest. A clan disgrace doesn't heed the passage of time or generations."

This she had never heard. Of course Clan G'ladheon hadn't existed for very long, nor was it of original Sacor Clan lineage. She sprinkled water over her hands from her water skin to clean off sticky peach juice. She would have to be careful in this life not to disgrace any of her descendants.

"Will someone repair the D'Yer Wall?"

"I don't know if we can." A troubled expression crossed Alton's face. "As I said, much of the craft that went into the wall has been forgotten. Something must be done, though. I can't imagine what evil has found its way through it already."

Karigan could. She had met it.

They cleaned up the remnants of their picnic and rode for another hour, the long valley still stretching below them.

This must have been some lake, Karigan thought, listening to the rustle of meadow grass in a breeze. Bees droned on the lupine. Whether or not the lake had been drained, it was still a pleasant place.

"Look below," Alton said, pointing into the valley. "I think that is the king's hunt."

Tiny mounted figures trotted below. Smaller white spots moved just ahead of the horses.

"This should help." Alton removed a brass telescope from a leather case attached to his saddle. D'Yer was no impoverished aristocratic clan if it possessed even one such looking piece. "The dogs seem to be on the scent of some quarry." Politely, after a brief glance, he passed the telescope to Karigan.

She took it into her hands dubiously. The last time she had looked into one was at Seven Chimneys where she had seen disturbing images of her past, present, and future. The last time she had seen a telescope was on the balcony of the castle during the ball. When Zachary had looked through, one of those future images had become apparent.

Six Hillander terriers bounded through the tall grass up front. They stopped to sniff the ground, pink tongues lolling, then sprinted off on a scent. The hunting party followed slowly behind, King Zachary in the lead with bow and arrow nocked. He was garbed in light mail, a short hunting sword girded at his side, and the silver fillet rested on his brow. His almond eyes scanned the meadow intently. Behind him rode a standard bearer in livery, holding aloft the Clan Hillander terrier banner, identical to the one that hung in the throne room.

Some well dressed men, who seemed more intent on conversation than hunting, hung behind, sipping at flasks probably filled with wine. They waved their bows about to add emphasis to whatever they were discussing. Among them was the lord-governor of Mirwell, dressed in scarlet and accompanied by his stoic aide and a guard.

Miscellaneous provincial soldiers and guards in silver and black rode with the nobles, boredom blanking their faces of expression. Weapons ranged about the group, their expressions, in contrast, wary and attentive. Karigan counted four of them, though there may have been more out of sight.

"You call that hunting?" She passed the telescope back to Alton. "It looks more like a procession to me."

Alton shrugged and looked through the eyepiece again. "The king considers this relaxing. He doesn't have any of his advisors present, there are no servants milling about, and the nobles are too drunk for rhetoric. No one is nagging him about the state of the country."

Karigan hooked a strand of hair behind her ear. When she had addressed King Zachary in the throne room that day, had her complaints been considered nagging?

"It wouldn't have been politic of him not to include a few nobles. They don't seem to be annoying him. The soldiers are a must. He is probably enjoying himself thoroughly, and his dogs are getting a little exercise."

Whatever.

Alton continued to watch through the telescope, his

brow furrowing. "Now that's strange," he said. "I won-der what's got the dogs riled up. Certainly not a hare."

Karigan shielded her eyes from the sun and looked down into the valley. Without the telescope, all she could see were little white dots scattering in all directions. Barking came to her distantly. The horses screwed on their haunches, ruining the orderly formation they had been walking in. A black-clad figure fell from his mount.

Alton pulled the scope away from his eye, as if he couldn't believe what he had just seen and needed to confirm it with his bare eyes.

"What is it?" Karigan asked.

Alton handed her the scope. The scene was chaotic. Dogs were nearly trampled by rearing horses. The king shouted orders at the dogs. Weapons galloped to the king's side with swords bare. The useless guards were too busy fighting for control of their steeds to be of any help. The figure she had seen fall lay still in the grass. A Weapon. Two arrows protruded from his chest.

Karigan, like Alton, took the scope away from her eye in disbelief. On the opposite ridge, and farther along their own, metal glinted in the sun.

By Breyan's gold, they're under attack!

Alton saw the reflection, too, and took the telescope from her. "Aeryc and Aeryon, have mercy. Those are groundmites."

⋘ BLACK ARROWS ⋙

Mirwell yawned.

"Are you tiring, my lord?" D'rang asked.

Mirwell surveyed the valley. The hunters moved at an excruciatingly slow pace. They waded through the tall grass in search of hare or small rodents at the absolute worst time of the day, with the sun still high in the sky and the critters burrowed away to where even Zachary's fine terriers could not dig them out. Even if it was the right time of the day, the noisy nobles would scare even the deafest of game to the far reaches of the country.

"I am not tired, D'rang," he said. "I'm bored. Though I believe things will get interesting very shortly." He glanced at Beryl. He had hoped for things to grow interesting between the two of them, but now she didn't even talk, except to say "yes, my lord." She was no better than the boy who had tended him during his bath the other night. Beryl's beautiful eyes were glassy and vacant. Whatever the Gray One had done to her, he had removed or hidden her spark of life and personality.

Mirwell squinted at the ridges on either side of the valley, which formed an excellent place for an ambush. The Gray One's forces could hide beyond the ridges and then, when the time came, trap Zachary and his nobles in the bottom. The valley was narrowing even now.

"Let us pause here," he said, "and see what unfolds. I have no wish to get caught in the thick of things."

"Yes, my lord," Beryl said in a deadpan voice. She

eined her horse in reflex and sat there staring straight
ahead.

Then, as if on cue, a Weapon fell from his horse, impaled by two arrows. The drunken nobles hauled on the
reins of their panicked steeds. At least a few lord-governors would die today, eliminating possible contenders for
the throne and leaving their provinces in disarray. Mirwell had hoped more would join the hunt, but they knew
from past years what a bore it was.

A bore no longer, he thought.

Twenty to thirty metal-clad figures swarmed over each
ridge toward the valley floor. The brave little terriers
charged the groundmites as if the instinct to attack the
creatures had been bred into them. Nobles fell to the
ground with arrows bristling from them like pins in a
pin cushion.

"Who is that?" Alton asked. He pointed at the opposite ridge and passed Karigan the scope.

She trained it where he pointed. At first she saw no
one among the trees and tall grasses, but then a solitary
figure standing there became discernible. Just barely. He
was dressed in gray. She nearly dropped the telescope.

"You know him?" Alton asked.

"I've encountered him," she replied, overcome by
shakiness. "A gray rider. The Shadow Man." Condor
shifted his weight and pawed the ground, his ears laid
back. "We've got to do something."

"I agree, but what? We would most likely get ourselves killed down there."

Karigan grabbed only air where the hilt of her saber
should have been. It was the one thing that had not been
returned to her. "We must stop that gray rider. He uses
terrible black arrows. They're magic . . . and evil. We
must stop him."

Alton loosed his saber from his saddle sheath. "Well,"

he said with a rueful smile, "I was tired of being left out of the action. My family will kill me if they find out about this. And if I survive."

Karigan saw that he was about to charge down into the midst of the ambush. "Don't go yet. I'm going to ask for help."

She freed the little velvet pouch from her belt and drew out the bunchberry flower, now with only three petals left on it. Alton held himself taut, ready to ride into the valley to fight for the king, but watched Karigan with his head cocked at a quizzical angle to see how she hoped to find help.

She plucked a petal from the flower and threw it into the breeze. It floated into the sky and was whisked away by the air currents. "Please bring help," Karigan said.

Alton snorted in disbelief. "If that isn't the most outrageous—" Night Hawk reared, and he fought to keep his seat. "Now what?"

What Alton D'Yer considered to be outrageous was blown away by a gathering of wispy, shifting spirits who arrayed themselves before Karigan. F'ryan Coblebay, dead F'ryan, stood frontmost. The faces of his companions stirred and changed as if under water, their voices a breathy babble. Alton blanched, enabled by some whim of the shadow world to perceive the dead, too.

"F'ryan," he said. "How—?"

F'ryan did not acknowledge the young lord, as if he must keep each movement to the barest minimum. Instead, he stood before Karigan. *I have come to help one last time,* he said. *One last time for the Wild Ride.*

The Wild Ride, the other ghosts echoed.

Alton glanced at Karigan, stricken, and she knew exactly how he felt.

In the valley, several nobles had been slain, though the rest attempted to repel the attackers, but mostly in vain. The remainder of the guards and Weapons left them unprotected and ringed the king, and though several groundmites lay dead, the odds were impossible.

You must end the pain, F'ryan said to Karigan. *Soon*

I will fade and be enslaved by him. He swept his pallid hand across the valley where the gray rider stood unseen without the aid of the telescope. *So many have already fallen to him. You must break the arrows. Break all the arrows.*

Break arrows, the ghosts echoed.

It is the last time for the Wild Ride, F'ryan said.

The Wild Ride! The Wild Ride! The Wild Ride!

"Hang on for your life," Karigan warned Alton. His wide eyes told her he was clearly frightened.

Condor and Night Hawk sprang down the hill after the ghosts, and it was as Karigan remembered. Everything wheeled past her as an indistinct blur in streamers of color. But this time the ghosts remained hushed and grave, intent upon their goal. Their passage was like a rustle of wind across the grasses, for this Wild Ride lasted only moments, and when it ended, they stood on the opposite ridge abreast of the Shadow Man. The ghosts seethed and wavered behind them. Alton was still white from the shock, his features taut, but he was in one piece.

The Shadow Man gazed into the valley. He leaned on his longbow and held in his hand in a casual, careless way, a black arrow. The spectral breeze of the ghosts fluttered his gray cloak. He turned to them, and although his features lay shrouded in the shadow of his hood, Karigan felt his gaze upon her.

She licked her lips, seized by fear and dread, wondering what it was the ghosts expected her to do against this one who possessed dark magic. She hadn't even her saber to use.

Alton overcame his fears first. He sat tall in his saddle, and with the most aristocratic bearing he could summon, he commanded, "Call off your attack."

Soft laughter trickled from beneath the Shadow Man's hood. "What a pretty hero you make, Lord D'Yer." The Shadow Man tossed his hood back, revealing deep golden hair that seemed to shine with a halo beneath the sun.

"The Eletian!" Karigan said.

Eletian, Eletian, Eletian, the ghosts babbled.

"I see the shades have come to your aid again, Karigan G'ladheon, but to what end? Here they have placed you within my grasp. Of you I shall make another slave."

The ghosts shrieked like the winter wind in the fury of a tempest; their otherworldly voices rose in a crescendo to an unbearable, piercing whine, and they began to spin around Karigan, Alton, and the Shadow Man, in a dizzying blur of white like a cyclone. The faster they revolved, the more high-pitched their voices rang, until it was almost beyond the hearing of living beings. Alton and Karigan covered their ears, the horses dancing beneath them and rolling their eyes.

The Shadow Man stood still, undismayed by the spirits' display, and uttered quietly words that had not been heard for hundreds of years, words of evil summoning that had never been spoken since the end of the Long War. And yet he spoke these words with ease.

The wail of the ghosts died abruptly, and they split apart, fell away, and reassembled in a mass behind Karigan and Alton, waiting. Waiting for what?

A new moaning grew as if from the very earth, and resonated in the air all around them. The trees trembled, and a gloom materialized behind the Shadow Man. Shawdell spoke the harsh words again, and the Green Rider ghosts seemed to cringe.

"What—" Alton began. His hair twisted and turned in a spirit wind. "What could ghosts be afraid of?"

"Other ghosts," Karigan said.

A host of the dead formed behind Shawdell, merging and separating among themselves. Their moaning was worse than a dirge, low and leaden and despairing. Slowly they passed around and over Shawdell intent on facing the Green Rider ghosts. They were young and old, some in uniforms, others dressed in the plain clothes of commoners.

Karigan and Alton put their hands in front of their faces as if to ward off the spirits as they surged toward them. But the ghosts passed by and between them. Karigan uncovered her eyes, but too soon. A spirit with the visage of a matronly, older woman, walked straight through her. Karigan felt the spirit as a blast of cold, like stepping into a winter cold room.

Each of Shawdell's spirits was impaled by two black arrows.

The faint trumpet of a battle horn could be heard, muffled as if an echo of time, and then there was the distant ring of blades being drawn, and still the low dreadful moan. The spirits streamed all around them like a fog on a hilltop shaped and reshaped by the wind.

Shawdell stood unflinching as the ghostly battle was waged around him.

The horses trembled, their necks lathered in a foamy sweat, barely tolerating the spirits that swarmed and moaned about them. Karigan watched as Alton slid off his unsettled horse and grimly dodged the ghosts to put himself in front of her and Condor. He stood erect and proud before the Eletian and drew his blade. Karigan wished he wouldn't put himself in the line of fire, further endangering himself. She jumped off Condor to stand beside him and lend support. They were in this together. He glanced briefly at her and she saw the apprehension in his eyes.

To Shawdell, he said, "You will stop this, traitor."

"Traitor?" Shawdell chuckled. "I owe allegiance to none, and certainly not to a mortal kingdom like Sacoridia."

The spirit of a young boy tottered by, and reached out to unravel an old Green Rider. Karigan rubbed her eyes and tried to put the ghosts out of her mind. "Then why were you trying to court favor with King Zachary?"

"Court favor? Sacoridia borders *Kanmorhan Vane,* the single, greatest concentration of power left in this world. Your king refused to take advantage of the situation, but Prince Amilton comprehends what it means."

"What has Eletia to gain?" Alton asked, his eyes betraying incredulity.

"Eletia? A land of fools always hiding, always hiding among their trees. I serve myself, but never Eletia. It is time for old powers to rise again. And you, my lord Alton D'Yer, threaten those powers. You possess the skills to repair the breach in your ancestral wall."

Faster than the eye could follow, and with the spirits aswirl about him, Shawdell raised his bow, speaking in whispers as if to himself, and loosed his arrow. Karigan cried out. Alton dropped his sword and raised his hand, palm outward, as if to stop the arrow. And he did. An arm's length from his breast, the arrow smacked some invisible barrier and dropped to the ground. All three looked at the arrow in utter amazement.

"I . . . I imagined a granite wall," Alton said.

"Your Greenie defenses are impressive," Shawdell said, "but like the D'Yer wall, they are not enough."

Before Alton had time to react, Shawdell nocked another arrow, drew it back, and shot. This time the arrow skimmed across the invisible wall and penetrated, piercing Alton's side. Alton wavered on his feet before crumpling to the ground.

With a cry of dismay, Karigan knelt by his side. The arrow had not pierced him deeply, but who knew what magic was at work?

The trumpeting of a horn shattered the air—not the trumpet of the dead—but clear, ringing notes of the living, and Karigan felt hope build inside her. Shawdell glanced down into the valley where five still defended the king. Their swords slashed at more than twice as many of the enemy, and as the horn sounded again, the fighting seemed to pause. Watching the scene through the embattled ghosts was like looking through a veil.

Nine Green Riders flew from the north end of the valley. Unmistakable red hair streamed behind the first and foremost Rider. Behind her, another Rider blared the horn. Somehow they had known to come!

"A handful of Greenies," Shawdell said, "should not change my plans overmuch."

Karigan grabbed Alton's sword and with an angry

rowl, lunged at Shawdell. He dropped his bow and met er with his own sword. When the two blades pinged ogether, Karigan felt shock waves tingle through her rms. How stupid, she thought, to use a saber against a ong sword. He easily countered every move she made, is pale blue eyes steady, and his lips curved up in a arody of a smile. He was enjoying this!

He toyed with her, let her exert herself. He parried er blows, neither defending himself, exactly, or at-acking. Just playing. He had the reach of her, and in quick succession, sliced the brass buttons off her great-coat. Karigan tried harder, tried to remember everything he had learned, but the harder she tried, the more Shaw-dell looked like laughing. He could have killed her ong ago.

Then the saber snapped. She looked stupidly at the agged shards.

"Those sabers are no match for a sword wrought Ages go by the smiths of Mornhavon the Black," Shawdell aid, slipping his into its sheath. "And your fledgling kills are nothing to me. I've been at the sword four undred years and twice that, and I've access to power one of you can reach. *I broke the D'Yer Wall.*"

A black orb like the one Karigan had seen in her oom at the Fallen Tree Inn in North formed just above Shawdell's upturned palm. It pulsated and rotated, and epelled the light. He hurled it at her.

Karigan dodged to the side, but the ball struck her houlder. The sensation was like the shattering of a glass vindow, fragments flying through the air, flying through er. Pain crackled through every nerve ending in her oody and she crashed to the ground in agony. Black, opy fire wrapped around her and she tried to scream, out her voice was stuck in her throat.

"This should hold you for a time," Shawdell told her, "while I attend to other matters." He took up the bow nd faced the valley, gazing intently at the scene below.

Laren Mapstone and her Riders had blown past Tomas
Mirwell and his aide and guard. Mirwell may have mas-
terminded this ambush on King Zachary, but he did not
pose a serious threat in the immediate battle. She would
deal with him later, and gladly. The groundmites, on the
other hand, pushed hard on King Zachary and his guards.
Only the skill of the remarkable Weapons had set back
the crude slashing of the snarling groundmites.

A great mist had settled on the ridge to the east. It
shifted in some unnatural way. Then, in response to a
blast from Patrici's horn, a distant sequence of notes, the
battle call of the Green Riders, sounded from the mist.
A figure loomed out of the mist, like a rider on a rearing
horse, her hair flowing behind her, and she held her horn
high as if in salute.

Fly, Riders, fly, a chorus of far-off voices chanted.

What was it Laren had said about the First Rider?

She didn't know how much time had elapsed since
then, for they had engaged the groundmites. The mud-
colored, hulking creatures cowered beneath the flying
hooves of enraged messenger horses. Several fell to
Rider sabers. Then the king's banner fell, was trampled
underfoot, and the groundmites rallied and fought back.
They growled through sharp teeth and beat their swords
on black shields in defiance. Before the Long War, Mornhavon the Black had bred these creatures to be unthink-
ing killers.

Laren was aware of some of her people being hauled
from their saddles and falling beneath the blades of
groundmites. Horses were hacked down, their Riders
never reemerging. Grimly she fought on, pounding
through the thick skull of one groundmite, and slashing
the throat of another. Her sword notched on the black
breastplate of one, and when his sharp claw rent through
her trousers and into the flesh of her calf, she drove the
sword through his eye.

It seemed to rain blood, and Laren lost count of how
many of the enemy she killed. One grabbed for Bluebird's bridle, she hacked his claw off. The din of metal

against metal was punctuated by grunts and shouts. Foremost in Laren's mind was to stand by the king's side and defend him, and she mindlessly hacked at groundmites to reach her goal.

She wondered in some distant corner of her mind if all her training, all her years in the messenger service, had come down to this base savagery, of indiscriminate thrusts and hacks. There was no fine technique here as was taught by the arms masters, and no sense of time. Just forward momentum and another groundmite to kill.

When there were quite suddenly no more before her, she stopped, blinking in surprise. The few remaining groundmites fled, throwing down their weapons as they ran, in the end no match for the mounted Riders. One of the surviving Green Riders began to chase after them, but Laren yelled, "Halt. Enough. We need your help here." She set him to helping the wounded.

Just two of her people remained mounted. All around her lay the dead and wounded, and it wasn't easy to know which was which. She shook her head in disbelief. Her people . . . She was responsible for them, for *this*. She swallowed, forcing back emotions that must wait for another, private time. She was still a captain of the messenger service, and there was work yet to be done.

She glanced at the king, who was leaning wearily against his horse. Of his original hunting party, only one haggard Weapon stood beside him. She saw the lines of grief and pain on Zachary's face, and when his eyes met hers, he said, "Mirwell."

Laren nodded in understanding and wheeled Bluebird around. She galloped her exhausted horse across the valley, fearing Mirwell would escape.

She found him sitting calmly upon his horse watching her approach with interest. She pulled Bluebird up before him.

"Well, well, Captain," he said.

Laren pointed her bloody saber at him. "I know your part in this, *Lord-Governor*."

The guard D'rang sat nervously playing with his reins,

but Beryl sat there unmoving, her eyes glassy and empty. Her winged horse brooch was missing. The captain tried to read her, but found nothing but a barrier, a very dark barrier.

"I have anticipated the moment when we could meet this way," Mirwell said, "when I didn't have to hide my thoughts from you."

"Oh, I've known well enough how you've felt about me," Laren said with a tight smile. "I just had to read the expression on your face, but you kept your other secrets well enough. It's all over."

"I daresay it is not." Mirwell glanced up at the ridge and Laren followed his gaze.

Through the gloom of ghosts, two figures could be seen battling one another. Gold hair flashed on one of the combatants—the Eletian of course. The other was not so easy to make out at first, but then the clash of ghosts shifted, and through a thinning of the supernatural fog, she could see her.

"Karigan," she whispered.

"Yes, the very same Greenie who made off with the message," Mirwell said. "I'll be very glad when the Gray One finishes her off, for all the trouble she has caused me. Her family will suffer when I take L'Petrie Province, you can believe that. Merchant clan, humph."

Laren wasn't paying attention. She considered riding up the ridge to help Karigan, but somehow, she felt that it was beyond her, that in the end, she would be of no help. It was Karigan's battle. Hers and the Eletian's. Instead, she looked to Mirwell again.

"Dismount," she told him. Only D'rang complied, and the governor glared at him.

"Spence," Mirwell said. "The captain has annoyed me for the last time. Do you understand?"

"Yes, my lord." Beryl drew her long sword.

Laren looked incredulously from Beryl to Mirwell. "What have you done to her?"

Mirwell smiled at Beryl like an indulgent parent. "Nothing," he said. "Or at least, less than I would have liked. But the Gray One wished to ensure her loyalty to the great province of Mirwell and its lord."

Beryl held her sword at the ready, her expression deadpan.

"Beryl," Laren said. "It's me, Captain Mapstone."

Beryl did not even blink before she swung the blade. The captain barely deflected the blow. Bluebird backed off to help weaken its force. Laren licked her lips. Beryl had been on the verge of initiating swordmaster training when the brooch had called her. Her skill with the sword was well known.

"Kill her, Spence," Mirwell said.

"Yes, my lord."

Beryl jammed her heels into her horse, and she sprang broadside into Bluebird. Laren felt the strain of bones in her leg, reawakening the pain of the bloody wound inflicted on her by the groundmite. Bluebird fought to maintain his footing.

The long sword came again, swinging like a scythe. Laren backed and backed under the assault. The exhausting run and the melee with the groundmites had tired her beyond reason, slowing her reflexes. Oh, how her body hurt.

A hard blow jangled the nerves all the way to Laren's teeth, and she knew that soon, Beryl would take her. The tip of the long sword swished perilously close to her chest and when she brought her saber in closer to guard herself, she realized her mistake, for the move was not completed. It was an advanced technique swordmasters called the "curve." It took great strength and control, after sweeping the sword across the opponent's chest, to reverse the momentum of the slash and bring it back across the opponent's neck.

Laren ducked, but not enough, and she felt a burning across her scalp, and then she was blinded by her own blood running into her eyes. She rubbed them, but Beryl rammed her horse into Bluebird again. The poor exhausted horse toppled over, and Laren rolled clear. She felt around for her saber, but a boot stepped on her hand.

Laren blinked her eyes clear. Beryl stood above her with the sword raised. Mirwell's laughter could be heard over her own hard breaths.

Karigan's head buzzed and she fought against fainting, wrapped in the searing pain. The energy of the Eletian's magic burned her inside and out like hot, writhing coals. She saw images of her charred flesh exploding open and molten fire pouring out.

She saw other images of the Berry sisters, weaving between the pale faces of ghosts, looking at her kindly, clucking and shaking their heads. *The child looks out of sorts,* Miss Bunch said. *Do not be too harsh on her,* Miss Bay said. *She may have failed, but she did try.* Arms Master Rendle shared a cup of tea with the ladies. *You forgot to watch your back,* he told her.

Her friend Estral sat in her dorm room plucking a lute. *I will write a song in your memory,* she assured her. Abram Rust sat next to her and blew smoke rings. *The tree fell long ago,* he said.

Torne and Garroty crowded her vision, pushing away even the ghosts. *You deserve this. Die, Greenie.*

And the ghosts whispered, *Break the arrows.*

Die, Greenie, Torne said. *Die.*

Break the arrows.

Karigan stopped struggling. She just wanted to sleep and not wake up. Why did everyone keep nagging her?

Break the arrows. She felt the pressure of all those ghosts crowding her.

Shawdell nocked an arrow to the bow string. His lips moved as if he spoke a prayer over it.

Karigan saw an image of King Zachary sitting on his throne patting a ghost dog on his lap. The ghosts massed behind him and oozed around the edges of his chair.

He looked up toward the ceiling where an artist lay on scaffolding, painting his portrait. He opened his mouth to speak, but it was not his voice she heard.

"This is for your king," the Eletian said.

The Eletian blurred in her tearing eyes. He stood erect and drew the bow string taut.

"One arrow to kill him," he gloated.

Karigan fought the agony of his magic on her. She staggered to her feet.

"And the other to enslave him."

Karigan tackled Shawdell as he loosed the arrow. It flew wild. She attempted to get a hold on him, and they struggled on the ground for a moment, limbs and bow entangled. Shawdell threw her off.

She tumbled through ghosts, feeling their cold presences pass through her. An old man with an arrow in his throat leered over her. He held a hoe over his head as if to strike her. F'ryan Coblebay pushed the spirit and it dissipated.

Break the arrows.

The Eletian faced Karigan, his features drawn with anger. He drew his sword once again.

This time, Karigan did not have a saber with which to defend herself, and it did not look like Shawdell was in the mood to play anymore. It was hard to think amidst the burning coils of his spell. She could toss a bunchberry petal to the wind, but by the time help arrived, Shawdell would have her sliced into a hundred pieces. The sprig of bayberry might make her feel better, but it was no defense against Shawdell. The winged horse brooch she wore pinned to her shirt had certainly been no advantage against him before.

There was only one more thing. She dipped her hand into her pocket and felt the smooth cool sphere she always kept there.

Immediately the spell shattered to pieces. Tendrils of black burning filaments fell to the ground, scorching and burrowing into the soil. No more burning hot coals. No more boiling flesh. When she looked at her skin, it was smooth and untouched.

But Shawdell still held the sword.

Use what is available to you, the king had told her following their game of Intrigue. She drew the moonstone out. It was all she had.

At first the stone did nothing, and all Karigan could do was back away from Shawdell's intent advance. Then the stone flared to life in a single, silver blade of light. Shawdell stopped his advance in surprise.

It was like a sword in her hand. She shifted it this way and that and it swept through the air as a well-made blade should. Now she advanced, and Shawdell met her.

Their swords did not clang when they touched as two metal blades would, rather they hummed as if resonating against one another, light and dark. Silver sparks cascaded about them and a thread of smoke curled up from Shawdell's sword.

The light of the moonstone grew within and without her, drawing on her strength and memory; gathering together everything she had ever learned about survival and putting that knowledge in her immediate grasp. It was as if all her experiences during her long journey had finally come full circle in a combination that guided her hands and feet with a confidence and a competence she had not known before.

When their swords crossed and they pushed on one another, Shawdell hissed, "Eletia has truly failed if it relies on a weak mortal to fight its battles."

Karigan pushed him away with a grunt and battered him with another volley of blows.

"Eletian moonlight is nothing over the power of Mornhavon the Black!" Shawdell shouted.

In a calm, quiet voice, Karigan answered, "Eletia has nothing to do with it."

The ghosts stood as supernatural witnesses in a fluctuating, gray ring about the two combatants.

Shawdell cut low at Karigan's knees, she whipped the moonbeam blade in a luminous arc and blocked it. She thrust at his chest, but he sidled away and swung back with a slash to her stomach. It went back and forth like this, this oddly silent sword fight.

Karigan used many techniques she learned from Arms Master Rendle and F'ryan Coblebay. The ghost had shown her more than anyone when he had claimed her body during her fight with Torne. She had felt how to move her body in a precise way when wielding a sword. She had learned how to anticipate and meet the enemy. Rendle and F'ryan had taught her well, and she owed her survival in this duel, thus far, to them. One element was missing, however, that would help her overcome Shawdell. It was what the cargo master, Sevano, had taught her: unpredictability.

As they traded blows, Karigan awaited the appropriate moment. It came in the form of an especially hard blow delivered by Shawdell.

Karigan stumbled back and fell to her knees as if stunned. She looked up at Shawdell with beseeching eyes, holding her breath, the sword tip to the ground in the position of surrender.

Shawdell laughed in triumph and brought his own sword down like an ax intended to split her in half.

Karigan loosed a bloodcurdling scream of suppressed rage, closed in on him, and wrapped her arms about his waist. The sword swung far too wide to touch her. She knocked him over and rolled away.

Quick as a cat, Shawdell was on his feet again. The ploy had failed, and now he would expect anything from her.

Where Karigan's instincts of survival and her experiences once helped her, they now faded away, leaving her drained and feeling hopeless. She could not go on much longer. She saw in Shawdell's sparkling eyes that he knew.

The light of Laurelyn had been made Ages ago to face the dark, to repel and defeat it. A thousand years ago, Eletian warriors of the League had carried blades of light to turn the tide of the dark. The light would not tolerate the dark then, nor would it now.

The blade of light intensified rather than diminished at Karigan's despair. Hope flared within her as if she were part of the light. The whole ridge ignited in brilliance, more brilliant than sunlight, and the ghosts, shadows of the afterlife, blanched. Shawdell's triumphant look turned to one of uncertainty, and Karigan sprang forward.

With all her power and might, she chopped down on Shawdell's blade. There was an explosion of light that went beyond the brilliance of a silver moonbeam—it was a crystallized, pure whiteness that blinded the eye.

Then she thrust at him and cut deep. Shawdell floundered back. He held a shattered sword in one hand and held his stomach to keep his guts from spilling out with the other. He opened his mouth to speak, but only blood poured out.

Karigan panted. "You underestimate the will of mortals to survive. You've underestimated all along."

But even as she watched, the folds of flesh around his gashed belly began to knit together beneath his hand. Though blood still spilled from his lips, he said, "And you underestimate the dark powers, girl. Your moonbeam is nothing."

As if in angry response, the moonbeam sword coalesced upon itself into a bright shining sphere. The light grew and flared with multiple rays of light, seeking, searching. Shawdell dropped his useless sword hilt to shield his eyes and staggered backward. As on the silver moon night when she had seen him walking after the ball, he seemed protected by a black shield. But this time, the shield fluctuated, thinning here, and thickening there. The more his shield faltered, the more the moonbeams grew and probed for a weakness. And stabbed.

Shawdell screamed, and his gray tunic darkened with blood. He backed away, still holding his half-healed belly and flailing his other arm madly as if he were being attacked by a hive of bees. His gray horse appeared from the woods, and he staggered after it, fighting the moon-beam all the way.

He crawled onto the horse's back like a wounded spider and urged it into a gallop. The blade of light streaked after him into the woods.

Shawdell's slave spirits howled plaintively, and disappeared. The Green Rider ghosts merged and faded. Somewhere in the valley, a Green Rider captain watched incredulously as her assailant dropped her sword in mid-strike.

Karigan closed her eyes for a moment. When she opened them, she looked at her palm. The moonstone was no more than a handful of crystalline fragments glittering in the sun. The moonbeam was gone forever. She slipped the fragments into her velvet pouch.

Karigan sagged to the ground next to Alton D'Yer. She brushed hair away from his wan face. He breathed shallowly, still alive despite the arrow in his side. She didn't know how to help him, but held his hand and spoke quiet, encouraging words, not knowing if he even heard her.

In time, Captain Mapstone limped up the ridge toward her, leading her horse behind her. Her green uniform was splayed with blood—that of her enemies, Karigan concluded, though there was an ugly gash above her brow and blood stained her face like a mask. The captain gazed wearily at her, at the two messenger horses, and at Alton D'Yer sprawled on the ground. She dropped the reins of her horse and knelt beside Alton.

"He still lives," she said in surprise. She yanked the arrow from his side and quickly wadded the wound with cloth. "The wound itself is nothing, but who knows what evil this arrow is tainted with. He is in fever now."

"Give it to me."

"What?" Captain Mapstone gazed at Karigan's outstretched hand, not comprehending.

"The arrow," Karigan said. "Give it to me."

The captain looked at it doubtfully for a moment, but complied when she observed Karigan's determined expression. Karigan touched the arrow reluctantly. She could feel the taint of death in it, the torture. Before that taint could seep through her skin, she broke the arrow on her knee.

"What?" Captain Mapstone raised a brow, but when Alton coughed and groaned, she returned her attention to him.

Karigan walked down into the valley among the carnage, across the blood slick grasses. The dead lay in mockery to the beautiful lupine that wavered in a breeze. The Sacoridian dead had been separated from the groundmites. She detached herself from the gore, and searched for those impaled by black arrows. When she found the arrows, she broke them.

When she dropped the remnants of the last arrow to the ground, she found herself by King Zachary. He knelt amidst the Sacoridian dead, his people, and sobbed into his hand. The other hung at an awkward angle at his side as if his arm had been broken. Nearby, six white corpses lay in a row, including the smiling terrier, Finder.

She looked away, not wishing to intrude on his grief, and walked to where Condor stood at the edge of the battlefield, his head hanging low. Karigan stumbled over a groundmite shield emblazoned with a dead, black tree. What it could portend, she did not know, and was too tired to think about it.

⮞ THE NEXT MOVE ⮜

Karigan jerked awake with a cry. The sun had moved its way over the west ridge, angling deep shadows across the waving grasses and lupine of the valley of the Lost Lake, which had once been the Mirror of the Moon, *Indura Luin*. Ravens circled in the sky, waiting to alight on the battlefield; waiting to see what scraps of gore they could feed on. The encroaching shadows chilled Karigan and she shivered.

"You all right?" Captain Mapstone sat next to her, huddled beneath her shortcoat which was draped over her shoulders.

Karigan sat up and nodded. She had been overcome by a great weariness not long after Horse Marshal Martel's fifty light horse had trotted into the valley, all shining helms and breast plates, the horses held in perfect formation. Their display of decorum would have impressed any parade spectator.

However, when the soldiers saw the black smoke pluming from the pyre, flames licking the corpses of groundmites, and when they saw the wounded, their decorum faltered. Eyes popped open, oaths were sworn, some made the sign of the half moon, and others simply stopped in their tracks.

Feeble from blood loss and hard pressed to even stand, Captain Mapstone had limped up to the horse marshal and shouted, "Get off those horses and help us!" She must have sounded half crazed to them, but she had sounded just the way Karigan felt. She wanted to shout and scream, too.

The cavalry soldiers practically fell over one another to make themselves useful. A mender among them set the king's broken arm and attended the wounded. The soldiers began the grisly task of caring for the dead.

Common soldiers and nobles alike were laid out side by side. "They were all warriors of Sacoridia today," the king said. "As such, they were all equals, and heroes all."

Karigan had set to work to help the soldiers build a cairn over the dead, but as she bent to pick up a rock, she was assailed by dizziness and her knees buckled. That was when she must have taken the nap.

"No . . . I passed out, didn't I?"

Captain Mapstone nodded. "Whatever it was you did on the ridge today to that . . . Eletian, it must have sapped your strength."

Karigan rubbed her temples to stave off a ferocious headache. "Some ending to a perfectly good picnic."

The captain tugged her shortcoat more snugly about her. "The king lives. I would not say that was a bad ending."

Some distance away, King Zachary spoke with the horse marshal. His broken arm was splinted and bound securely to his chest, but he was quite alive.

"If you hadn't come when you did . . ." Karigan began.

"The king would be dead?" The captain cocked her head as if considering. "Perhaps. Perhaps not. One cannot predict other outcomes so easily."

"You cracked the code in F'ryan Coblebay's letter?"

"Yes." Captain Mapstone went on to explain how she and two other Riders had worked for many hours to find the hidden message. "It told of an Eletian who could not be trusted, and that the king's brother would take the throne by force. The attempt on the king was to coincide with his annual hunt. When we learned Shawdell was missing after the king had left with his party, we became concerned. More than concerned, in fact. A Rider reported seeing a band of groundmites in this area."

Captain Mapstone gazed sadly at the few Riders left alive. Two tended three wounded, including Alton

D'Yer. The rest were disappearing beneath the stone cairn being raised by the cavalry soldiers. She cradled a dented silver horn in her lap. "I wish we could have come sooner."

Karigan winced. "If I had given you the letter sooner—"

The captain reached over and patted her on the knee. "I don't think any of us would have suspected the letter was more than it seemed—an expression of love from F'ryan Coblebay to one he cared about tremendously. Much in that letter was genuine. Perhaps F'ryan knew Lady Estora would find it strange and bring it to one of us. It seems he knew he wouldn't make it back to Sacor City himself."

"Why was it in code?" Karigan asked.

"It revealed Beryl Spencer. It was also a form of misdirection, I believe, in case F'ryan was ever captured. It would survive in its seeming irrelevance, and the false message would be of equal unimportance because the information was old. Unfortunately, it did not help F'ryan in the end."

Captain Mapstone gazed at the horn in her lap. "We cannot dwell on what might have been. Don't blame yourself, Karigan, about not getting the real message to us sooner. You were right before. You are not a Green Rider, at least not a trained Green Rider and we—I was at fault to assume you would know how things worked. If it helps, let me say that you, more than anyone else, helped save the king today."

"Thank you," Karigan whispered.

"I'm not sure you are the one who should be doing the thanking." The captain's hand slipped unconsciously to the bandage that bound her head wound. "We owe you much. Even the dead do." She held out her other hand and it gleamed with gold. Gold winged horse brooches.

Karigan was astonished. "You took them? You took them from—?"

"From the dead? Yes. Like Joy's brooch you brought

back to us, they always find their way home. These brooches are curious things. More curious than you know. New Riders will be called to the service, and they will wear these same brooches. With the brooches they will discover new talents and use them. When they retire from the service, or die, the brooch will call out to someone new. It has always been this way."

"But I wasn't called," Karigan said.

"Are you so sure?" The captain smiled. "The calling to become a Rider comes in a variety of ways. Perhaps you are right about it being the situation: F'ryan's dying, you being right there." She shrugged. "Their qualities are peculiar. They seem to attract strange adventures and extraordinary people to the wearer. Some believe it is just the nature of the job, of being a king's messenger, yet others believe it is the magic."

Karigan touched her brooch. It felt like cold metal, that was all, yet she knew what it was capable of. "What do you believe?"

"What do I believe? I believe in all kinds of possibilities. But as far as the brooches go, it is the rare moment that life has been dull for me since I first pinned one on some twenty years ago."

The captain unfolded her legs, and in what looked like an agonizing movement that shone clearly in her taut features, she stood up. She covered the pain with another smile, but Karigan could see it in her eyes.

"Come," Captain Mapstone said, "and we will find out what happens next."

Karigan raised herself from the sweet grasses and followed in the tracks of the captain who limped on ahead. *You, more than anyone, helped save the king today,* the captain had said. Karigan had tossed a bunchberry petal to the breeze. It was supposed to bring a friend in need, and though she had thought so at the time, the arrival of the Green Riders had not been the result of the bunchberry petal. Did the bunchberry petals lose their efficacy after a certain amount of time?

She no sooner asked herself the question when some-

thing small and white, like a snowflake, drifted out of
the sky. She held her hand out and the bunchberry petal
settled on her palm.

*How do I interpret this? Am I my own friend in need?
I can depend on myself?* She blew it off her palm, smiling
for the first time in hours.

She could depend on herself, yet hadn't she been surrounded by friends the entire time? Friends who had
helped her along in her journey or who tried to protect
her? Where would she be without them?

She paused and called out to the captain. "I'll join you
in a moment."

Captain Mapstone nodded, and Karigan walked over
to where the wounded rested. Among them, huddled in
a coarse blanket, slept Alton D'Yer. In the dusk his expression was one of peace without a hint of the day's
strivings; no sign of pain or worry; simply the release of
sleep, and with it, a certain innocence.

Karigan shuddered to think of what black arrows
might have done to this young man. She had seen it all
too vividly, too many times. First F'ryan Coblebay, then
Joy Overway, and those who died today. It was not simply death, but a twisted, dark, and tortured path. What
made Alton different from the others was that she had
grown to know him, while the others had been strangers.
With Alton, she could put a face with a name; a face
that was alive with laughter and dreams and the future.

She knelt beside him, and when he shifted in his sleep,
she adjusted the blanket about his shoulders.

Today he had stood between her and black arrows.
Her fingers brushed his cheek and she felt the warmth
of him.

"Thank you, Alton," she whispered. "I only hope I'm
worthy of what you did for me today. You are a true
friend." And perhaps more than a friend, but confusion
fluttered in her heart at the thought.

She made sure he rested as comfortably as possible on
the ground where he slept, the regular rise and fall of
his chest reassuring. She left him reluctantly and joined

the able-bodied survivors of the ambush who sat in a circle in the waning sun. Among them were Horse Marshal Martel, a couple of his officers, and Beryl Spencer.

It was as if the king and his followers had become primitive hunters, back to the dark days before Sacoridia was what it had become, when folk sat in council on the rough ground, and told the news of the lands in stories by a fire.

"I've posted sentries should any of the enemy decide to return." Horse Marshal Martel sat very erect in his shortcoat of deep navy, a red sash knotted at his waist. Silver buttons and a gorget about his neck gleamed in the dwindling light. His gold marshal's shoulder cords, and the red-plumed helmet placed carefully in the grass beside him, made him an impeccably well turned out officer, though he had discarded his breast plate earlier. Even the formal uniform of the Green Riders did not compare to his field uniform. "We should make camp for the night."

"It sounds sensible," King Zachary said. "It would be preferable not to move the wounded tonight, at least not far, and I think most of us are deeply tired. However, I am concerned about what my brother is up to."

"You should be, Excellency," Beryl Spencer said. "He planned to march on your castle with more than twice what you have garrisoned there."

Martel glanced at Captain Mapstone. "Do you trust her word? Is she not the one who tried to kill you?"

The captain nodded tiredly. "She speaks the truth. The compulsion placed on her by the Eletian is mostly gone, as far as I can tell. There is still a residue of the spell, but I believe it is fading. Besides, the message brought to us by Karigan confirms Amilton's intent."

Karigan squirmed as the horse marshal's light gray eyes fell on her.

"Then we ride," he said.

"Just like that?" the captain asked. "You won't know anything about the prince's force or its position."

Martel stuck his chin out resolutely. It was covered by

a dense but closely cropped flaxen beard. "My soldiers are well trained in reconnaissance, not to mention fighting if it comes to—"

"With all due respect, Marshal," Beryl broke in, "your soldiers almost panicked at the sight of this battle's aftermath. You expect them to face five hundred of the enemy?"

"Beryl—" Captain Mapstone said in warning.

Martel's eyes flashed in anger. "I will not have this Rider insult—"

King Zachary raised his hand to stop them. "Hold, my friends, hold. Captain Mapstone is right. We cannot rush in without knowing what we are up against. And the horse marshal is right, too. His riders are trained for reconnaissance."

"Do we know something of what we're up against, then?" asked one of the horse marshal's officers.

"Major?" said King Zachary.

Beryl inclined her head to the king. "Before we left Mirwellton—the governor and I—" She hastened a quick glance at the old man who sat some distance away with D'rang under the watchful eyes of cavalry guards. "—the governor mustered Mirwellian regulars and hired some merc companies to follow the prince to take the castle."

"Even with thousands of soldiers," King Zachary said, "he would be hard-pressed to take the castle. It is well fortified."

"And the castle has been warned," Captain Mapstone added.

"He was prepared for a siege, my lord, and do not forget he knows the castle almost as well as you. And there is one other thing . . ." Beryl looked about the group with haunted eyes. "You, my lord, were not the only one to have someone inside the enemy's court."

"What?" Zachary cried.

"Crowe," Captain Mapstone snarled. "It must be him."

"The castellan?" Martel's expression was incredulous.

"Yes," Beryl said. "On two occasions I tried to warn you. Once when Rider M'farthon delivered the ball and banquet invitation to Lord Mirwell, and a second time when I tried to speak to Karigan after the ball. Both times I was thwarted."

Karigan tensed as Beryl glanced at her, but the Rider's expression was not accusatory.

"I left Crowe in charge," Zachary muttered.

"It is because of him we arrived so late," Martel said. "He kept delaying me."

To Karigan, a shadow seemed to drop over the king. Another betrayal. First his brother, then one of his liege lords. Now one of his most trusted advisors. In his eyes, she could see him asking himself why, but he would never voice it. He could not, at least not now, for he was king and his duty was to lead fearlessly. In an odd way, his hurt pleased her, for it made him human and not simply a king with a hard visage who ruled without compassion. She hoped the intrigue and betrayals would never make him indifferent and callous to his people.

"I can send a small detachment for reconnaissance," Martel was saying. "They would not be detected in the dark. Once we know what your brother has achieved, we can plan our next move."

The king sighed. "If he has taken the castle, it means exile for me until I can muster a force large enough to retake it."

"I will be with you, my lord," Martel said with his fist to his heart. The others in the circle added their resounding agreement.

King Zachary was visibly touched. "Then there is nothing more for today, except to get some reconn—"

A shout went up from among some of Martel's soldiers on the perimeter. "Rider coming!"

Hands fell to swords and the group ringed themselves around the king.

"It's a Green Rider!"

All relaxed a bit with this news, but did not let down their guard. Soon, the approach of hoofbeats was clearly heard, and a Rider galloped at full speed into the valley. He hauled on the reins of his gray steed, dismounting simultaneously. He was a silhouette in the dusk as he approached with long strides. King Zachary's remaining Weapon, Rory, put himself between the messenger and the king.

"It's all right," Captain Mapstone said quietly. "I know him. It's Connly."

The young man's dark hair was plastered to his forehead with sweat. He had run his horse hard to reach them, and without slowing his stride, he came before the king and dropped to one knee.

"Sire," he said.

"Do you bear news, Messenger?"

"Yes, my lord." He stood up then and looked around at each of them. When his dark eyes rested on Karigan, they registered surprise. Just as quickly, his gaze shifted back to the king. "My lord, the castle has been taken."

The king seemed to sink into himself. Exclamations of dismay passed among the others.

"But I warned Captain Able," Captain Mapstone said.

"Treachery was at work, then." Connly placed his hand on her sleeve. "I am sorry, but he and some others hang at the castle gates."

"He was a good man," Martel said.

The others stood silently in disbelief in the midst of chorusing peepers.

Finally, Captain Mapstone shook her head. "He was a good man, and a good friend. We've lost so many . . . good friends."

"Yet I am grateful," Connly said, "to have found my captain and my king alive. I suspect our enemies believe you were defeated here, but when they hear nothing of victory by sunrise, they may grow suspicious and send someone to look things over. It is not safe to stay."

"We can withdraw to another place," Martel said.

The king waved the idea off. "We will do that, but first I want to hear what Rider Connly knows of the takeover."

"Actually, very little, Excellency, except no one in the city is panicked."

The king smiled grimly. "Another day, another king. Just so long as it does not interfere with their lives."

"I was spending some time at an inn I frequent on Chantey Street," Connly explained, "after a vigorous run. Osric, another Rider, was filling me in on the strange happenings over the past couple of weeks. We heard the hoofbeats of Prince Amilton's army riding in, followed by siege engines and infantry. They simply marched through the city gates. No one was there to close them or defend them. The city went on about its business, people moving aside as the prince rode in. Some along the streets even cheered and hailed him."

Zachary winced. "Yes, my brother has always had his supporters."

"Very true, Sire, though there was a show of force at the castle gates. Osric and I followed the army, watching and trying to keep out of sight, of course."

"How did they get in?"

"They scaled the scaffolding set up for repair on the castle wall, my lord," Connly said. "They climbed over the wall and took Captain Able and killed many others. The guard seemed to lose its spirit then."

Zachary shook his head. "The scaffolding. Crowe told me the wall needed repair."

"Beyond that," Connly said, "I don't know what transpired behind the castle gates, except the gates were opened and the prince rode right through."

"How did you know where to find us?" the king asked.

"Osric had heard of the king's annual hunt, where it was headed, and of a bunch running off after you. I fled the city before anyone noticed me, hoping to find you alive and well. Osric is still in the city, trying to locate other Riders and regular militia who are still loyal."

"Well done, Connly," Captain Mapstone said. She turned to King Zachary and placed a hand on his shoulder. "You cannot blame yourself for this. This is your brother's doing."

"There was a time when I would have gladly given him the throne."

"I know, but you gave up your personal freedom to lead Sacoridia, so your brother would not destroy it."

"He may still."

The evening darkened a shade deeper, and the chorus of peepers quickened like a heartbeat.

"Is there anything else, Connly?" Beryl asked.

"Yes." He settled his gaze on Karigan, and a tremor of fear ran up her spine. "Your father came seeking you."

"*What?*" Karigan stood ramrod straight.

"This was our second meeting, as Captain Mapstone can attest. He thought the captain or I would have information about your whereabouts. He must have seen me on the street and followed me to the inn. This was before Prince Amilton and his army came through. Of course, I had heard of your remarkable journey and arrival, but little more than that. He was surprised and more than a little gratified to hear you were even alive. He questioned me as to where he could find you. Last I had heard, you were still at the castle. I sent him there to find you."

It took a moment for what he had said to sink in. "You sent my father to the castle *before* Prince Amilton arrived?"

Connly looked at his feet. "I'm sorry. I assume he got caught up in events, but I didn't know what was about to happen."

Karigan thought she was going to explode with anger and frustration, but she just turned away with clenched hands, missing the king's look of sympathy.

"We must think about our next move," Martel said.

"I think I have an idea," Beryl Spencer said, "but it means we are going to have to move fast, and it means we need someone to go inside the castle gates to look the situation over."

"I'll do it."

Everyone looked at Karigan in astonishment, and she stepped right up to Beryl, her expression one of sheer determination.

"Karigan—" the king started.

"I said I will do it. I'll get into the castle."

Beryl started to protest, but Captain Mapstone motioned her to silence. "Yes. Karigan will do it."

⋖⋗ WOMAN OF THE
SHADOWS ⋖⋗

The shadows absorbed Karigan.

She darted from the dark side of one
building to another. She was like a phantom, fading in
and out, and if anyone marked her passage through the
streets of Sacor City, they might discount it later as some
vision, or a trick of their eyes.

Karigan used her brooch to the full extent of its powers, using it to conceal herself from the armed militia of
Prince Amilton Hillander. Some roamed the open
streets, others stood on the city walls. But the city was
not closed, nor the populace molested. *Yet.* A wise move
on Amilton's part—the more he left folk to their ordinary lives, the quicker they would accept him as their
new king, and the less chance he would face a rebellion.

A few folk still meandered on the streets. Peddlers
closed up their hand carts and pushed them away for the
night. Others entered inns and pubs. A good portion of
the populace was in for the night, and they did not notice
if there was a green flicker where the gold light of their
lamps spilled out into the dark.

From time to time Karigan rested, sinking to the
ground in a darkened close or alley, struggling to catch
her breath and relieve herself of the suffocating gray
world she submerged herself into every time she used
the power of the brooch to fade out. Now she squatted
in the narrow close between a Chapel of the Moon and
a market, among the stinking refuse that hadn't sold in

the latter. Both buildings were dark and empty, and she felt safe enough that she could drop the invisibility for a few moments.

She mopped sweat from her brow with her sleeve. The headache was coming back and exhaustion made her body tremble. Would the day never end? Or had it become an eternal nightmare?

Black clouds drifted across the nearly halved moon, and she darted into the street again, fading out and avoiding the light pooling about the oil-burning street lamps.

As she trotted along, King Zachary's short hunting sword slapped her thigh, a constant reminder of him. He had protested her further involvement with his brother's takeover, but Captain Mapstone convinced him Karigan was the only one to complete this mission. When Karigan demonstrated the power of her brooch, he could not argue.

"I must go," Karigan had said. "If my father is there, he may be in danger."

King Zachary smiled. It was a smile saddened by too many things. "I hope he knows how fortunate he is to have a daughter like you."

"I am fortunate to have him as my father."

Zachary lifted his sword and baldric over his head and awkwardly, with one hand, placed it over her shoulder.

"You want me to take your sword?" Karigan asked incredulously.

"Alas, brave lady, it is but a hunting sword. Yet it will be better than nothing, for I see you are without your own."

He had put his hand on her shoulder, and she could see many things in his brown eyes. Things she did not wish to think about.

"Come back . . ." he began, and she thought he might have finished with "to me," but he turned hurriedly away without saying another word.

Karigan wrapped her hand around the hilt of the sword now. It was a fancy thing with an intricate guard and blade etched with a hunting scene. Hopefully she would not have to use it. A hunting sword it was, but she did not pursue sport.

Before she knew it, her tired feet brought her within the shadows of the castle gates. A curious sight greeted her there: the Anti-Monarchy Society, gathered together, as if making some sort of plan. She moved closer and heard the confident tones of Lorilie Dorran who stood in the middle of the group.

"We can't deny something big has happened," Lorilie said. "But even if Zachary is dead and his brother now rules, it shouldn't change our plans. After all, monarchy in all forms is tyranny, and this monarch seems more tyrannical than some."

Her supporters glanced toward the gates. The gates were wide open, but well guarded by soldiers in Mirwellian scarlet. Others stood watch in silhouette on the surrounding wall, archers among them. Torches illuminated corpses swaying from nooses on either side of the gates.

Karigan would have to move fast lest the torches break the spell of fading and arouse the Mirwellians to her presence. A pair of sentries marched back and forth beyond the gates, and she would have to time it just right.

The Anti-Monarchy Society broke its huddled grouping and defiantly faced the gates. As one voice, they chanted: "Monarchy is tyranny, no king is a good king. Monarchy is tyranny . . ."

The sentries beyond the gate passed one another, and Karigan sprinted across the draw bridge. She nearly ran into a hulking soldier who appeared out of nowhere in the gray mist of her vision. She veered just in time to miss him. She bolted over to the guardhouse and leaned against the cold, stone wall.

Boots swung above her head. Ropes creaked on timbers. The sound knotted her stomach. The hanged hovered above her like stiff marionettes some puppeteer had abandoned, the flickering of torches distorting their bloodless, wooden features.

The guard Karigan had nearly run into had simply

stepped out onto the drawbridge to get a better look at the Anti-Monarchy Society. Miraculously, he seemed unaware of her.

She felt her way around the guardhouse and watched the sentries pace back and forth beyond the gates once more.

Instead of running straight across the courtyard, she continued to edge along the guardhouse, hurrying past the open doorway where lamplight glowed, and under the portcullis. Once she was inside the gate, she adhered to the shadows of the inner castle wall. One of the sentries paused his rhythmic pacing. The other joined him.

"Something wrong?"

"No . . . Just . . . I thought I saw something by the guardhouse caught in the light."

His companion glanced in Karigan's general direction. "Nothing there. Torchlight can trick your eyes."

"I suppose, what with those corpses hanging about."

Karigan listened no further and sprinted across the courtyard. There was a breezeway here, that separated the outer courtyard from the ornamental gardens of the inner courtyard and connected two wings of the castle. A glance at the main entrance to the castle convinced her she would gain no entry there, for it was heavily guarded by Mirwellians.

She swung her legs over the low wall and into the breezeway. Surely some guards would patrol this way. No sooner had the thought entered her mind than guards appeared from either end of the breezeway bearing torches. They paced toward one another. Karigan dived over the low wall on the other side of the breezeway, and fell to the ground of the inner courtyard right into a clump of rose bushes.

She yelped involuntarily and bit her lower lip before more could spill out of her mouth. The sickeningly sweet fragrance of crushed roses thickened in the air about her.

A torch-bearing guard paused near her on the breezeway and waited for the other to join him.

"You hear something?" he asked.

"Nope," the other said affably. "Quiet as the dead. Only interesting place is the throne room."

The first guard snorted. "I would like to show some of those nobles a thing or two myself." He sniffed. "Phew. Just smell those roses."

The two moved off, conversing companionably, and Karigan breathed again. She plucked thorns out of her hands, arms, and legs, and stood up.

"I'm doing well," she muttered to herself with sarcasm as she unsnagged her coat from one of the bushes. "Vicious shrubs."

She trotted along the garden paths to where she remembered the ballroom was. Perhaps she could enter there, undetected. But when she reached the ballroom entrance, it was ablaze with light. Inside, soldiers in silver and black were jammed together under many watchful guards in scarlet.

She turned away, but the sound of a commotion just outside the doorway caught her attention. A guard pulled on the arm of a small, struggling prisoner.

"C'mon, li'l Greenie. Tagard wantsa li'l fun."

"Nooo!"

Mel? Karigan cursed silently. As a member of the Green Foot, Mel would be treated just like any of the other soldiers, or even worse.

The guard slapped the writhing girl and knocked her to the ground. Mel cried out again in a terrible sob.

Karigan knew the feeling. The helplessness of being under the power of someone much bigger and stronger than she. She could almost smell the foul Garroty and feel his hard, callused hands on her.

Without another thought, King Zachary's sword was in her grasp. Although it might ruin everything, she could not simply let the soldier hurt her friend. She knew . . . she knew the fear.

She crept up silently behind them, and though the light from the ballroom touched her, she was barely perceptible. The soldier was too busy with his prey anyway and would not have noticed Karigan even if she were fully visible. He giggled like a boy.

Karigan plunged the sword into his back.

There was no sound, no outcry from the soldier. He simply collapsed on top of Mel. Her cries were muffled beneath him. Karigan hoisted the man away, and Mel curled up into a ball in a fit of sobbing.

"Mel," Karigan whispered. She reached down and touched the girl. Mel cried louder and kicked out. "Mel! It's me, Karigan."

Mel rubbed her eyes. "Karigan?" Her tone was one of disbelief. "Where . . . ?"

Karigan touched her brooch. The gray world fell away and she sighed with weariness. No sooner had she appeared than Mel sprang over to her and wrapped her arms around her. The girl wept into her coat, her whole body wracked hard by sobs like unrelieved grief.

"Quietly now," Karigan said in a soothing whisper. She stroked Mel's hair and rubbed her back, keeping watch on the ballroom door, fearing they would be discovered at any moment.

"It w-was so t-terrible." Mel's whole body shuddered.

"You're fine now," Karigan said, still stroking. "You're fine."

Then Mel pushed away, sniffing, her face wet with tears. "It's . . . it's really you."

"Who did you think?" Karigan smiled down at her.

"I-I thought you went away, or were dead." Mel wrapped her arms around her again and a new freshet of tears began. "The captain's dead, isn't she, and King Zachary . . . ?"

"Absolutely not."

Mel stopped in mid-sob. "What?"

"They are both alive. We had some trouble, but we made it."

"Truly?"

Karigan nodded, and Mel wiped tears off her cheeks, a wide grin shining on her face. "Thank you, Karigan. You don't know how happy I am."

"I can guess," Karigan said. "We can't stay here. Those guards are going to miss this fellow soon." She pointed at the dead soldier. "Help me pull him into the bushes."

They each took an arm and dragged until he was concealed in the darkest shadows they could find beneath a clump of shrubbery.

"He didn't hurt you, did he?" Karigan asked.

Mel shook her head, then shivered a little. "He . . . he frightened me."

"I know," Karigan said. "Listen to me, you have got to get out of here. Is there somewhere you can hide?"

Mel thought for a moment. "Maybe at the stable."

"Good! You hide as well as you can, all right? There are some things I've got to take care of here, and it may be a while. Don't be scared, but don't come out of hiding. Do you understand?"

Mel nodded.

"Good." Karigan looked down at her friend, but her face blurred. She rocked on her feet, assailed by dizziness. She passed her hands over her eyes.

"You all right?" Mel asked. "You look . . . I don't know. Not good."

Karigan shrugged. "I'm fine. I've just been using my brooch an awful lot. Now you run. I've got some things to do."

Mel started away, but glanced over her shoulder at Karigan.

"Go," Karigan said, waving her off.

Mel disappeared across the courtyard and Karigan prayed she would reach safety unmolested. She sagged in the shadows herself, closing her eyes briefly and taking a breath. She just wanted a nice long sleep in a feather bed. But just as she thought she was at the end of her endurance, she pushed herself to continue.

She wandered the inner courtyard looking for an entrance into the castle. She did not use her brooch as long as no one was about to detect her. Every time she faded out, her headache intensified and the brooch sapped her energy.

She came to some great glass doors, an unusual contrast to the massive stone walls of the castle. In fact, there were many windows here that glimmered like black ice in the moonlight. Whatever the room beyond, it was dark, and no guards were nearby. She tried the latch, and it yielded easily to her touch. She took one last look behind her, and stepped inside.

She wished she had her moonstone now to reveal the room and aid her in navigating its vague expanse, but the moonstone was gone forever, just so much crushed crystal.

The room, she decided, was some sort of sun room or study. She could make out the shapes of bookshelves and the edges of heavy furniture. She wondered if this was a place King Zachary spent much time in.

She moved across the room with care, but still jammed her thigh on the edge of a table. She barely managed to suppress a cry of pain.

"I'll be black and blue from head to toe," she mumbled, rubbing her throbbing thigh.

She aimed for a bar of light that filtered beneath a door, and managed quite well without bumping into too many objects or knocking anything over. Once she reached the door, she dropped to her knees and peered through the space where the light came through, and she listened. She could not see or hear a soul.

Just in case someone was out there, she touched her brooch and faded out, then cracked the door open. The corridor outside was only dimly lit, and it was empty save for some old suits of armor standing at age-old attention.

She slipped out of the room, and using her own best judgment, headed in the direction she believed the throne room lay.

⋙ THE GHOST ⋘

Stevic G'ladheon was not sure he could take much more of the screaming. A few nobles had dared to defy Prince . . . no, he corrected himself, *King* Amilton. One noble lay dead with blood flowing out of his nose, ears, and mouth, a few others had given in to the strange power Amilton wielded before they met the same fate. Amilton would put his hands on their shoulders or heads. Bolts of black energy would spark and crackle around his hands, and the victim would cry out in pain.

"I pledge . . . my . . . undying loyalty," the most recent unfortunate said. It was a plump man on his knees with head bowed. Blood oozed from his nose.

The fire seemed to burn within and without Amilton. His "loyal" servants, the nobles who had capitulated, stood behind him in the throne room. The strange stone that hung at his throat glimmered, and at times, seemed to pulsate like a living thing.

Stevic and Sevano had found an alcove with a bench beneath one of the tall windows that marched down the length of the throne room. The bench was carved of stone, and was cold and uncomfortable, but it was better than standing among the sweating, shaking nobles. Amilton had dismissed him and Sevano as unimportant when he discovered they were lowly merchants. Yet they were not permitted to leave.

The old woman, Devon Wainwright, stood among the nobles. Stevic remembered her back to the time he had visited Queen Isen to petition for recognition of his clan.

Devon had been advisor even then, and as stern as a Weapon, but fair and careful in her judgments. She had aged a great deal in the time intervening, but her mind still seemed sharp. She talked quietly with a rather beautiful, statuesque woman with golden hair hanging long and loose to her waist. She wore black, a stark, mournful contrast to her features, as if a grieving widow. Soon Amilton would question their loyalties. Stevic hoped both would acquiesce without a fuss.

His seat was shrouded in shadow, and partially obscured by a thick pillar. If he remembered correctly from his previous visit, Weapons had stood guard in these alcoves. They were dark, he supposed, on purpose. He wondered what had become of King Zachary's Weapons. He wondered what had become of the king himself.

Likely the king and all his Weapons are dead.

Fleeting thoughts, like what Amilton's reign would do to commerce and relations with other countries streamed through his mind. But most of all, he wondered and worried about Karigan. He had been so close to finding her. The Rider Connly had told him some strange story of how Karigan came to Sacor City bearing a message for the king. Stevic was not clear on what Karigan was doing with a Green Rider message in the first place. Connly was vague on the details, for he had only just heard the story himself, but he seemed to think Karigan had survived many frightening adventures.

"Sevano," Stevic said, "do you believe those stories that Rider told us about Karigan?"

The old man grunted. "I believe he thought them true. And why not?"

Stevic shrugged. "My own daughter . . . a schoolgirl . . . facing brigands on the road?"

"A resourceful schoolgirl. We taught her to be so."

Stevic rubbed his upper lip thoughtfully. Connly had directed them to the castle where they sought out Captain Mapstone, but there was not a single Green Rider to be found. As they walked the castle grounds, they were nearly run down by the cavalry. They waited some time at Rider barracks for someone to appear, but no one did.

Then they resolved to speak with the king himself, but when they stepped outside, soldiers in silver and black were running wildly in all directions. Arrows whined over the castle wall and everyone was shouting. When an arrow took out a soldier right in their path, they retreated to the barracks to await the outcome. It was not long before soldiers wearing Mirwellian scarlet found them. They were mistaken for a noble and his guard and were taken to the throne room to be dealt with by Prince Amilton, and there they had been ever since.

Still one question remained unanswered: Where was Karigan? Had she made it off the castle grounds before the fighting broke out?

Stevic stretched his long legs before him and leaned back against the stone wall. Castellan Crowe's voice lilted as he made the pronouncement: "And L'Petrie Province joins His Majesty's grand purpose. . . ."

"There goes commerce," Sevano muttered.

"Our dear lord-governor is not the one to go against the current," Stevic said.

He allowed the shadows to hang about him. Amilton and Crowe were but distant things in a glittering light that did not include him. He gave up being surprised by Amilton's use of magic and by the treachery of Zachary's castellan, one of his most important advisors. He tried to ignore the scene of two guards in scarlet dragging away another body.

In the darkness, he imagined he saw a figure in green weaving in and out among the columns of the opposite wall. She was wraithlike and thin and hard looking. He could not see her clearly—she seemed to fade in and out of the light.

She carried herself like one who is hunted and keenly aware of all that is about her. She was self-possessed and unafraid. She turned to him and looked directly at him. Her features were filmy and blurred, but he felt her eyes on him, haunted eyes that had seen too much. Eyes he recognized.

He sat up straight, and his mouth fell open.

She drew her finger to her lips, then melted away into a shadow, became part of it, and did not reemerge.

Stevic's heart plunged. "Nooo," he moaned.

Sevano looked at him startled. "What's wrong?" he whispered.

"Karigan . . ."

"What about her?"

"She's dead, she's dead. . . ." Stevic put his face in his hands.

"What?"

"Her ghost." Stevic pointed a shaking finger where he had last seen her.

"Her ghost? Now look here. That Connly lad said she was alive."

"*Was.* She's dead now. I saw her ghost."

Stevic shook his head and put his ashen face in his trembling hands.

Jendara peered in each alcove along the east wall in search of the merchant. There had been something unsettlingly familiar about him, and she now took the opportunity to seek him out while King Amilton was preoccupied with terrorizing his nobles.

She found the man and his guard tucked away in one of the alcoves, and to her surprise, he was weeping, the cargo master's hand on his shoulder.

"You there," she said to the cargo master. Her voice was nasal and muffled from having her nose broken. "What is the problem?"

The cargo master looked at her with jaundiced eyes. "It is none of your nevermind," he said.

"I could cut your heart out before you drew your next breath, old man." Jendara unsheathed her sword and watched as comprehension dawned on the man's face when he saw the black band on her blade.

The cargo master looked up at her, but the disgust in his expression had only deepened. "What in life made you fall to such a level, Swordmaster?"

Jendara smiled, showing her canines. "You say I have fallen? Am I not the personal Weapon to the *king* of Sacoridia? It seems I have ascended to a higher place."

"*That* is no king." The cargo master pointed in the direction of the throne.

Swiftly, the blade tip pressed against the old man's throat. She watched his Adam's apple bob as he swallowed.

"Do you wish to die?" she asked him.

"I have no such wish," he said with equal intensity. "But I see it in *your* eyes."

Jendara laughed. "We become Weapons because we expect death."

"Then I will rephrase my question. What has made you such a bitter woman?"

"A man," she said.

She pushed the cargo master away with the flat of her blade. She gazed down on the overcome merchant. "Tell me what ails him, old man."

"Grief."

"Is that all? There is enough to go around these days."

"His daughter has been missing. Now he believes her to be dead."

"He believes? Doesn't he know?"

"He says he saw her ghost."

"What? Just now?"

"Aye."

There was a prickling on the back of Jendara's neck. She placed the tip of her sword beneath the grieving man's chin, and lifted it, tilting his face upward. Even in the shadows, she saw how striking his face was, how strong and well-formed, though drawn and creased with worries. The lines around his eyes suggested character and more merry days. There was also that nagging familiarity.

She grabbed his chin. The cargo master started, but she whipped her sword to his chest.

"Stand off," she told the old man. "I won't hurt your chief."

She shifted the merchant's face in the dim light. Yes, there it was in the dimples around his mouth, and perhaps the bright glint of his eyes. The shape of the face was different though. She dropped his chin, and then saw on his finger a familiar ring. She had worn its twin.

The girl's features must favor the mother, but the ring was unmistakable. A fine chill tingled up her spine. "She should have killed me," she whispered.

The merchant seemed to only just notice her. "What?"

She looked right into his eyes. "I know her."

Jendara swung around. Amilton had another noble on her knees. He was about to place his hands, hands full of magic, on her shoulders. Jendara would not interrupt him, and he would not notice her absence.

She stalked down the throne room, peering into every alcove, testing the air before her with her sword. The Greenie could be gone by now for all she knew.

Then, near the entryway, she saw it—a flickering light, a streak of green. Jendara pelted down the throne room and through the great doorway, past astonished guards. Here the corridor was well lit with lamps and candles, and the flames bent at the Greenie's retreat. Down the corridor she saw the Greenie run, transparent and ghostlike. No wonder the merchant thought his daughter dead.

Holding her sword before her, Jendara charged down the corridor after the Greenie, but when she rounded one corner into another corridor, she discovered it was darkened and the air thick with candle smoke.

Jendara peered through the hall and into the shadows. *Careful,* she thought. The Greenie could be armed.

The shape of a person loomed up on her left and in the blink of an eye she swung her sword into it. A suit of armor crashed to the floor. The helm rolled down the

corridor. Jendara narrowed her eyes as she stepped over
a leg of armor and extended every sense into the gloom,
but she heard nothing, saw nothing, felt not even a shift
in the air. She smelled nothing but candles.

Even then, however, another sense awakened in her,
like a peripheral vision of the mind. She perceived the
Greenie to her right, tight up against the wall. Jendara
shifted her eyes, but could see no one. Maybe there was
a deepening of a shadow against the wall.

She took a deep breath, and held her gaze straight
ahead, defying her greatest urge to take a direct look.
That would only alarm the Greenie. Instead, she slashed
out with her sword.

A cry of pain from the shadows confirmed her instinct
had been true, and she laughed in triumph. Now she
spun toward the Greenie, just in time for another suit of
armor to topple down on her.

It took Jendara some moments to realize she was on
the floor. Her body hurt, pummeled as it was by age-old
plate armor. She groaned and pushed the breast piece
away and untangled herself from the arms and legs.

She felt around for her sword on hands and knees,
and her hand fell into something wet. She brought her
fingers to her lips and dabbed them with her tongue.
Blood!

Jendara raised herself to her feet and trotted back to
the lit corridor. She grabbed a candle and took it into
the dim corridor. She found her sword next to the twisted
wreckage of armor. She looked in satisfaction at the
blood on its tip, and the drips of blood leading in a trail
down the corridor. Candle and sword in hand, she followed the trail like a hound on a scent.

⇜ BLOOD TRAIL ⇝

Karigan leaned in a darkened doorway, sucking in painful breaths. One hand clutched the door frame, the other closed on the wound beneath her ribs. It was not too deep, but it bled profusely and stung painfully.

Dim light glowed in an adjacent corridor, but she had to drop the invisibility to preserve any energy she had left. The slash to her side was not helping matters. She looked down, and in the darkness, discerned an even darker stain spreading across the front of her shirt. Crimson oozed between her fingers and pattered on the floor.

She leaned her head against the door frame and tried to catch her breath. Sweat poured down her face and burned her eyes. It would not be long before Jendara found her. She feared she would have to confront her this time, in a clash she had little hope of winning.

Light shimmered at the far end of the corridor. *No time to rest.* She shook off her light-headedness and reached to touch her brooch. It was her only—

Disembodied hands reached from behind through the darkness of the doorway. One clamped over her mouth before she could utter a scream, and the other grabbed her around her chest. Weakly she struggled against the iron grip. It drew her slowly, inexorably inward, into the night dark room behind.

Shhh, someone breathed into her ear.

She began to think she had fallen into the darkness of the unconscious realm, or it was simply the unlit room, but her body fell limp and felt as if it floated upward and away to the night sky, perhaps to the heavens to meet the gods.

Jendara smashed her hand into the wall until her knuckles bled. She had followed the Greenie swiftly, but the blood trail simply ended in the doorway of an empty storeroom. She scoured every inch of the room, but it remained undisturbed. No strange shadows, no invisible presences, no telltale drips of blood.

Jendara had to face it: she had failed.

She was thankful she had not told her lord of her little errand. She had no wish to exact more punishment from him. She was tired, so tired. But what else was there? She had been devoted to Amilton and his cause for years. She knew he could be cruel, but he had never punished her before the way he had the night of the silver moon. He was a different man, a different man from the smooth, dashing prince she had sworn her life to protect so long ago.

She had once been an innocent much like the Greenie when she was younger and a swordmaster in training. She was proud to serve Sacoridia and King Amigast. When she became a Weapon assigned to protect Prince Amilton, he swept her away with his charm. She lost her innocence then. She had made a choice. Reflecting on that choice and others, she knew she would still make them if she could do everything over again. That was where she and the Greenie differed, she supposed. The Greenie learned from her mistakes.

She left the empty room and stumped down the corridor, the candlelight like a shield around her.

When she reached the throne room, she found the merchant still sagging on his bench with the cargo master sitting stiff and resolute next to him, his arms crossed. Jendara thrust her bloodied sword tip in front of the merchant. He looked at it with bleary eyes.

"This is the blood of your daughter," she hissed. "She is no ghost."

She did not await his reaction and strode down the runner past the thinning ranks of defiant nobles. Among them was her old teacher Devon Wainwright, a mighty warrior in her day, but now blind as a possum and reduced to being Zachary's advisor in her dotage. Jendara shook her head. She had once admired Devon, but now saw only a wrinkled and bent crone. Jendara did not wish herself such a long life.

Crowe and King Amilton were speaking with a Mirwellian soldier and did not note her presence, for which she was grateful.

"What did they say?" Amilton's cheeks were flushed, and his eyes flashed. Energy crackled about his clenched fists.

"M-monarchy is tyranny, my lord." The soldier licked his lips and his eyes darted uncertainly from Crowe to Amilton.

"Who are they?"

"The Anti-Monarchy Society, my lord." It was Castellan Crowe who answered. He leaned on his staff of office, untroubled by the news. "Your brother spoke of them from time to time, but they were a nuisance at best and nothing more. He did order the leader arrested, but didn't pursue the matter. He became a little more concerned when they found much support in North, but other matters demanded his attention."

"Do they malign my name?" Amilton asked.

"Yes, my lord," the soldier said. "They wish to abolish rule by a monarch at all. This they shout into the night, and their leader attracts an audience with her speeches."

The crackling on Amilton's hands ceased, and he stroked his mustache. "You have archers up on the walls, don't you, Sergeant?"

"Yes, my lord."

"Then let them practice their aim."

"Very good, my lord." The soldier bowed and left the throne room at a trot.

Ignoring Jendara, Amilton's eyes fastened on the small group of nobles still standing before him. "Well, well. If my eyes do not deceive me."

He walked among them and circled the tall blonde in black, looking her up and down. "Lady Estora, how good to see you again."

Jendara watched as Amilton took the woman's pale hand in his and kissed it. The woman looked straight ahead, coolly ignoring him.

"You are beautiful as ever, my lady," Amilton said. His other hand trailed along her cheek and down her neck.

Jendara's knuckles whitened in clenched fists. It had always been this way, he looking at others than she.

"My lady," Amilton said in soft tones, as his face came unbearably close to the woman's. "My dear, dear heir of Coutre Province, I have some interesting ideas for you."

Karigan was falling, falling from the sky, and she jerked convulsively to stop herself.

She opened her eyes to the soft glow of a single candle. She had been asleep or unconscious, and lay on stone. The hard, cold surface made her back ache.

The candle did little to reveal the room she was in. It was stone, like everywhere else in the castle, and though she could not discern dimensions, she sensed the walls to be close and the space vaultlike. The candlelight glinted on glass—vials and jars on a shelf. The room smelled faintly of herbs and mustiness; the air was thick as if it had been closed up for some time.

The candlelight splayed across the ceiling. Glyphs and runes were carved there, so ancient they surpassed the old Sacoridian language. Crudely wrought images of Aeryc and Aeryon were also carved there, and others. One was of a creature—part man, part bird—the god Westrion who escorted souls to the stars; and another was of his great steed, Salvistar, the harbinger of strife and battle.

She lifted her head up to look around some more, but it throbbed and she moaned. "Where am I?"

"The preparation room," someone said.

Karigan's heart skipped a beat. "Who's there?"

The disembodied hands returned, this time accompanied by a disembodied face with familiar, stony features aglow in the candlelight.

"Fastion!"

The Weapon, who had so often guarded her door at Rider barracks, drew closer and she could make out the outlines of his broad frame. His black uniform had created the illusion of disembodiment.

"You are awake, then," he said.

"Yes. What do you mean this is a preparation room?"

"It is for the dead," he said. "It is here the royal death surgeons prepare the bodies of kings, queens, and the special ones chosen to reside in the Hall of Kings and Queens, or along Heroes Avenue. It is here they open the body from chin—" He put his finger to his chin and drew a line with it down to his stomach. "—to the gut so that the soul may escape the body and float to the heavens. It is an ancient rite."

Karigan sat up, heart pounding. Suddenly she feared Fastion. Here she was, laid out on the funerary slab of royalty, where they were embalmed and prepared for the grave. What did Fastion intend?

"Easy," Fastion said, "or you are going to start bleeding again." Then he must have recognized her fear, for he crossed his arms and said, "If I planned to prepare you for death, I wouldn't have bound up that sword wound, and your soul would have been in the heavens long ago."

Karigan tentatively touched her side where Jendara's blade had cut her. It was indeed bound with linens.

"Lots of bandages here," Fastion said.

"For wrapping the dead."

He nodded.

"I'm sorry I mistrusted you, but it has been a very long day, and this is strange. . . ."

"It is strange for me, too. This room has . . . memories for me." Fastion's eyes roamed the room as if in search of images of the past. "Before I became a Weapon for King Zachary, I was a tomb guard. I guarded King Amigast in his death, and watched over the surgeons lest they did something to damage him or impair his soul. As I said, the rites are ancient."

"I would like to get off this slab," Karigan said. It was too much.

Fastion put his hand on her shoulder and pressed her back. "I realize how uncomfortable this must be, but you have to rest while you can. You seem weak, and on more than account of blood loss. We can talk while you recover. But first, I need to know if you have news of the king."

"He lives."

Joy crossed Fastion's normally impassive face, and any doubt of his intentions faded completely. "Then there is hope," he said.

Karigan told him of the day's events, and about her purpose at the castle. "I must return to them and tell them what I've seen. My own father is trapped in the throne room with Amilton and Jendara."

"The traitor!" Fastion broke in with vehemence. "I would have taken her on in the corridor, but I had my arms full with you."

"Sorry," Karigan said.

"Do not apologize. I'm glad I could help after what you have told me. Killing Jendara would have brought me some satisfaction, but it would have raised an alarm and ruined all hope. You see, I've been trying to reach the tombs. I expect to find others there, more Weapons. I am hoping they have been forgotten by Amilton, or they have been able to resist attacks by his forces."

"How many do you think there are?" Karigan asked.

"Perhaps as many as twenty, but I would guess fewer.

As you know, one Weapon is worth four or more ordinary soldiers."

"Yes," Karigan said. "I do know."

Fastion looked pleased. "We may not possess Greenie magics, but we have our own skills. We have secrets."

Karigan lay in silence. The cold of the slab was getting to her, as was the closeness of the room. There was no telling how much time had been lost, but half the candle had dripped away as they spoke.

"Fastion," she said, "I've got to get back to the king and the others to let them know what I learned."

"Can you stand?"

She dropped her legs over the slab. Her head throbbed mightily. She nearly fell back on the slab.

"A little at a time," Fastion said.

He produced some dried meat and water left over from his own supper. It had been some time since midday when Karigan had sat with Alton beneath the sun at their picnic. Would she ever see the sun again? The food improved her spirits considerably, and she felt much stronger. Now she could stand, though she had to hold onto the slab at first to keep steady.

"I will guide you out," Fastion said. "You must tell the king when you see him to remember the Heroes Portal. He must have walked those paths when a boy. His grandmother would have seen to it. I will try to reach the tombs and assemble all the Weapons I can. There, on Heroes Avenue, we shall meet you and the king."

"The tombs . . . ?"

"Yes."

Karigan had a vague suspicion she would never truly extricate herself from dealings with the dead. Ghosts, killings, and now tombs.

Fastion led Karigan through black corridors and a series of rooms, then down more corridors. He relied only on a single candle to light the way.

"Why is it so dark here?" Karigan asked. "Isn't this part of the castle used?"

"No longer," the Weapon said. "This section could

house hundreds, and it once did. Troops, mostly, were garrisoned here in more restless days."

"A very long time ago, then."

"Yes. We Weapons know it all, all the corridors and rooms. We must. Quite a lot of history back here. There are even some Green Rider relics. I keep meaning to tell Captain Mapstone, but I get tied up in my duties and forget."

The route Fastion took seemed like that of an endless cave or maze. When one candle melted down, he lit another. Their footsteps were hollow on the stone-flagged floor. Time seemed not to exist in this netherworld.

They passed numerous doors. Motheaten tapestries rustled on the walls as they walked by, and their feet stirred up dust. They caught the glow of a rat's eye in the candlelight as it scurried across the corridor.

"The servants really ought to clean down here," Fastion muttered.

Beside the tapestries, rusted arms and shields hung on the walls. The shields bore the devices of regiments: the evergreen, the sea dog, the wild rose, the catamount, the black bear, and the eagle. One shield of green featured the gold winged horse.

"So the Green Riders were once garrisoned with the rest of the militia," Karigan said.

"At war time, yes. Green Riders served not only as couriers, but in other capacities, such as light cavalry. There are other things that are not disclosed in the history books, so I can only guess."

Karigan could, too. Capacities like the one Beryl Spencer served in. "You sound like a historian," she said.

Fastion glanced at her with a smile. "I am versed in more than weaponry skills."

Karigan smiled back, abashed.

Finally, Fastion stopped at a heavy door bound in iron. "This opens into the main courtyard," he said, "so you must take care. We're some couple hundred yards from the main entrance and the gates. There are apt to be soldiers all about, but not directly guarding this door. It is somewhat . . . obscure."

He turned and pulled on a huge iron ring, and if Karigan was expecting the hinges to creak and shriek with age, she was to be disappointed, for someone had made a point of oiling them.

Fresh night air rolled into the corridor, and Karigan breathed deeply, finally feeling she was going to be freed of the tomblike atmosphere of the castle.

"I would use your . . . er . . . ability," Fastion said, "to get across the courtyard. Have you a horse?"

"He's down in the city," she said.

"Good. Remember, the Heroes Portal. The king should remember it. May Aeryc and Aeryon guide you."

"And you," Karigan said.

With some regret, she touched her brooch and stepped out into the night. The door closed shut behind her, and she was on her own. Shrubbery concealed the doorway, and she peered around it. Soldiers milled around, walking here and there to whatever business called them to duty at this late hour.

There was not enough light to reveal her, and she darted across the courtyard at a trot to the inner wall. She hugged it until she neared the guardhouse and gate. Someone barked orders to those standing on the wall, but she was not going to wait around to find out what those orders were about.

She watched the sentries cross paths, gauged where the shadows were deepest beneath the portcullis, and she ran. As her feet thudded on the draw bridge, she heard the command, "Ready arrows!"

"Oh, no," she groaned.

Across the moat, the Anti-Monarchy Society shouted slogans and shook fists. A crowd had assembled to watch.

"Find your sights, wait for my mark," the soldier commanded.

Karigan pounded across the bridge and headed straight for the Anti-Monarchy Society. She could imagine the archers, poised between the crenellations atop the wall,

olding their bowstrings taut. It would be slaughter. The
Anti-Monarchy Society was grouped at an easy arrow's
ight from the wall, and the streetlamps made them visi-
le targets.

Karigan dropped her invisibility as she charged them
nd no few mouths fell open.

"Run!" she shouted. "They're going to—"

"Loose arrows!" The command rang through the
ight.

Arrows rained from the sky, impaling members of the
Anti-Monarchy Society and the crowd, skidding along
he paving stones of the street, or sticking in the ground.
creams and cries surrounded Karigan. The terrified liv-
ng stampeded the wounded and dead. Karigan was jos-
led from every side by the panicked onrush of people.

And again, the command rang out: "Loose arrows!"

People dropped on either side of Karigan. An arrow
kimmed her shoulder. When she came to the first build-
ng beyond the castle wall, she veered around it to safety.
A dozen or so other people had done likewise, Lorilie
Dorran among them. She was on the ground, an arrow
ammed in her thigh. She gasped in pain. Two of her
ollowers hovered solicitously over her.

"King Zachary would never have done this," Lorilie
aid.

Karigan strode over to her. Her own side was stinging
rom her desperate run. When her shadow fell across
Lorilie, the charismatic leader of the Anti-Monarchy So-
iety looked up at her.

"Perhaps you should support King Zachary rather than
nalign him," Karigan said. "What you've got now is a
eal tyrant claiming the throne."

Lorilie squinted through her pain. "I remember you,
ister. North. You were there. You . . . you are a
Green Rider?"

Karigan shook her head. "I am not your sister, nor am
a Green Rider."

"All monarchy is tyranny."

Karigan glanced over her shoulder at the bodies bristled with arrows lying in the street. Some people were trying to drag themselves along, others knelt on the ground wailing.

"Is this worth it?" Karigan asked her, gesturing at the wounded and dead.

"Yes," Lorilie whispered fiercely. "Yes. They died for me; they died for the cause. Their sacrifice will only strengthen it."

The woman was despicable. "Believe what you will then." Karigan whirled around and ran, disappearing into the shadows as she went.

⊰ HEROES AVENUE ⊱

Karigan rode Condor through the city, vanishing only if she saw Mirwellians or mercenaries, but otherwise heedless of others who might see her. Some in the city spoke of seeing the restless spirit of the First Rider rush by on her fiery steed. The First Rider, they said, was angered by the overthrow of King Zachary. Some heard only pounding hooves and a passing breeze. Others saw the Rider's ghostly figure, or a streak of green.

Karigan blew through the final gates of the city, riding across the countryside like a demon until she reached the thicket of woods where she had left the others. As she pulled up on the reins, a single figure stood there, cloaked and hooded in gray.

"No!" Karigan cried. The Shadow Man! If he was here, that meant the others must be in danger. She drew the king's sword and ran Condor straight at the figure. The Shadow Man jumped to the side just in time.

Karigan reined Condor around for another pass, but the figure cried out, "Karigan! Stop! It's me." Captain Mapstone pulled back the hood, revealing her bandaged head.

Karigan dismounted, relieved but weary, and led Condor toward her.

"I'm sorry," Captain Mapstone said. "I wasn't expecting you just then. Connly found this cloak in the city while you were gone, and we thought it might prove useful for Beryl's plan."

The others emerged from the woods.

"At least we know it works," Beryl said.

The king looked Karigan up and down. "You've been hurt," he said. He took her elbow apprehensively.

Karigan then realized she was on her knees. A line of blood had seeped through Fastion's bandage. Helping hands lifted her to her feet, and led her into the woods.

"It looks worse than it is," she said. "It's the brooch. . . . I'm exhausted."

The mender pushed between Captain Mapstone and the king. "I'll be the judge of that," she said.

They sat Karigan down on a blanket, allowing her to lean against the trunk of a tree. The mender checked her wound with gentle hands.

"I have a terrible headache from the brooch," Karigan said.

"I've roots for you that should help the pain." The mender rebandaged the wound and said, "It is not deep, but if you keep riding around the countryside, it won't knit together."

"Couldn't help it," Karigan said.

The mender rolled her eyes. "You Riders are all alike. You make the worst patients. Next to other menders, of course." Then she gave Captain Mapstone a stern look. "I know you have questions to ask, but she is in need of rest. Don't push her."

Karigan eased herself against the tree trunk, glad at least, to be visible and among friends again.

"Do you feel able to talk?" the king asked. His eyes were wide with concern as he gazed down at her.

I must look beyond redemption, she thought with some amusement. The exertion of battle and having walked through those old, dusty castle corridors made a hot bath seem a heavenly dream. "I have a lot to report," she said.

The king and captain glanced at one another, then beckoned Horse Marshal Martel, Beryl Spencer, and Connly over. They sat in a semicircle about Karigan as she told them, as briefly as possible, of her adventures. When she described her encounter with Mel, Captain

Mapstone's face fell and she looked away. She seemed little relieved when Karigan told her Mel was safe when she last saw her.

"The castle . . . Rider barracks is no place for a child to grow up," Captain Mapstone said.

Beryl placed her hand on the captain's shoulder. "She loves you, and that's what matters."

Karigan told of Prince Amilton and how he used magic to torture, kill, and coerce the nobles. "Magic surrounded his hands and . . . and it was like what the Eletian used." *On me,* she did not add. "My father was in the throne room with the others. He seemed fine, but I didn't dare talk to him."

She recounted her narrow escape from Jendara and how she received the wound. She told of Fastion's help.

"The Heroes Portal," Zachary murmured. "I remember. Yes, it's perfect. Good old Fastion! His years as a tomb guard have served him, and served us, well."

The others did not understand what he was talking about, and he didn't enlighten them other than to say, "It is another way in."

When she told of the attack on the Anti-Monarchy Society, Zachary said, "My brother has turned into a despot of the worst sort. I fear that he will not confine his brutality to those within and around the castle. The city may be in peace right now, but how long before he extends his reach among ordinary citizens and into the provinces?"

While the king, the captain, and the others talked among themselves, Karigan dozed off. Their distant voices became the babble of ghosts, hanging on the fringes of the living world. Her dreams followed dark routes, dim passages of stone and earth. The ghost babbles shivered up and down the walls in whispery echoes. She entered a vaultlike room where pale blue light hovered over a stone slab. Glyphs and carvings of funerary rites on tablets covered the walls. Similar figures ornamented the base of the slab.

Karigan walked over to the slab, sat on it, swung her

legs up onto it, and lay down. Disembodied hands pulled a gauzy shroud over her.

"No!" Karigan sat up, wincing at the soreness of her side.

"You're all right," said a soothing voice.

Karigan blinked. She felt the fresh air of night blowing through her hair and made out the outlines of branches against the starry night. The king was sitting beside her, pulling a blanket over her.

"I thought you might get cold," he said.

Karigan pushed her hair out of her eyes. "Th-thanks. I had a dream. . . ."

He nodded. "You have been through a great many things today. I shouldn't be surprised if you do have dreams."

"Where are the others?"

"Major Spencer, Captain Mapstone, Connly, and Mirwell are preparing to enter the city."

"What?"

The king absently ran his hands through his hair. His silver fillet was missing. Without it, he seemed an ordinary man with a shock of amber hair falling into his eyes, but he was a haggard man, tired and careworn. He seemed to have aged years over the course of a day.

"They are taking my head and crown to my brother." He smiled impishly.

"What?"

"It is part of Beryl's plan to infiltrate the throne room. My brother knows little of her true affiliations . . . as of yet. Captain Mapstone will be cloaked as the Eletian, and Connly volunteered to take the part of the Mirwellian guard. You see, with our outnumbered forces, our only hope is to win the castle from within."

"But the lord-governor," Karigan said, "how will he cooperate?"

"Beryl said she would see to it."

"Is that it? I mean the whole plan?"

"Oh, no." Zachary seemed to enjoy telling her the plan. Despite his haggard appearance, there was a light in his brown eyes. "Horse Marshal Martel, a good number of his soldiers, and I will enter the Heroes Portal and infiltrate the castle that way. Alas, unlike Connly and Captain Mapstone, we have no disguise. Upon reaching the throne room, I shall reclaim the crown, and Mirwell will order his troops to regroup and return home."

"What about me?" Karigan asked.

"Hmm?"

"What part do I play?"

"You have already done more than your share," he said. "You will rest here with the day's other wounded, and the remainder of Marshal Martel's troops. Should we fail . . . well, I can depend on you to move these people out of harm's way."

"No," Karigan said.

The king raised a brow. "No?"

Karigan shoved the blanket off and raised herself to her feet. "I'm going with you. King or not, you can't stop me. My father is being held in the throne room."

"You are wounded and exhausted," Zachary said. "I don't want you to slow us down."

"You have a broken arm," Karigan retorted. "Who will be slowing who?"

The king's eyebrows shot up, and his mouth was quirked in a half smile he couldn't quite hide. It was as if he wanted to laugh, but he knew better than to do so.

"I see," he said.

Horse Marshal Martel appeared at the king's side, his face impassive. "I told you, my lord, we should have left her while she was asleep."

"I should have listened more closely," he said.

"I suppose she would have followed us," the marshal said. "Captain Mapstone tells me the girl operates on pure spunk, and from what I've seen, I cannot argue."

Karigan glowered at both men. "The appreciation I get for—"

The king bent close to her, and in a sober tone, he said, "I am indebted to you, brave lady, more times over than I can count. I did not wish to belittle your accomplishments. If you wish to join us, I will not deny you. But also know, I could be leading you to your death."

Without his fillet, she had almost forgotten he was king. Just as seriously as he, she said, "I must go."

The moon was at its apex and beginning to slide into the western sky as King Zachary, Karigan, Horse Marshal Martel, the Weapon Rory, and about twenty-five cavalry soldiers rode in a circumference around the outskirts of Sacor City, far enough to be out of eyeshot and hearing of guards on the walls. They rode in silence, and they rode without light save that cast by the moon.

High on its hill, the castle sat at the center of it all, its stony facade rotating, changing angles as they rode. Tiny lights twinkled about it, making it appear as some celestial palace of the night rather than a behemoth of granite constructed by mere humans and anchored firmly to the earth.

On the northeast side, they slowed their horses to a walk. The king and his Weapon Rory rode in front, quietly consulting with one another.

A single white obelisk, cracked and splotched by yellow lichens, marked the spot where an age-old road began. Horse hooves clicked and clattered on blocks of granite paving stones. Grasses and saplings grew up through the cracks between the stones. An ancient grove of hemlock bowed over the path, plunging it into an even deeper darkness than the bare night.

They came upon a stone slab set beside the path, and all at once, Karigan could feel the cold stone on her back, like the slab in the preparation room. Only this one was covered with thick mosses, lichens, and a layer of dead leaves. A fern grew from the base.

This was a coffin rest, the king explained. A rest for those who bore the one to be interred in Heroes Avenue.

The group rode on, like silent mourners until they

came to a rock ledge that loomed above them and was overhung with dripping mosses. Another obelisk stood like an accusing finger next to a round portal of iron embedded in the ledge.

King Zachary faced those who followed him with a grim smile. "You follow the ancient path only the dead, royalty, and those who care for the dead are permitted. This entrance has been forgotten by most and has lain mostly unused for a century at least. The dead, alas, keep their own company."

He sat without speaking for some moments as water trickled down the ledge to a puddle beside him. "When I was a boy, my grandmother, Queen Isen, brought me here so I could learn the stories of Sacoridia's bravest heroes. I was terrified then, and I am none too comfortable now. To say the least, it is disturbing to see the inside of your tomb while you still live and breathe."

Karigan shifted uneasily on Condor's back. The night seemed to crackle with premonition: the accusatory obelisk telling them to turn back, the iron portal with the glyph of Westrion on it.

"Beyond this portal," Zachary said, "lies the domain of the dead from which only members of the royal family and Weapons may re-emerge. All others who trespass must spend the remainder of their lives along its somber avenues tending the dead, never to see the light of the living day again."

The cavalry soldiers exchanged worried glances and whispered among themselves.

"However," the king said, "I am in a position to change the rules for one night under these circumstances in which we ride. It would be different, perhaps, if we were entering the Halls of Kings and Queens where the royalty sleeps. Heroes Avenue is slightly more permissible; more forgiving to an intrusion of the living." He looked at each person as if he could look right into their souls. Karigan was not warmed by his gaze. "Here we shall leave the horses."

As one, the soldiers dismounted. They gathered together bundles of torches they had brought with them, and King Zachary smiled. "Leave them," he said. "We enter a tomb, not a cave."

The soldiers murmured uncertainly and shrugged. Rory ran his hands over the portal and pushed on the glyph of Westrion. It swung open easily, with just a minimal scraping of iron on granite, thanks, no doubt, to the vigilance of the Weapons who guarded the tombs. A breath of cool air issued out, thick with the scent of earth and rock.

One by one they filed into the round opening wide enough for a coffin and pallbearers. The corridor they entered was tubelike. Although it was not lit, light shone at the far end, and it was enough for them to see by.

Miraculously the shaft was dry and the speckled grain of the granite walls smooth and uncracked. Although the underground world was not damp, a heavy cold penetrated through Karigan's coat and into her very bones.

"The craftmanship," the horse marshal murmured.

"It has never been matched," King Zachary said. "The tombs may have been delved before even the time of the Kmaernians."

The tube opened into a larger, low-ceilinged chamber lit by flickering lamps. To Karigan, it felt as if the earth above pressed down on them. The taller among them had to bow their heads in order not to bump them on the ceiling. Another coffin rest stood in the middle of the room, its base decorated with the now familiar glyphs and ancient Sacoridian script. Several corridors branched off from this chamber, but only one was lit.

Five black-clad Weapons dressed in padded tunics and trousers and fur-lined cloaks, awaited them there, and fell on their knees before the king.

"Rise," he told them. "What news have you?"

A woman stepped forward and inclined her head. "I am Sergeant Brienne Quinn, my lord," she said. "Weapon Fastion sent us to await you here. We are honored by your presence."

Zachary nodded. "Where is Fastion?"

"He keeps watch above at the main portal, guarding it lest Prince Amilton thinks to assault this place."

"And how many are with him?"

"Another ten, my lord."

"Excellent. No one will get past them."

Brienne beamed with pride. "It is our sacred duty to protect those who rest here."

"Let us go then. Lead on, Sergeant."

"Yes, my lord." Brienne turned smartly on her heel and walked to the front. One Weapon stayed with her, the other three dropped to the rear, much to the relief of the cavalry soldiers by the expressions on their faces. The Weapons seemed content to leave Rory as the king's personal guard. Though they would fight to the death for the king, their place was as tomb guards. Others cared for the living.

They followed another shaft, but this one was square with lamps fitted in alcoves along the way. The walls were a riot of colors, painted with battle scenes and heroic images. Armor-clad knights charged the field on battle horses, pennons rippling on lowered lances. Others, dressed in full mail, battled dark enemies with swords. Some stood at rest, their fingers shaped in the sign of the crescent moon.

"These walls could tell stories," Marshal Martel said. He shifted his helm beneath his arm. "I wouldn't be surprised if they held more knowledge than all the repositories of Selium."

The mention of the school Karigan had run away from was jarring. It had been a lifetime ago, her time at Selium. Perhaps it had been a different life altogether. She certainly felt like a different person from that schoolgirl who had run away for some petty reason she could hardly remember.

They emerged into another chamber, this one vast and wide, still maintaining the low ceiling which was supported by many square, granite pillars. There were rows of granite slabs. None were occupied.

"It seems no one has been interred for a while," Horse Marshal Martel said.

King Zachary overheard and replied, "We've been at peace for so long. We've had few heroes."

They passed into another such room, and another. Each was brightly lit, hardly the dark, shadowy tomb Karigan had envisioned. The stone floor was polished, no cobwebs hung in doorways, dust did not swirl about their feet. Though cold, the air was good and vented without the stench of decay or bones. The unused section of the castle Fastion had led her through was far gloomier, more funereal than this place.

Even so, Karigan felt tense. She felt as if someone watched their procession with unfriendly eyes. Sometimes she caught the movement of a shadow out of the corner of her own eye, but when she looked, it was gone. It was as if someone were flitting from behind one funeral slab to another. No one else seemed to notice, so she kept her peace for the time being. Tombs and lamplight and exhaustion could produce strange visions.

The next room was not empty. Shrouded forms lay like sleepers beneath gauzy linen sheets. Others, in full gleaming armor, lay with weapons drawn at their feet. Some were encased in sarcophagi with carved effigies on the lids.

In the next room, and the rooms after that, every slab was filled. There were rows upon rows of shrouded dead. Karigan kept her eyes to Horse Marshal Martel's back, or to the floor. Somehow, dealing with the spirits of the dead was easier than walking among their long-abandoned remains. She felt very mortal, very small.

Their path gradually shifted upward and it seemed they had walked miles.

"Sacoridia certainly has its share of heroes," the marshal remarked. Unlike Karigan, he did not have trouble looking around at his surroundings.

"Wars," King Zachary said. "Some date from the Long War and before." He smiled back at them. "Few know the magnitude of what Sacor City rests on."

"A good thing," Marshal Martel said.

Karigan sneaked a peek and saw the jutting angles of bones beneath one shroud. Another lumpy form was bound in linens.

The king paused, then whispered something to Brienne.

"Yes," she said, and pointed to a far corner.

King Zachary turned to Karigan and beckoned her to follow. He walked off among the slabs in the direction Brienne had pointed. Karigan hesitated with a sense of loathing to walk among those desiccated, brittle husks. With her jaw clenched, she plunged after him, avoiding direct contact with the slabs, and keeping her eyes to the floor.

In the far corner, the king stopped by a slab, and peered down at its occupant. Upon it rested a linen-wrapped form, covered by a shroud. A length of green-and-blue plaid fabric was draped over it from hips to toes. The head was tightly wrapped with sunken depressions where the eyes had been.

Mounted on the wall behind the remains were a two-handed great sword, a battle ax, and a saber. Above the corpse, painted on the ceiling, was the portrait of a woman astride a big bay stallion. She wore the plaid about her shoulders and carried the saber, and a shield bearing the gold winged horse on a field of green.

Warmth blossomed on Karigan's chest where her brooch was pinned. She touched it. It was hot and seemed to sing—not audibly—but she could feel it sing through her.

"The First Rider," King Zachary said. "She was a great hero of the Long War. I know such time has passed that Green Riders have lost some of their glory and few recognize their worth. But they come of great lineage."

Karigan's head spun. The walls seemed to close in even tighter. Hoofbeats drummed in her ears. She wanted to run away, she—

"I will likely have need of my sword before the night is over," the king was saying. He flexed his good arm.

"I'm fortunate that groundmite broke my shield arm and not my sword arm."

"I, uh . . ." Karigan said, suddenly wondering why he wanted his sword now. She lifted the baldric over her head and handed it to him.

"I shouldn't think the First Rider would begrudge you borrowing one of her swords," the king said.

Karigan took a sharp intake of breath. "I can't!"

"Why not? She doesn't need it and you do."

"I—I . . ." She backed away until she bumped into another of the horrible slabs behind her. She jumped as if the corpse had pinched her.

"I don't want you to go up above unarmed," the king said. "Pick a sword."

Karigan hooked a strand of hair behind her ear. "I—" But the king's face was set. "Uh, all right," she said.

She edged around the slab and gazed at the weapons. The great sword was almost taller than she. The First Rider must have been a tall and powerful woman. She reached for the saber.

The thrum of hoofbeats intensified as she did so, as if urging her to take it. The brooch sang in resonance as Karigan's fingers closed around the hilt. The sword came off the wall easily and weighed well in her hand. The hoofbeats dissipated, and the vibrations of the brooch eased. She sighed in relief.

A bundle of gray-and-white robes, like a corpse springing to life, arose from behind one of the slabs and launched on her. They toppled to the hard granite floor and rolled. The creature tussled with her, grabbing for the sword. Karigan was so shocked she let it go. The mass of robes scurried away and huddled at the king's feet, cradling the sword.

Rory and Brienne were there in moments, towering over the quivering heap.

"Are you all right?" the king asked Karigan. He stretched out a hand to help her rise to her feet.

The wind had been knocked out of her and her side

ached, but she suffered mostly from shock. She nodded, looking curiously at the creature that had attacked her.

Brienne's hands were on her hips and her expression was severe. "Agemon!" she said.

The ragged bundle quavered at her voice and she rolled her eyes in annoyance.

"Sheathe your sword," she told Rory.

He obeyed without question.

She addressed the bundle again. "Agemon, do not hinder the king."

The bundle shifted and whimpered.

"Nervous as a winter hare," Rory commented.

"He is a caretaker," Brienne said. "They are overwhelmed by the living."

"Yes, yes," the creature whined.

"Arise, Agemon," the king said in a commanding voice.

The quivering mass stood up and turned into an old man with long gray hair and a curiously pale, unwrinkled face. His robes, though not old or worn, were of muted and dusty tones, like that of the linen-wrapped dead. He held the sword possessively to his chest, and adjusted a pair of specs on the tip of his nose.

"You need not fear us," King Zachary said.

"Honored," the man squeaked. "Honored to have you, great king, and your Black Shield. But these others. These blues, this green. These do not belong in the presence of the great ones. These colors do not belong unless they be heroes. Unless they are dead."

"I tolerate their presence," King Zachary said. "And among them are heroes worthy of traveling these avenues."

"But they live," the man said desperately. "They breathe. They contaminate the dead."

Zachary placed his hand on the little man's shoulder. "I've the right to bring them here. I've broken no taboo."

"They must stay and be caretakers. They must never see the living sun again."

"No," Zachary said. "They come with me. They all protect me. They all protect the tombs."

"As you say, my lord. As you say." Agemon adjusted his specs again, his features full of despair. "But this one," and he pointed at Karigan, "has touched the great Ambriodhe's sword. She must stay."

"No," the king said. "You must give her the sword back, and she must leave with me. I promise the sword will be returned. I don't think the First Rider will mind."

"I don't know, I don't know." Agemon shook his head his expression of despair deepening.

"Give it to her," Brienne snapped.

Agemon jumped, then thrust the sword out to Karigan. Karigan took it and stepped back.

He gave her a wizened look, his eyes shifting from her head to her toes as if to deem whether or not she was worthy. "She is touched by the dead already, anyway. I guess I will not mind."

His pronouncement was like a cold hand on the back of Karigan's neck.

Agemon turned back to the king. "The Birdman will not be happy about this."

"Westrion understands," King Zachary said. He glanced at Brienne. "We haven't the time to debate it."

"Understood, my lord." She took Agemon's arm and pulled him aside. "Agemon, you must continue your duties. Do you understand?"

"Yes, yes." He waved her off and started ambling down the corridor. "I polish the great Heath's armor. Yes, yes. Heath the Ironhanded. I polish his armor."

Brienne sighed. "I'm sorry, my lord, but he is the chief caretaker, and he feels responsible for the intrusion of the undead."

"I know," King Zachary said. "I suppose the others are too timid to come forward."

She smiled. "They are. Some won't even talk to *us*."

"How many are down here?" Karigan asked, wondering with revulsion how anyone could live in this mass tomb.

"Perhaps fifty, perhaps a hundred. It is difficult to say, for they are secretive. Some have family that have lived here for generations. From time to time, we try to move families up above, but often enough they can't adjust. The move goes against anything they have learned about not seeing the living light."

Karigan frowned with distaste. "Where do they live?"

"Not too far removed from the dead, in their own chambers. It is their way. It has always been so."

"Shall we move on?" King Zachary suggested. "I am guessing Beryl and Captain Mapstone are somewhere within the city walls by now. It would not be well for them if we were late."

⊰ A WEAPON'S WRATH ⊱

Remember, old man," Beryl said, "I will have a dagger to your back the whole time. If you speak one wrong word, I will use it."

Mirwell sat hunched in his saddle, bone-weary and cold under the blanket of night. The city lamps held no warmth, only an icy glow. If only he had his bear pelt to throw over his shoulders. His Beryl Spencer of old would have fetched it for him without hesitation, but now she wasn't his. She never was.

She rode knee to knee with him as they approached the second city gate. Mapstone rode behind, her gray hood drawn over her face, and next to her, the Rider Connly dressed in D'rang's scarlet uniform. To complete the illusion, Mapstone rode Connly's gray mare.

If Mirwell were a less pragmatic man, he might have been amused by the irony of his situation. He and Beryl had virtually switched roles, he now the captive, she the captor. He had been fooled by her pretty face, hard work, and seemingly unfeigned loyalty. She had been the spy in House Mirwell all along while he thought her to be his most trustworthy officer, above Captain Immerez and all others.

Mirwell admitted it to himself: he had been duped. Yet the ultimate move of the game of Intrigue had not been played out. He still possessed the Gray One's magic words of power to use at the most appropriate moment.

They halted before the city gate, and the guards in his own color of scarlet held a lantern up to see who rode in.

"Lord Mirwell!" the guard said in surprise. "And

Major Spencer." He and the others bowed. "We are glad to see you. Prince . . . I mean King Amilton was concerned about you, seeing how late it is. He sent word for us to keep watch."

"Then send a messenger up to the castle and tell him we come," Beryl said. "Tell the king we bring him a great prize."

"Yes, Major."

The lantern light showed on Beryl's ruthless smile. A great prize indeed, Mirwell thought. He glanced back at the basket Mapstone carried. How long before their ruse would be discovered?

At Beryl's signal, Mirwell prodded his horse forward and he rode beside her through the gate. The guards bowed respectfully, but he knew their eyes were on the gray-cloaked figure riding behind bearing the basket. Ahead of them, a messenger rode off at a canter, and the clatter of hooves receded into the night.

Beryl might be pleased by her little charade, but Mirwell could reveal it at any moment knowing that whatever happened to him, his soldiers would see to her death. She had promised to kill him should he reveal their deception, and he knew she spoke the truth. But he must exercise patience and play along for now. He was not ready to sacrifice himself. He still had one move to make, and her plan, after all, was flawed.

"Don't you think someone will not see through your plan?" he asked her. "Amilton has met the Gray One," he said. "That woman is not the Gray One."

His pronouncement was met with soft laughter from behind. "No," Captain Mapstone said in a low voice, "I am the *Green* One. We need but little time in the throne room to accomplish what we must. It won't matter who we really are."

A pity Beryl had not killed the woman during the battle. It was unfortunate timing the spell broke when it did. Such things could be rectified, however.

"You are Mirwellian born, aren't you?" he asked Beryl.

"Yes," she said.

"Don't you wish to see our province as great as it once was? Don't you wish to feel the glory?"

Beryl surveyed the quiet streets, her expression cool and unreadable, just as he had seen it so many times when he believed her to be his loyal aide. She shifted the reins to one hand, and rested the other on her knee. "Do you remember," she said, "a young soldier named Riley who served in your house guard?"

"Riley? No, but there would be no reason for me to."

"It was some ten years ago. He was a simple private who did his job honestly and with good faith. His officers had nothing to complain about. He believed in the greatness of Mirwell Province and he thought it superior to any other. Then one day, someone in your household marred the leather of a new saddle you favored. You did not know who it was, but you decided to make an example of someone. You chose Riley. You cut off both his hands so he would not drop another saddle. Do you remember?"

Mirwell thought hard, but could not remember the incident, or could not distinguish it from many others of a similar nature. "I do not. I suppose you are going to tell me this Riley was your father."

"No," Beryl said, watching the street ahead. "My father died in one of your bloody tourneys just before I was born. Riley Spencer was my brother. He was proud to serve House Mirwell, as our father had, but you took that away from him. The glory died. When he returned home, he lived for a few years, but a man without hands cannot plow his land. He could find no use for himself and killed himself. But he had already died, I think, of a broken heart."

Mirwell snorted. "How does a man with no hands kill himself?"

Beryl looked at him with baleful eyes. "He threw himself off a cliff."

"A weak man, then. It is good I removed him from service. Only a weak man would allow his infirmity to get the better of him." Mirwell scratched at his gray streaked beard. "I suppose you want me to ask forgiveness?"

"No. I would not expect you to. I know you."

The castle loomed upon its hill over the sleeping city. The horses climbed steadily, their hooves clacking hollowly on the empty street. The moon had begun its descent into the western sky.

Mirwell shifted uncomfortably on his horse, his bones protesting at this late night ride. "Yes," he said. "You know me well enough. Evidently better than I knew you. I had thought you wanted to see Mirwell restored to greatness the same as I did."

"Oh, but I do," Beryl said. "That is why I have done what I have done. I wanted to see Mirwell become a great province once again. Everything I have done has been for the province."

"Then I don't understand—"

"Of course you don't." Beryl shook her head emphatically. "We envision two different provinces. Yours would be oversized and bloodthirsty, interested in glory only."

"And yours?"

"Mine . . ." Her voice grew very quiet again. "I envision a province without Mirwells. Without Mirwells who seek glory from blood."

Mirwell's belly shook as he laughed. "What would you call the province then? Spencer Province?"

"No," she said. "There are other clans."

She was clearly obsessed, Mirwell decided.

As they rode by silent houses and shops empty of all light, he said, "Your visions and dreams are one thing, my dear, but if your timing is off, or if someone notices the Gray One is quite a bit shorter than *he* used to be, or if one of D'rang's comrades notices he looks different, then your scheme will fail utterly and will bring about Zachary's destruction. You will never see the province you envision."

Beryl twisted in her saddle and smiled coldly at him. "Nor will you. Should the plan fail, I am taking you down with me."

"You are," Mirwell said, "more like me than you know."

"I am a Green Rider," she said, looking ahead at the brightly lit castle gates emerging out of the darkness. "I will do what I can to fix what you have tried to destroy. We are not alike at all."

"How I never knew you to be a spy . . ." Mirwell shook his head.

Beryl grinned at him, amusement dancing in her eyes. "As a Green Rider, I am gifted with the ability of deception, to assume a role. You were not difficult to deceive."

Stevic paced in agitated circles, his cloak aswirl about his ankles.

"You've got to stop," Sevano told him. "You don't want to attract *his* attention."

Stevic paused and peered down the length of the throne room where Amilton sat in his chair. Another dead, or nearly dead noble, at the base of his dais was being dragged away. The ranks of those whose loyalty was to be tested was thinning rapidly. Amilton had put the Lady Estora in reserve. She had been placed in a chair next to the dais. Amilton reclined in the throne chair, his fingers pyramided as he gazed at the half dozen nobles before him. In the shadow of his chair stood the woman Jendara.

Stevic turned on his cargo master. "Sevano, I've got to talk to her."

"You do not," Sevano said.

"She said Karigan wasn't dead. She had blood . . . blood on her sword. How do you think it makes me feel?"

Sevano grabbed his arm roughly and pulled him close. "I can guess how it makes you feel. Aye, I can. I know also that it makes you reckless."

"Then I've got to get out of here. I've got to find

Karigan. If she is somewhere here in the castle . . . Somewhere hurt . . ."

Sevano dropped his arm. "How do we get out of here?" He glanced meaningfully at the soldiers guarding the doors.

"We walk out. After all, I am but a simple merchant."

Sevano snorted.

"We've got to try, old friend."

"And bring about unwanted attention?"

"They won't even notice us."

Sevano rolled his eyes. "Aeryc and Aeryon have mercy on fools."

They turned toward the entranceway as one, and with matching strides, walked down the runner. The guards watched their approach with some interest, but did not move to intercept them. Stevic thought they might actually make their way out, but just as they drew abreast of the guards, pikes were crossed in their path.

One of the guards smirked. "No one leaves but the dead. Orders of the king."

Stevic and Sevano turned on their heels and headed back.

"So much for that," Sevano said.

"It was worth a try," Stevic said.

Instead of returning to their half hidden alcove, Stevic walked past it and approached the throne more closely.

"What are you doing?" Sevano whispered.

"I want to see if I can talk to that Jendara woman." He paused a few paces from the remaining nobles.

Amilton's attention was presently on Lady Estora. He twined his fingers through her shining gold hair. "Wine, my dear?"

In a soft but firm voice, she replied, "I am not your dear."

Amilton's face went white with rage. He grabbed a handful of her hair and yanked her head close to his lips, and she screamed.

"You are," he said, "whatever I tell you." Then he

pushed her away, and she curled up in her chair with
a sob.

Amilton looked as if he were about to say more, but
a soldier entered the throne room at a trot. He fell to
his knee before Amilton.

"My lord," he said, panting hard. "Lord-Governor
Mirwell rides through the city. He brings you a great
prize."

Amilton stood, triumph shining on his face. "Sacoridia
is mine," he crowed. "They did it! They defeated my
brother."

Stevic's shoulders drooped. He could feel it from the
others, too, from Sevano and the old woman, Devon,
from Lady Estora, and even the nobles who had sworn
themselves to Amilton. He could sense their loss of hope.

Fastion clapped Karigan on the shoulder. "Good to see
you again. Thank you for bringing the king."

Karigan smiled weakly. "He brought himself."

But Fastion did not hear. He was already talking to
Brienne, the king, Marshal Martel, and about ten other
Weapons. They had left behind the hundreds of slabs
encumbered with the dead. She could see a row of slabs
through the open doorway from where she sat in an ante-
room. Several chairs and a coffin rest were the only
pieces of furniture here. Glyphs and runes similar to
those she had seen throughout Heroes Avenue ornamented the walls here as well. Some were covered by
more recent tapestries depicting heroic events, or of
Westrion carrying souls off to the heavens. A statuette
of Aeryc holding the sickle moon stood by the fireplace.

The roaring fire felt good to Karigan. The penetrating
cold of the underground tomb had clung relentlessly to
her, and she wondered if she would ever be able to shake
it off completely. She watched the blaze. The fire was
alive and warm compared to the denizens of Heroes Av-

enue. The bare sword lying across her knees reflected dancing flames. She wished it was her old sword . . . F'ryan Coblebay's. He had been hero enough. But to take the First Rider's from her tomb? She shuddered, and this time not with the cold.

"We must go on," King Zachary said to them all. "We must not miss our appointed time."

They all waited by a set of double doors, again wide enough to admit the dead and pall bearers. Fastion and Brienne stepped through into a dark outer room. In moments, they returned.

"It is secured, my lord," Fastion said.

One by one they slipped into the darkness of the outer room. The air was immediately warmer. It was as if Karigan had been released by the grips of the tomb and its dead. The ceiling vaulted into a high arch instead of pressing down on her, and she could breathe easier.

The room was a Chapel of the Moon with religious tapestries hung on the walls, and a coffin rest which must also serve as an altar. Wood benches faced the coffin rest. Unlike the tombs, there were no glyphs, no images of Westrion. The chapel must have been built long after the tombs, and it was not one used by the royal family. It was plain and lacked the heraldry of the ruling clans. Instead, there was a shield of black and silver upon the wall. A chapel for common soldiers and their families.

They had left the tombs behind, but in the glimmer of Brienne's lamp, she saw four figures strewn on the floor and one slumped over a bench. They wore the colors of Mirwell. There had been no sounds of fighting or cries as the soldiers died. Weapons might not possess magical talents, but as Fastion had once said, they had their secrets.

"There will be more soldiers outside the chapel," Fastion said.

"Then we shall not go that way," King Zachary said. Fastion nodded.

"My lord," Brienne said, "we understand the dire situation you are going into, but we are sworn to protect the dead. I must leave a few Weapons at least to guard the entrance to the tombs."

"I know," he said. "I would not want to see the caretakers harmed, nor the sanctity of the tombs desecrated. Besides, there are relics of the past down there that should not be handled. Their disturbance should prove more disastrous than a simple coup."

"My lord?" Marshal Martel queried. "A *simple* coup?"

Zachary smiled at the Horse Marshal. "You said yourself that the tombs must store more history than all the repositories of Selium."

"I did say that."

"There are artifacts in the tombs, Marshal, thousands of years old, that possess powers no longer understood."

The Horse Marshal raised his eyebrows. "I see."

And now so did Karigan. The Weapons did not simply guard the husks of old heroes and kings and their treasures, but protected objects of power in sacred trust, against those who might misuse them. Like Amilton.

Brienne picked four Weapons and sent them back to the tombs. Without another word, Fastion walked behind the coffin rest, lifted a tapestry, and pressed his hand against the wall. A new current of air, damp and musty, filled the chapel as a portion of the wall slid open.

"And I thought I knew the castle fairly well," Marshal Martel said.

King Zachary grinned at him. "There is much, much more you don't know. This is an old corridor once used by priests. It has since been abandoned and very few know of it. When my father brought me here, I was not one to remain idle. I explored the castle and the grounds while my brother played the dandy in court. My restlessness serves me now."

He disappeared into the passage. When Karigan passed through, she slipped on the damp floor. Brienne caught her elbow and held her upright.

"Thanks," Karigan said.

The wavering lamplight cast strange shadows against

the moist walls. Cobwebs fluttered from the ceiling. How odd the tombs remained so dry when this simple passage dripped.

"Where are we?" Karigan asked.

"Near the roof of the earth," Brienne said.

Amilton's announcement still rang in Stevic's ears when the old woman, Devon, said, "You are no king, but a young whelp who knows nothing about running a country."

Amilton looked down on her with distaste. "Have you anything important to say, old hag, or do you simply wish to mock me?"

"I served your grandmother, your father, and your brother," she said. "They are not of your ilk. I wonder if Amigast was truly your father at all."

Amilton's hands crackled with magic. Stevic thought he was going to pounce on the old woman, but he threw his head back and laughed instead. "Why should I listen to this? I am king now. What can your small voice do to harm me?"

Castellan Crowe cleared his throat. "My lord. The Weapons."

"What about them?" Amilton said.

"They follow her. She oversees them."

Amilton stepped down from his dais and faced the castellan. "Do you see any Weapons here besides my Jendara?" His hand swept the expanse of the throne room. "My soldiers will root them out, and they will be given the same choice as these others: serve me or die."

Crowe licked his lips nervously. "They will not succumb so easily. Th-they will listen to *her* guidance." He dipped the tip of his staff in Devon's direction.

Now Devon's laugh echoed in the room. "That is why I seek death."

Crowe's eyes grew round. "If she dies by your hands,

my lord, you will turn the other Weapons against you, and bring their wrath upon you."

Amilton stalked over to Devon. "Stop laughing, crone. Weapons are eternally loyal to the king of Sacoridia."

"You assume much about those who serve you." Devon's voice was now quiet and controlled. "The Weapons, as you call us, come from an ancient, ancient order. Yes, we are intensely loyal to our monarchs, and we will freely kill those who threaten them, but we have our own traditions and codes. We are swordmasters and Black Shields, we obey the precepts of our order."

"I've heard whisperings of Weapon secrets," Amilton said with a dismissive wave of his hand. "You are more superstitious than one might credit you with. It is no reason to go against the rightful king."

"The rightful king?" Devon spat. "You are *false.*"

Stevic glanced at Amilton's Weapon. She had moved imperceptibly closer to Amilton, her eyes watching Devon's every move.

"Jendara," Amilton said, "this woman raves."

Jendara shook her head. "No, my lord. Everything is as she says. Except about you being false," she added hastily. "If she dies, the wrath of the Weapons shall be upon us."

"Well, well," Devon said, squinting her eyes in Jendara's direction. "Amilton's dog speaks. It was my student once."

"I was, old woman," Jendara said. "Now I am far stronger and faster than you ever were."

"Still spiteful because I spoke against you becoming a Weapon?" Devon clucked. "Such a long while ago. Yes, you may be quite the swordmaster. I won't deny it. But I see my other intuition about you was right. I spoke against you because I believed you hadn't the character to be a Weapon. After all this time I was right."

"You are too caught up in superstitions, old hag."

Devon crouched over, then from beneath her robes, she drew a bright sword with a black band about the blade. She held it before her and said, "I seek death. May it be yours before it is mine."

Jendara leaped in front of Amilton to shield him. Stevic and Sevano stepped back. Lady Estora watched wide-eyed from her chair.

Devon's blade slashed through the air gracefully. Despite her age, she moved with enviable agility and strength. The problem was her sight. Her blade flew far off the mark.

Jendara laughed and sidestepped away from Devon. "Over here, old hag!"

Devon looked disconcerted, then moved confidently toward Jendara's voice.

As Devon approached, Jendara sprang away. "Over here, old hag!"

Devon changed course again and again, seeking Jendara's voice. Jendara moved about the room, luring her away from Amilton and trying to tire her out. A few of the nobles, forgetting their new allegiance to the self-proclaimed king, shouted encouragement and directions to Devon. It only seemed to confuse her as she looked this way and that.

"You are too slow, old hag," Jendara said.

But in saying so, she nearly lost her life. Devon sprang at her, her sword humming through the air.

Stevic clenched his fists, his body rigid. "Someone should help her."

Sevano touched his wrist and shook his head. "You must let them finish it," he said. "And look around you."

The dozen or so soldiers stationed in the throne room watched the proceedings attentively. The two with crossbows had bolts cranked to the ready should anyone make a wrong move.

"This is between the two Weapons," Sevano said.

"But Devon will—"

"She seeks it," Sevano said. "This is the way Weapons like to die. They do not want to die in their sleep, they do not want to die of old age. Devon can do the most good by having the Jendara woman kill her or by killing Amilton."

Stevic shook his head. It was painful to watch the old woman being goaded around the throne room as if a cloth had been tied about her eyes.

"Come, old hag," Jendara taunted, darting from side to side.

Castellan Crowe banged the butt of his staff on the floor. "This is quite enough," he said. "We can lock her up if we don't want to kill her."

Devon suddenly veered off course away from Jendara's taunts. She pivoted and thrust her sword at the unmoving target of Castellan Crowe.

"Traitor!" she bellowed. She drove her sword through him until the hilt met his breastbone.

Crowe's eyes went wide, then rolled to the back of his head. His staff clattered to the stone floor, and he folded over into a clump. Devon jerked her sword from his body. The length of the blade was stained red. The whole of the throne room went silent. One of the soldiers aimed his crossbow at Devon.

"No," Jendara told him. She circled around Devon, stepping over Crowe's body. "Well done, old hag. If he served as a traitor to Zachary, who is to say he would not betray King Amilton? Hmmm?" Jendara circled around and around, Devon following her with the tip of her sword. "But he was unarmed and unmoving. Can you get me?"

Devon answered with her sword and this time Jendara met her. Their blades hissed and clanged, their feet barely moving, their swords just extensions of their arms.

"I see you have not allowed your dotage to enfeeble your reflexes," Jendara said.

"Every day I practice." Devon slashed at Jendara's neck, but Jendara blocked it.

All in the throne room stood as silent witnesses to the fight. The nobles had quieted after Crowe's death, and watched apprehensively, at the same time relieved Amilton's attention was fixed elsewhere. Indeed, he seemed thoroughly entertained by the spectacle and had resumed his seat in the throne chair. He leaned over the arm, murmuring to Lady Estora and stroking her cheek, his eyes all the while following Jendara and Devon. Estora shuddered at his touch and closed her eyes tight. Whatever words he spoke were for her ears alone.

Jendara continued to toy with Devon. For her, it was a simple exercise to block and parry the old woman's moves. Devon, on the other hand, was slowing down, her movements faltering. Her breath rasped loudly.

"Tiring, are we?" Jendara said. "Put your sword down, and you can rest. King Amilton will see to it you are comfortable."

"I will not stop . . ." Devon said between breaths. Her body shook. "I will not stop until one of us dies."

"Then your heart will burst first."

Devon paused, and a smile crossed her face. "My heart is strong as ever, and more pure than any. You will meet your fate as Saverill did, traitor, and may Aeryc and Aeryon judge you as they will."

Devon leaped at Jendara, and Jendara held her sword up ready to fend off another blow, but it did not come. Devon dropped her sword and ran herself onto Jendara's blade.

Jendara's face turned a sickly white beneath all the bruises. She watched as Devon slid slowly off her blade and sank to the floor.

The silence in the throne room was broken by Amilton's low laughter. "Well, well, Jendara. The wrath of the Weapons will be upon you."

Her expression remained one of disbelief, and now fear. She glanced at Amilton. "They will be upon you, too."

"I think not," he said.

Before he could say more, a soldier entered through the great oaken doors and trotted down the runner. He bowed before Amilton.

"My lord, the Lord-Governor Mirwell has arrived."

A smile split Amilton's face. "Excellent. Send him in."

The half moon was just discernible through one of the tall windows on the west side of the throne room. Stevic calculated they were into the wee hours of the morning and it seemed the nightmare was no closer to ending. It had only deepened.

He watched as the stout old lord-governor, looking gray and haggard, limped into the throne room. An officer in scarlet kept to his side, supporting him as he made his slow, awkward way down the runner. They were followed by another soldier with his helm visor down, and someone cloaked entirely in gray. Stevic felt dread as he looked upon that one, for he carried a basket, its bottom stained with blood.

⇜ DECEPTION ⇝

It was as if all in the throne room were frozen in time as Mirwell and his companions halted before Amilton. The nobles, guards, Mirwell, and even Amilton, stood rigid and pillarlike. Only the light and shadows showed life as the flames of oil lamps flinched in a draft as though the dark of night threatened to deny them even that simple golden glow. Stevic wondered how the night could possibly get worse.

"It is about time you arrived," Amilton said. "I began to worry our plan had failed."

The Mirwellian officer inclined her head. "Everything went as expected, my lord, but the strain of battle on Lord Mirwell delayed us."

Mirwell glared at the woman. He tried to shake his arm loose of her, but she clung to him.

"My lord Mirwell," she said with an edge to her voice, "you are exhausted." Then she looked about the throne room, briefly eyeing the corpses of Devon and Crowe, and the nobles huddling together. Her face showed little surprise. "Would it be possible for someone to find a chair for Lord Mirwell?"

Amilton clapped his hands and a guard came forward. "Get a chair."

"Yes, m'lord." The soldier trotted down the runner and through the double doors.

Amilton gazed past Mirwell, his eyes settling on the gray cloaked figure. "You have brought something for me, my friend Master Gray One?"

Stevic held his breath as the gray-cloaked figure took

one precise step after another, his booted feet making not a sound on the floor, the hem of his cloak swaying at his ankles. He stopped an arm's span from Amilton and reached beneath the folds of his cloak. A gleaming circlet of silver clenched in a gray gloved hand emerged. The night, Stevic decided, had gotten worse. Much worse.

"Finally!" Amilton's voice rang out in the stock stillness of the throne room. He reached for the fillet eagerly, but stopped himself. An impish smile crossed his face. "I would have my Lady Estora do the honor of crowning me."

He walked to her and took her hand. Obediently she stood up and allowed him to lead her to the Gray One. To Stevic, she seemed to be walking in a trance.

"You have been a good friend, Master Gray One." Amilton stroked the black stone at his throat as he spoke. "You have brought me gifts that have made me strong and powerful."

The gray hood nodded, and the gloved hand held the crown out so it shone like a ring of light.

"My lady Estora," Amilton said, "would you do me the honor?"

Lady Estora blinked as if just waking up. She glanced at the Gray One, then at the crown, and back to Amilton.

"No." Her voice was so quiet that Stevic had to strain to hear her.

"What?" Amilton's brows drew together, his anger aroused once again. He was as volatile as a blacksmith's forge.

Lady Estora lifted her chin defiantly and in a louder and stronger voice, she said, "*No*. I'd sooner spit on you than crown you. You will never be the king your father or brother was."

Amilton's fist flung out, and Lady Estora dropped to her hands and knees with a cry. Mirwell's cold officer watched impassively, and the lord-governor leered as if enjoying some private joke. They were monsters, the lot of them.

Stevic schooled himself to silence, to still his outrage and frustration at Amilton's cruelty. He was helpless against the magic of Amilton Hillander, helpless to stop him.

As a clan chief and one of the leading merchants of Sacoridia, powerlessness was not something Stevic G'ladheon was accustomed to. He had always faced problems quickly and decisively, whether it was averting a clan feud by intervening with tact and a few well-chosen words, or defending cargo trains from thieves. Inaction, in his mind, equated disaster. This time, however, the stakes went far beyond guarding cargo and even his own life. He must exercise restraint and patience, for action could mean disaster.

Yet, he was not helpless to render aid and he crept cautiously to the woman huddled on the floor hiding her face with her arm. He knelt beside her and took her face into his hands. Her lip bled, her fair features would be bruised, but nothing worse, though this was likely the worst treatment she had ever received in her whole life.

"Can you stand?" he whispered.

His estimation of the woman surged as she steeled herself and nodded. Not a single tear threatened to spill from her eyes, though he could feel the trembling of her body as he helped her rise.

Amilton seized the fillet from the Gray One himself and held it high above his head for all to see. "I am king!" He walked among the cowering nobles, displaying the crown so there was no mistaking it.

"It is my birthright," he said. "I would have been king if my brother had not usurped me." He slowly lowered the crown onto his head. "Aeryc and Aeryon as my witnesses, I name myself *King* of Sacoridia."

Silence. Silence and dread as palpable as the granite walls that surrounded them.

Amilton glared at the nobles, prompting them to clap with great enthusiasm.

"You had better clap," Stevic whispered to Lady Estora.

"I cannot applaud for . . . for *that*," she said, gesturing at Amilton.

"I should not like to see him get any angrier with you," Stevic said. She reluctantly joined in.

Amilton strutted around and among the nobles, ensuring that each person got a good look at him with the crown on. He then climbed up onto the dais and stood tall and straight. "My dear Lord Mirwell," he said, "you have served me faithfully. I grant you, as you requested, the lands comprising Adolind and L'Petrie Provinces."

Lord Nethan L'Petrie emitted a strangled cry. Mirwell's own response was a throaty chuckle.

"Now we are truly doomed," Sevano whispered to Stevic.

It was one outrage after another, Stevic thought.

Amilton seemed pleased with himself for bestowing such a gift. He was likely even more pleased he possessed the power to do so.

"Master Gray One," he said, "I see you have brought me yet another gift. I should have liked to have heard my brother's screams as he died, but you have done well."

The Gray One held out the basket and a hush fell over the throne room. Lady Estora groaned beside Stevic. "All hope is truly lost."

Mirwell laughed.

Amilton snapped his head at him. "What is it?"

"Go ahead," Mirwell said. "Look in the basket. The Gray One carried it all this way for you."

Amilton smiled tentatively. He unclasped the basket's fastener and opened the lid. He reached inside.

Lady Estora pressed her face into Stevic's shoulder. "I can't bear to look. I just can't."

Stevic could not either. *It gets worse and worse,* he thought. But he caught an amused gleam in the Mirwellian officer's eye as she exchanged glances with the soldier behind her, and such a curious expression crossed Amilton's face, that Stevic found he could not avert his gaze.

Amilton drew out a round bloody mass. "What jest is

this?" he hissed. A headless chicken still dripping blood dangled from his hand.

Mirwell laughed again and Amilton turned his fiery gaze on the old man. The chicken hit the floor with a soft, wet sound. "Tell me why you laugh, Mirwell."

"Where is my chair?" he demanded.

Amilton blinked, not comprehending.

What in the name of Aeryc is going on? Stevic wondered.

"Imbecile." Mirwell's eyes were dark. "I ask you, where is my chair? The guard you sent after it . . . where is he?"

Amilton glanced about wildly. "Guard!" he cried, but the man did not reappear. The remaining guards shifted nervously.

"There are those who are not what they seem," Mirwell said. "You think you have won the game, but your opponent has deceived you with his strategy."

Understanding dawned slowly on Amilton's features. A muscle spasmed in his cheek.

Everything fell to stillness again; the air did not stir, and the light did not flicker. Those who watched held their breaths in the uncertain atmosphere, waiting to see what Amilton would do next. Stevic felt caught in the clutches of some spell and thought he must burst, his inaction gnawing at him with new ferocity.

Amilton broke the spell. He faced the Gray One squarely. His cheek twitched again. With a trembling hand, he reached out and threw back the Gray One's hood.

"Captain Mapstone!" Stevic said in surprise.

The Green Rider folded her arms and grinned.

Amilton's face took on a deathly pallor and he staggered back as if struck. A confused babble broke out among the nobles.

Amilton's lower lip quivered. "Guards!" he shouted, but only half of them appeared, looking just as bewildered as he by the turn of events. "Jen-Jendara!" She did not answer. She had vanished completely, and she had done so with such stealth that no one had seen her go.

Amilton groped at his black stone, and it seemed to calm him. Color slowly crept back into his cheeks. His guards stood uneasily about him, their swords drawn.

A tapestry not far from the throne fluttered aside, and two black-clad Weapons, followed by a very much alive King Zachary, entered. The king looked exhausted beyond measure and as if his bound and splinted arm pained him.

"Aeryc and Aeryon preserve us," Lady Estora said.

"Breyan's gold!" The darkness that had pressed down on Stevic dissipated and was replaced by a lightness of heart. "I never believed in miracles . . ."

The clack and whiz of a crossbow broke the stunned silence. The bolt hit its mark with a loud *thwack* and King Zachary staggered backward, but did not fall. He glanced down in disbelief at the bolt stuck in his splint. By the time everyone looked to see who had fired it, the soldier lay dead on the floor with his throat slashed open, and a third Weapon stepped out of the shadows.

King Zachary wrenched the bolt out of his splint, and a cheer went up among the nobles. The king waved everyone to silence and faced his brother. "You are unfit to rule. Give up."

"Hear, hear!" cried the nobles. A convivial mood took them and their courage swelled with the king's presence and brave words.

Zachary motioned them to silence again, and fixed his attention on his brother. "My soldiers and Weapons stand ready to retake the castle."

"Your soldiers are being held prisoner, or are dead."

"Others are seeing to their release."

"Then if you want the crown, take it off my head."

Amilton's voice was a low growl, like that of a cornered wolf. His eyes were half slits. He stroked his stone and it glowed with a black aura. He swept his hand out. *Slam! Slam! Slam!* The lights dimmed and flickered with the onrush of air as the great oak doors of the entrance, followed by the secret door Zachary had come through, shut in quick succession.

Amilton closed his eyes and took a deep breath. The stone flared with power, and he flung his arms wide as if to embrace it. Moments later, the power slowly ebbed away to a glimmer. He dropped his arms to his sides. When he opened his eyes, gasps issued from those who stood before him. His eyes were no longer brown, but light blue.

"Now," he said, "no one can enter or leave." His facial muscles relaxed and the fire burning within him cooled. Each movement he made was controlled, steady; more like a wild predator stalking its choice of prey.

Stevic had seen Amilton demonstrate his power several times already this night, but it still raised the hairs on his arms. And why were his eyes blue? That had never happened before.

The nobles, who had begun to see a return of sanity with King Zachary's miraculous arrival, now spoke nervously among themselves, their feet shuffling on the stone floor. Captain Mapstone, Stevic noted, was looking less certain.

Two of the Weapons approached Amilton with their hands on the hilts of their swords.

Black energy pulsated to life about Amilton's hands. The Weapons drew their swords. Amilton flung his hands out, and strands of black energy surged off his fingertips. The ropy tendrils of magic twisted up their sword blades and forked into their faces. It knocked them senseless to the floor.

The third Weapon hesitated, and when Amilton cast his gaze his way, he stopped his advance altogether.

"Fools." Two voices in unison, issued from Amilton's mouth. One of his own biting tenor, the other was lighter and melodious.

Amilton's blue eyes rested on King Zachary. With a flick of his hand, Zachary fell hard to his knees. Captain Mapstone started forward to aid him, but he shook his head. "Stay put, Laren," he said. Of Amilton he asked, "What has happened to you, brother?"

Amilton held his hands up before him, letting the magic weave between his fingers. "We have learned much," he said with the strange double voice. "Together we combine our strengths."

We? Stevic wondered. *Our?*

Zachary attempted to stand, but Amilton's hand swept down, and the king fell to his knees again.

"You must observe proper obeisance," Amilton said.

"You are not a king," Zachary replied.

The Amilton of old would have exploded with fury, but now he simply gazed down at his brother with cold, alien eyes. "You may capitulate now and save yourself pain. Or you may make life not worth living for you and your minions." He turned his attention to Captain Mapstone. Stretching out his hand, he clenched it into a fist.

Captain Mapstone's eyes bulged, and she clasped her throat, gasping for air. Her breaths were raspy and ineffective. She sank to her knees.

"Stop!" Zachary said.

Amilton dropped his hand, and the captain fell the rest of the way to the floor, panting and gagging. Stevic thrust Lady Estora into Sevano's arms and stepped over to her, his heart hammering against his chest.

"Are you all right?" he whispered.

She was white around the lips, but she looked up at him with wide hazel eyes. A strand of red hair had escaped her braid and fallen across her pale face. For the first time since he had met her, she looked truly frightened. She opened her mouth to speak, but could only choke. He helped her to sit up.

"Does this mean you capitulate?" Amilton asked.

"Your argument is with me," Zachary said. "Leave my people out of it."

Amilton's eyebrows bobbed up in mock surprise. "We think not, not after your spies and messengers have hurt us. One nearly destroyed us. They must all be punished, but it is up to you how severely."

King Zachary's gaze roved over the worried nobles, his injured Weapons, Captain Mapstone, and the woman who assumed the role of the Mirwellian officer. His brown eyes even settled on Stevic and held him for a fleeting moment. It was enough time for Stevic to sense the grave consideration in the king's eyes and to mark how his features were carved by grief.

It was enough to break Stevic down to despair, but the king held himself with such unbending dignity, though he was forced to his knees at the tyrant's feet like a common dog, that Stevic felt strangely uplifted.

"I have loved this land from birth," King Zachary said. His voice was calm and firm. "The rugged seacoast, the heart of the Green Cloak, and the mountains. The land shapes the people, and the descendants of the Sacor Clans are strong." He looked up at his brother. "You should know that. Whatever evil you are in league with will not take Sacoridia so easily."

King Zachary turned his gaze back to his people. Now his expression was fierce. "The people who defend me and stand with me serve Sacoridia first—always first. We serve out of love. Therefore, for the sake of Sacoridia, though it means I may sacrifice myself and a few others, I dare not capitulate."

"Well said, Sire," the Mirwellian officer said.

Others murmured their agreement and Stevic found himself adding his voice to theirs. There was no better man to be king, he thought, than this man who knelt humbly when all others should be on their knees before him.

"And *we*," Amilton said, "are not displeased."

One by one, lamps along the west wall blinked out, throwing the room into half shadows. Stevic wondered what new, terrible torment was about to come upon them, but Amilton appeared just as surprised as everyone else. His eyes searched the wall as if he were trying

to see something. For once, he was not the source of
strange happenings.

Captain Mapstone grabbed handfuls of Stevic's cloak
and drew him close to her. She tried to speak, but could
only choke and wheeze. Finally, she mouthed one
word: *Karigan.*

Stevic's heart leaped and he looked wildly about. He
saw no one, but more lamps blinked out. And King Zachary vanished.

Karigan placed her hand on the king's shoulder, and he
started at the unexpected touch.

"Shhh," she whispered to him.

Karigan absorbed him into the gray world, and he became a filmy ghost in her vision. She bent and whispered
into his ear, "You are invisible."

His shoulder flexed and jerked beneath her hand. He
looked up at her . . . through her . . . with startled eyes.
"Karigan! I cannot see you."

"Shhh."

He staggered to his feet and nearly broke contact with
her to charge at his brother, but she grabbed his arm.
"No. We must be touching, or the spell will break. And
you will not stop him by simply leaping on him."

Indeed, Amilton—or should she say Amilton-Shawdell?—
had become more than he seemed. With the spell of
fading upon her, she could see the transparent form of
the Eletian overlapping Amilton. She was not sure if he
could see her, but he did not seem to. When she had
last disappeared in his presence, he had vanished from
her own sight, but now it was not so.

The Eletian's image flickered and waned, and he was
hunched as if in considerable pain. Blood soaked his gray
cloak. *Good,* she thought, and she wished him more pain
and then some, but Amilton stood with him lending him
strength. A direct current of power, like a bloated vein,
flowed from Amilton's stone and into the Eletian's chest.

Amilton-Shawdell glanced vaguely in their direction, but his eyes did not fall on them. So far he seemed blind to them. He put his hands on his lips. "It seems the Greenie has decided to join us."

Karigan backed away, drawing the king with her. "Slowly," she breathed in the king's ear, "so no one detects movement."

"I thought I told you to stay with the horse marshal," the king whispered.

Karigan grinned though he could not see it. "And miss the fun?" Just before Amilton had slammed all the doors shut, she had vanished in the secret corridor, and against Marshal Martel's protests, slipped into the throne room. A good thing, too, or she would have been cut off from her father and the king.

A black ball of energy, the type of which Karigan was already too familiar with, formed above Amilton-Shawdell's hand. He smashed it on the floor very near where they had stood. Currents of energy slithered away like black snakes.

Karigan guided the king into a shadowed alcove.

"Do you see the Eletian?" she asked.

"The Eletian! No. I thought you destroyed him."

The king must not see the world as she could even when under the spell of the brooch. Karigan bit her lip. "He was not destroyed. Now he stands with your brother, weakened, but feeding off him."

"The eyes and voice were familiar to me." Zachary leaned against the pillar, this new despair weighing down his shoulders.

"Come out of hiding," Amilton-Shawdell said. "We shall see you soon anyway. Why not preserve your strength?"

"If he is weak now, how can we stop him before he gets stronger?" Zachary asked. "Even Brienne and Rory could not close in on him."

Karigan gripped hard on the hilt of the sword of the First Rider as she thought. "Perhaps we must force him to expend a large amount of energy at once. Using my magic has a weakening effect on me, and maybe it is the same for him."

Zachary did not look pleased by her answer. His features in the dimness of her gray sight were taut.

"It's that," Karigan said, "or we try to get that black stone away from him. That is where the power is coming from."

Amilton-Shawdell paced in front of the throne chair, his eyes darting into the shadows. The half light of the chamber skewed the shadows of the assembled into monstrous shapes on the walls and ceiling.

"We could send our guards to relight the lamps," Amilton-Shawdell said, "but we would hate to destroy such an appropriate ambiance."

The king glanced at her . . . through her . . . with concern. His eyes were blackened sockets in her gray world.

"Can you sustain this?" he asked.

Karigan sighed, deeply tired. The events of the day and night combined had taken their toll on her long hours ago. Her gray vision had turned leaden, and though she did not wish to admit it and thus disappoint the king, she felt as though she might drop from the weight of the magic she used, "Not much longer."

"Perhaps we can persuade you to come forward," Amilton-Shawdell said. His eyes scanned the assembled as if searching for someone. "You there!" He pointed into the group before him and beckoned with his finger. Stevic G'ladheon walked forward with halting steps as if he were trying to resist but could not.

Karigan clenched the king's wrist hard.

"Uh . . . ." The king grimaced, and squirmed in her grip. "I will hold onto you. You are crushing my good wrist."

Karigan obeyed only half aware as he fumbled for her hand. "This is peculiar," he muttered. "I talk to a pillar and hold onto air."

Karigan wasn't listening. Her attention was riveted on her father.

"Yes," Amilton-Shawdell said. "This one is related to

he Greenie, is he not?" He stepped close to Stevic, look-
ng him up and down. "A merchant. A merchant by the
name of G'ladheon. We know this name." Another black
ball of magic formed over his hand.

A small gasp left Karigan's lips.

"Your offspring," Amilton-Shawdell said, "knows well
now this feels."

He lobbed the ball at Stevic. The magic exploded on
his chest and ropy tendrils of black twined around his
shoulders and arms. Stevic threw his head back in a silent
howl of agony.

⊰ THE FINAL PLAY ⊱

The tangle of black currents snared Karigan's father. They blanketed his chest and wove between his arms. They rippled down his legs and up his spine. Her father could not move, he could not speak, he couldn't even scream.

When Karigan wavered on her feet, the king's grip firmed and steadied her. She knew her father's pain. She knew it too well, but how could she choose between protecting the king and helping her own father?

The king made the decision for her. "You had better go help your father," he said. "I cannot defeat my brother by hiding in the shadows anyway."

She looked at him, at his earnest expression, and she knew she looked upon a man unlike any other. This was why he must be king; this was why he had to succeed. "I'm sorry," she said, her voice hoarse.

"I know," the king said, "though it is not your doing. The heavens know there has been enough suffering this night." And he let her go.

Karigan strode from her hiding place on shaky legs. "I am here," she said, dropping the cloak of invisibility as she went. The colors of the normal world collided into place in her vision, and the startled expressions of those who watched sharpened as though a veil had been lifted from their faces. She felt exposed as if she had suddenly shed all her clothes.

She halted before Amilton-Shawdell. The Eletian was now gone from her sight except in the light blue coloring of Amilton's eyes. She did not permit herself even a brief glance at her father trapped in his agony, for she would snap if she looked, lose her self-control, and reveal her weakness to the tyrant who stood before her. Then all would be lost.

She licked her lips and tried to put on her best merchant's face, a mask that gave nothing away. "Release my father," she said.

Amilton-Shawdell lifted a brow.

"I came out like you wanted," Karigan said. "You let him go."

"I rather like this," he said. "You trying not to show your pain. Why should I let him go?"

Karigan trembled with anger. "He has done nothing to you."

"But you have."

"Then punish me!"

Amilton-Shawdell smiled. "Such spirit," he said. "We shall reward you with what you request—your father's relief from pain, and your own punishment." With a flick of his hand the magical currents dissolved.

Karigan hastened to her father's side to support him just as his legs gave out. Sevano took the other side.

"Father?" she said.

His eyes shot around the throne room, unfocused. He swayed on his feet. "What?"

She shook him gently. "Father, it's me, Karigan."

He looked down at her, at first without recognition. Slowly his eyes focused. "Kari?"

She embraced him soundly, and all she had held pent up since leaving Selium threatened to gush out then and there; the hurts and struggles, the loneliness. Yet she knew this was not the time to give in to her emotions. She pressed into him hard. When she looked up, his cheeks were wet.

"Touching," Amilton-Shawdell said. His double voice carried thick overtones of mockery. "One's father is so very important, is he not?"

King Zachary emerged from the shadows, not stopping until he reached the dais. He craned his neck to look up at Amilton-Shawdell. "Our father ignored me. He loved *you*. He loved you even after you made too many mistakes. It was me he felt less for."

"He named you king."

"Yes, because he loved Sacoridia, too."

Amilton-Shawdell waved his hand dismissively. "It is all in the past. Other matters interest us now."

"Yes, there are two of you now, isn't there? But soon there will be only one, isn't that right?"

"One? We are together. We work for one purpose."

"The man who was my brother will be no more," Zachary said.

Amilton-Shawdell rocked on his feet, his forehead crinkling and jaw clenched. Veins bulged on his neck, and his hands curled into balls as if he strove with himself for mastery. A black glow blossomed around the stone at his throat, and his blue eyes flared. In a moment the struggle was over. His features smoothed over and his hands relaxed.

"We wish it." He stepped down the dais and stood face-to-face with his brother. "We have learned to draw on the powers of *Kanmorhan Vane*. They strengthen and unite us. You were a fool to refuse this partnership."

"Not I," Zachary said. "For all Father ignored me, we both shared a great love for this land. You would destroy it. An opening in the D'Yer Wall will cause a great blight and all that is living will perish or be perverted. We will return to the darkest, most primitive of times. The Black Ages will return though we left them behind a thousand years ago."

"In destroying we shall renew."

"You will renew the evil of Mornhavon the Black, and I will not allow it."

Karigan held her breath as the two brothers fixed their eyes on one another, each reading deep into the other's soul.

Zachary's hand lashed out, and he snatched the black stone. Then he froze, just short of yanking it off its gold chain, unable to release it. Bolts of energy burst between

is fingers and coiled up his arm. His mouth gaped open
a silent scream.

Another current erupted from the stone and fused into
Amilton-Shawdell's chest. He closed his eyes and inhaled
deeply as if taking in fresh air. His hair acquired a radiant golden sheen.

Fastion ran full tilt across the throne room to aid the
king. With the flick of Amilton-Shawdell's hand, a bolt
of energy tossed Fastion across the width of the throne
room and against a pillar. The Weapon crumpled to
the floor.

Karigan knit her eyebrows together. She watched in
disbelief, shaking her head. "No," she muttered. "This
isn't right."

"What?" Her father was still addled from his ordeal.

"I was wrong." Her voice raised an octave in urgency.
"Using the magic doesn't exhaust him, it feeds him. It
empowers him."

Amilton-Shawdell's intensity grew and spread out from
him like a black aura that pushed away the light. Zachary's eyes bulged, but he remained unmoving, statue
still, trapped in a web of magical currents.

Captain Mapstone drew her sword, but Mirwell caught
her arm. "The final play of Intrigue!" he shouted.

Beryl raised her hand to strike him, but he turned on
her. "*Axium cor helio dast, Mor au havon!*" The words
rumbled from his throat like thunder, and Karigan
thought the very air must splinter beneath their weight.

Expression drained from Beryl's face. She bowed to
Mirwell. "Command me, my lord."

"Kill Captain Mapstone."

Her sword sprang into her hand. The clash of steel rang
in the distilled atmosphere of the throne room. Connly
intervened to help the captain repel Beryl's attack, but
she used her sword in a mindless and savage way, causing
them both to fall back. Her sword tore and thrust with
a life of its own, and the two did all they could to simply
defend themselves. Mirwell chortled.

Karigan had to help the king.

She tore loose of her father's grip. With the sword o
the First Rider clenched in her hand she charged toward
King Zachary and Amilton-Shawdell.

"Kari!" her father shouted. "Look out!"

Something snarled and hurtled out of the shadows a
her, knocking her down. Karigan sprawled on her side
the sword skittering across the floor out of reach. She
took a couple of deep breaths to get air back into he
lungs and raised herself to her elbow. Jendara knelt o
one knee beside her, her sword tip pressed against he
chest. Footsteps approached from behind.

"Back off, merchant," Jendara said, her eyes neve
leaving Karigan. Her jaw was set, her eyes narrowed. She
looked a raptor ready to plunge on its prey with talon
spread. "Back off, or my sword will taste more of he
blood, and yours as well."

Karigan sensed her father hesitating behind her. "Go,"
she said. "She means it." She heard his feet pad away
and the low tones of his voice as he exchanged word
with Sevano.

Karigan gazed up the length of Jendara's bright blade
"You shouldn't stop me," she said.

"You should have killed me when you had a chance,"
Jendara replied.

"It was not my way." Proud Jendara had diminished
it seemed to Karigan, as if her spirit had been beaten
out of her. Her fierce hawklike features sagged and were
marred by bruises, cuts, and swelling. Had she guessed
wrong about Jendara all that while ago? Had she guessed
wrong that there was enough good in her worth saving
Or had F'ryan Coblebay been right? Jendara had no
killed her outright and that was something, she supposed
a gleam of hope.

The din of Captain Mapstone's fight with Beryl seemed
to shake Jendara from her thoughts. "I cannot let you
interfere with King Amilton," she said. "We have
worked too hard and waited too long for him to claim
what has always been his by right."

"Your king is dying."

Jendara glanced over her shoulder, the ringlets of her lush russet hair shimmering. She seemed to hesitate and Karigan took the advantage—not with a weapon for she had none, but with words.

"When I fade out, I can see it; I can see the Eletian. The stone he wears binds them together, but soon the Eletian will absorb Amilton completely. There will be no King Amilton. No Amilton, period. If you stop me, there won't be a King Zachary either. Just the Eletian. Who knows what will become of Sacoridia then."

Jendara shook her head. A variety of emotions battled in her eyes.

"You must see it yourself," Karigan said, feeling the time pass like blood gouting from a wound. "Is he the same man you pledged to protect? Or has he changed?" Her voice took on a tone of desperation. With every passing moment, the Eletian grew stronger, and King Zachary came closer to dying. She could not let him die. Yet there was little she could do on the wrong end of Jendara's sword. She would not escape a second time. "He is dying, don't you understand? They are both dying! They are being sacrificed to augment the Eletian's power."

Jendara's eyes searched hers. She pursed her lips. Then with a growl she stood up and drove her sword home into its sheath. She grasped Karigan's wrist and hauled her to her feet.

"I know it," she said. "I guess I have known it. He is not who he was. What will you do?"

"Separate them."

Jendara snatched up the sword of the First Rider and thrust the hilt into Karigan's hand. As Karigan took it, their fingers brushed and in a bare half-second, Karigan understood Jendara's own sacrifice. No matter how this ended, it would not go well for her.

"Jendara . . ."

"I've made the right decision for once," Jendara said. She pushed Karigan in the direction of the dais. "There is no time to lose."

Karigan had been wrong. Jendara's spirit had not diminished, but had grown brighter. Yet she had not been wrong that there was still goodness to be found in the woman. She turned to the king and his brother.

King Zachary's back was arched, blood trickling from his nose. His cheeks had gone hollow, his flesh pasty, and his hair had dulled as if his very life force was leaking away. In contrast, Amilton-Shawdell's expression was exultant. His hair was now completely golden.

The sword in Karigan's hand repelled the dark of Amilton-Shawdell as it must have Ages ago in the hands of the First Rider during the Long War. She passed into the aura of darkness, and the magic hummed all about her and prickled her flesh.

She raised the blade above her head and struck downward. She cleaved through the gold chain that bound the black stone to Amilton-Shawdell's neck.

King Zachary toppled away like a stiff column of granite. The black stone slipped from his hand. When it hit the floor, black energy flared up in a curtain around Karigan as if she were in the eye of a storm of black lightning. A tendril of magic arced across the ceiling scorching a black, jagged line through the portrait of King Amigast Hillander.

The last thing Karigan heard was the terrible dual scream of Amilton-Shawdell. Then the world went white.

❖ TRIAD ❖

Karigan was stretched out on a cold, hard surface. Her eyes fluttered open to white. Gauzy white. Linen tickled her nose and eyelashes.

"Gods!" She tore off the shroud and sat up panting. The sight that met her eyes was not much more reassuring.

She was surrounded by a milky white landscape and sky—if they could be called such. White plains stretched infinitely in all directions. The sky possessed no sun, clouds, or moon, it was simply white. There was no differentiation, no horizon, no undulating terrain, no defining lines. Nothing broke or blemished the all-pervasive white.

Even the green of her uniform was washed out as if this strange place could not endure color. Her skin had gone pale.

Worse still, suspended above her by no means she could detect, was a portrait of herself like a mirror image, only like a sleeper with her eyes shut and hands folded across her chest. A death portrait.

"Gods!"

Karigan rolled off the stone slab. It looked exactly like the ones she had seen along Heroes Avenue inscribed with funerary symbols, and tablets adhered to the base depicting scenes from the deceased's life. The tablets on this slab showed images of her journey. She fought the creature of *Kanmorhan Vane* on one tablet, on another she faced off with Torne, and in a third she rode Condor at full gallop.

She put her hand to her temple. "Is this death?" Her voice sounded small and muffled.

A moving, billowing vapor rolled and tumbled across the plain. In no time it converged upon her and wisped about her, obscuring the white world with yet another layer of cottony white. It enveloped and pressed in on her. She turned round and round, looking for a clearing or point of reference, but the vapor was all pervasive. Attempts to wave it away simply caused it to swirl and eddy in dizzying patterns. She paused, breathless. The vapor moved by her in ragged shreds, and as quickly as it came, it drifted away and unveiled two rows of funeral slabs, each laden with an occupant.

Not again, she thought with foreboding.

She passed between the slabs slowly. The shrouds draped the corpses in such a way that she could clearly discern the outlines of their features: Fastion, Mel, King Zachary, Sevano, Captain Mapstone, her father . . .

With a cry she clawed the shroud off her father. It rustled to the ground beside her. She shook him and patted his cheeks, but his flesh was cold, his body stiff.

"No!"

Light, musical laughter rippled around her. "Dead," a voice said. The Eletian.

Karigan looked in all directions, but no one was there. "If this is death," she shouted, "where are all the other spirits?"

"Dead." His voice tolled like a sonorous bell.

On the verge of weeping, Karigan went to Captain Mapstone's slab. She peeled back the shroud. Here the captain looked far more peaceful in death than she ever had in life. She was dressed in her full formal uniform with its gold captain's cords on the shoulders, and silken sash tied around her waist. She clasped the hilt of her saber in her hands. Her winged horse brooch gleamed coldly in the white light of the world.

Karigan's own brooch resonated, and without knowing how she knew to do so, she touched the captain's brooch. "I am not dead," she said.

A voice in her head responded, *True.*

"I am dead."

False.

"Dead!" the Eletian cried.

False.

"You must not disturb the dead."

Karigan snatched her hand away from the captain's brooch and turned, heart thumping, to find Agemon of the tombs observing her. He carried a cloth in his hands and bent over Captain Mapstone to polish her saber.

"Where are we?" she asked him, relieved to see another living being, even if it was Agemon.

Agemon hummed tunelessly as he polished.

"Agemon!"

The little man faltered and gazed at her with a perplexed expression. "Huh?"

"*Where* are we?"

He peered at her through his specs. "It is a transitional place."

Karigan licked her lips. Her mouth was dry and the vapor had left an acrid taste in it. "Why are we here?" She gestured at the corpses.

"They are," he said, "what could be."

Not dead yet, she thought, but could be.

"Agemon," she said, "you must show me the way back."

"I cannot."

"Why?" Desperation crept back into her voice. "I need to go back. I need to help the others, the king—"

He looked her up and down and clucked. "I attend the dead. You are touched by the dead, but not dead. Not yet."

"Agemon!" She clutched his sleeve. "Please! Show me the way out."

He simply stared at her with his frightened hare expression until she let him go. He readjusted his robes and waggled the specs on the end of his nose.

"You cannot leave once you enter," he said.

False, the voice vibrated in her mind.

"Do not forget the sword," he said, "or *she* will be unhappy."

He pointed into the distance. Thunderous hooves clamored in her ears after so much silence. Far off, a horse and rider galloped across the plain in silhouette. In moments they disappeared. Karigan glanced down at Captain Mapstone. The saber clenched in her hands was no longer her own, but that of the First Rider. Karigan pried it from her stiff fingers.

At the sound of humming, Karigan pivoted just in time to see Agemon scuttling away, his legs working beneath his long robes.

"Agemon! Wait!" She darted after him, but no matter how fast she ran, she could not gain on him. He grew smaller and smaller as the gulf between them expanded, his aimless humming fading until he disappeared altogether.

"Agemon!" Karigan wailed, but the heaviness of the white air muted her voice.

Behind her, the vaporous mist, noiseless and suffuse, billowed in again and obscured the funeral slabs. When the cloud wafted away, nothing remained save the endless white plains.

Out of breath, Karigan collapsed to the white ground. She drew her legs up close and rested her head on her knees. She sat like this for a time, resting, willing herself to stave off despair. It could have been minutes she sat there, it could have been hours.

Eventually she stood up and walked. There was nothing else to do but walk across the colorless plain. Short, white grass crunched beneath her feet. Otherwise, nothing fed her senses. She wondered if she simply walked in place for she could not identify any changes in her surroundings.

She recalled the sprig of bayberry she carried tucked away in an inner pocket of her greatcoat and took it out. A gift given to her so she could remember the vast expanses of the northern forest and the green, living things. So she could remember friends.

The sprig of bayberry defied the bleaching effect of the world and Karigan's eyes feasted on it. She rubbed a smooth leaf between her fingers. Its sweet scent brought back the bright blueberry blue eyes of the Berry sisters, and the green needles of a giant pine tree which had towered over Abram Rust. It brought back the earthy smell of the forest after a rain, and of pine needles baking in the sun.

Karigan rejoiced in the reawakening of her senses, of touching something real in this dull unreality.

As if in response to her rising spirits, a dark blotch appeared on the plain before her. Her pace quickened into a trot. Her strides brought the splotch closer as though she had taken great leaps instead of steps. The splotch turned into two figures who sat hunched over a table.

Karigan slackened her pace, hope turning into dismay. Amilton sat in one chair and the Eletian in another. A third chair was left unoccupied. The table and chairs were made of ordinary wood, or appeared to be. On the table, a game of Intrigue was set up. Like the bayberry sprig, the pieces retained their true colors: blue, green, red.

Amilton leaned over an army of red pieces, his eyes darting here and there over the board. He wrung his hands anxiously, reached out to move a piece, hesitated, and snatched his hand back. He muttered to himself unaware of Karigan's presence. Shawdell the Eletian, in contrast, leaned casually back in his chair, watching her approach with interest.

"Won't you join us?" he asked.

Karigan adjusted her grip on the sword. "Why are we here?"

The Eletian smiled his dazzling smile. In this place he was not bloodied or injured from their previous encounter at the Lost Lake, nor was he the ghostly image she had seen overlapping Amilton in the throne room.

"Would you believe anything I told you?" he asked.

"I will judge your words for myself."

"You will not like what you hear."

"Just explain," Karigan said.

"All right." Shawdell's voice was quiet. "With your actions, you have released wild magic and it has torn the wall between the worlds. You brought us here."

"What do you mean between the worlds?"

"This is a place of passage, neither here nor there. It is not of the earth, nor of your mortal heavens. You have touched it before when you rode with the ghosts, but only the borders. You did not cross over. Many others touch it with their dreams or in death. Some find their way here with magic, but that is rare. This place is not always of the corporeal, but often of images and symbols."

"I don't believe you."

Shawdell shrugged. "As you wish, though I suspect if you consulted Captain Mapstone's brooch, you would know the truth of my words. How else would you explain all this?"

The brooch was gone, and it did not speak to her, but it did not matter. All that mattered was leaving this place, getting back to the king. "How do we get back?" she asked.

Shawdell mocked her with his light and musical laughter. "You would trust me with the answer? You who will not believe the truth about where we are?" She glared at him, and he stopped laughing. He leaned forward and drew his eyebrows together in an expression of the utmost gravity. "To leave, we must finish the game. You must sit down and play. Won't you have a seat?" He gestured at the empty chair.

Karigan ignored the proffered chair but looked the game board over. On her side of the board, green pieces stood in formation. She looked closely, for their features were familiar. One carried a great ax on his shoulder— Abram Rust. Miss Bayberry leaned on a cane. Somial, Softfeather, Arms Master Rendle, the little boy Dusty, and others she knew all had their places. King Zachary sat upon the green throne. Weapons stood behind him with hands on the hilts of their swords. Captain Mapstone and Beryl Spencer faced one another with their swords drawn.

Several pieces lay in the dead position: F'ryan Coblebay, Joy Overway, and numerous other Green Riders, Weapons, and soldiers.

Amilton's pieces consisted of Mirwellian soldiers and mercenaries. There was one-handed Captain Immerez flanked by Sarge and Thursgad. Mirwell faced the battling Captain Mapstone and Beryl Spencer. Jendara stood just outside the action.

The very image of Amilton sat on the red throne. Likewise, Shawdell sat on the blue throne. The two pieces were close together. A black thread of energy flowed between them. One more piece stood before them, a green piece. Karigan did not need to look at it closely to know who it represented.

Shawdell's pieces thronged on the borders of the green king's realm. They were groundmites and other twisted creatures with hideous faces, wings, and claws. Denizens, no doubt, of *Kanmorhan Vane.*

"I don't want to play," Karigan said.

"I thought you wanted to leave this place," Shawdell said. "You must win the game to leave."

"No," Karigan said.

"No? You are the Triad. You have been throughout, the unexpected player of the game, the player none of us knew how to counter—not Mirwell, Amilton, or myself. Zachary, however, managed to woo you to his side early on."

"Don't twist it," Karigan said. "I chose—"

"We never knew what you would do next," Shawdell said as if he had not heard her. "Other pieces supported you, and others hindered you. I suppose it is too late for me to coax you to our side? We would make an incomparable match."

His smile was charming, his eyes warm. He held his hand out to her. Karigan recoiled.

"I could show you things you never dreamed of," he

said. "I could give you power a thousand times that of the horse trinket you wear. A simple mortal king like Zachary is not good enough for you. You've a temperament that requires much, much more." He folded his hands on the table, and with earnest eyes, he said, "It pains me to admit it, but I find you most intriguing for a mortal, Karigan G'ladheon. What do you think about immortality? I have the power to grant it."

Karigan sputtered, her mind awhirl and appalled by all he implied. "Is that what you offered Amilton? Immortality?" She glanced at the prince who was oblivious to everything but the game board.

"What I offered Amilton is between him and me, and needless to say, it is quite different than what I offer you."

This couldn't be happening, could it? Immortality? To spend all her days with Shawdell the Eletian? The one who unthinkingly killed so many for his own purposes? She could never cross over to his side. This one thing at least, she knew.

"I made my choice long ago," she said. "I made my choice free of false promises and coercion."

Shawdell's expression was one of genuine regret. "My promises are not false. I wish you would join me, for we could share more than power." He paused to allow his words time to sink in. "Since you have refused my offer, there is no alternative. I ask again, won't you finish the game?"

Karigan hated Intrigue. She always lost. By rising to Shawdell's challenge, she doomed King Zachary, her father, all her friends. She doomed Sacoridia.

She nodded toward Amilton who still muttered to himself and dithered over the game board. "Why doesn't he make a move?"

"He moves when I give him leave," Shawdell said.

"And when do you move?"

Shawdell crooked a golden eyebrow. "I move when you sit down to play."

"You mean everything is just . . . stalled?"

"It is a stalemate."

"And if I refuse to sit?"

Shawdell slowly smiled. "We share an eternity in this place. But if you play the game, you have a chance to win."

"Why don't you use your magic?" Karigan asked.

"Play the game," Shawdell said.

"Why don't you use your magic?" she repeated.

Shawdell's posture grew rigid. Amilton, too, tensed and his murmuring increased in urgency.

"Play the game," Shawdell said. "It is the only way you can leave."

Karigan laughed, giddy with sudden insight. The essence of her insight, the only truth to be found in this unreality, was far more mundane than simple magic. She was the Triad, the random element. She could spur the game on, or maintain the stalemate. She controlled the game.

"I won't break the stalemate," she said. The colorful game pieces reflected on the shiny blade of the First Rider. She bent close to Shawdell and whispered, "You are too weak to break it yourself."

And if this place was a combination of symbols, images, and the corporeal . . .

She raised the sword over her head. Shawdell quailed. The sword slashed down like a scythe.

It plummeted down between the enthroned pieces of Amilton and Shawdell, severing the black thread that linked them. The blade bit into the cork game board and green, blue, and red pieces scattered. The sword carved deep into the table and through it. A roar grew louder and louder in Karigan's ears like a great whoosh of air— the screams of Shawdell and Amilton.

The table split into two neatly sliced halves. Shawdell and Amilton, one the mirror of the other, brought their arms up as if to ward off some invisible blow, their faces averted. Cracks crazed their images and they shattered into thousands of tiny fragments.

Still the sword descended. It plowed into the white

earth and sank deep. It kept sinking. The ground engulfed the blade, the hilt, her hand. It swallowed her wrist and forearm and elbow. Still the sword descended. The ground took her shoulder. It took her all the way.

The blade rang on the stone floor of the throne room.

Gold links from the chain that had held the black stone around Amilton's neck rained to the floor in pieces. The black stone bounced again, and when it struck the floor, it cracked.

Wild magic escaped from it.

The magic crackled and shot across the room in a black streak, hungry and vengeful. It found Karigan's sword and sizzled up the blade. She flung it aside, but still the tendrils leaped off it and lashed onto her like a live creature, a predator sustained by the screams of Shawdell and Amilton.

She added her own scream as the wild magic twined around her torso and around each limb. It pulsed on her flesh, strangling the life from her. The other faces in the throne room blurred in her tearing eyes.

Amilton's arms were outstretched to the ceiling as if he reached for his father painted there. Even without her brooch, Karigan could see the ghostly, bloodied figure of the Eletian being drawn out of him.

A black current of magic burrowed through Karigan's flesh and into her shoulder. She writhed as the black thing sank deeper, crawled under her skin, wriggled in her muscle.

Smoke drifted up from the fabric of her coat. She smelled her own burning flesh. Old hurts reignited: the burns on her wrists from the creature of *Kanmorhan Vane,* the bite of Immerez's whip on her shoulder, the countless knocks, bruises, scrapes, abuses . . . Her side was wet with blood.

The thing probed deeper, and she moaned with pain. She knew with some part of her that it sought out her heart and strove to twist and twine like poison through every sinew of her body.

On the periphery of her vision, a shadow with a sword looked down at her with steely eyes. The shadow tossed her mane of russet hair over her shoulder, and turned to the screaming Amilton. The sword streamed through the air like the tail of a falling star and plunged into Amilton. The scream stopped short though its residue clung to the stone walls of the throne room.

Amilton crumpled. The silver fillet fell from his head and rolled across the floor to King Zachary's feet. It spun there like a coin until he grasped it with a trembling hand.

The Eletian faded from existence like a puff of smoke.

Karigan groaned as the last vestiges of magic left her body and the accompanying pain dissipated. Her father's face clarified in her hazy vision as he looked down at her. Sevano, and some blonde, green-eyed lady who looked vaguely familiar, also gazed down on her.

"Kari?" her father said hoarsely.

"Uh . . ." was all she could say.

He clasped her hand. His hand was warm and its weathered texture felt good to her. It felt real. "Can you sit up?" he asked.

She raised herself to her elbows and shook her head to clear it. Pain lingered, but its intensity was a distant thing. Her whole body felt battered; it was too difficult to pinpoint one single hurt more significant than the others. Where the current of magic had entered her shoulder, she felt nothing at all.

She let her father and Sevano help her to her feet. Shakily she hooked a strand of hair behind her ear.

An odd gray light stole the contrast of oil lamp and night from the throne room. With some surprise she realized morning had finally dawned and its dusky light had brightened the east side windows.

Nobles murmured among themselves in weary tones. Brienne and Rory stirred on the floor, grimacing and rubbing their eyes. Fastion crouched by them. Captain Mapstone sat beside a dazed Beryl Spencer who cradled her head in her hands. Connly held his sword to the jowls of Tomas Mirwell.

Jendara stood over the body of Amilton Hillander. Her bloodied sword hung loose in her hand. She shook her head and tossed the sword aside. The clatter of metal on stone woke everyone up. All eyes fell on her. Her eyes found Karigan.

"We are even, Greenie," she said.

Karigan opened her mouth to speak, but just then, the throne room doors burst open and Weapons and soldiers dressed in silver and black spilled into the room. The door hidden behind the tapestry opened as well and Weapons, followed by Horse Marshal Martel and his cavalry soldiers, issued in. The opening of the doors dissipated the last of the spell that had cloaked the room.

Horse Marshal Martel and the Weapons sought out the king to ensure he was well. Karigan could not tell from where she stood, but he seemed well, at least as well as she was. He looked dazed and exhausted, with blood staining his mustache and beard.

"We need some menders here," Marshal Martel said to one of his officers, "and double quick."

A Weapon knelt by the corpse of Devon Wainwright. Others joined him, and they spoke in low voices. They stood and turned to the king. "We seek the one who has killed Devon."

Before the king could respond, Jendara stepped forward and said, "I did."

Swords hissed out of sheaths. A black ring of Weapons closed in on her.

"I know you, traitor," one said. "Devon was our teacher."

"You shall suffer Saverill's fate," another said.

Jendara stared coldly at each of her captors. "I was once Devon's student, too. I learned much from her." She looked them over critically, as if gauging them, as if they had fallen far beneath her standards.

Then she lunged.

One of the Weapons reacted by raising his sword to stop her. Jendara did not stop.

"N-no," Karigan cried, but her father enclosed her in his arms and swept her down the throne room runner, and through the great oaken doors.

⋙ HOMEWARD ⋘

Karigan walked along the pasture fence, in the bright blue silks her father had given her, feeling odd after so long wearing the uniform of the messenger service. The silk felt light and billowy on her skin, as if she wore nothing at all.

She squinted in the sun, watching Condor frisk with some other horses. He cantered across the pasture, his tail held high like a flag and his ears pricked forward. Karigan laughed aloud when he halted in his tracks to roll and grunt in a patch of mud. Mel would not be happy when it came time to groom him.

"Carefree, aren't they?"

Karigan turned in surprise to find Beryl Spencer standing behind her. Incredibly she still wore her scarlet uniform with the incongruous winged horse brooch fastened to her shortcoat. She held the reins to a bay mare tacked with saddlebags for long travel. The mare's ears flopped back and forth and she nickered at the frolicking horses.

Beryl patted the horse's neck. "This is Luna Moth," she said. "I just call her Luna. She would much prefer to be playing with her friends rather than leaving."

"Where are you off to?"

Beryl glanced at the reins in her hands, then back up at Karigan. "Now that old Lord Mirwell is under lock and key and those in his army who will not be executed are marching home, I thought I would return to Mirwell Province and see what good I could do there. After all, I still hold an officer's commission in the provincial army."

"You can't be serious," Karigan said. "They must know the part you played."

Beryl smiled brightly, an expression Karigan had never seen on the serious woman's face before. "It is generally believed Green Riders are a reckless lot, always galloping off into trouble. More or less it is true, and hopelessly so." She shrugged. "It may be no one in Mirwell is aware of my . . . affiliations. After all, anyone privy to the information has been killed or locked up, and may yet face execution."

"It isn't just recklessness," Karigan said. "You're endangering yourself."

"Perhaps, but maybe the new lord-governor will welcome one who can help him ease into his new position. After all, no one knows that position better than I. Besides, King Zachary desires a liaison to watch over Mirwell Province, and, shall we say, influence the new lord-governor's loyalties."

Karigan frowned. Her old nemesis from school, Timas Mirwell, was going to be lord-governor. In a way, his actions had precipitated the ultimate fall of his father: he had caused her to run away from Selium, which caused her to meet F'ryan Coblebay, which caused her to carry the message . . .

"Bad things may await me in Mirwell," Beryl said, "but I can't try to change the province from here. Besides, I can be quite persuasive." She touched her brooch. "How about you? What will you do? I know Captain Mapstone is keen to swear you in. We're so short of Riders now."

Karigan smoothed some breeze tousled hair out of her face. "This afternoon I leave for Corsa with my father," she said. "I could be leading my own cargo trains within the year."

Beryl reached out and clasped Karigan's hand. "Good luck," she said. "I find it hard to imagine you as a merchant. It sounds rather tame."

"Good luck to you," Karigan replied. "Watch your back around Timas."

Beryl stuck her toe in the stirrup and mounted Luna gracefully. "That's Lord Timas to you." She grinned, and with a wave of her hand, she was off.

Karigan snorted. *Lord Timas?* She did not envy Beryl.

Her wanderings led her into the quiet of the inner courtyard gardens. She sat cross-legged on a stone bench warmed by the sun, and cupped her chin in her hands, intent on watching bees crawl in and out of the rose blossoms. A hummingbird buzzed by and chased another from a blossom. It was hard to believe she had killed a man in this peaceful place not so long ago.

She rubbed the cold spot on her shoulder, the spot that stayed cold despite the heat that beat down on her. It was the place the tendril of black magic had scored her flesh, and although her various bruises, bumps, strains, and even the sword slash, were taking care of themselves, this wound was slow to heal. The skin was punctured and burned, but did not hurt. On the contrary, it lacked feeling. The menders did not understand it. They applied a variety of poultices, but nothing seemed to have much of an effect on it.

So absorbed in her thoughts was she that she did not hear the approach of another until a shadow fell on her. She gazed up and discovered the tall blonde, green-eyed lady she had seen in the throne room. She was familiar, but Karigan couldn't place just where they had met before.

"Hello," the woman said. "Am I intruding?"

"No," Karigan said.

"May I sit?"

Karigan dropped her feet to the ground and moved over so there was room on the bench for two.

"I almost did not recognize you without the green uniform," the woman said. Her own gown of aqua and deep gold was a summery contrast to the black Karigan remembered her wearing in the throne room.

Karigan tried to figure out who she was. The accent was eastern, her bearing that of nobility. "I'm sorry," she said, "but have we met before?"

The woman's eyes danced. "Yes, under very mysterious circumstances.'

Recognition struck Karigan, and she wondered how she had missed it before. "Lady Estora!"

"I am glad for this opportunity to talk to you without a veil on so you would know who it was you helped. I wish to tell you what a comfort it has been to have F'ryan's final letter."

Karigan smiled. "I'm glad I could help."

"I now know what else that letter contained. Captain Mapstone told me all about it, and all you endured to bring it." Lady Estora's eyebrows became set and her tone more serious. "You know, that night in the throne room, I saw much in you that reminded me of F'ryan."

"I didn't know him," Karigan said. "At least not well."

Lady Estora seemed to search for the right words. "You were not going to let anything stop you, and you did not. That was very like F'ryan."

Karigan looked at her knees. "I couldn't stop. I was afraid. I was afraid for my father, I was afraid for the king, and I was afraid for me. If I stopped . . ." She spread her hands wide for Lady Estora to come to her own conclusion.

Lady Estora studied her thoughtfully.

"Something wrong?" Karigan asked.

"No." Lady Estora shook her head and her hair shimmered in the sunshine like a river of gold. "F'ryan was never, forgive me, strong enough to admit fear. He shrugged it off like nothing, but I could see it in his eyes."

They sat in silence for a while, lumpy white clouds sailing across the sky far above, and a toad scampering beneath some bushes. A hummingbird darted from blossom to blossom with whirring wings. All of these small details of life Karigan had taken for granted.

Presently Lady Estora asked, "Will you be staying in Sacor City?"

Karigan shook her head. "No, I'm returning to Corsa. You?"

"My father wants me to find a good suitor." Lady Estora rolled her eyes. "Coutre Province is isolated by the Wingsong Range and a treacherous stretch of coast. He thought I'd have a better chance of meeting a fine young nobleman here. I thought if you were staying, we could be friends."

Karigan smiled regretfully. "I—"

But now Lady Estora was gazing across the courtyard. "I believe someone is waiting to speak to you."

Karigan followed her gaze. Standing at the far end of the courtyard was King Zachary watching her expectantly. She pushed her hair behind her ear and licked her lips nervously. Why did the king make her feel so out of sorts?

"You had better go," Lady Estora said. "It is not good to keep a king waiting."

Karigan smiled weakly and bid Lady Estora farewell. She walked the gravel path amid shrubbery and flower beds. As she approached, a Weapon stepped in her way to intercept her.

"It's all right, Wilson," the king said. "This is Karigan G'ladheon."

The Weapon's expression brightened, and he bowed. "I am usually guarding the tombs," he said, "but recent upheavals have me on duty here. There has been much talk down below of your deeds."

Karigan reddened. Before she could respond, however, Wilson slipped away to a discreet distance, leaving her and the king to stare awkwardly at one another. King Zachary looked well, but as if he had aged years. There were new lines crossing his brow and hollows beneath his eyes. She could not imagine the strain he had been under dealing with his brother's betrayal and death. The treachery of those he believed loyal, and the deaths of those who had remained loyal, had undoubtedly taken their toll on him as well.

Finally he said, "Would you walk with me?" Karigan fell into step with him on the gravel pathway. "I have just stepped outside for some fresh air," he said. "It seems summer has finally found us."

"Yes," Karigan said.

Another silence fell between them.

"I—" he began.

"We—" she said.

They stopped and glanced at one another.

"Karigan," he said, "I still haven't heard a full account of what went on in the throne room that night. I was a bit dazed, you know, when you broke the spell binding my brother to the Eletian. It seems you and my brother vanished momentarily. Laren—Captain Mapstone—seems to think it wasn't the power of your brooch. Where did you go? What happened?"

Karigan felt the energy drain from her. She disliked revisiting that night for it hounded her in her dreams and intruded on her waking thoughts. Over the last week she had found too much idle time to mull over what could have been. What if she had made the wrong choice? What if she had taken the Eletian up on his challenge to a game of Intrigue? What if she had lost? The vicious whirl of what-ifs exhausted her.

She started to turn away, but the king caught her arm. "Please," he said.

She nodded. "It is still strange to me."

And there in the courtyard, among the fragrant flowers, the buzz of bees, and the trill of birdsong; she told King Zachary of her experiences in the white void in which she had been trapped. The longer she talked, the wider his eyes grew. Her heart grew lighter as her words poured out. She realized, as she spoke, she had made the only choice she could have possibly made, and that none of the alternatives would have made sense to her then, or ever. In relating her experiences to the king she also learned she did not have to carry the burden of those choices by herself.

"I have heard," he said when she finished, "there are many layers to the world. The domain of the gods is one layer. The world of the afterlife is another. I have also heard that when you use magic, you enter yet another layer. Perhaps this is what happened."

"I don't know," Karigan said. "Agemon called it a transitional place."

The king shifted the sling on his shoulder. "Karigan, you have astonished me time and again. I am more grateful than you know for all that you have done. Without you, my brother would have taken all and destroyed Sacoridia."

"Jendara," Karigan said, "stopped your brother."

"She killed my brother, but it is you who stopped him and the Eletian. I know there was an understanding of some kind between you and Jendara, but know that in the end, she found the most merciful way out for herself. The justice of Weapons is ancient and brutal. Despite her final act, the Weapons would have branded her a traitor, and she would have suffered a great deal prior to execution."

Karigan glanced down at her feet. "I know. I hope she wasn't buried in some unmarked grave."

"She is where she deserves, interred beside my brother in the Halls of Kings and Queens, albeit along a more obscure avenue. But I do not wish to speak of tombs." The song of a chickadee perched on a slender white birch lilted across the courtyard. The king put his fingers beneath her chin and raised her face into the sunlight. "I'm asking you, no, imploring you, to reconsider joining the Green Riders. Your valor will not be forgotten."

"I can't—" she began.

He cut her off. "I simply ask you to reconsider. Go spend time with your family and think about it. If you return to Selium to finish your schooling, all the better."

"I'm not going back there," she said. "That's how I got into this mess in the first place."

The king's brown eyes danced with amusement. "A Green Rider should soon be handing Dean Geyer a message sealed with the royal mark, explaining how erroneously he judged you. You are free to return there."

Karigan wasn't sure whether to be relieved or annoyed that she no longer had an excuse to stay away from Selium. It would not do to appear ungrateful, however. "Thank you," she murmured.

He grinned with a lightness she did not expect, and he took her hand into his. "Your deeds will not be forgotten, brave lady." He kissed her hand and bowed.

With that, he turned away, his cloak rustling behind him as he strode off.

Karigan returned to her room at Rider barracks feeling rather giddy and blushing madly. Her saddlebags were packed and there was little to do but await her father. She sighed and leaned against the window frame. The wind bent the grasses of the pasture and horses grazed in the distance.

The king. He stirred up feelings in her that she would rather not think about. She was leaving Sacor City to be a merchant. Or, was she simply running away again?

She would miss Sacor City, but she would miss the people even more: King Zachary, Mel, Captain Mapstone, Fastion, and Alton D'Yer. Alton had left the city two days ago for his ancestral home. He was supposed to help figure out how to mend the breach in the D'Yer Wall. He was sorry she had decided not to stay on, and he made her promise to visit frequently. After the Battle of the Lost Lake and the discovery of his shielding talent, he finally felt like a proper Green Rider.

The door creaked open, and her father strode in looking resplendent in a cloak of sky blue. He placed his hands on his hips and smiled broadly at her. "Ready?" he asked.

She grinned and crossed the floor to embrace him. He felt as he always had with his arms around her: strong and safe and warm. "I'm glad you're here," she said.

Her father laughed aloud. "I am glad we both are."

Karigan pulled away and looked up at him. "What has you in such good spirits?"

"I've had some meetings with Captain Mapstone. She has told me many things about your journey—things you had not told me. It took seeing it through the captain's eyes for me to realize how much you've grown."

Karigan made a face. "I am Karigan G'ladheon, merchant."

"I told the captain that. She is short on messengers and thought I could talk you into joining up. I told her you were returning to Corsa with me. Even so, she insisted upon riding out of the city with us."

Karigan threw her saddlebags over her shoulder. She was pleased the captain was joining them, and she could tell by the sparkle in her father's eye that he, too, was pleased.

They found Captain Mapstone by the stable holding the reins to Bluebird. She looked well and rested. Only a small bandage on her forehead and a slight limp hinted at the battle she had endured. According to Mel, it had been no easy task keeping the captain quiet while she recuperated. The menders had their hands full with her, and many had simply thrown their hands up in exasperation when she stubbornly disobeyed their instructions.

Mel and Sevano led the other horses out of the stable. Karigan hugged Mel soundly. The girl was as cheerful as ever, but Karigan wondered if the night of the takeover ever plagued her dreams. She would not talk about it, but preoccupied herself with chores around the stables, or running about the castle with messages.

"It seems like we keep saying good-bye," Karigan said.

"You'll be back," Mel said.

"I'm not too sure about that."

Mel grinned and handed over Condor's reins. "The

captain is thinking about sending me to Selium for school."

Karigan patted her friend on the shoulder. In a low voice she said, "A little advice if you go: don't ever think about running away."

Mel chuckled and hurried off into the stable.

The foursome mounted and rode in silence across the castle grounds and through the gates. Captain Able and his guardsmen who had swung from nooses at the gate had been removed and buried with honor. Still, Karigan couldn't help but feel a certain dread when she passed beneath the portcullis.

In the city, the added security was evident everywhere. Soldiers in silver and black patrolled the streets in pairs and questioned travelers, particularly Mirwellians, at the gates. However, the hawking of merchandise from streetside booths, and the singing and playing of buskers, and the bustle of people flowing this way and that had not changed.

Captain Mapstone nosed Bluebird alongside Condor. Karigan's father and the cargo master rode on ahead. The captain twisted in her saddle so she could look directly at Karigan. Her hazel eyes were intent. "I am sure King Zachary requested you to join the messenger service," she said. "Add my invitation as well."

Stevic G'ladheon overheard and opened his mouth to protest, but the captain forestalled him with a stern glance. "Hold, merchant. You agreed to let me have my say."

He pursed his lips, but could not contain himself. "Yes, and a lot more."

"You made a bargain, if you recall," Captain Mapstone said.

Karigan raised her eyebrows. "Bargain?"

"I found you, more or less," the captain explained. "Your father agreed long ago to reoutfit my unit—which happens to be the whole of the messenger service—if I found you." She turned her hazel eyes back on Stevic. "Remember, make them conservative and *green*."

Stevic rolled his eyes. "Aeryc and Aeryon preserve me from making deals with Green Riders." He shook his head and turned his attention back to the road ahead.

"Them?" Karigan asked, mystified.

"Uniforms." The captain smiled smugly. They rode for a bit more and the smile faded to a more thoughtful expression. "Karigan, please consider joining us. You have shown rare courage, and we would be proud to have you."

Karigan worked the reins between her fingers and looked down at her hands. She felt the pull of the Green Riders, but didn't understand it. She needed some time to think it over. "No, I don't—"

The captain cut her off. "You do not have to decide now. I won't pressure you. I believe you will feel enough pressure in . . . well, other ways."

The captain did not explain further and the conversation shifted to more inconsequential things for the duration of the ride through the city. She rode with them through the last gate, then halted.

"I have some things for you," she said to Karigan. She reached behind herself and unfastened a saddle sheath complete with saber. She presented it to Karigan. "This isn't the blade of the First Rider though I think you deserve to carry it. Agemon of the tombs demanded its return. This was F'ryan's."

Karigan ran her fingers across the worn leather sheath. "I recognize it."

"You have his brooch and horse," Captain Mapstone said. "It seems logical for you to have his sword as well. I think he would be pleased."

"Thank you," Karigan said.

"One more thing." Captain Mapstone's expression became grave and she scratched at her neck scar. "I saw you after the Battle of the Lost Lake. I saw what you did with those black arrows. Here." She handed Karigan an oblong bundle wrapped in cloth. "These are the arrows that killed F'ryan. I'm not sure why you broke all the others, but I have a feeling it would be a good idea to break these as well."

Karigan took the bundle and clasped Captain Mapstone's hand. "Thank you for everything."

"Good-bye, Karigan. I hope your journey home is far more pleasant than any other you have taken lately."

Karigan watched as the captain rode Bluebird back through the gate. She turned Condor away, away from Sacor City, away from the imposing castle atop its hill and the man who inhabited it. She rode with her father and Sevano and left everything that had happened far behind.

When they reached the spot where she and Alton had picnicked by the Lost Lake, she dismounted Condor and walked alone into the cool shade of the beech tree. She unwrapped the arrows.

She shuddered as her fingers touched the black wood of the shafts. Blood still crusted on the steel tips. Without ceremony, she broke the arrows over her knee and let the pieces drop to the ground.

F'ryan Coblebay appeared before her, very faint, his luminescence fading. She could see meadow grass waving through him. *Thank you*, he said. No arrows protruded from his back now, no blood flowed. His face was not creased with pain. *Others remain enslaved, but you have helped many. Now I, too, may go home.* He turned and walked away, fading out as he went until he was no longer there.

Karigan mounted Condor and reined him up beside her father. He smiled at her and reached over to squeeze her knee.

Karigan touched the winged horse brooch fastened to her shirt and sighed.

"Let's go home," she said.

Kristen Britain

GREEN RIDER

As Karigan G'ladheon, on the run from school, makes her way through the deep forest, a galloping horse plunges out of the brush, its rider impaled by two black arrows. With his dying breath, he tells her he is a Green Rider, one of the king's special messengers. Giving her his green coat with its symbolic brooch of office, he makes Karigan swear to deliver the message he was carrying. Pursued by unknown assassins, following a path only the horse seems to know, Karigan finds herself thrust into in a world of danger and complex magic.... 0-88677-858-1

FIRST RIDER'S CALL

With evil forces once again at large in the kingdom and with the messenger service depleted and weakened, can Karigan reach through the walls of time to get help from the First Rider, a woman dead for a millennium? 0-7564-0209-3

To Order Call: 1-800-788-6262